THE SISTERS MONTCLAIR

ALSO BY CATHY HOLTON

Revenge of the Kudzu Debutantes

Secret Lives of the Kudzu Debutantes

Beach Trip

Summer in the South

THE SISTERS MONTCLAIR

A Novel

CATHY HOLTON

Branwell Books

2012 Branwell Books Trade Paperback Edition

Copyright © 2011 by Cathy Holton

Published in the United States by Branwell Books, Chattanooga, Tennessee

ISBN 978-1-938529-00-9

Library of Congress Control Number: 2012907487

Printed in the United States of America

www.branwellbooks.com

Designed by Rebecca Swift

Layout by Cheryl Perez

Also available in eBook formats from Branwell Books.
(eBook ISBN 978-1-938529-01-6)

For Mark

One

§§§

October, 1934

*C*ome home. Your sister has lost her mind.

Her mother's words seem to echo in the room around her. Alice could almost hear the breathless pauses in her voice, the undercurrent of tension and pleading in her tone. Her mother wrote the way she spoke. Alice crumpled the letter in her lap.

Well, why should she? Go home, that is.

She was in college now, away from home for the first time in her life, and surely her sisters were no longer her concern. She had felt when she came up to Sweet Briar a year ago that she was leaving her old life behind and beginning anew. Reinventing herself as the person she wanted to be, not the dutiful oldest daughter who must always watch after her little sisters, escort them to school on the streetcar, make sure they had money in their pockets for the return trip. Laura, with her cloud hair and angelic face, always wandering off into the street, lost in her own dreamy world. And Adeline, the youngest, difficult and stubborn and determined to have her own way.

And now Laura was sixteen and Adeline was thirteen, old enough to take care of themselves, and it was unfair that Mother would expect Alice to come home. As if there was anything *she* could do to prevent her sister from falling in love with an unsuitable man and running off with him against their parents' wishes.

Really, it was unfair of Mother to even ask.

Alice felt her mother had an ulterior motive in asking her to return, just as she had an ulterior motive in refusing. The simple truth was, and Alice would admit this to herself even if she wouldn't to anyone else, she didn't want to come home because she didn't want to see Bill Whittington.

She had let him kiss her at a cotillion party in August and now something seemed to have been settled between them, something Alice was loathe to acknowledge or accept. The fact was, she didn't even like him. He made her nervous, with his fine clothes and manners, and the slightly condescending way he had of speaking to her, as if he expected her to be dazzled by his charm. He was five years older than she, and he and all his friends had been to college and had come home to join their fathers' businesses. Or spend their fathers' money, in Bill Whittington's case. His grandfather had been one of the first millionaires in Chattanooga and he had grown up in a sprawling mansion staffed with servants. He and his friends were from Lookout Mountain, which was where the old money resided, and Alice was from Signal Mountain, which was where the people who ran Chattanooga, the doctors, lawyers, and engineers, lived.

Her father, Roderick, did not like it when she voiced this distinction. *You have nothing to be ashamed of*, he would say gruffly. *Your people were here in this valley long before the Whittingtons arrived*. The Montclairs had been in the Tennessee Valley from the time of the Indian Removal, long before the first carpetbaggers came to town and made their fortunes. Her father was a lawyer and he had business dealings with many of the Lookout Mountain crowd but he let Alice know she was never to feel socially inferior to any of them. Her mother had been a Jordan, which was one of the Old Carpetbagger Families (as her father called them privately), so Alice at least had some connection to Lookout Mountain. But despite her father's admonition, she always felt slightly out of place with Bill Whittington and his gentlemen friends. As if they were all laughing at some joke she wasn't privy to.

Alice had no intention of returning to Chattanooga and settling down with Bill Whittington, or anyone else for that matter. She liked boys well enough; she liked dancing with them, and flirting with them, but she didn't like being told what to do or how to do it, and it seemed to her that that was a husband's sole purpose.

Two days after she let Bill Whittington kiss her she came home from a party to find her parents on their way down to Ringgold, Georgia to rescue Laura from yet another undesirable suitor. The lovebirds had gone down there to get married because Georgia didn't require a blood test.

Watching her parents drive away, Alice decided that once she graduated from Sweet Briar, she would never come home again. She would never get married.

She would travel the world and live life to its fullest, and above all else, she would avoid love like the plague.

Two

§§§

It was one of the largest houses she'd ever seen, rambling along the western brow of Lookout Mountain. More like a hotel, really, than a house. Stella Nightingale pulled to the side of the road and checked the address. *This was the son's house*. He lived next door to his ninety-four year old mother, Charlotte had told her. Stella put the car in reverse and backed slowly along the street. She'd been driving for half an hour along this road that ran up the front of the mountain and meandered along the brow past houses that looked like they belonged in Beverly Hills.

She could see now why she had missed the house. It was smaller than the others, more like a cottage really, sandwiched in between the two mansions on either side. Larger than anything Stella had ever lived in but smaller than most on the mountain. It sat down slightly from the street, with a high pitched roof and a circular drive in front. Stella pulled into the drive and parked in front of the garage beside another small, forlorn-looking car. The other caretaker was named *Janice*, Charlotte had said. She was the one who would be showing Stella the ropes.

"She's been with Miss Alice the longest so it's best that she train you."

The whole time Charlotte was talking, Stella was thinking, *Do I really want this job*? But jobs were not easy to come by these days, especially for girls like her, so she kept her mouth shut and nodded her head politely as Charlotte explained the routine. Miss Alice was hard of hearing and she was *particular*. She wasn't *difficult*, of course, (said with a nervous laugh) she just liked things done a certain *way*. Her way. She had her own little *routines*, and that was the important thing, to keep Miss Alice on her routines. Not to shake her up. She got upset over small things so it was important to follow the routine to a tee. (Another nervous laugh).

Stella had answered the ad on Craigslist because it had stated clearly that she would be a "companion." An in-home caregiver, not a nurse. No bathing the client, no insulin shots, no ass-wiping. The client was ninety-four years old and walked with a walker and the caregivers were only there to make meals and make sure she didn't fall. There was a housekeeper to do the cleaning. Her son, Sawyer, who lived next door, did all of the shopping. The job was for two twelve hour day shifts, eight to eight on Wednesday and Thursdays, and the ad claimed that the client kept mostly to her room so caregivers were on their own for much of the time.

It had sounded like the perfect job for a college student; plenty of time to study and write term papers. The interview process was brutal, a twelve page application, an online psychological test, and a background check. Stella had never expected to make it through, especially through the psychological test. She had been surprised when Charlotte, the head of the agency, called to tell her she was hired.

It seemed they were as desperate to have her, as she was to have the job.

The house was deceptively large inside. The ceilings were nine feet tall and the rooms along the back, the living room, dining room, and sunroom, all had French doors leading to a wide verandah overlooking the valley. The view was spectacular, the valley bathed in sunlight, the Tennessee River meandering like a snake, and the distant mountains of the Cumberland Plateau rising into a violet sky. Despite its view, the house had a fusty, over-heated smell. Stella stood in the wide foyer staring at an oil portrait that hung on the wall of a somber dark-haired young woman. In the library to her right she could hear the sound of two female voices, one low and well-modulated with the aristocratic accent her mother had always dismissively called "Plantation South," and the other higher-pitched, too loud, twittering.

"Miss Alice, the new girl is here and I want you to be nice to her," Janice said.

"New girl? What new girl?"

"The one who's taking Martha's place."

"I don't like Martha."

"I know. That's why she's not coming back. Now you sit here and write your letters and I'll show the new girl around and then bring her in and introduce you."

"Oh, all right then."

Janice came hurrying out of the library, a small nervous-looking woman, smiling brightly. "Follow me. I'll show you the kitchen." Her eyes swept Stella, came to rest, pointedly, on her lip ring and her hair, dyed an unnatural shade of black, and then skittered away.

Stella followed her down a long narrow hallway through a butler's pantry to the kitchen. Janice was talking the whole time. *Miss Alice likes this, Miss Alice doesn't like that.* "You're not to eat her food. Bring your own lunch and dinner from home. She'll tell you what she wants to eat. Here's her routine," Janice said, opening a three-ring binder that contained accounts of all the minutiae of Miss Alice's daily life, down to the time and quantity of her bowel movements. "She exercises twice a day, morning and afternoons, five complete laps of the ground floor." Janice took a glass down from the cupboard. "These glasses are for Miss Alice only. You can use the ones on the bottom shelf. You have to walk behind her as she walks to make sure she doesn't fall. Before you begin, fill one of these glasses with ice up to here, just here, do you see where I'm pointing? The rest with water. Put the glass on the table and cover it with a napkin. That way, when Miss Alice needs to hydrate as she's making her laps, she can just pick it up off the table. The rest of the time, she has a little bell and she'll ring it if she needs you."

Stella thought, *I'll call Charlotte tonight and tell her I can't take the job.*

"Are there any questions?" Janice said brightly.

"No. I don't think so."

"Don't worry," Janice said, laughing. "You'll do fine."

Her financial aid hadn't come through, not in the amount her counselor had told her anyway, and now she was short on tuition for the spring semester. Short on tuition and short on money for books, food, and housing, too. It was the way her chaotic life always went. If things could go wrong, they would. She should have been used to poverty by now, she'd been on her own since she was sixteen, she should have developed thick skin, calluses, a devil-may-care attitude. But she wasn't like that. Poverty wasn't like that. It wore you down, permeated your clothes, your skin, like a fine powder. After awhile you gave it off like a stench.

Just once, Stella wanted life to be easy.

She deserved it, damn it. If anyone deserved an easy life, it was her.

Alice Montclair Whittington was nothing like she had expected. She had expected Joan Crawford in a padded-shoulder suit, but Alice was thin, of medium height, with a cloud of white hair. She wore a green knit dress and a pink sweater, and a pair of tennis shoes with pink socks. Her eyes were a faded blue but Stella saw something move in their depths, something sharp and fierce. Those pale eyes fixed on Stella's face while Janice twittered on, speaking in an overly-loud and jovial voice, as if she was talking to an unruly child.

When Janice had finished, Alice looked at Stella and said, "I hear you're from Alabama"

"That's right."

"Well, I'm sorry for you."

Stella stared at her a beat. "It could be worse," she said.

"I don't see how."

Alice was sitting in a wingback chair next to a wall of bookcases. Janice stood behind her.

"Now, Miss Alice," she said nervously.

Alice ignored Janice and continued her perusal of Stella. "What's that mark on your arm?"

"This?" Stella hesitated, and then pushed up her sleeve so the old woman could see. "It's a tattoo. It's the Sanskrit symbol for peace."

"You young ones are always marking up your skin. Do you know what that will look like when you get to be my age?"

Stella pulled her sleeve down. "I try not to think about it."

Behind the chair, Janice frowned, giving her head a warning shake.

Alice brightened, slanting her eyes up at Stella. "Ever do this kind of work before?"

"Nope."

"But you think you can handle it?"

"It's not brain surgery. I can handle it."

"They say I'm difficult."

"I'm used to difficult people."

"I'm not difficult. I just like things done a certain way."

"I understand."

Alice folded her hands in her lap. She gave Stella a sly look. "You'd be a pretty girl if you'd do something with your hair."

"And you'd be a nice old lady if you'd stop saying things you shouldn't."

Behind Alice's shoulder, Janice's mouth fell open in shock. The clock on the mantle ticked steadily. Stella thought, *I never even had a chance to ask what the hourly rate was.*

Without warning, Alice Montclair Whittington put her head back and laughed.

The girl reminded her of someone. She had suffered; you could see it in her eyes, in the fierce, wary expression on her face. The girl's face was heart-shaped; a sign of beauty in

Alice's generation but less so now, with their celebration of thin, blade-faced women with over-full lips. The girl reminded Alice of someone but she couldn't remember who.

Memory was like that. It shuffled in and out of her consciousness like an old servant. One moment she might be looking at the angelic expression of a blonde child in a sepia-tinted photograph, and the next moment she remembered, with all the fresh anguish of grief, that the child was her own son, long grown now and dead.

Alice watched the girl's face as Janice explained the dreary routines of this dreary house. The girl listened attentively, eyes hooded, chin dropped slightly, and Alice was reminded again of someone she'd known long ago. Memory stirred, began its lumbering progress along the dusty corridors of her mind toward the shuttered room where something unpleasant waited.

No.

Alice closed her eyes and let it go, sinking once more into blessed oblivion.

Stella and Janice were standing in the library when Alice's sister, Adeline, drove up. Stella watched her through the window, listening half-heartedly to Janice describe the routines of the house, still in shock that, despite her inappropriate comment to Alice, she'd been offered the job. Adeline came in carrying a bag of chili-cheese Coneys that she'd picked up at the Sonic Drive-In. She was well-dressed and looked every bit the aristocrat, handing the greasy bag to Janice and saying, "There are three in the bag. Make sure they *all* go in the refrigerator."

Janice took the bag gratefully, without so much as a grimace, but Stella blushed.

"I'm Alice's sister," Adeline said, her eyes sweeping Stella. "Who are you?" The disapproval in her face was obvious. She didn't even try to hide it.

"I'm Stella."

Alice said, "She's my new caregiver. She's taking the place of that other one. The one I didn't like."

They looked as different from each other as sisters could look, although Janice had warned Stella that Adeline visited often, and that she and Miss Alice quarreled like children.

"Done this kind of work before have you?" Adeline asked Stella.

Stella frowned slightly. "No."

"I didn't think so."

"Stop interrogating her, Adeline. I don't come to your house and interrogate the help."

The help. Stella blushed again and followed Janice into the kitchen. The whole time she stood listening to Janice give instructions on how to make meals, Stella was thinking, *I won't be back.*

But later, as she was leaving, walking past the library door, Alice called to her, "Are you coming back tomorrow?"

Something hopeful and hesitant in her voice made Stella stop. She raised her chin and stared boldly at Adeline, and then at Alice, giving her a tight little smile.

"Of course I'll be back," she said, lifting one hand carelessly, and turning, she walked out.

They watched her through the library windows climb into her small rusty car and drive away. The January sky was darkening, pressing down on the roofs of the houses across the street.

Adeline said, "She has a tattoo."

"It's the Sanskrit symbol for peace."

"The what?"

"The tattoo. It's Sanskrit."

"She has a ring through her lip."

"They all do these days."

"Only the bad ones. Did you hide the silver?"

"I like her," Alice said. "I think I'll keep her."

All the way back to Josh's apartment Stella rehearsed in her head what she would say to Charlotte. She would tell her another job had come up. She would tell her her school schedule had changed. But then, in the middle of imagining what excuses she would use to not take the job, Stella remembered her promise to Alice. She remembered Adeline's expression of open dislike and she felt a tremor of resentment. All her life, people had been looking at her the way Adeline had looked at her.

As if being poor was a crime.

It was one of the reasons why, despite the odds, she'd gotten her GED. It was one of the reasons she'd enrolled in college. To make something of herself, to rise above poverty and hardship through her own merits, without any help from anyone. To use education to get what so many people around her seemed to take for granted; a good job, a roof over her head, food on the table.

A life of her own.

Josh was sitting on the sofa playing Halo when she got home. The apartment was a townhouse, with a living room and dining room in front and a kitchen in back, and two bedrooms and a bath upstairs. The downstairs was crowded with several sofas and easy chairs that Josh had picked up from neighbors who were moving out. He was a packrat, but he paid the rent on time and kept food on the table, which was more than her previous boyfriends had been able to do. The sex wasn't great, but it was good enough.

"Did you get the job?" he said, without looking up.

"Have you ever seen that movie, *Driving Miss Daisy*?"

"Yeah." He frowned. "I mean, I think so."

"Okay. Well, I'd be the Morgan Freeman character."

He chuckled but she could see that he had no idea what she was talking about. He kept his attention fixed on the screen.

"Why aren't you at work?"

He glanced at her and then back at the TV. "I stayed out late last night and didn't feel like going in. I called in sick."

"Nice."

"You can do that when you've been gainfully employed for awhile."

She refused to let him rattle her. She said benignly, "One of the perks of full-time employment, I guess."

"Yeah," he said. "You should try it."

She went into the kitchen and opened the refrigerator, pulling out a beer. She stood for a moment at the kitchen window, staring out at the hard-packed dirt yard and the roofs of dilapidated houses and the distant ridge tops, dark against the winter sky. This part of Chattanooga was hilly and well-settled, with small shotgun-style cottages perched on the sides of steep ravines, and here and there, a rambling old Victorian cut up into small apartments. After a few minutes she went back into the front room and slumped down in one of the overstuffed chairs facing the TV.

"Did you pick up some more beer?" he said, without looking up from his game.

"No, I forgot."

"You can run out later."

She hadn't forgotten. She didn't have the money for beer. She didn't have the money for anything. She owed him two months' rent, which of course, was what he was pissed about.

"So when do you start?"

"If I took the job, I'd start tomorrow."

He glanced at her and then back at the TV. "What do you mean, *if* you took it? You have any other job offers recently?"

Asshole. He knew she'd been looking, had been trying since Christmas to find a part-time job to supplement her meager work study earnings. Still, it couldn't be easy for him either, having to support her. He worked as a computer tech for a local insurance company and although the money was good, it wasn't good enough to support two.

She felt a mind-numbing weariness come over her. She stared moodily at the screen, remembering Alice's statement to her sister. *I don't come over to your house and interrogate the help.* The help. That's what she would be; a servant at the beck and call of a rich old lady with a little silver bell. How humiliating would that be? Still, compared to everything else she'd faced, was facing now, what difference did it make?

"I'll probably take the job until I can find something else," she said.

"Good girl," he said. "What's it pay?"

She told him. He shrugged, not looking at her. "Not too bad. That should buy a few groceries." He seemed in a better mood now that he knew she'd have some money coming in.

She put her head back and closed her eyes. In the apartment next door, a child began to wail.

"Speaking of groceries," he said. "What's for supper?"

I don't know, fucker, what's for supper?

That's what she wanted to say. She spent a lot of time fantasizing about saying things like that to him. But reality kept her mute. She was tired of sleeping on the flea-infested sofas of people she barely knew.

She got up and, without another word, went into the kitchen to see what she could make.

Alice was already dressed and sitting up in bed when Stella arrived the following morning. She was wearing the same clothes she had worn yesterday and she had a crossword puzzle book open on her lap.

"Good morning, Alice."

Alice looked up. "Oh, hello," she said. "Who are you?"

"I'm Stella. The new girl." The room was large and sunny and filled with twin beds and assorted pieces of French provincial furniture. Through a door to her left, Stella could see a small bathroom.

"Oh, you're the new girl. I don't know anything. I just do what they tell me."

"Okay. I'm going to clock in now."

"You better clock in," Alice said. "What's her name just left."

The night caregiver, a young woman named Elaine, was waiting for Stella in the kitchen. She rolled her eyes and said, "We're having a difficult day today."

"Oh?" Stella said.

The girl looked like she might cry. Her hair was long and dark and she wore it in a thick braid down her back. "Well, to start with, she wouldn't change her clothes. She has a bad habit of wearing the same thing over and over again. I try to explain to her about germs but she won't listen to me."

Stella thought, *What's the big deal*? The old woman had been around for ninety-four years and if germs hadn't killed her by now, they probably wouldn't.

"Promise me you'll try to get her to pick out something clean to wear," Elaine said, giving her a dark, reproachful look. "You'll have to lay her clothes out when you get her ready for bed. See if she'll let you pick something clean."

"Sure," Stella said. "I'll see what I can do."

After Elaine left, she walked through the sunny rooms of the spacious house, marveling at their size and cleanliness, the perfect order, the dark mahogany furniture and oriental carpets, the smell of lemon wax and leather. Books and flowers and silver framed photographs filled every room. Everywhere there were crystal bowls and silver trays inscribed with thanks from Alice's various charities; Big Brothers Big Sisters, The Salvation Army, the Little Theater. In the valley below, the city of Chattanooga sprawled along the banks of the Tennessee. Stella went into the library and helped herself to *Billy Bathgate* and a biography of Jackie Kennedy, taking both into the glass-walled sunroom to read. There was a baby monitor on the table and she could hear Alice turning the pages of her book, whispering under her breath the words she was trying to find in the crosswords.

A few minutes later the bell rang and Stella walked to the other side of the house. Alice was sitting on the edge of the bed.

"I'd like to go to the bathroom, please," she said and Stella hurried over with the walker. She had been told to keep the walker on the other side of the room so Alice couldn't get up without assistance. It seemed a dirty trick to play on an obviously independent woman, to put her walking aid where she couldn't reach it. But so did hovering outside the opened bathroom door and waiting for Alice to relieve herself. *Whatever you do, don't let her go in there alone and close the door*, Janice had said. *But don't let her think you're spying on her either. We try to give her as much privacy as we can.*

Alice went to the sink afterwards and washed her hands. Then she hobbled out, sliding the walker in front of her. Stella went into the bathroom as discreetly as she could and flushed the toilet and turned off the light. She picked up a wet bath cloth from the edge of the tub, and emptied the clothes hamper of a towel and pair of white cotton panties. Janice had told her to take the laundry down to the basement first thing every morning.

She walked down the steep basement stairs holding the clothes in front of her. The basement was cool and dark and smelled of mold. She followed a narrow corridor that opened on one side to a small low-ceilinged bedroom with twin beds and, further on, a half bath. *Servant's quarters*, Stella guessed. Not the kind of place where you'd stash family members although it was certainly nicer than some places Stella had slept. Further on down the corridor to the left, was the laundry room.

A gray, slanting light filled the room, falling from high dusty windows. Beneath the windows, a laundry rack stood covered in hanging towels and bath cloths. On the adjacent wall, a washer and dryer crowded beneath a pair of cupboards, and beside them stood an old galvanized soaking tub. In the bottom of the tub was a shallow plastic pan filled with soaking panties. Stella dropped Alice's underwear here and sprayed them lightly with presoak. She hung Alice's towel and bath cloth on the rack. The room was dark and strange-smelling. This part of the house, low-ceilinged and cramped, was different from the rest. There was a feeling here of lives lived in quiet desperation, of secrets kept, and old sorrows unaired. Standing there Stella was overcome by a sense of despair, a sudden desire to flee not only the basement, but also the house.

She shivered and stepped back, and turning, hurried along the corridor and up the steep steps to the kitchen, fighting an overwhelming urge, the whole time, to turn and look behind her.

Alice was to exercise twice a day, taking five laps around the house which, owing to the size of the rooms, was a good distance. On that first morning she rang the bell around nine-thirty and Stella hurried back to the bedroom.

"Are you ready to exercise?" Alice asked, rising unsteadily to her feet.

"Sure," Stella said, positioning the walker so she could reach it.

Alice pushed the walker in front of her, the wheels complaining softly. Someone had stuck tennis balls on the back legs of the walker to make it easier to push along the darkly polished floors. Stella walked just to the side and slightly behind her, trying to make sure the walker didn't catch on any of the oriental rugs. While she walked, Alice complained about Elaine, the night caregiver. "She's terrified of germs," Alice said. *"Oh, Alice, you can't wear that,"* Alice mimicked in a high falsetto voice. *"That dress is crawling with germs."*

Stella wasn't sure whether to laugh or comment, so she stayed quiet. As soon as she could, she changed the subject. "Do you like exercising?" she asked Alice.

"I guess so. I don't mind too much. These are the exercises they wanted me to do at Cantor," Alice said. "I told the doctor I could do them just as well at home."

"How long ago were you at Cantor Hospital?"

"How old am I?"

"Ninety-four. I think."

"Okay, then. Four years ago. Sometimes I forget things. The doctor wanted me to wear one of those patches that make you remember all the time but I told him, if I can't remember something I'll just call my friend Weesie or my sister Adeline. Between the three of us, we have a pretty good memory."

Stella laughed.

"I lived by myself until I was ninety."

"Really?" Stella said. "That's awesome."

"Ninety years old and I'd never fallen a day in my life, and I'm walking out of a restaurant with my grandsons and I just fell over. Just fell over backwards and hit my head on the pavement. Can you believe that? Anyway, when I woke up I was at Cantor Hospital on the wing where they put the stroke victims. And they slapped this patch on my arm and it made me sick as a dog. I haven't thrown up since I was eight years old and all of a sudden, I've got the dry heaves.

When the doctor comes in, I say, *'Doctor, why have you put this patch on my arm?'*

And he says, 'Why, Miss Alice, that's to keep you from losing your mind.'

And I say, 'Well, I've already lost my mind. And it makes me so sick I can't stand up. I will not wear it.'

And he says, 'Now, Miss Alice, I'm the doctor and you must do as I say.'

I say, 'I want to go home.'

'Well, as soon as you go to the bathroom on your own, I'll release you. But not until then.'

'I will not go to the bathroom here. I have a perfectly good bathroom back at my home.' (She stopped walking and looked at Stella, shaking her head at the unfairness of this memory.) "They wanted me to use a bathroom women *and* men had used." She shook her head fiercely, her cheeks pink with indignation. "Well?" she said. "Would you use a bathroom strange men had used?"

Stella couldn't bring herself to tell Alice about some of the bathrooms she had used. Alice had no understanding of the desperate ways some people lived. That much was apparent.

'The doctor says, I won't release you until you've used the bathroom on your own. And it says here on your chart that you're refusing to do your exercises.'

'I can do my exercises at home.'

'The therapist says you're having trouble with that hip. You know we can replace that hip if it's bothering you.'

'Doctor, I came in to this world with all my original parts and I plan on going out with all my original parts.'

'Well I can't release you until you go to the bathroom and do your exercises.'

'They tell me you got your medical degree from Alabama.'

'That's right. The University of Alabama.'

*'Isn't that where they train doctors by letting them practice on
animals?'*

He never batted an eye. *'That's so we'll know how to deal
with crotchety old patients who won't do as they're told.'"*

Alice looked sideways at Stella. A crooked grin spread
slowly across her face.

"I knew then I was going to like him," she said.

After they'd finished walking, they did Alice's calisthenic
exercises in her bedroom. Her "Slide and Glides," she called
them. She stood in the bathroom doorway, holding onto the
frame, and slid one foot out ten times, followed by the other
foot. Stella did the same, standing in the bedroom doorway.
When they had finished, Alice sat down on the edge of her bed
and stood up again, ten times.

"What do you call this?" Stella said, mimicking her with a
series of squats.

"Jump ups," Alice said.

She was breathless. When she finished the jump ups she
sat for a moment on the edge of the bed, catching her breath
and rolling her head slowly on her neck. "Whew-ee," she said.
"I'm worn out."

Stella helped her put her sweater back on and then got her
situated in bed with her crossword puzzle book opened on her
lap. Heading back to the kitchen, Stella paused in the doorway,
looking at Alice curiously.

"So who won? You or the doctor?"

"What?" Alice said.

"At Cantor Hospital. Who won, you or the doctor?"

Alice gave her a sly look. Her eyes were blue and cloudy
as seawater. "Who do you think?" she said. "When my son,

Sawyer, came to visit I told him about my conversation with the doctor and how he said I couldn't leave."

'*Pack your bag, Al,*' Sawyer said. '*We're breaking you out of here.*'"

The day followed a strict, invariable routine. After exercise, around 10:30, came snack, a diet coke in a bottle and a packet of Ritz crackers with cheese, carefully cut open along the side, both served on a white paper napkin. Alice preferred to spend her mornings in her room, sitting up in one of the twin beds with her crossword puzzle books spread out around her. Between the beds stood a small nightstand holding a lamp, a clock, her snack, and a little red Salvation Army bell that she rang whenever she needed Stella.

Lunch was at 12:30 and was basically deli or convenience food heated up and served at a carefully set table in the kitchen. The table was actually a desk facing a wall of built in glass shelves filled with photographs and collectibles and a few tarnished golf trophies. Alice preferred chicken and turkey to beef and fish, and along with this, two vegetables, a fresh fruit cup, cider or lemonade, followed by a scoop of ice cream. Alice's appetite was hearty but she preferred small portions, and Stella, looking at Alice's binder and realizing that a lot of the caregivers gave her the same thing every day, tried to spice up lunch by including a few fresh herbs and tomatoes, a variety of canned vegetables.

"Oh, how pretty it looks," Alice said, looking down at the plate Stella had made and waiting for Stella to pull the chair out so she could sit down. Stella felt her face flush with pleasure. She had brought a peanut butter sandwich for lunch, and had set a place beside Alice's, and after Alice said a quick prayer, she picked up her sandwich and began to eat.

Alice sat very still with her hands in her lap, staring straight ahead at the wall. "Bib me," she said.

Stella put the sandwich down and looked at her. "Sorry?"

Alice pointed with one bony finger at a plastic baby bib folded on a corner of the desk. Stella got up and tied the bib carefully around Alice's neck.

"I don't know whose idea this was," Alice said. "I just do as I'm told."

They ate for awhile in silence. Stella quickly learned that Alice's hearing, like her mind, seemed to come and go. It was best to simply wait and let Alice begin the conversation because asking questions irritated her. She was a good lip reader but she couldn't read lips with Stella sitting beside her and it frustrated her. At other times, Alice's hearing would become suddenly acute, and she would hear the distant chiming of a clock or some whispered comment made by Stella.

While she ate, Stella stared at a funny card of an old woman in a flowered dress and tennis shoes wielding a baseball bat displayed prominently on the shelf above them.

Alice said, "My son, Roddy, gave that to me for my birthday."

"How many children do you have, Alice?"

"Three." She frowned, her face clouding slightly, and said, "Two." She pointed at another photograph, higher up on the shelves, of an attractive middle-aged couple. "That's Roddy and his wife, Hadley. She's cut her hair since then. She looks better now." Alice stared at the photograph a moment and then continued eating. "She's a real talented sculptor. I've never known a sculptor before. She did a bust of Roddy and I walked into the dining room and thought, '*Oh my God, she's cut Roddy's head off.*' It was that real. Now she's got heads of Roddy all over the lawn."

"Does she sell her sculptures?"

Alice turned slowly and stared at Stella. "Who would want a head of Roddy?"

"No, I mean, does she do other people?"

"No. Just Roddy."

After Alice finished her lunch, Stella fixed her a scoop of ice cream. She was still nervous around the old woman, afraid she might say the wrong thing or show her lack of refinement through some inadvertent word or action. She felt guarded around Alice, carefully weighing her words before speaking. It made her feel, at times, tongue-tied and stupid.

When Stella sat down again, she pointed at a tarnished brass golf trophy in the glass case that read, *Duffer's Trophy*. "Is that your husband's?"

Alice thought this was funny. She chuckled for a moment, her shoulders shaking. "Bill Whittington must be turning over in his grave," she said. She spooned her ice cream, her lips moving slowly. "He was a golfing fanatic. We used to have to sit on the back row of Sunday services so he could sneak out early to get to the club. He didn't believe women should play golf, and on the day I won the *Duffer's Trophy*, he was furious. I and Louise Parramore had gone along with Bill and Baxter Parramore for a club couples' tournament. It made Bill Whittington mad, the way Louise and I didn't take it seriously, the way we sat in the back of the cart giggling. And when I won the *Duffer's Trophy* and got up and made a pretty little speech, he was so embarrassed. On the way home, he said '*Good God, Alice, it's not a compliment to win the Duffer's Trophy. It means you have no business being on a golf course.*' But I didn't care. I put it right up on the front shelf where everyone could see it, right up beside his trophies. We had a cabinet filled with his golf trophies but I put most of them in the attic when he died."

Stella had a sudden image of Alice and Louise Parramore giggling in the back of the golf cart, while their husbands looked on in stern disapproval.

She grinned. "Alice," she said. "I bet you were something."

"Oh, I was something, all right." Alice smiled serenely. She finished her ice cream and pushed the bowl away, bending her neck meekly, like a child.

"De-bib me," she said.

After lunch, it was nap time. Alice lay down on the top coverlet of one of the twin beds with her tennis shoes on, and Stella wrapped her up like a mummy.

"Night, night," Alice said, and a few minutes later, she was breathing deeply.

Stella wandered the quiet house. She didn't believe in ghosts, but if she had, she would have expected them to reside in a house like this, filled with the prized possessions of people long dead. The oil portrait of the young woman in the foyer was Alice's great-great-grandmother who had died at the age of twenty-eight giving birth to her sixth child. Alice had told her the story earlier that morning, as they began their exercise circuit.

"My great-great-grandfather is supposed to have said, *I killed her. I loved her too much*. He was broken-hearted. Her name was Alice, too. I'm named for her, and as a girl the story of her death horrified me. Love seemed to me a mysterious and dangerous emotion. I used to stand in front of her portrait and vow never to fall in love. Never to marry."

"So what happened?" Stella said.

Alice turned her head and let her blue eyes rest for a moment on Stella's face.

"Life," she said. "Life happened."

Stella wandered slowly through the large living room, trying not to touch anything, her arms crossed behind her back. An old-fashioned sofa, low and wide with intricately carved feet, faced the fireplace which was flanked by two chintz-covered wingback chairs. An assortment of pillows covered the sofa's back, framing a black velvet cushion that read, *Queen of Everything*. On all the tables and book cases scattered throughout the room there were silver framed photographs of a dark-haired man with black-rimmed glasses. *Bill Whittington*, Stella guessed. He was dressed always in a suit, and there was a pompous, self-satisfied air about him that Stella didn't like. He was a small man but you could see that he had been vain and fastidious about his appearance. Oddly, there were no photographs of Alice as a young woman. There were a few of her as a child, and one or two of her as a middle-aged woman, but nothing else. The room, with its many photographs of Bill Whittington covering the tables and shelves, seemed almost like a shrine.

On the dining room sideboard there were more silver-framed photographs of children and grandchildren, some sporting Alice's clear blue eyes and blonde hair. Others resembled her husband, with their dark hair and eyes and their broad lantern jaws. Stella, who had only seen one photograph of her grandmother as a girl, was amazed, looking at the Whittington clan, at the certain passing of genetic material from one generation to the next.

On the far wall near the dining room windows was an oil portrait of a young woman in a blue evening gown. Her hair was blonde and she wore it pulled back in the style of Grace Kelly. She was strikingly beautiful, and her face was turned slightly to the side, so that she seemed to be gazing off into the distance with a mild, dreamy expression on her face, a slight smile curving her lips. Stella had noticed the portrait several times as she and Alice made their rounds this morning, but she had not walked close enough to see it clearly. It hung on the wall above a mahogany chest cluttered with silver serving pieces.

Staring at the portrait Stella became gradually aware of the creaking of floorboards behind her, as if someone was walking along the hall. She turned and stared, and the creaking stopped. She stood for a moment listening intently, but heard nothing besides the distant whirring of the refrigerator.

She turned back to the portrait. The young woman's face seemed oddly familiar, and feeling a slight tremor, a cold touch at the nape of her neck, she thought, *Now, who does she remind me of?*

She wandered into the sunroom and picked up the biography of Jacqueline Kennedy Onassis. *"She was a Sweet Briar alum, too,"* Alice had told her. *"I never met her but I used to get fund raising letters from her all the time."* She sat down in a small upholstered chair. Sunlight fell in wide swaths across the tiled floor. After some time, drowsy with the heat and the soft sound of Alice's breathing on the monitor, Stella closed her eyes. She folded her hands on the book nestled in her lap. How pleasant to live like this, removed completely from the cares of the world, shut up behind thick protective walls like a princess in an enchanted castle.

After awhile, Stella dozed.

She awoke gradually to the sound of whispering on the monitor. It had been continuing steadily, she realized, coming out of sleep into wakefulness. She had heard it in her dreams. It was a deep voice she heard now, low and hoarse and anguished.

Laura. Oh my God, Laura.

Stella sat up. The book slid out of her lap onto the floor with a loud clap. She was instantly awake, the hair on her arms rising. The voice she had heard was so tormented that she could feel it like a tremor along her spine.

She leaned forward, listening intently. The only sound now was Alice's soft breathing, followed a few minutes later by the noise of the bedsprings giving as she rolled over. The sudden, loud ringing of the bell made Stella jump.

"Jesus," she said.

She got up quickly, walking down the long dark hallway, past the locked front door, to Alice's bedroom. The elderly woman was sitting on the edge of her bed, her hands in her lap, her hair standing up behind her head like a dove's wing. She looked confused, disturbed.

"Alice, are you okay?"

"I need to go to the bathroom, please."

She helped Alice to the bathroom and then got her settled again on the bed, her puzzle books spread around her. She seemed less confused now, more aware of her surroundings, yet there was a distance in her gaze, a slump of defeat in her shoulders.

"*Family Feud* is on at four," Alice said.

Stella stopped in the doorway and looked at her.

"You have to turn it on for me because I don't know how to use the clicker."

"I can do that," Stella said, wondering now if she had dreamed the voice on the monitor. With the sunlight streaming into the bedroom it seemed impossible that she had heard what she thought she heard.

"But first we have to do our exercises."

"Yes," Stella said. She stood in the doorway, hesitating.

"And after that, you'll need to check the mail."

"Okay."

"And get me my Ensure."

"All right."

"I'll ring when I'm ready to walk."

Stella went out. Halfway down the long hallway to the kitchen she stopped, her hand to her throat. The heavy front door, which she had passed just a short time before, stood wide open.

The dream hovered at the edge of her consciousness, buzzing around her like a swarm of angry bees. The memory of it faded but the feelings it evoked did not. Alice sat on the edge of the bed, stunned, frozen. The dreams were becoming more insistent now, trying to tell her something, to wake her from her self-imposed slumber.

Yesterday, she had seen Bill Whittington. He was standing in the doorway watching her with a severe expression as if to say, *Look at you. Didn't I say you would end this way?*

She drew herself up and turned her head and when she looked again, he was gone.

And now the girl with the heart-shaped face was there, standing in the doorway and smiling her sad smile, and her face was so familiar it caused a stirring in Alice's heart and a quickening of her breath, so much like the beloved's face, and yet not her at all.

Are you all right? the girl's expression seemed to say.

No, I am not all right, Alice thought. *I will never be all right.*

Stella was surprised how tired she was at the end of that first day. The bell rang continuously. Alice could not close the blinds or change the channel on the TV or pick up a large book without assistance. Stella had brought her laptop but she hadn't opened it, spending the entire day reading and dozing and listening for the sound of the bell, the strange creaking noises of the old house.

After dinner she got Alice settled in her room with *Wheel of Fortune* blaring on the television, and she went back to the kitchen and washed the dishes and put them away in the cabinets. Alice had so few dishes and it seemed ridiculous to stack them in the cavernous dishwasher and so she washed everything by hand. The light was dying in the west and a rosy glow filled the kitchen. Stella stood at the sink feeling exhausted and sleepy. It was seven-thirty and the night caregiver would arrive at eight. She tried to remember what Janice had told her about getting Alice ready for bed.

"It's like taking care of a big old baby," Alice said, as Stella helped her undress. She put her arms up so Stella could pull her dress over her head, but at the last minute she said impatiently, "Wait a minute, wait a minute." Her head reappeared from the dress and she carefully pulled each sleeve off at the wrist. "There," she said. "Now it's right side out." She sat on the edge of the bed in her slip and tennis shoes watching while Stella neatly folded the dress.

"Would you like to wear a different dress tomorrow?" Stella asked.

"No I would not."

Alice pointed at the pink sweater that lay folded on the bed beside her. "Here, take this and hang it on the back of that chair."

Stella took the green dress and folded it neatly over a small chair in the corner. Then she took the pink sweater and arranged it carefully across the back.

Behind her Alice said in a querulous voice, "Wait. What are you doing?"

"You said to hang it on the back of the chair."

"Why do you have my sweater? Where did you get that?"

"You were wearing it. You gave it to me to hang up."

"Sweaters belong in that closet over there."

"Okay. I'll hang it in the closet then."

"Oh, that's right. I was wearing it. Put it on the back of that chair."

Her tone was different than it had been earlier in the day, impatient, petulant. She was like a stranger sitting there, her eyes fixed suspiciously on Stella. Stella helped her take off her tennis shoes and Alice went into the bathroom and brushed her teeth. Stella pulled down the bed covers the way Janice had showed her. Alice came out of the bathroom, pushing the walker in front of her. She sat on the edge of the bed in her slip and socks with her hair standing up around her head in curly wisps. Stella laid Alice's nightgown out on the bed beside her and then she began to smooth baby oil on Alice's arms, shoulders, and legs. Her skin was mottled and purple with bruises and it soaked up the oil like old parchment.

"Did you ever see such a mess?" Alice said, staring down at her helpless body.

Stella, embarrassed, said, "Does this help with the dryness?" The old woman seemed to be coming in and out of awareness. Twice she looked at Stella as if she had no idea who she was and once she called her, *Martha*.

"Put some of that in my hand," Alice said, holding out one cupped hand twisted with arthritis. "So I can put it on my face."

Stella tried to tap some into her palm but the oil wouldn't come. Alice sighed. Stella tried again. Alice made a low whistling sound, an obvious expression of disgust, and Stella felt her face warm.

She gave a more vigorous squeeze and this time the oil spurted out of the bottle into Alice's palm and ran down onto her slip.

"Oh, Lord," Alice said.

Stella quickly capped the bottle and dabbed at Alice's slip with a Kleenex. It was embarrassing and yet comical, too. She giggled nervously.

"Sorry," she said.

Alice watched her, gingerly applying the oil to her face. "I don't know that you're cut out to be a caregiver," she said.

"I'll get it, Alice. I promise. I'm fairly intelligent."

"I'll be the judge of that," Alice said serenely.

Three

§§§

T he next morning Stella cornered Elaine in the kitchen before she clocked out.

"I have to ask you something," Stella said. "I hope you won't think I'm crazy."

"You didn't get her to change her dress."

"What? Oh, no, I asked her but she said no."

Elaine stared, her eyes blue and emotionless.

Stella hesitated. "Have you ever heard footsteps in the hallway? Or had a strange feeling down in the basement?"

Elaine gave Stella a long, inscrutable look. "Are you asking me if the house is haunted? Because I've been here three years and I've never seen or heard anything out of the ordinary." She crossed her arms over her chest, considering. "There was an evening caregiver a few years ago who woke up in the middle of the night and swore she saw an Indian standing in her room. She left and never came back. And there was another one who said she saw a man wearing plaid pants watching her in the basement. But they're the only ones I know of."

"I heard whispering on the monitor."

Elaine's expression was mildly condescending and Stella wished now she hadn't said anything. She was a psychology major and she'd taken enough classes to know that ghostly hallucinations are often projections of inner emotional turmoil. Given that definition, it was amazing that she didn't see phantoms everywhere.

Elaine gave a slight shrug. "Alice talks in her sleep. I've heard her."

"But this voice was low and very – husky. It didn't sound like her."

"Her voice is fairly deep." Elaine smirked suddenly and Stella understood why Alice didn't like her.

She said, "Did Alice have a daughter?"

Elaine stopped smiling and shook her head. "No. Three sons. Although one is dead and we don't ever talk about him. Sam, I think his name was. Her husband's been dead a long time, too, and we don't ever talk about him either."

"Okay, well, thanks. I feel a lot better knowing that you've never seen or heard anything weird."

"If there's nothing else," Elaine said, gathering her crochet and stuffing it into her sewing bag. "I guess I'll clock out." She picked up the phone and called in and Stella went over and wrote her name in the book and read through Elaine's notes from the night before. *Alice seemed restless*, she had written. *She didn't sleep well. Once she got up without waiting for me and went into the bathroom and turned on the light. Very sarcastic this morning.*

"Oh, one other thing," Elaine said behind her, and Stella turned. "When she takes off that green dress tonight, take it and put it immediately in the clothes hamper. The thing is crawling with germs. I won't have her wearing it again until it's been washed."

Despite Elaine's comments in the notebook, Alice seemed rather chipper and happy to see her.

"You came back," she said when Stella poked her head in the room.

"Of course I came back. Are you used to people not coming back?"

"Some don't."

"Well, I'm not like that."

"I can see that you're not." She waved her hand at the newspaper lying on the other twin bed. "You're welcome to read it, if you like."

"Thank you," Stella said, picking up the paper. "Is there anything good to report?"

"Just the usual death and destruction," Alice said cheerfully.

"Oh, good. I like reading about death and destruction."

She took the paper out to the sunroom and sat drinking a cup of coffee and staring at the sunny valley below. She shouldn't be reading the paper at all; she should be working on a term paper due in her *Psychology of Gender* class. The class met on Tuesdays and Thursdays and now that Stella was sitting with Alice on Wednesdays and Thursdays, she would have to miss the Thursday morning session. At least temporarily, until she found some other kind of work. She stirred guiltily, remembering Alice's comment this morning about her not coming back. Still, some things couldn't be helped. She had told Charlotte specifically that she couldn't work Thursday mornings because of her class and yet Charlotte had scheduled her anyway. Her professor was cool and Stella felt certain that once she had explained the situation, she'd be allowed to pick up notes from some other student. *But who to ask?* Stella kept to herself, she didn't socialize with the other girls in her class, many of whom had started out together as freshmen, reinforcing their friendships through rush parties and trips to Destin. Stella had never had the time, or the money, for any of that. It was everything she could do just to keep up with her class work, given the number of hours she had to work.

The reality was she couldn't have done it without the help of Professor Dillard who was also her advisor. Professor Dillard had taken Stella under her wing and seen to it that she was allowed to take *Psychology of Gender* even though she hadn't taken the prerequisite *Women as Victims* class. And she would make allowances, Stella felt certain, for her current situation, too.

She had been lucky with teachers. Even during grade school back in Alabama, there'd always been at least one teacher each year who took an interest in her. She was smart and quietly attentive, and she made good grades all the way up until her junior year of high school when everything she knew, or thought she knew, came crashing down around her. Even then it had been Charlie Chesmore, her Honors English teacher, who had taken her aside and demanded to know if she was having trouble at home.

Professor Dillard would make allowances for her for spending Thursdays with Alice Whittington, but she would expect Stella to find someone whose notes she could copy. And the only person Stella could even remotely imagine asking was Luke Morgan.

He was the only male student in her *Psychology of Gender* class; the upper level psychology classes were filled primarily with women, and this made him a great favorite with both the professor and the other students.

"*Tell us what you think from a male perspective, Mr. Morgan,*" Professor Dillard would say when explaining some controversy over cultural and psycho-biological influences. He'd been in Stella's *Serial Killers in History* class in the fall, but he'd let his hair grow out over the Christmas holidays and now it fell in soft brown waves around his face. When asked a question, he would always pause thoughtfully before replying in a deep, melodic voice, and everyone in the class would turn their heads to listen.

Last Tuesday he had answered one of Professor Dillard's questions in a way that made the whole class laugh. Turning to look at him, Stella had found his eyes fixed intently on her. He was sitting a row behind her, they were separated by a group of giggling sorority girls, but he had stared at Stella in such a frank, steady manner that even the sorority girls had turned around to look at her. Stella quickly dipped her head, letting her hair drop around her face like a curtain.

Afterwards, she sat quietly while the rest of the class filed out. He was not the sort she was usually attracted to; he seemed too clean-cut and sincere and his eyes were kind. She had the feeling, sitting there, that he would be waiting for her when she went out, and this thought caused a flutter of dread, but also nervous anticipation, in the pit of her stomach.

She thought of the way he had stared at her, jaunty, appreciative, as if the comment he had made, and the laughter it caused, had been a gift for her. It was pleasant to picture him waiting, perhaps as nervous as she was, pretending to hunt for something in his backpack while listening for the sound of her footsteps.

But when she finally gathered her courage and her backpack and walked out, hopeful and wary, the hallway was empty.

That morning as they walked around the house, Alice told her a story about going on the train from Sweet Briar to New York during the nineteen-thirties.

"You couldn't tell me anything when I was young," Alice said. "I thought I knew it all. I went to college at Sweet Briar. Have you ever heard of it? When I asked one of the other caregivers she said, *Never heard of it.*"

"I've heard of it," Stella said firmly.

"Do you go to college?"

"Yes. UTC. I'm putting myself through."

"Very commendable," Alice said.

She slid the walker out in front of her in a steady, rhythmic manner. She was quiet for the next lap and Stella was afraid she'd forgotten about the story.

"So you went up on the train from Sweet Briar?" she said, prompting Alice. She had come to enjoy Alice's stories, the unpredictability of them, the humorous overtones, the glimpses of Alice as a young woman, strong and determined and fearless.

"What?"

"The train."

"What train?"

"The one that you took from Sweet Briar to New York. You were telling me about a trip you made in the nineteen-thirties."

"Oh yes," Alice said. "Anyway, I was going up on the train with my friend, Clarice, up to New York. Several of my school friends were from the city and I used to go up there a lot on the weekends. Oh, they were wild, those Yankee girls. It was shocking the things we could get up to without proper chaperones. Their parents mostly let us alone to do as we pleased and I wasn't used to all that freedom. Anyway, we left Sweet Briar in the morning and by mid-afternoon I was hungry. But when we got to the dining car there weren't any open tables. A porter came up to us and said, *'That lady over there said you could share her table.'*

She seemed nice enough, but kept asking us all kinds of questions. I was a sociology major, you see, and I knew everything there was to know about everything. And I told her what I thought about the New Deal and the WPA and the CCC.

When we got back to our berth, Clarice said, *'Say, I know who that lady was.'* And she pulled out a magazine and sure enough we'd been talking to Eleanor Roosevelt. The president's wife.

I said, *'I should have known from her teeth,'* and Clarice just laughed and laughed."

Stella stopped just inside the living room doorway. She stared at the slowly retreating Alice. "Are you telling me," she said in a loud voice, hurrying to catch up. "Are you telling me you had lunch on the train with *Eleanor Roosevelt*?"

Alice paused in front of the French doors, staring down at the steep wooded lot that sloped precariously toward the valley below. "When I got home, I told my father and my grandfather. My father was a lawyer and my grandfather owned a bank. And when I told them all the things I'd said to the First Lady about social security and union protection programs, my grandfather shook his head and said to my father, *"Law, Roderick, is this what comes of educating girls? Is all my money going to educate future socialists?"*

Stella stepped up beside her, still feeling the shock of her revelation. "Alice, do you know how incredible that is? You're probably one of only a few people still living who can say they ever had lunch with Eleanor Roosevelt." They stood looking at the hazy mountains and the distant, snaking glint of the river.

"Well, I don't know about that," Alice said.

"You should write a book."

"No one would read it."

Alice turned, sliding the walker in front of her. Halfway across the living room she stopped again and pointed to a framed photograph that lay, face up, on the coffee table. It was of a group of school children, lined up in three neat rows in front of a bricked school building. The girls all wore their hair with bangs and two points that curved forward on their cheeks, and the boys wore their hair slicked back from their faces. They were all dressed in white, white dresses for the girls and white shirts and knickers for the boys. "Can you pick me out of that group of scallywags?" Alice said.

Stella let go of the mental image of Eleanor Roosevelt and picked up the photograph. She held it up and studied it carefully. There were several girls who looked like what she imagined Alice must have looked, but one in particular, a tall girl with blonde hair and a stubborn, mischievous expression, caught her attention. She was standing on the back row with the boys, her arms crossed over her chest.

"That one," Stella said, pointing.

Alice chuckled. "That's right," she said. "You're the only one who's ever guessed right the first time. That was at Miss Fenimore's School. It was downtown by the river in those days. My mother was so displeased when she saw me standing with my arms crossed on my chest. That was considered very unladylike in those days."

"I thought you lived on Signal Mountain."

"Only in the summer. During the school year my father rented a house downtown so my sister and I could go to school at Miss Fenimore's. Later, I went to Marymount Academy for Girls and I didn't like that so much, shut up all day with only females. In those days, both Westover and Smithson were boys' schools. Westover wasn't coed like it is today, or I'd have wanted to go there. Of course my family was all Westover people but the Whittingtons were Smithson people. So when I married Bill, I had to become a Smithson person, too. My sons all went to Smithson."

"And your granddaughters went to Marymount?"

Alice gave a long fluttering sigh. "That's right," she said.

There were three prep schools in town; Marymount, Westover, and Smithson. Marymount was all girls, Smithson was all boys, and Westover was co-ed. The elite of Chattanooga sent their children to one of these three from sixth grade on; it was one of the ways of determining what social class you were from. When adult Chattanoogans met each other for the first time and asked, *What school did you go to?* they weren't asking about college. Competition to get in was fierce, especially at Westover which only accepted fifty boys and fifty girls each year. The rivalry between Westover and Smithson was legendary, sustained by over one hundred years of fierce competition. Stella had had a girl who graduated from Marymount in one of her classes at the university, a thin, sweet girl who'd flunked out of Sarah Lawrence (*I was homesick*, she'd told Stella mournfully) after only one semester. She was congenial and well-educated and extremely naive, the kind of girl who could recite Sylvia Plath, but didn't have a clue when a guy in class was hitting on her.

Alice began to walk again and Stella put the photograph down carefully and followed her. Alice was almost to her bedroom when she stopped and turned her head. "My son Roddy's writing a book."

"Oh really?" Stella said. "What about?"

"The family. He won't let anyone read it. Not until he's finished."

"When will that be?"

"He doesn't know. He says the muse will tell him."

Something in her expression made Stella laugh. "I hope it's not one of those *Mommie Dearest* books."

"It probably is," Alice said, shoving the walker out in front of her. "It's probably best that I not read it."

Later that morning Alice's son, Sawyer, came by to get her grocery list which was kept on the refrigerator door. He was tall and blonde with a big booming voice and a jovial manner. He went back to Alice's bedroom and Stella could hear them on the baby monitor.

"Al, I've come for your grocery list," he said.

"Oh, hello," Alice said. "Is it time to write bills?"

"No, Al. That's the first of the month."

"What?"

"We write bills on the first of the month. Not today."

"Do you still have my checkbook?"

"Yes. But we don't write bills today."

"Oh. Not today? Okay then."

"I've come for your grocery list."

"Oh, you've come for my grocery list?"

"That's right."

"Well, I don't know what's on it. They write down what they think I should eat. I just do as I'm told."

"Now, Al."

"I like that new one though. That new caregiver. She's very smart."

"Is she? Well, that's good."

"She has a tattoo."

"That's nice.'

"It's the Sanskrit symbol for peace."

"Okay well, I've come for the list. I'm going to Wal-Mart."

"Okay then. I don't have anything else to report."

"I'll see you later."

"Make sure you put Rum Raisin ice cream on that list," Alice called after him.

She wouldn't eat bread but Alice had a weakness for ice cream. The notebook said she wasn't to be given any unless she'd eaten her lunch or dinner first. Stella made her a plate of chicken salad, coleslaw, and yellow squash with onions for lunch. She cut up some watermelon and put it in a small ramekin beside Alice's plate.

"Oh, doesn't this look lovely?" Alice said, sitting down.

Stella smiled, pleased, and sat down beside her. Alice folded her hands in her lap and sat staring straight ahead at the wall.

"Is something wrong?" Stella said.

"Bib me," Alice said.

"Oh, sorry. I keep forgetting." Stella stood and unfolded the plastic bib and tied it around Alice's neck. Half-way through tying it, she began to giggle.

"There," she said. "You're bibbed."

"I'm bibbed," Alice said. She slid her eyes up at Stella and snickered like an evil child.

Stella sat down again and they bowed their heads, but Alice had trouble with the prayer, snorting several times so that Stella had to bite her lip to get through it.

Afterwards, they unfolded their napkins on their laps and ate for awhile in silence.

"Did you like school when you were a girl?" Stella asked, remembering the old photograph.

Alice turned her head slowly, giving her a long look. Her eyes were pale blue, as faded as washed denim. "I liked Miss Fenimore's School all right. I wasn't so happy with Marymount."

"I wouldn't like it either," Stella said. "An all-girls school, I mean."

"You got used to it," Alice said. "Weesie was there, and later, my sister."

Stella slowly chewed her peanut butter sandwich, looking down at her plate. She had broken the rules and helped herself to some grapes in Alice's refrigerator. "I hear those are pretty expensive schools. I had a girl in one of my classes who had gone to Marymount."

"In those days, the tuition at Marymount was $100 a year. $50 if you had a sister who went there. Now, of course, it's over $20,000. And I should know since I paid for all my grandchildren's tuitions."

"Well, that was nice of you."

Alice chewed thoughtfully, her blue eyes fixed on the calendar that hung on the wall in front of her. "At Marymount we used to have these Sugar and Spice Parties," she said.

"Sugar and Spice Party? What's that?"

"It's where you sit down with a bunch of girls and everyone says something they like about you and something they don't."

"That sounds cruel."

Alice snorted. "It could be. You had to have a strong temperament to get through it. I was pretty good at it but my sister used to go home in tears. She was always tender-hearted."

Stella snorted. She couldn't imagine Adeline ever having a tender heart. She also couldn't imagine attending a school that cost twenty thousand dollars a year. She had seen *The Dead Poets Society*, had secretly harbored a desire to go off to a boarding school where everyone wore uniforms and lived on a campus with soaring Gothic architecture. A place where being smart and scholarly was encouraged.

She plucked absently at one of the grapes, pulling it off its stem. How different might her life have been if she'd had even a few of the advantages Alice's grandchildren had had? If she could be certain of success in life, knowing that she could not fail?

"I wasn't really cut out for a girls' school," Alice said, following her own meandering train of thought. "I always liked playing with the boys. In those days girls were supposed to be sweet and dainty but I always liked climbing trees and riding bareback and playing football. I was what my Grandfather Jordan liked to call, a *bearcat*. Mother was always fussing at me about acting ladylike but I couldn't seem to manage it."

She broke off, chewing slowly, her eyes fixed on the calendar above the desk.

"Yeah, I know what you mean," Stella said. "When I was little, we moved around a lot. I was always the new kid in school. So I learned early on to go up to the bully on the playground the first day of school and just punch him in the face. We'd go down in a heap of flying fists, and I usually got the worst of it, of course, but it seemed to prevent any future problems. Everyone figured I was crazy enough to be left alone."

Alice turned her head slowly and looked at her, her expression a mixture of shocked disapproval and consternation. "I'm not talking about physical altercations," she said. "Girls and boys didn't fist fight in my day. It was considered a sign of bad breeding. I'm talking about how I liked playing with boys, I wanted to be one of them, I envied them their carefree ways and their freedom. It always seemed to me that my Cousin Dob got away with murder while I was the one stuck having to obey the rules and regulations." She raised her voice in a high, wheedling tone. "Young ladies don't do this, young ladies don't do that," she said, as if imitating a scolding adult.

Bad breeding. It was the kind of comment Stella would have expected someone from Alice's social class to make. She had a sudden desire to shock the old lady, to watch her eyes widen and her chin tremble. Where would Stella have been if she hadn't learned to fight in those early days, what would have happened to her if she hadn't known how to take care of herself, to pack up with others to survive the pimps, dealers, and perverts? People like Alice Whittington had no idea how the other ninety percent of the world lived. Money smoothed the way, made troubles bearable, took away the suffocating daily worries and fears. It created an artificial world where everything was shiny clean and fair.

"Of course, there was one boy I never much cared for. Charlie Gaskins. You may have heard of him. His family lived next door to us down on the river."

"Let me guess," Stella said. "Is Gaskins Park named for him?"

"Yes."

"I knew it," Stella said.

"He used to throw rocks at me over the fence and Mother wouldn't let me heave them back."

A boy who threw rocks. How terrible.

Stella didn't finish the rest of her sandwich. She wrapped it up in a napkin for later. Outside the window, the distant whine of a leaf-blower broke the mid-day stillness.

Alice ate slowly and when she had finished her lunch, she sat back with her hands in her lap. "I'll have my ice cream now," she said.

Stella stood and gathered the plates. "What kind?"

"Surprise me."

"Consider yourself surprised," Stella said, taking the plates to the sink and flipping on the hot water. She poured detergent into the water until foamy mounds appeared, and then she tossed the bottle back under the sink.

The girl's voice was low and smooth like water running in a brook and Alice had to turn her head to hear it. The girl didn't shout and bully her like the other caregivers, talking to her like she was a belligerent child. She spoke in a normal voice which meant that Alice couldn't hear her at all unless she turned her head so her good ear might catch the wispy threads of the girl's voice, or faced her so she might read her lips. Usually low-talkers irritated Alice but the girl spoke with heart, she wasn't condescending, and so Alice was willing to put up with the extra work involved with sitting beside her at lunch.

Besides, despite her admission of fistfights on the playground, there was something gentle about the girl, something she took great pains to hide, that made Alice feel vaguely protective of her. She was the kind who would give her last dollar to a bum on the street corner, the kind who took in every stray dog or cat who showed up at her door. She had seen the girl's arm when she lifted her sleeve that day in the library, had seen the claw marks and silvery scars, and she'd known immediately that the girl was a cat lover. Alice couldn't abide cats, and she really wasn't too fond of dogs either, at least not in the house.

One of her boys had had a dog, hadn't he? No, that's right. Bill wouldn't allow dogs. They were dirty and they carried disease in their saliva, he'd said. *Bill.* Funny, how at times like this, she could hear his voice but could not see his face. Memory was both a curse, and a blessing, coming as it did now in unexpected and irrepressible swells. It was probably her age, which she constantly forgot, (she was always amazed at her withered image in the mirror) that caused the daydreams to come to her, shiny and reflective, like shards of broken glass.

She was overcome suddenly by a wave of intense recollection, a memory of the man she had loved in her youth. She remembered his green eyes, and the small silvery scar below his right eyebrow, and the width of his chest and shoulders, covered by a sheen of sweat, as he reared above her. And yet she could not remember his face. Only the intense emotion aroused in her by his hands, by his mouth. Remembering now those first tentative attempts at lovemaking, his practiced movements and her own gradual ratcheting of desire, she was suffused by a delicate shame.

She might not have married Bill. Her life could have taken a different track altogether. In her youth she had conjured this incessantly, this shadowy other-life that could have been hers, imagining a life free of duty and restraint, but with its own achievements and pitfalls. Yet who's to say this other life would have been any different? Who's to say that, regardless of the path she took, she wouldn't wind up learning the same thing about herself? That caution and duty were what she would always choose to build her life on, what she would always come back to.

And now the girl was talking, she could hear the tinkling lilt of her voice, and turning her head, Alice caught the tail end of what she'd said. It was faint and muffled, like talking underwater, and Alice could barely make it out. Already the memory of the man she'd loved was fading, was gone. The girl was smiling, her lip ring glinting beneath the overhead lights and her black hair falling around her familiar face. There was a bitter taste in Alice's mouth. She felt a growing sense of alarm. The girl had awakened something in her; Alice could feel it low and rumbling.

She felt a shift, a sudden dislodging, and a surge of memories like a rockslide, came tumbling down around her, crushing her with their weight.

Charlie Gaskins had a stutter and so Alice's mother would not let her throw rocks at him. Alice would be standing at the edge of her yard down near the river and Charlie would come out and start lobbing stones over the fence and mewling like a cat. If she retaliated, he would go inside and call to his mother, and she would go next door and complain to Mother.

"Shame on you," Mrs. Gaskins would hiss at Alice as she walked by. "Shame on you, a big girl like you, picking on an afflicted child."

Alice wanted to shout, "Shame on your afflicted child for throwing stones at me," but she would clamp her mouth shut and keep quiet.

And later when she went to Marymount Academy for Girls with Charlie's twin sister, Adele, it was the same thing. Mrs. Gaskins could not bear for the other girls to be mean to Adele, even though Adele spoke perfectly well and had no need of parental protection. The result of all of this was that Adele and Charlie grew up as mean as snakes. No one wanted to play with them.

It was Adele who first came up with the Sugar and Spice Parties. None of the other girls wanted to go to Adele's parties and so Mrs. Gaskins would get on the phone and call around to their mothers, and at the appointed time, the cars would pull up in front of the Gaskins house and out would step girls with big bows in their hair, walking dejectedly toward the Gaskins front door.

If Mrs. Gaskins was present, Adele would be catty to the other girls, and would have temper tantrums if she lost at games. But when Mrs. Gaskins left the room, Alice would walk up and stick her fist in Adele's face and say, "We don't like you. We're only here because our mothers made us comes." Alice was the only one who could make Adele cry.

When Alice was a senior in high school and had long out-grown Sugar and Spice Parties, Adele was still having her mother call around to make sure her invited guests showed up. At one particular party in October of 1932, Alice brought her sister, Laura. It was a

Cat Rat Party; the senior girls were Cats and had been assigned to care for a freshman sister, known as a Rat. Alice had insisted that she be assigned to Laura because she knew she was the only one who could handle her. Laura wasn't like other girls.

And because she knew this, and because the other girls knew it too, Alice was apprehensive this particular evening, feeling herself to be outgunned and outmaneuvered. She stood at the edge of the grand room with its mullioned windows overlooking the river, searching for Laura who had slipped away not long after they arrived. A crowd of senior girls and their Rats were dancing to "I've Got the World on a String." Alice wore a black leotard and tights and ballet slippers and she had carefully painted whiskers on her face with a charcoal stick. Laura had dressed in a pink tutu with her long slender legs encased in white tights and her blonde hair lying loose around her shoulders and cascading down her back. She had refused to paint her face with whiskers, even at Mother's insistence that, "all the other girls will be painted up and you will look like a fool."

And now she was gone, she had disappeared into the crowd, and Alice had a sick feeling in the pit of her stomach. The last thing Mother had said to her as they left the house was, "Don't let her out of your sight."

She made her way slowly around the room, adopting a false, casual manner, stopping to sample hors d'oeuvres and chat with several of the girls. Laura was not in the room. Alice was certain of that. The next logical place to look would be the kitchen where her sister could often be found sitting and chatting with the servants, and if she wasn't there, chances were good she'd given Alice the slip, and had left the house for an assignation with some unknown beau.

Heat rose in her face at this thought, followed by a quick stab of anger at her sister, and at her mother for making her responsible for Laura's actions. Always responsible for Laura. Always having to stop her from making some catastrophic mistake that would bring shame and despair down on the rest of them.

"Looking for someone?" Adele stood at the edge of a group of girls who were all staring at Alice.

Alice sipped her punch. "No," she said.

"Because if you're looking for your sister, I saw her disappear up the stairs with my brother not five minutes after you got here."

Alice stared at her above the rim of her punch glass. She set the glass down carefully on a table. "Maybe you should have said something."

"Why should I?"

"Because your brother is three years older than my sister."

"What difference does that make? Your sister will go with anyone."

For a moment Alice thought she might strike her. Her hand tingled with the imagined slap, the weight of her flesh against Adele's rouged cheek. But then she saw the faces of the girls arrayed behind Adele, their expressions closed, accusing.

"My sister is a good girl," Alice said serenely.

"She's not," Adele said.

"Everybody knows she's not."

"My mother says she's boy crazy."

"My mother says girls like her always end badly."

"Your mothers are a bunch of jealous old biddies," Alice said, turning away from them.

She could feel the weight of their eyes as she climbed the stairs. She walked slowly, deliberately, with no apparent concern. At the top of the stairs, out of view of the living room, she paused. She heard giggling at the end of the hallway, and she followed the sound to a closed door. Turning the knob, she put her shoulder against the door and shoved hard to open it.

Laura sat on the edge of the bed, naked from the waist up, her pink tutu bunched around her hips. Her lips were red and swollen and her hair rose like a cloud around her lovely face with its expression of guileless innocence.

"Sister," she said sweetly.

Charlie Gaskins knelt in front for her. "G-get out!" he said.

Alice picked up a wooden globe and hurled it at him. She followed this with a copy of "Shakespeare's Sonnets" and "The Divine Comedy" which caught him in the temple, causing him to cry out and hold his head in his hands. She crossed the room and took Laura by the arm and yanked her upright, pulling up the straps of her tutu. She pushed her sister ahead of her into the hallway. In the doorway, she turned and looked at Charlie.

"If you touch my sister again I'll kill you."

They went quickly down the backstairs, through the kitchen, and out the back door into the cool night air. Laura was crying softly. Her hair glowed in the moonlight.

"I like him," she said.

"No, you don't."

"He's nice."

"No, he isn't." *Alice took Laura by the shoulders and shook her.* "He's not nice," *she said.* "And it's the fact that you don't see this that makes you so dangerous."

"I'm sorry, Sister."

She seemed so innocent, so completely bewildered by her crime that Alice couldn't bear it. She let her go.

"Stop crying. Fix your hair." *She stroked Laura's cheek, laying her fingers on the small birthmark on her neck.*

Laura nuzzled her face against Alice's hand. She sighed. "I feel sorry for him," *she said.*

Alice took Laura's hands and held them tightly. "Promise me you won't see him again. Promise me you won't be alone with him."

"All right."

"Promise."

"I promise."

Alice helped her fix her hair. She brushed the tears off Laura's cheeks. "Don't tell Mother."

"I won't," *Laura said. She took Alice's hand in both her own.* "You're a good sister," *she said.* "You look out for me."

"I'll always look out for you," *Alice said.*

Stella wasn't sure if she had offended Alice by asking too many questions at lunch. Or maybe it was her laughter when Alice mentioned that her sister had a "tender heart." Adeline had the least tender heart of anyone Stella could imagine but sisters were often loyal to one another, and Alice might not take kindly to any criticism of Adeline, however slight.

Or maybe it was something else Stella had said or done that had caused Alice to sit quietly through the remainder of lunch, slowly eating her ice cream and staring at the wall. Alice seemed a very private person, the kind who set wide boundaries around herself, and Stella wondered now if she had trespassed those boundaries in some crucial, although unintentional, way.

Yet, whatever it was that had upset her during lunch seemed to pass. Alice seemed herself again as soon as they left the kitchen and walked down the wide hallway to the bedroom. As she lay down for her nap, she looked up at Stella with her cold pale eyes and said, "Night, night."

Stella smiled. "Sweet dreams," she said.

She went out into the sunroom to do her homework. Despite being behind in all of her classes, she couldn't bring herself to open her backpack. Instead she sat staring drowsily out the long windows, wondering if she should just go ahead and chuck it all, drop out of school, quit fucking around and get a full-time job, something that would at least allow her to pay rent and maybe buy a good used car. She had lasted longer in school than anyone predicted; she had nothing to prove to anyone. Not even to herself.

She was so far behind now, she would probably never catch up and she was tired of the grind, the worry over money, the constant stress over trying to keep up. Last night Josh had come into the kitchen as she was packing her lunch for Alice's and he had bitched her out about not contributing for groceries. Or anything else, for that matter. And really, she couldn't blame him. She was nothing more than a kept woman, something she had always sworn she'd never be. She'd sworn she'd never become dependent on a man like her mother had been, and yet here she was, making the same mistakes Candy had made. How was that for family tradition?

No, it seemed dropping out was her only option. It was time to grow up, to step into the real world of forty-hour work weeks and groceries and bills stacked up on the kitchen table.

And yet. She paused, considering.

To give up the dream now filled her with a sense of dejection. The truth of the matter was she could see herself counseling troubled girls. She could imagine herself making a difference in patients' lives. *Dr. Nightingale.* It had a nice ring to it.

And besides, if she dropped out now, she would still have two years of school loans to pay off. A crushing, unforgivable debt and nothing to show for it.

She sighed and pulled her backpack toward her. She took out her *Psychology of Gender* textbook, and spent the next thirty minutes reading and making careful notes. She would send an email to Professor Dillard this evening explaining her absence from class today. She would ask Luke Morgan on Tuesday if she could copy his notes. This thought, so casually arrived at this morning, now roused a wave of unexpected nervousness. She put her pen down and rubbed her eyes, trying to imagine how she would ask him. After class? During class? Follow him out into the quad where the giggling sorority girls wouldn't see her? She was so caught up trying to imagine how she would ambush him without appearing nervous or desperate that she only gradually became aware of whispering on the monitor.

Immediately, she stopped daydreaming and listened.

It was a low, repetitive sound. More like a murmur or a meditative chant. As she listened, Stella gradually became aware of individual words.

Oh Lord, no. No.

It was Alice's voice. Low and anguished, but still Alice. Stella was relieved to realize this, and yet the suffering was so intense that Stella felt a catch in her throat, listening.

Oh Lord, Laura.

Stella closed her book.

Please. Oh Lord, please.

Stella shoved the book in her backpack. She got up and walked down the long, wide hallway to the bedroom but by the time she arrived, Alice was lying quietly on her back, sleeping peacefully.

She slept for a long time and after she awoke, Alice seemed groggy and confused. Twice she called Stella, *Mary Ann*, and as they walked through the living room on their afternoon walk, Alice stopped and looked at a collection of photographs on a long sofa table. She pointed to one silver frame and Stella picked it up so she could see it better.

"Who is that woman and those two children?" Alice said.

Stella looked at the photo. "Isn't that your sister?"

Alice's face clouded. She said, "My sister?"

"Adeline."

She was quiet for a moment, staring. Then she made an impatient gesture with one hand. "Go put it in the bedroom and I'll ask Sawyer when he comes if he knows who it is." Alice sat down in a wingback chair near the fireplace and waited for Stella to do as she was told. When she came back, they continued their walk.

Alice said, "There was this girl in the neighborhood where we lived when I was raising my family. Do you know the house I'm speaking of? It was a big house over on Hammond."

"So you didn't raise your children in this house?"

Alice stopped and turned her head, giving her a disdainful look. "Of course not," she snapped. "I had a big house and two servants over on Hammond Road. I didn't move to this house until after Bill Whittington died. After the children were grown. I've lived in this house for ten years." She shook her head. "Twenty years. Oh I don't know. A long time." She started walking again.

Behind her, Stella said gently, "So there was this girl in your neighborhood?"

"She was a homely little thing. Pitiful really, for a girl to look like that. The other girls weren't very nice to her, I'm afraid."

"They usually aren't."

"The family's name was Shufflebottom."

"Shufflebottom?"

Alice chuckled. "When I came home and told Bill Whittington he said, '*Alice, someone is pulling your leg.*'"

"I can see why he would think that."

"But that was their name. The father liked to work in the yard. He was from up there in Yankee Land but despite this he made a good citizen, he sang in the choir and kept his yard nice."

She stopped at the desk in the kitchen and picked up the glass of ice water Stella had waiting for her. She drank heavily and then set it down again.

"They make me drink a lot of water," Alice said. "They say I have to hydrate."

"Well, they say that's good for you."

"It's ridiculous. *Hydrate*. Why don't they just say, *Drink some water*. And why do you have this napkin resting on the top of my glass?"

"I was told to do it that way. I was told that was what you wanted."

"Well, it's not."

"Okay," Stella said. "No more napkins then."

Alice shoved her walker out in front of her and they moved off into the dining room.

After a few minutes, Stella said, "So what happened to the Shufflebottom girl?"

"She was very smart in school. She went away to college and never came back. I don't know where this story is going. I forgot what I was going to say."

"So you never heard from her again? You don't know what happened to her?"

"Oh, I know all right. Her mother wrote me a letter. That's right, now I remember. I'm telling you this because I need to sit in the library after we exercise and write a letter to the poor little Shufflebottom girl's mother."

"Did something happen to the poor little Shufflebottom girl?"

Alice stopped and looked at her. "What number are we on?"

"Four."

"So I can go through the door?"

"Yes."

The door was a short cut from the butler's pantry through the dining room that ended the walking for the day.

"Oh goody," Alice said. She went through the dining room and into the living room and shuffled off toward the library.

"So what happened to the poor little Shufflebottom girl?" Stella asked, following her. She felt it was good to keep Alice on topic; she thought it might help to improve her memory.

"She grew up to work for that group of diplomats in New York that Roosevelt started."

"The United Nations?"

"Yes. That one."

"Wow. So her life was a success after all."

"Well, I wouldn't say that. She married a black man."

Stella was quiet and Alice sighed. "I know, I know," she said. "It's a different world."

"Yes," Stella said firmly. "It is. Thank God."

They walked a few more feet and then Alice said, "I've always been a champion of colored folk."

"Have you?" Someone had moved the coffee table. Stella pushed it out of the way with her foot so Alice could get by.

"I was on the Board of Big Brothers and Big Sisters for over twenty years."

"Well, that's good."

"You don't need to take that tone with me."

"What tone?" Stella said mildly.

She got Alice settled in the wingback chair near the window in the library, setting her walker up against the wall, out of the way.

"Push that chair over closer to me," Alice said. "No, not that one. That one," she said, pointing emphatically. "I use it as a desk."

"Can I get you anything else?"

"No. I'll just sit here and write my letter. I'll ring you when I need you." She picked up a little gold bell on the table beside her, and then set it down again.

"Okay," Stella said. She stopped at the bookcase on her way out, perusing the titles. The library was filled with good books, volumes on history and biography and literature by writers like Tolstoy and E.L. Doctorow.

"I don't know who's been moving things around in here," Alice said.

"It wasn't me," Stella said.

"Someone's moved everything around and now I can't find anything."

Stella took down a collection of Flannery O'Connor short stories. "Do you mind if I read this?" she said.

"Help yourself." Alice rummaged around on the chair beside her, which was stacked with envelopes and stamps and engraved note cards. She stopped suddenly and looked up at Stella, her expression curious, intent. "Do you have a young man?" she said.

"I suppose so. Yes."

"Do you love him?"

Stella opened the book and began to flip through the pages. "He's all right."

"Not exactly a ringing endorsement."

"I'm only twenty-one."

"That's old enough to know whether or not you love someone."

Stella looked up from the book. They stared at each other in silence and then Alice said, "Will you marry him?"

"I'm not marrying anyone. I'm never getting married."

Alice snorted and turned back to her letter. "I wish I had a dollar for every time I've heard that one," she said.

After supper, Stella finished washing up and had just settled down for more reading in the sunroom when Alice rang the bell. When she appeared in the bedroom doorway, Alice looked up at her and said, "Do you know how to put me to bed?"

"Yes, ma'am. I did it last night."

"You did? Oh, all right then." The old woman seemed bewildered, frail, her white hair standing up around her head like whipped egg whites. Alice's frailty affected Stella, made her feel oddly tender. It must be terrible for an intelligent woman, a reader, to lose her memory the way Alice seemed to have lost hers. Although it wasn't a permanent loss. Memory seemed to come and go, flowing and ebbing like waves on a beach. Sometimes she was sharp and quick and lucid; her stories of the past, down to the minutest detail, were proof of that.

Stella brought the walker and Alice went into the bathroom to brush her teeth. *Wheel of Fortune* blared on the television.

And her stories weren't lies, like some old people told, they weren't made up, because she told the same ones over and over again, and the details were always the same. So she was remembering events as they actually happened; she wasn't making stuff up.

As she came hobbling out of the bathroom, Alice said, "I'll wear something else tomorrow." She sat down on the edge of the bed. "Turn on that light. No, that one on the wall. Okay, now open the closet door."

Stella did as she instructed, sliding the door open. A long line of neatly-ironed pastel knit dresses hung on hangers.

"Okay, now grab that blue one. No, not that one, the blue one."

"This one?"

"No. The blue one! The blue one!"

"I'm not sure where you're pointing."

"Oh, for heaven's sakes," Alice said.

Stella pulled out a pale lavender dress with large buttons down the front. "*This* one?"

"Yes. That one. Now, put it over the chair. And take this one and put it in the hamper to be cleaned. Elaine will be so happy because now I won't be wearing a dress with germs on it. That girl drives me crazy with her phobia about *germs*."

Alice stood unsteadily and pulled her dress up around her hips and Stella hurried over to help her. After Alice was dressed in her cotton knit nightgown (*My K-Mart special*, she called it) and settled in bed, Stella rubbed oil on her arms and legs. Alice was quiet through most of this, staring at the TV. When she had finished, Stella went into the bathroom to wash her hands, and when she came back out, Alice was staring at the silver framed photograph on the nightstand.

"What's that doing in here?" she said.

"You told me to put it there. This afternoon when we were walking."

"I did?"

"Yes. Do you know who is in the picture?"

Alice gave her a scornful look. "Of course I do," she said. "That's my sister, Adeline. My sister Adeline and two of her daughters."

Stella put the cap back on the baby oil. "I thought it might be."

"Put it out in the living room," Alice said. "It doesn't belong in here."

After she'd gotten Alice settled in bed watching *Jeopardy*, Stella walked out into the sunroom to find Adeline sitting in a chair, flipping through a magazine. Stella was so startled she jumped, putting a hand to her throat.

Adeline glanced at her and then back at the magazine. "Sorry," she said. "I didn't mean to scare you."

"I didn't hear you come in," Stella said, slowly advancing into the room.

"You might want to lock that front door," Adeline said.

"I thought it was locked."

"Apparently not."

Stella was quiet a moment, staring at the older woman who continued to flip casually through *The New Yorker*. "Do you want me to tell Alice you're here?"

"No, I'm having lunch with her tomorrow. I'll talk to her then." Adeline wore a pair of tailored pants and a white ruffled blouse. She looked very stylish. "I just came by to check on things." She closed the magazine on her lap. "How is she?"

"She's fine." Stella stood by one of the chairs, not certain whether she should sit or continue standing. Adeline made her nervous. "A little forgetful today."

"Aren't we all sometimes?" Her tone was sharp but her expression was bland, impassive.

"Yes." Stella had the feeling that Adeline had stopped by hoping to catch her in some transgression; eating food out of the refrigerator or loading valuables into her purse. Some offense that would lead to a swift and certain firing.

"The other girl will be here soon?" Adeline said.

"Yes. At eight o'clock."

"So how was your first week?"

"It was good. I enjoy Alice's company."

Adeline seemed surprised. "Do you?"

"Yes."

"How unusual. She goes through caregivers fairly quickly. Some don't even last the first day."

Stella gave a careless shrug. "I'm tougher than that," she said.

"Obviously."

Outside the windows, the lights of the valley glimmered in the darkness. Deep within the house, a sound caught Stella's attention, the soft bang of a closing door. She turned her head to listen.

Adeline said, "Any problems to relate?"

"Well." Stella hesitated, unsure whether she should mention it. Adeline was staring at her, her expression cool, unreadable. Stella took a deep breath and went on. "She has nightmares. When she naps in the afternoons. I heard her on the monitor." She should just shut up. The woman was looking at her in the same way people in authority often looked at her. Hostility mixed with distrust. Underlying it all, fear. She should just shut up but Adeline's expression made her bold.

"Someone named Laura," she said evenly. "She has nightmares about someone named Laura."

Adeline's expression changed; a flicker of something and then a sphinx-like composure descending. She picked up the magazine on her lap and opened it again.

"You must be mistaken," she said coldly.

Four

§§§

On Friday morning Stella missed her nine o'clock class. She lay in bed long after Josh had left for work, imagining how angry he'd be if he came in and found her still in bed. She was not allowed to sleep in if he wasn't. It was an unspoken rule in the house. And it was not a class she could afford to miss, either. Stella knew this, and yet she couldn't bring herself to rise and get dressed and jump on her bike and pedal to campus. She lay in bed with her arms behind her head, watching as the sunlight pushed between the broken slats of the mini-blinds and climbed the walls.

It was going to be one of her dark days. She could feel despair like a hard lump in her stomach, a lump that would swell and spread gradually through her chest until it nearly choked her. She would carry it around for days, feeling weighed down, oppressed, marked by a secret shame. Josh had no patience with her moods; he took it as a personal affront, an indication he was doing something wrong. Not feeding her enough, not providing a safe roof over her head, not making her cry out in bed. She hid it from him as best she could.

On Friday night when he came home she had managed to rise and dress herself and mop the kitchen floor. A pot of chili bubbled on the stove.

"What's this?" he said, lifting the lid of the pot and sniffing.

"Cincinnati Chili."

"Smells good." He sat down at the table and waited for her to fix him a bowl. She took a cold beer out of the refrigerator and set it down on the table in front of him.

He looked at her. "Aren't you eating?"

"I'm not hungry."

He drank thirstily and then set the beer down and began to eat. She sat across from him with one knee drawn up, smoking a cigarette and staring out the window at the darkening sky.

"Did you make cornbread?" he said.

She got up and went to the cupboard and took down a box of saltines and set it on the table.

"You know I like cornbread with my chili."

She thought, *I mopped the fucking floor. I didn't have time to make cornbread*. She said, "Sorry." She didn't have time to fight with him, a fight that, once begun, might go on for days. She had too much work to catch up on. She slid back into her chair.

He stared at her a minute and then went back to eating.

"We're going out," he said. "Macklin's having a bonfire."

"I don't feel like a party tonight."

"You never feel like a party."

"I'm tired."

"It's Friday night."

"I need to study. I'm behind in most of my classes."

"Go on. Get showered and change your clothes." He didn't look at her again but there was no mistaking his tone.

His jaw jutted obstinately over his bowl; a stubborn expression settled on his face.

She sighed and stubbed out her cigarette.

"I told Macklin we'd bring the beer," he said.

Macklin and Jessica lived a few miles from them in a neighborhood of small Victorian cottages fallen on hard times. The house needed a fresh coat of paint but it sat on a large lot with a wide patchy lawn surrounded by a picket fence. A huge oak spread its branches protectively over the house. At the top of its tall crown, a rude tree house had been built using scrap lumber and a series of climbing ropes and ladders, so that the entire structure looked like something built by the Lost Boys in Neverland. The house was haunted by the spirit of an old man who had hung himself from the tree, the neighbors told Macklin and Jessica on the day they moved in and began the tree house, and Stella did not like going over there. It was always dirty and it smelled of dog, and there was an air of sadness and loss about the place that affected her deeply.

But Macklin and Jessica were two of Josh's oldest friends, they had all three gone to high school together, and so there was nothing for it. The bonfire was in full swing by the time they arrived. A ring of lawn chairs had been drawn up around the fire pit in the side yard and the night sky was cold and bright with stars and a thin sliver of moon.

"All right! The beer's here!" Macklin shouted when he saw them coming across the lawn dragging the cooler behind them. There were perhaps a dozen people gathered around the fire smoking weed and passing a bottle of Jack Daniels between them. Someone played an acoustic guitar. Stella greeted those she knew and then grabbed a can of PBR from the cooler and walked over to the far side of the fire. She sat down with her back against the ancient oak, watching the others. The firelight cast fantastic shadows in the branches of the old tree.

She put her head back and closed her eyes. An image of Alice Whittington came stubbornly into view. An image of Alice as a girl, attractive and well-dressed, climbing on the train and heading for New York, unaware that she would soon have lunch with Eleanor Roosevelt. Why did some peoples' lives turn out like that, magical and unexpected, almost as if their fate was nothing more than some marvelous movie script? While others struggled to escape their destiny, feeling it always at their backs like a cold wind.

She opened her eyes. Sparks drifted like fire flies on the cool night air.

Karma. What a joke. There was no rhyme or reason to anything that happened, no order to the universe, only chaos. The sooner she accepted this and moved on with her life, the better off she'd be.

When she first left home, she had fallen in with a group of Birmingham street kids down on Third Avenue. On cold winter nights they would stand around a burn barrel trying to keep warm and telling their stories. It had seemed romantic to her, at first, the nomadic life, huddling like gypsies around fires at night, bellies empty, stories waiting to be told. But the romance had quickly paled. She found she had no stomach for panhandling, for running from the cops, for fighting off junkies. The drugs scared her, the ease with which you could fall into addiction, the things people would do for a fix. She knew that once she went down that road there would be no turning back, and she felt there were other quicker ways to end herself. She fell in with two rough girls from Chicago, Sam and Rocha, who took her under their wings. Rocha was small and feminine with short spiky blonde hair, and Sam was not. She had scars on her neck that she never spoke of and she carried a switchblade in her boot. At night they slept under bridges or in abandoned houses in Norwood, and during the day they hung out with other kids at Linn Park, raiding restaurant dumpsters for food.

In April, Rocha announced that she and Sam were hitchhiking to San Francisco. They left the following morning. Stella, lonely and homesick, walked to a pay phone and called her mother.

"Well, we were just talking about you," her mother said. In the background Stella could hear her little brothers arguing.

"How're George and Anthony?"

"They're fine. Can't you hear that racket?" She put her hand over the receiver and Stella heard her shout, "You boys pipe down, I'm trying to talk to someone on the telephone." She didn't say, *I'm trying to talk to your sister on the telephone.*

"I'm hungry," Stella said.

"Have you been taking care of yourself?"

"I'm sick."

"Where are you?"

"Birmingham."

"Still there? I thought you might have moved on. You always liked to travel. Remember when you were little and we used to hit the road? We went through Birmingham years ago. Do you remember? It was before I met your step dad. Before I had George and Anthony. You and I were coming through on our way to Tuscaloosa and we stopped and stayed the night with a friend of mine. Rena. I wonder what ever happened to her?"

"I want to come home."

"You can't do that."

"Why?"

"You know why."

In the background, Anthony began to cry. Stella's mother said, "You boys stop fighting! I mean it; I'm going to take a switch to you." She came back on and said, "I have to go. These boys are driving me crazy. You take care of yourself now, you hear? You're a big girl, and real smart, and you know how to do that. You'll be fine. I have to go now but thanks for calling." She hung up.

A semi-truck went by, its headlights sweeping the wet pavement. Behind the brightly-lit Waffle House, a lone dog nosed along the dumpster, looking for scraps.

Stella stood, for a moment, with the phone cradled against her chest. Then she hung it up carefully, and turning, picked up the bag at her feet and went out into the cool, gray morning.

They were all drunk; Stella could see that from where she sat. Josh was laughing and gesturing wildly, the way he always did when he drank too much and was spoiling for a fight. The bonfire had begun to die down, no one was willing to chop any more wood, and Stella was cold. She pulled her knees up and wrapped her arms around them. The chill night air, the smell of wood smoke and damp vegetation reminded her of being on the road. An unpleasant reminder. She supposed that for the rest of her life, however short or long that might be, these smells would carry unpleasant memories, a reminder of the baggage from her former life that she would never be able to discard, no matter how hard she tried. She wondered how people managed it, those lucky few who seemed able to transcend their childhoods. She supposed that was why she'd been drawn to the study of psychology.

Physician, heal thyself.

Josh was looking for her; she could see him peering through the smoke at the sparse crowd, weaving on his feet. He put his head back and began to shout, "Stell-a!" in his best Stanley Kowalski imitation, even though he had no idea who Stanley Kowalski was, he'd never seen *A Streetcar Named Desire*. But he'd seen John Belushi on *Saturday Night Live*. Beside him, a boy with blonde dreadlocks put his head back and began to bellow, "Stell-a!"

Stella rested her forehead on one knee. She half-wished now that she'd had more to drink, had taken the bottle of Jack Daniels and settled down with it. But she had a test on Monday morning and she'd missed class today and she was determined to study all weekend. Which is why she hadn't wanted to get drunk. Which is why she hadn't wanted to come to this damn bonfire in the first place.

Besides, it was dangerous drinking during one of her dark moods. There was no telling what she might say. There was no telling what might come spilling out.

Josh had seen her and was gesturing impatiently for her to come over. He put his arm around the shoulders of the boy who was still shouting, "Stella-a!" and pointed at her with a beer bottle. The boy stopped shouting and grinned. He raised his beer bottle, motioning for Stella to join them.

She sighed and stood up and walked over. Several people were passed out on the ground or sprawled in lawn chairs. The fire sputtered weakly, casting a dim light.

"Where've you been all evening?" Josh said.

"Over there taking it easy."

"So you're Stella?" the blonde boy said. "Cool name, by the way."

"Thanks. It was my mother's idea."

"She a big John Belushi fan?"

"No. Marlon Brando."

"Who?"

"You've been antisocial the whole night," Josh said. He tipped his beer, his eyes narrowing as he watched her.

"Give me the keys," she said holding out her hand. "I'm sober. I can drive."

Josh wiped his mouth. He let his beer dangle from the tips of his fingers. "I'm not going anywhere and neither is my fucking car," he said.

"I'll take you home," the blonde boy said.

"She's not going anywhere."

"Okay, man. That's cool." The boy, hearing the menace in Josh's tone, held his hands up and backed away, still grinning at Stella.

They watched him move around to the other side of the fire.

"Don't be an asshole," Stella said to Josh.

"I'm not being an asshole. You are."

Stella stared at the dying fire. She could make it better, just by giving in. By going up to him and putting her arms around him. Then everything would be ok. He'd be pleased, satisfied of her allegiance, and she'd be off the hook. But tonight, stubbornly, she didn't want to submit to Josh or anyone else, for that matter.

"Look," she said. "I'm tired. I've got a test to study for."

"I've got a test to study for," he said in a falsetto voice, lifting his beer.

She turned and walked off.

"Where do you think you're going?" he said.

"To sleep in the car."

"Not in my car, you're not."

"Fuck you."

"Fuck you," he shouted after her.

She didn't sleep in the car after all; she walked home. The next morning she awoke to a suffocating feeling of remorse. She had learned long ago to keep unacceptable parts of herself hidden away, to make herself pleasant and accomodating. It had kept her from being arrested, it had secured her a bunk for the night at shelters that weren't allowed to take in teens, it had led, finally, to someone taking enough of an interest in her to get her off the streets and back into school.

And she had risked everything last night by walking away from Josh.

The apartment with Josh was the only home she'd had in the past three years and she didn't want to lose it. She didn't want to go back to the old way of life. She had a chance now that she hadn't had before; a chance to finish college and make a better life for herself. She was grateful to him for taking her in, for providing the kind of stability she'd been looking for since she left home; food in her belly, a chance to better herself, a safe place to sleep at night. He was a great-looking guy with a steady job and he was good to her most of the time. A lot nicer to her than other boyfriends had been. It was simple when you broke it down into basics. When you didn't let yourself get caught up with all of the *what ifs* and *why nots*.

She got up and, in a flurry of activity, cleaned the apartment, washed the laundry, and took a pound of ground beef out of the freezer to thaw for dinner. Then she took a shower, and dressing in a pair of tight jeans and a low cut sweater, she carefully applied make up to her face. If the thought occurred to her that she was more like her mother than she cared to admit, she quickly discarded it.

Mid-afternoon, Josh arrived home in a foul mood, hung over and dirty and still angry about last night. He didn't speak to her, going up to take a shower and then falling across the freshly-made bed, where he slept for three hours.

When he woke up she had dinner made, spaghetti and meatballs, one of his favorites, and afterwards she sat on his lap and kissed him and through a series of contrived but insistent actions, managed to convince them both that everything was all right between them.

On Tuesday, she waited after class for Luke Morgan. He had gone up to speak to Professor Dillard as the class was filing out, and Stella had filed out with them and then, turning, had gone back and hovered outside the door, waiting.

He was smiling when he came out but he had his head down and he didn't see her. She came up behind him and touched him lightly on the shoulder.

"Oh, hello," he said. He was tall and spare, with a wide chest and shoulders like a swimmer.

"I need to borrow your notes." She had rehearsed it but now that she was looking at him, it came out all wrong, rushed and hurried and slightly arrogant.

"Yeah, I know. Professor Dillard told me." His eyes were a luminous gray. He stared at her with an expression of curious fascination, as if she was some exotic creature he had stumbled upon. This thought caused a nervous stir in Stella's chest.

"How did Professor Dillard know?" she said.

"She said you had emailed her and asked if you could copy someone's notes for a few weeks and she asked me if I'd be willing." She thought she detected amusement in his voice and she forced herself to meet his eyes. They stood in the middle of the corridor staring at each other. He grinned at her expression.

"I don't mind," he said. "Really." He turned and began to walk slowly and she fell into step beside him, her backpack bumping gently against her hip.

"But how did she know I was going to ask you?" The fact that she could be so easily read by Professor Dillard bothered Stella.

"I don't know that she did. I think she asked me because she knows me. Professor Dillard is my godmother. She and my mother went to school together. She's why I'm here in Chattanooga. I came down last summer to visit her and never left. I'm auditing her class."

"Why?"

He laughed. "Because I'm a filmmaker and I'm interested in what drives people to do the things they do. *Psychology of Gender* seemed the perfect class. I figured I might learn something about the way people think."

The hallway was crowded with students hurrying to class and Stella had to weave in and out of the traffic. Without saying anything, he moved to the outside so she could hug the inside wall.

"So you've already graduated?" she said, heaving her backpack higher on her shoulder.

"Yes. NYU."

"Wow."

He grinned. "Don't say it like that."

"I'm impressed, that's all." Of course it made perfect sense. He had seemed so different from everyone else, so self-contained and confident. He spoke well, too. She imagined a prep school background, country club parties, family ski vacations to Aspen. The kind of life she'd read about in books and seen on reality television shows, and could only dimly imagine. He and Alice Whittington would, no doubt, get on well.

"So you like Chattanooga?"

"I do." He was very tall; she had to bend her neck to look up at him.

"I'm into climbing," he said. "I climbed Sintra in Portugal. And I've done a lot of climbing out west, The Buttermilks in California and Indian Creek in Utah, but Chattanooga has some of the best bouldering around."

"Really?"

"You sound surprised." He smiled down at her and she thought again how striking he was, not really handsome in a classic sense, but attractive.

"Well, I mean, it's a great place," she said. "I've been here for almost five years and I like it a lot. I'm not much of a wilderness person, I guess." *You wouldn't be either*, she thought, *if you'd spent as much time as I have living in it.*

"Do you want to get a cup of coffee?"

"I don't know. I have a class at twelve."

He looked at his cell phone. "That should give you forty minutes."

She slid her backpack up on her shoulder. "All right," she said.

He was from upstate New York. His parents were diplomats of some kind and he'd spent time in England at boarding school before returning to the states for college. Since graduating he'd done a documentary on Angola Prison and now he was putting together a documentary on his travels through the South.

"No one finds the South interesting," she said. "It's nothing but a bunch of snake handlers and debutantes."

"But that's what makes it so fascinating. The contradictions. And everyone has a story. The oral tradition down here is very strong. I sit in the Waffle House at the foot of Signal Mountain and I listen to people talk. You wouldn't believe some of the stories I hear."

"Actually, I would." She tapped one finger absently against the plastic lid of her cup.

He sipped his coffee, then set it down again. "So what about you?"

"Me?" She looked up in surprise.

"What's your story?" His eyes were formidable. She could see how people, looking into their cool gray depths, would confess to anything. She'd have to be careful around him. She'd have to watch herself.

"I don't have a story."

He laughed. "I know that's not true. I knew the moment I saw you, there was something unusual about you. And now, you see, you're being coy. You've turned it into a challenge so I'll have no choice but to obsess over it and hound you and carry around a big DVR to stick in your face every chance I get."

He flushed a dull red and she looked down at her hands. They both grinned at the vague sexual connotation of his statement.

"Sorry," he said. "A DVR is a camera."

"Yeah, I kind of hoped it was."

The coffee shop was crowded with students laughing and chattering, rushing, bleary-eyed, on their way to class.

"You know I won't stop asking you," he said. "Until I know your story. Where you come from. Where you hope to go. All the dark dreary secrets of your childhood."

"Alabama," she said quickly. "That's where I come from."

"Birmingham?"

"No. I mean, yes. I didn't grow up there but I lived there once. For a brief time." Her voice trailed off and she turned her head and stared out the wide glass windows at a patch of rolling lawn bordered by shrubs.

"I'll make a deal with you," she said finally. "Each time I meet you to copy your notes, I'll tell you one thing about me."

He stuck his hand across the table and she took it, giving it a firm shake. Gently he turned her hand over, palm up. "Start with this," he said.

"What?" she said, swiftly withdrawing her hand.

"Your arm. Start with that."

"It's a tattoo. Everyone has one."

"Not the tattoo," he said softly. "The other."

She pulled her sleeve down and stood, gathering her backpack. "This isn't going to work," she said.

He opened his binder and took out four sheets of paper and held them out to her. She hesitated, not looking at him, and then took them. "I'll copy them at the library," she said.

He wrote his cell number down on a piece of paper and gave it to her. "Call me," he said. "I'll meet you."

She put the slip and the notes in her backpack and walked off, and it wasn't until she had reached the door that she had the courage to look back over her shoulder.

He was sitting where she had left him, staring after her with an unreadable expression on his face.

Five

§§§

December, 1934

There was no hope for it. Alice would have to go home. Her mother would hound her until she did, driving her crazy with her slow drips of guilt, her endless wash of tears. It was worse than a Chinese Water Torture, reading her mother's wild letters.

This one is a grease monkey, she had written. *She met him at the County fair. I thought the last one, a rail road drummer, was bad but this one is worse. She will ruin us.*

Alice lay back on the bed and closed her eyes. It was all she had ever wanted; to get away from *this,* to start fresh where no one knew her. To be a nameless face in a sea of nameless faces. She had recently read a novel, *What Mad Pursuit,* about a cynical female reporter who travels the world in search of personal fulfillment, immersing herself in bohemian society. She has many love affairs but refuses to submit to marriage, and it occurred to Alice, reading the novel with a rising sense of wonder and excitement, that she could be happy living this way. It seemed to her that only in work would she find the freedom and joy in living that she sought. She could be happy traveling the world alone and writing, the slave of no man. She and Clarice had already made plans to go to New York after graduation and now here she was being dragged back into this endless family drama.

Come home. She'll listen to you. You're the only one she'll listen to.

At least she'd be spared any future acquaintance with Bill Whittington. He'd written her three letters since August and she hadn't responded to any of them, and now he'd gone definitively quiet.

Your sister is crazy in love.

Alice, apparently, wasn't made that way. At least she'd be spared that.

Mother was waiting for her at the train station wearing her fur coat and a black hat with a veil to hide her swollen face.

"Thank God you've come," was all she said, motioning for Simon to collect Alice's bags and put them in the car. They were both quiet on the ride home, Alice pushed into one corner of the luxurious automobile, her face turned toward the glass, and her mother pushed into the opposite corner, lost in her own thoughts. It had snowed the night before and a light dusting lay across the lawns and sidewalks, turning to slush in the streets. Children on sleds raced down the hills of the Country Club and in the distance the river was a gray fog. They turned into Riverview and the car began its slow ascent towards Ash Hill, past stately mansions with curved drives set back on wide sweeping lawns. Her father had bought the estate the year Alice went off to Sweet Briar. Ash Hill had belonged to a former governor of Tennessee and it had a swimming pool and a tennis court and ten bedrooms. It had seemed the height of folly to buy such a large estate during the middle of the Great Depression, but Roderick Montclair was a canny businessman and he'd had the cash to invest in real estate when so many did not. Ash Hill was a house Alice's mother had always admired. As a girl she had attended Cotillions there and when it came on the market Roderick had bought it as a gift for his wife's thirty-eighth birthday.

The house had been decorated for Christmas and lights shone merrily from the windows as they turned into the long drive.

"Home sweet home," Alice said.

Her mother sighed, pulling at the tips of her gloves. "If only it was," she said.

After Laura was rescued from the railroad drummer who'd tried to elope with her to Ringgold, Georgia, things had quieted down for awhile. Her parents had arrived in time; the justice of the peace's wife had taken one look at Laura and said to her husband, "This girl is underage," and he'd refused to go through with the ceremony. Roderick had the drummer arrested on some petty charge and secreted out of town one night, put on the train by the Sheriff and two of his stone-faced deputies who warned him not to return. Mother took Laura off for a rest cure to a sanitarium in Nashville which was rumored to be "very nice," but the first evening Laura cried hysterically and clung to Mother's skirt, and on the second night they had her so sedated she didn't recognize her at all. They had dressed her in a coarse nightgown that Mother found "cheap" and when they brought Laura's dinner in on a tray, the utensils were "dirty", and on the third day one of the other female residents lifted her nightgown to expose her naked nether regions, and that was the end of the rest cure. Laura came home on the train with Mother and there was no more talk of sanitariums.

Laura was quietly subdued for awhile but the family was not relieved by this. They had learned that this was the course her illness ran; periods of great excitement and impulsiveness followed by days when she could not drag herself out of bed. Mother worried over her incessantly. The flightiness came in through her side of the family, her own mother had been "high strung," and she had an aunt who had accidentally overdosed on laudanum, leaving a husband and five small children.

As worrisome as they were, Laura's high-spirited moods were better tolerated by her mother than the days when she lay in a darkened bedroom with the blinds drawn and her face turned toward the wall. There was something frightening and insidious about these periods of pronounced lethargy, as if Laura might be under some kind of a strange sleeping spell from which she might never awake.

After they returned from Nashville, Laura stayed home from school, refusing to see anyone, refusing to eat, sleeping fourteen to sixteen hours a day. And then one night, without warning, she rose and carefully dressed herself and went out to the county fair with Adeline and a group of her giggling friends. There on a dance stage strung with lights like fallen stars, she was asked to dance by a dark-haired, green-eyed man named Brendan Burke.

And just as quickly as they had begun, Laura's sleeping days were over.

The house was quiet when they arrived home but there was a pleasant smell of baking bread. Distantly, Alice could hear the faint lilting sound of Laura's laughter. Simon took Alice's bags up to her room and her mother followed, first laying her gloved hand on Alice's arm. "Talk to her," she said. "But don't let her know I've asked you. She is so tired of being hounded by her father and me. She won't listen to a word we say."

"Have you met this boy?"

"He's not a boy. He's a man," her mother said stiffly. "And no, I haven't met him but your father has had words with him. He has some kind of a shop. A shop where they sell gasoline and repair motorcars. You know the kind of place. He's older than she and entirely unsuitable."

"I'll take your word for it," Alice said. She watched her mother slowly climb the stairs. Then turning, she followed the sound of her sister's laughter. She found her sitting in the kitchen with Nell, who was baking yeast rolls. When she saw Alice, Laura jumped up and flung her arms around her sister.

"You've come home," she said. "Oh, look, Nell she's come home."

"Are you hungry, Miss Alice? I can make you a sandwich."

"No thanks, Nell. I ate on the train." She held Laura at arm's length, studying her flushed face, her ethereal, fragile beauty. Her eyes were large and very blue.

"Have you come home to stay?"

Alice smiled and dropped her sister's hands. "Would you like it if I had?"

"Only if you wanted to be here. I wouldn't want you to come home for any other reason." Laura frowned and tucked a stray curl behind one ear, watching as Nell pinched off pieces of dough and rounded them into smooth shapes between her palms.

"I thought we might take a ride," Alice said.

"Oh?" Laura said.

"I have some Christmas shopping to do."

"But I'm helping Nell bake bread."

"You go on," Nell said. "I'll be fine."

"Well, all right." Laura untied her apron and folded it neatly over the back of a chair. "Let me get my coat and my pocket book."

"I'll meet you in the garage," Alice said.

Alice drove her father's little Willys coupe and they parked downtown in front of Goldman's Department Store. It was the most exclusive store in town, taking up a whole city block with the bottom windows blazing with their annual Christmas display. Women in fur coats hurried in dragging excited children behind them. It was as if the Depression had never happened. Alice and Laura went inside and shopped for a dressing gown for Roderick and a pair of gloves for Mother. When they were finished they went up to the fourth floor for hot chocolate in the Ladies Tea Room.

"So, how've you been?" Alice asked, looking around to see if she saw anyone she knew in the crowded room.

Laura stirred cream in her hot chocolate. She tapped the spoon gingerly against the side of the cup. "I've been fine," she said.

"How's school?"

"I hate school."

"I did, too, at your age. That will change."

"I don't think so," Laura said.

The waiter brought a plate of cookies and Alice got up and went over and talked to a group of girls she'd gone to school with.

When she returned to the table, Laura was sitting with her chin on one hand, gazing out the frosted window at the busy street below.

"Lord, these small towns," Alice said in a low voice. "You can't go anywhere without seeing someone you know."

"I hate it," Laura said.

"Oh, well, now it's not so bad as that," Alice said. She coughed delicately, opening her napkin on her lap.

"Everyone knows everyone else's business."

"Yes, I suppose that's true."

"I can't wait to get away from here."

Alice smiled brilliantly. "I know just how you feel," she said.

Later, they drove down by the river and parked and watched the fog roll off the water. The sky was a gun-metal gray. A flock of starlings darted back and forth across the water like a school of fish. Laura sat stiffly on the seat as if suspecting that Alice had been sent to scold her, and so Alice didn't. Instead she talked of Sweet Briar and going off to New York after graduation.

"How wonderful," Laura said, smiling gently and turning her face to the glass. She seemed more relaxed now. "Maybe I can visit you."

"I'll say," Alice said. "You can come anytime you like."

"But aren't you going to marry Bill Whittington?"

"What?" Alice said. Heat rose in her face. "Who told you that?"

"Mother."

"Well, Mother doesn't know everything," Alice said sharply. A distant barge, slow and ponderous, passed on the river. They both began to giggle.

After that, it was better between them. Alice didn't ask about the unsuitable beau, and Laura didn't ask about Bill Whittington. They talked for awhile about Adeline, how Father and Mother spoiled her, giving into her temper tantrums the way they never had with them. And Alice talked about the Yankee girls she had met up at Sweet Briar, how they were so outspoken and sure of themselves in the way that Southern girls never were. How they smoked cigarettes in public and went away unchaperoned for weekends with boys, and Laura, wide-eyed, shook her head and said wistfully, "Don't you wish we could be like them?"

Alice pulled a compact out of her purse and carefully reapplied her lip rouge. "Oh, I don't know," she said.

Laura's breath fogged the air in front of her and she turned and blew on the glass and wrote, *B.B. + L.M.* with a heart around it, and then wiped it clean. Alice, embarrassed, pretended not to see.

"All my life, I've wanted to be someone else," Laura said.

"We should probably head home," Alice said, closing the compact. "Mother will be worried."

"Wait," Laura said, shyly touching Alice's arm. "Let's go one other place first. There's someone I want you to meet."

Alice felt a slight tremor of dismay. There was no use stopping now; she had come this far and she might as well see it through to the end. She carefully slid the compact back into her beaded bag.

"All right," she said.

They drove past the Smithson School through the Missionary Ridge Tunnel to Brainerd. Above them, the lights of the houses on Missionary Ridge twinkled merrily. Evening was coming on quickly. Alice followed Laura's instructions and pulled up in front of a small, steep-roofed garage with a couple of gas pumps outside. The bell rang as they pulled up and the door opened and a man in a gray jumpsuit stepped out into the gathering gloom. He was smoking a cigarette, its tip glowing feebly, and he took it out of his mouth and crushed it under his toe, walking toward them with his hands thrust deep in his pockets, his shoulders rounded against the cold.

Laura rolled down her window. "Hello," she said, and he stopped for a moment and stared, and then came on slowly, his cap pulled low on his forehead.

"Hello," he said. He came around to Alice's window. "Fill her up?" he said, and she said through the glass, "Yes."

"Roll it down," Laura said. Her face was pale under her cloche hat. "The window. Roll it down."

"It's cold," Alice said, but she did as her sister asked. He stuck the nozzle in the tank and then came around to clean the windshield. She could see his face now in the slanting light from the garage window. His expression was fierce, intolerant, challenging. Briefly, through the glass, their eyes met.

Laura leaned over and said, "Brendan. This is my sister. Alice."

He took a rag out of his pocket and wiped his hand and held it out to her. Alice, after a slight hesitation, took it.

"Brendan Burke," he said.

He seemed to be laughing at her; she sensed it in his tone.

"How do you do," she said coldly.

"We've been Christmas shopping," Laura said.

"Have you?" His eyes were an unusual shade of green, pale and luminous like sun-lit water.

"We thought we might see a picture show tonight," Laura said, laughing. "Do you want to come?"

Alice, shocked, looked at her sister and then said with some confusion, "Mother will be expecting us home tonight. It's nearly Christmas."

The station door opened and a young man came hurrying out, pulling on his cap. "Sorry, Mr. Burke," he called, putting his hand on the nozzle. "I didn't hear the bell."

"That's all right, Billy."

"Please say you'll come," Laura said, leaning across Alice's lap and smiling up at him.

"Laura!" Alice said.

He looked at Alice. "I can't," he said.

Laura pushed herself back into the corner, pouting.

"What do I owe you?" Alice said, lifting her purse. She could feel her face burning in humiliation at her sister's behavior. She wanted to meet his gaze but she felt herself to be at a distinct disadvantage.

"You can pay Billy," he said, and without another word, he thrust his hands deep into his pockets and walked off toward the station, whistling.

"Really, Laura, how could you?" They drove swiftly through the dimly-lit streets. Alice was rigid with anger, remembering his expression through the windshield glass, the careless way he had walked off. "You practically threw yourself at him."

"I did throw myself at him."

"And you're proud of that?" Alice turned her head and looked at her sister who sat with her forehead resting against the window glass.

"I love him."

"Oh, Laura."

"I don't care what Mother says, or Father. Or you."

"He's not – suitable."

She turned her head and stared at Alice, her eyes fierce, mouth drawn up tight. "You don't even know him."

"I know enough."

"You always said not to judge people by how much money they had."

"I'm not talking about money, Laura. Be reasonable."

"I don't have to be reasonable," Laura said, pulling her coat tightly around her throat. "I love him."

The episode colored all of Christmas. Alice went around sunk in despair, avoiding Laura when she could, pretending to be merry and unconcerned, when she couldn't. Laura had always been so malleable, so willing to bend herself to Alice's will, and this new streak of stubbornness was disturbing. Ash Hill, Chattanooga, the people in her life, felt suddenly removed and distant. It was as if Alice's whole world had been turned inexplicably upside down; things she had taken for granted, small truths she had accepted without question, now felt false. She drifted, rudderless, through the holidays; attending parties and helping her parents keep a close watch on Laura.

There was nothing they could do, short of locking her in the cellar, to prevent Laura's escapes. There were too many windows to be climbed out of, too many doors to be opened and closed softly. These trysts never lasted long; Laura returned most evenings by midnight. Twice Alice caught her on the landing, her shoes in her hands, tiptoeing off to bed. Both times Alice stood staring, hoping to shame her, but Laura said nothing, pushing boldly past and going off to bed without a word.

Alice could put a stop to it. She could tell her father; but Roderick was a proud man, there was no telling what he might do. She could go herself and appeal to Brendan Burke as a gentleman. But her father had already tried that. He had, no doubt, offered inducements; money, patronage, gifts. He had most likely issued threats, too, although Alice could not imagine Brendan Burke responding to those.

She remembered his face that night under the lights, his expression of intense yet curious scrutiny, as if he were looking deep inside her to find that one thing, she wished above all else, to keep hidden.

She did not return to Sweet Briar in January. Her mother had slipped into one of her black moods, staying in bed most days behind a closed door, and if Alice left there would have been no one to order the meals, or arrange Adeline's busy social life, or see to it that Laura returned to school. Alice went around to see the headmistress and together they worked out a plan whereby Laura could return to school and graduate with her class.

In February she ran into Bill Whittington at a dance at the Country Club. He was there with Isabelle Aubrey, another of the wealthy Lookout Mountain crowd, and Alice was there with Bud Case. Bill Whittington gave her the cold shoulder at first, but later he asked her to dance, and because she obviously didn't care to dance with him, he was smitten. He stayed close to her elbow the rest of the evening, ignoring his date and trying to impress her with his smooth talk about bogeying the back nine. It was obvious that he and most of his friends spent their days golfing and they were all proud of this fact and stood around boasting about who had had the better game. Listening to them, Alice stifled a yawn. Isabelle stood beside Bill hanging on his every word, her lips slightly parted, ready at the least provocation to break into gales of giggles. Alice imagined Isabelle and Bill's future life together, the stately home on Lookout Mountain, the long dining table surrounded by a bevy of good-looking children, endless charity events and golf tournaments, the kind of life Alice's mother had settled for. The kind of life Alice had decided she never wanted for herself. Bud Case was nice enough, Alice's friend Sally had arranged for Bud to escort her, but he was a bank clerk from East Ridge and Alice could see that Bill Whittington and his wealthy friends intimidated him.

Afterwards, they all went out to a juke joint on the river. Bud said goodnight, he had to work the next morning, so Bill offered to drive Alice home. She tried to decline but she'd had enough Singapore Slings to make her tongue-tied and light-headed, and so she smiled at Isabelle, who was giving her a cool, appraising look, and said, "Sure. Why not?" She raised her glass in a cocky salute.

Later, when the smoke and the noise and the smell of tightly-packed, perspiring bodies became too much for her, she went to the ladies room and then stumbled out into the cool evening. She had stopped drinking some time before and the brisk night air sobered her immediately. In the distance, the river glistened in the moonlight. She followed a graveled path down to the water's edge, past a dimly-lit bricked patio to a pair of wooden chairs facing the water. She sat for a long time watching the dark, swiftly moving river and listening to *Dixie Vagabond* and the rhythmic thumping of the dancers' feet. From time to time the door would bang open and she would hear a woman's soft laughter, or a man's gruff voice, and then the sound of their feet on the graveled drive. Once she heard Bill Whittington calling for her. She pulled her feet up and slumped down in her chair, and he went around to the parking lot, calling her name. A moment later Isabelle came out looking for him and Alice could hear their low, angry voices in the drive. Bill said, "Oh, calm down, will you? I promised to see her home, that's all." They went back inside, the door banging loudly behind them. Alice sighed and put her feet down, wrapping her arms more tightly around herself.

"Who are you hiding from?"

The voice, deep, overtly masculine, had come from behind her. Startled, she raised her head and looked around. She could see a figure in a hat sitting at a nearby picnic table, his cigarette glowing feebly.

"I'm not hiding from anyone."

He made a short, dismissive sound.

She was not frightened, although perhaps she should have been. "How long have you been sitting there?"

"Long enough to know you're hiding from someone."

"I told you, I'm not." She stood abruptly. He rose, too, stubbing his cigarette under his toe, and something in his mannerism, in his spare yet sturdy build, seemed familiar to her.

"You don't recognize me, do you?"

"Should I?" She took a step up the graveled walk, but stopped. She would have to walk past him to get back to the juke joint and she was suddenly hesitant to do that. *What had she been thinking, coming out here alone? It was dangerous. Dangerous and foolish.*

He took his hat off and stepped forward into the light slanting across the lawn, and she recognized Brendan Burke.

"I didn't mean to startle you," he said.

She felt a quiver of anger followed quickly by a wash of relief. "No? Then why are you sitting in the dark? You should have announced yourself."

"If I had announced myself, I would have spoiled the vision of you in the moonlight." His teeth glimmered in the dim light. "You would have left, like you're doing now."

She walked slowly up the path. She could see him clearly in the wash of light from the patio. He looked different than he had that night at the garage, standing there in a dark suit with his hair combed off his face, his pale, straight part shining in the moonlight.

He fell into step beside her. "I'm fairly harmless," he said.

"That's not what I hear."

"You've been talking to the wrong people."

She stopped and looked at him, holding his gaze. "My sister is only sixteen years old," she said.

His expression changed then, became closed and wary. He raised one hand and indicated an empty table and two chairs on the patio. "I'd like to talk to you about her."

She hesitated. She didn't want to hear what he had to say about Laura, about himself and Laura. As if realizing this, he said in a coldly polite manner, "Please. I'll only take a few minutes of your time."

He pulled out a chair for her and she sat down. "You're cold," he said.

"No."

He took off his coat and draped it around her shoulders and then sat down facing her.

The coat was warm and smelled faintly of cologne and tobacco and whiskey. A good, manly smell.

"It's my father you should be speaking to," she said.

"I've spoken to your father. Several times."

"Oh?"

"Would you like a drink?"

"No. Thanks."

The table was near the door, partially hidden by a trellis. If Bill Whittington came looking for her now, she'd have no choice but to answer.

He cleared his throat and stared out at the dark river as if considering how to begin. After a moment, he sat back. "Do you mind if I smoke?"

"Go ahead."

He pointed vaguely at her. "They're in the breast pocket," he said, and she felt her face flush, fumbling in his coat.

She pulled out a silver case, took out a cigarette, and stuck it between her lips. "Do you mind?"

"Of course not."

She passed the case to him and he lit her cigarette and then his. They both leaned back in their chairs, smoking quietly.

"Your sister is a fine girl," he said abruptly. She made a restless movement with one hand and he said quickly, "I met her at the county fair. I saw her across a crowded dance floor and I asked her to dance. I didn't know how old she was." He put his head back as he exhaled, looking up at the stars. After a moment, he dropped his chin, taking a long drag on his cigarette. "And later, when I found out who she was and how old she was, I broke it off."

She exhaled slowly, watching him with narrowed eyes. "You broke it off?"

"That's right."

"Well, that's odd because she sneaks out of the house several nights a week and comes dragging home around midnight. Are you saying she isn't with you?"

"Sometimes she's with me. But never alone. I'm never alone with her. I don't date her. I haven't dated her since your father came to see me. She finds out where I'm going to be, I don't know how, and she just shows up. It doesn't matter where I am or who I'm with." He looked at her. "Sometimes I'm with another girl. It doesn't matter."

Alice felt her face heat up with the shock of his words. She waited until she was certain she could control the trembling of her voice. "So you're saying my sister is a hopeless flirt."

"I'm saying she's young. It's a school girl fascination. She'll outgrow it. She'll find some nice boy her own age and settle down and forget all about it."

Alice thought of Laura's expression those nights when she caught her on the landing, her shoes in her hands. Laura wasn't like a school girl at all. There was something timeless about Laura, something ancient and knowing.

Alice tapped her cigarette in the ashtray. "How old are you?'

"Twenty-five. How old are you?"

"Nineteen. Almost twenty." She'd misjudged him, she could see that clearly now. Laura had been right. He was entirely suitable. "You didn't grow up here?"

"No," he said. He smiled faintly, fixing her with a direct gaze. "Kansas. I came down here with my father after my mother died."

"And the gas station is his?"

"No. The gas station is mine. Bought and paid for by me without any help from anyone." He said this firmly, as if trying to make a point. He continued to stare at Alice and their eyes met, held.

The door banged open and Bill Whittington walked out. He stood for a moment, letting his eyes adjust to the darkness. "There you are," he said.

Alice stirred, putting out her cigarette. "I needed some air," she said.

He stepped around the trellis, noticing Brendan for the first time, and stopped. "Who are you?" he said.

Brendan exhaled, casually stubbing his cigarette in the ashtray. He rose slowly, extending his hand. "Brendan Burke."

Bill hesitated and then took it. "Bill Whittington." They shook, briefly, and then let their arms drop back against their sides. "Burke," Bill said. "Are you related to the Burkes in Riverview?"

"No."

"I didn't think so." He turned to Alice. "Are you ready to go?"

"Almost."

"I should see you home. Your parents will be worried." He hadn't thought about her parents before; it was only now that he saw her with Brendan Burke that they occurred to him.

"We were having a private conversation," Brendan said.

Bill stared at him for several moments without speaking. "I promised to see Miss Montclair home."

"I suppose it's up to Miss Montclair who sees her home."

Alice stood and slid Brendan's coat off her shoulders. He stepped closer to her. His fingers brushed hers, taking the coat, and she felt a tremor pass through her.

His voice, when he spoke, was low and smooth. "When can I see you again?"

She took a deep breath and turned away.

"Goodbye, Mr. Burke," she said.

Six

§§§

Several weeks after Stella began working for Alice, Alice's cousin, "Dob" Montclair called to say he was coming up for a visit. Dob lived down in Riverview, the exclusive area close to the country club, and he made his own mustard relish. Once a week he brought a bag of hotdogs and homemade relish up to Alice.

"Pray that he brings Ann with him," Alice said to Stella.

"Who's Ann?"

"His wife. She keeps him from talking too much. She tells him when it's time to go. He's a retired lawyer and he talks just like he was trying a case in court. After awhile I get tired of listening to him. He's eighty-nine years old and he and Ann are taking an evening philosophy class at the college. Did you know that once you turn sixty-five you can go to college for free? Well, anyway, I feel sorry for the poor professor because Ann says Dob harangues him the entire class and no one else can get a word in edgewise."

"Where'd he get a name like Dob?"

"It's a nickname. His real name is Robert."

Stella frowned. "Why didn't they call him Bob then?" she said.

"I don't know," Alice snapped. "Maybe because his name is Dob. Just like his grandfather and his great-grandfather before that."

They sat in the library waiting for him. It was a sunny day, unseasonably warm for early spring, and a patch of bright blue sky was visible beyond the roof tops of the grand houses. At the house across the street, a lone yard man with a leaf blower moved slowly behind the wrought iron fence and stone pillars of the drive, leaves cascading at his feet like an unfurled carpet. A verandah with white columns covered in wisteria stood on one side of the large house, and beyond that, a gaily splashing fountain. An old golden retriever walked stiffly around the fountain, nosing the mossy bricks with a studied, incurious air.

Stella felt warm and drowsy in the bright sunshine falling through the library windows. She closed her eyes, resting them, and then opened them again. Alice sat with her chin on her palm, staring fixedly out the window. Her white curls were nearly translucent in the sunlight and her face was like old parchment, lined and tissue-thin. Lulled by the distant hum of the leaf blower, Stella let her eyelids droop.

"Oh Lord," Alice said sturdily. "He didn't bring Ann."

Stella sat up, glancing out the window at a Honda Accord that had pulled into the drive. "Do you want me to come in and make up some excuse after you've spent twenty minutes with him?" she asked Alice.

"I like the way you think," Alice said, pulling herself to a standing position.

Stella helped Alice get settled in one of the wingback chairs in the living room, and then she went to open the front door.

"Hi. I'm Stella. Alice is waiting for you in the living room."

"Hello, hello," Dob said, handing her a plastic bag filled with hot dogs. He was a little stoop-shouldered man with thick glasses and a lively expression. He looked like that cartoon character from the sixties. *Mr. Magoo.*

He went ahead of her into the living room. "Hello, old girl," he called to Alice in a loud booming voice. He was dressed in a t-shirt, a pair of shorts, and tennis shoes. His legs were bowed but muscular. *He works out at five-thirty every morning at the YMCA*, Alice had told her.

Stella took the bag of hot dogs to the kitchen and put them in the refrigerator. She could hear Dob and Alice in the living room, Dob talking in a loud, slow voice and Alice answering when she could get a word in.

"Do you remember Teddy Franklin?" Dob said.

"No, I don't believe I do."

"Yes, you do. The Franklins lived down in Riverview. They had four boys. Teddy, who was the oldest, then Lem, Sam, and Whitfield."

"I don't recall."

"Sure you do, Alice! How could you forget Teddy Franklin? He was your age. He married the Ammons girl." His voice became increasingly loud and irritated as he quizzed Alice and her answers fell short of his expectations.

"Well, what about him?" Alice said finally.

"He died."

"He's dead?"

"That's right. Last night at home."

"Well, I'm sorry to hear that. I read the obituaries every day to see if I know anyone who's passed. It's getting to be a pretty regular occurrence."

"The Franklins lived in that big house on the corner, next door to the Susongs."

"If you say so."

"Damn it, Al, I know you must remember. Little Teddy Franklin? Had the lazy eye? You used to call him Wimpy? Wimpy Franklin."

"Now that rings a bell," Alice said.

She was giving as good as she got, although Stella could hear the exasperation in her voice. She checked the wall clock and went over and opened the three-ring binder and began to read what the night caregiver had written. *Miss Alice had a restless night. She talked quite a bit in her sleep. In the middle of the night she sat up and said, "You should have announced your presence." This morning when I asked her, she said she'd been dreaming about her childhood.*

Dob had moved on from talking about Teddy Franklin and now he was relating a story about when he was a boy, and overheard Alice's father and another man talking at the bank.

"Your father had taken me down to the drug store to get an ice cream cone and we had stopped in at the bank on our way home," he said.

"Yes," Alice said. "He often did that."

"Do you remember script?"

"What?"

"Script! Do you remember script?"

"Well, no, I don't guess I do."

"Back during the Depression counties used to issue script to pay their employees. And I remember that man at the bank arguing with your father; it was the first time I'd ever heard anyone openly argue with him, about whether to take script in payment of services. Your father said, '*It's as good as paper money,*' and this man said, '*No, he didn't believe he'd take it.*' It was an eye-opener to me, having someone dispute your father like that."

"I guess it would be," Alice said.

"Well, I found out later, the county paid their schoolteachers with script. And you know, Al, schoolteachers have to eat like the rest of us. So the big landowners were going around and buying up script for 30 cents on the dollar from the teachers and other poor folks, and then they were turning around and paying their taxes with script! Now, Alice, that wasn't right! It just wasn't right!" He finished with a loud, agitated hoot, his voice cracking slightly like a lawyer summing up his case before an indifferent jury.

"No, I don't guess it was," Alice said serenely.

"It burns me up, just thinking about it."

"I guess the good old days weren't always so good."

"No, they were not."

Stella closed the binder, listening. Dob's voice had risen steadily to a shout. Stella had noticed that Alice and her family talked to each other like this; loud and bullying. There was a sly edge of humor to their teasing, just the slightest hint of cruelty. She had thought it disrespectful, at first, to hear Sawyer talking to his mother this way, but Stella had quickly learned that Alice seemed to expect it, she seemed to appreciate it. Sentimentality would not have been tolerated in the Whittington house anymore than it had been tolerated in Stella's childhood home, although perhaps for different reasons. Among the Whittingtons it would have been considered cowardly, and among the Nightingales it was unheard of.

We are all products of our childhood, Stella thought, paraphrasing Harlow. Baby monkeys deprived of maternal contact in the first weeks of life, will never develop normal brains and social relationships.

Dob said, "I talked to Adeline and she says she and Ann and Weesie are taking you to lunch tomorrow."

"Who?" Alice said.

"Adeline! Your sister, Adeline! And Ann, my wife. And Weesie, your childhood friend."

"Oh, they're taking me to lunch tomorrow."

He sighed loudly. "Yes, I know that, Alice. That's what I just said."

"Or I'm taking them, more likely. That's the way it usually is."

He said, "Do you remember that time our fathers took us to the county fair and we got sick eating candy apples?"

"I don't guess I do."

"Sure you do, Alice! You remember that!"

"If you say so."

"*Think, Alice, think*! I was only five and you were ten and you teased me because I was too scared to ride on the Tilt-A-Whirl. And you called me a big baby and made me cry."

"That sounds about right."

"I know you can remember that day. It was in the fall. We were there with our fathers!"

He was shouting again and Stella couldn't stand it anymore. She walked into the living room and said, "Alice, I hate to bother you but you were supposed to call Weesie. Remember?"

Alice looked up at her with a blank expression. "What?" she said. "Why do I need to call Weesie?"

"To make arrangements for tomorrow. Remember?"

"I've already talked to Weesie," she said irritably. "It seems silly to call her again when I've already talked to her.

You know I don't like talking on the telephone, you know…" She stopped suddenly. "Oh," she said, looking at Stella. "Oh, that's right. I need to call Weesie."

"Well, I should probably go," Dob said.

"Oh, yes," Alice said, stirring. "I remember now." She grinned at Stella. "I need to call Weesie."

Dob rose, motioning for Alice to stay seated. "No, no, don't stand up unless she's there to help you," Dob said.

"I don't need her to help me," Alice snapped. "I do jump ups every morning."

"Jump ups? That sounds dangerous. You shouldn't put too much strain on your heart, Alice. You shouldn't jump up too fast because all the blood leaves your brain." And he began a long, haranguing discourse on the limitations of the circulatory system in the elderly.

"I know what I'm doing," Alice said when she finally got a word in.

"Well, I don't want you to fall because I cannot lift you if you do!"

"Nobody's asking you to lift me," Alice said in a voice heavy with sarcasm.

"She's pretty good at getting herself up," Stella said. "She's in good shape really." Stella smiled encouragingly at Alice, who rose slowly with theatrical dignity.

"Well, okay then, I'll leave you to your phone call," Dob said, turning and walking stiff-legged out of the room. He stopped in the doorway, looking back. The overhead lights reflected off his thick glasses, off his shiny speckled scalp beneath its thin covering of hair. "Don't forget the hotdogs," he said. "You can have one for lunch."

Alice didn't hear him. She swiveled her head and said loudly to Stella, "What an ordeal. Thank goodness he's gone."

Stella averted her eyes, sure that Dob had heard Alice. But he said nothing, and turning, walked out.

"He's a real character," Stella said to Alice at lunch.

"Who?"

"Your cousin. Dob."

"That's one way of putting it." Alice chewed slowly, moving her black-eyed peas around on her plate with a fork. She had decided she didn't want a hotdog for lunch after all. "His father and my father were brothers. We grew up together on Signal Mountain. We lived on one side of my grandparents and Dob's family lived on the other side. All three houses are still standing." She turned to Stella. "Have you ever been up there?"

"To Signal? A couple of times. I don't know it very well." Why would she know it? Only rich people lived up there, rich people who drove expensive foreign cars and played tennis all day. Not like Lookout though, with its old families and old money. Flashy and extravagant, Signal flaunted its money the way Lookout did not have to.

"Great-grandfather Sawyer built a summer home up there. It was at the top of the W-road. Do you know it?" Her pale eyes settled curiously on Stella. Stella shook her head. The W-road was a narrow, winding road that ran up the back side of the mountain. A couple of treacherous switchbacks at the summit gave it its name. Stella had been up it a couple of times but she had never driven it; she would have been too nervous to drive it.

"Half of his children were in Texas and half were in New York, and so he built the summer home as a half-way place where we could all gather. I can remember going with grandmother to open up the house. It had a bowling alley and my cousins and I all thought that was wonderful. The house is still standing. Sawyer took me up there and we drove by and the house and the property still look the same, only someone has painted it green. I don't think great-grandfather Sawyer would have liked that. Alice Sawyer was his mother. She's the one in the portrait in the foyer. She's who I'm named for."

Her face took on a serene expression. She was obviously lost in her memories and Stella was quiet, allowing her to roam through the past undisturbed. Stella tried to imagine the large house surrounded by wide lawns and big trees, with a crowd of children dressed in white running around in bare feet. *Like something out of an old movie,* she thought. *Cheaper by the Dozen* or *Little Women.* Something about a large, happy family where children are encouraged and valued and spoiled. Stella had cousins but she'd never met them. She'd only seen her grandmother a couple of times. She was a large, slow-moving woman who lived in a trailer on the outskirts of Maynardsville. The last time they visited, she and Stella's mother had gotten into a loud argument over a ceramic cookie jar that Stella's mother had broken as a child.

Alice stirred. She set her fork down and touched her napkin to her lips. "Dob's always getting arrested when he drives through Atlanta. I don't know why. It's almost as if the police are looking for him, as if they know his car. He's always on his cell phone driving on the expressway. You know how crazy Atlanta traffic is, people zipping by at eighty miles an hour. Last time he called me and we were talking and he said, *'Damn, Alice, I'm fixing to get arrested,'* and then the phone went dead."

"What'd they get him for?"

"I don't know. Belligerence probably."

Stella laughed. "Yeah, I can see that."

"He's always had his own way of doing things. When he was a boy he went through some wild times, hopping freight cars and traveling around. His father got so tired of getting calls from little country jails telling him to come get Dob. He was a lawyer, like my father. They were brothers and law partners. Anyway, the last time Uncle Danforth got a phone call from some little country town sheriff, he said, *Keep him for a few days.* He wanted Dob to get a real taste of what being a jailbird was like. And after that he didn't hop any more freight cars."

Stella had never spent any time in jail but she'd spent time in shelters. She wondered if Dob had fond memories of his days on the road. She'd noticed how old people tended to romanticize their youth; if you listened to old people talk it was as if nothing bad had ever happened to them.

"What about you?" Alice turned her head and let her eyes settle on Stella. "What about your family? Do you have any brothers or sisters?"

"Two brothers. Two little brothers."

"That's nice."

"Yes."

"You don't have any children do you?"

"Good Lord, Alice, I'm only twenty-one!"

Alice smirked and raised one eyebrow. "Well, I had my first at twenty-two. That was common in those days."

"And I'm not married either. I have no intention of ever getting married! Marriage is an archaic institution."

Alice went back to eating. She chewed silently, staring at the wall calendar that showed a mother rhesus monkey with a baby monkey glued to its back. "My sister married a Yankee," she said finally.

"Really?" It was all Stella could think to say. She was embarrassed by her outburst, her insistence that she would never marry. Sometimes things came spilling out when she least expected them.

"Of course we did everything we could to stop her, but Adeline had a mind of her own. Despite our disappointment, my mother and I went to visit her in Cleveland, Ohio. It was cold. Snowy and cold. For some reason, my sister's mother-in-law, Mrs. Marr, insisted on having a *Welcome to Cleveland* cocktail party for us. The first thing she said to my mother, after taking a good long look at my sister and I, was *'Goodness, do they have the same father?'*

My mother's expression never wavered. *'Apparently,'* she said dryly."

Stella put her head back and laughed. Alice grinned, slanting her eyes up at her. "Mother did not suffer fools gladly," she said.

They ate for awhile in silence, each lost in her own thoughts. Stella had brought some of the leftover chili for lunch and she'd fixed Alice a plate of barbecue pork and black-eyed peas and collard greens.

"But Adeline came back to Chattanooga?"

Alice looked at her. "What?" she said.

"Adeline. She moved back to Chattanooga."

"Oh yes, eventually. After Brooks died, she came back."

"Was Adeline the only one who ever left Chattanooga?" Stella asked.

"No. Bill and I moved to Mobile during the War. He was stationed down there. They found out he was a good golfer and they'd send all the big brass down there to relax and recuperate and play golf with Bill Whittington. It was our only war time assignment."

"Well, at least he did his part."

Alice made a wry face. "I suppose you could say that. He had a fine time. I hated it. It was the kind of place where if you weren't from Mobile, you weren't anybody. Since I didn't have too many friends, I decided to start a garden. '*Grow some collard greens, Alice!*' Bill Whittington said. '*You'll feel better about yourself.*' And so I did. I tended that garden all summer. I never was a gardener, you know, I never had a green thumb, but I threw myself into it. I had a big straw hat I used to wear to ward off sunstroke because it's hot as Hades in Mobile, Alabama. I've never worked so hard in all my life. When it came time to pick them, I went outside one morning, and they were all gone. Some one had snuck into my garden in the middle of the night and stolen all my collard greens."

The image of Alice in a straw hat was too much for her. Stella put her napkin over her mouth. She said, "Oh, no, that's terrible!"

Alice stared rigidly at the wall, her chin trembling slightly.

"And that's all I have to say about Mobile, Alabama," she said.

That afternoon during her nap Alice dreamed of collard greens, big, green heads like plump pillows lying around her feet. She was standing in a field of them, collard plants stretching in all directions as far as the eye could see. A storm was coming, she could see dark clouds gathering on the horizon, and she was afraid for the plants, afraid she would not be able to shelter them from the storm, to keep them from harm. There were so many of them and just one of her and she seemed to be rooted to the spot, unable to move, unable to do anything except watch helplessly as the dark clouds rolled in.

The plants were trembling and making mewling noises like kittens and when she looked down the collards had turned into baby heads, big, fat-cheeked, blue-eyed baby heads looking up at her, in alarm and expectation, all waiting anxiously for her to gather them up in her arms.

Later, coming out of the dream into wakefulness, Alice remembered a morning at breakfast.

It was during the war and they were living in Mobile. Bill was playing golf with a four-star general at nine and he was in a chipper mood. Alice sat at the breakfast table with the baby, Sawyer, on her lap, watching bleary-eyed as Sam played battleship with his Corn Flakes. In the kitchen behind them, the girl, Winnie, fried an egg for Roddy who had decided he wouldn't have Corn Flakes after all this morning.

"Well then, you'll have no breakfast," Alice said when he steadfastly refused his Corn Flakes. Roddy was a stubborn, opinionated child determined to have his own way, much like Adeline had been. He and Alice didn't get on too well.

"If the boy wants an egg, then let him have an egg," Bill said from behind his raised newspaper. He sat at the end of the table like a king trying to keep order among his unruly subjects.

"Winnie needs to wash the baby bottles," Alice said.

Bill let a corner of the paper drop so she could see his eyes, glinting behind his dark-framed glasses. "Well, she can wash the baby bottles after she makes the boy a fried egg." He went back to reading his paper.

He spoiled Roddy because he had "spunk" (which was what Bill called male temper tantrums); unlike Sam who was gentle and quiet.

Roddy spent all day running over the neighborhood with other boys, but Sam stayed close to Alice, helping her with Sawyer, brushing her hair when she was tired, going through magazines and helping her pick recipes for Winnie to try for supper.

In the kitchen, Winnie knocked a sauce pan off the counter and it clattered loudly on the floor. Alice sighed. Winnie was just a girl, she'd had no previous service experience, but it was impossible to find experienced help now that they'd all found factory jobs. The whole world seemed to be turning itself upside down because of this War. Alice didn't know how things would ever go back to being the way they'd been before. The only one who seemed to be enjoying himself was Bill Whittington.

Winnie came in carrying a plate with a fried egg, burnt and gelatinous, staring up at them like an eye. She set it down in front of Roddy, glancing nervously at Bill, and then turned and hurried back to the kitchen.

"It's burnt," Roddy said.

"It's not burnt," Alice said, shifting the baby on her lap. He had taken hold of the collar of her dressing gown and was staring at it with fixed fascination.

"It's burnt and I will not eat it." Roddy pushed the plate away and folded his arms across his chest.

"You will eat it," Alice said.

Bill put the paper down and picked up the plate. "Winnie," he called briskly, and she stuck her head out of the kitchen and said nervously, "Yes, sir?"

"Have you ever made a fried egg?"

"Well, yes, sir."

"Here's how it should look. It should be creamy white, with just a hint of golden color around the edges. And the yolk should be orange and when you stick a fork in it, it should burst and flow across the plate like Vesuvius. Do you understand, Winnie? Vesuvius?"

"Yes, Mr. Whittington."

"Take this then and try again." He waited for Winnie to take the plate and return to the kitchen, and then he leaned across the table and said in a low voice, "And that, Alice, is how you handle the help."

Marriage was every bit as dreadful as she'd imagined it would be. There were days when Alice could barely bring herself to get out of bed, when the noise and disorder and loneliness of her household became almost too great for her to bear. The house they were renting was a small cottage with only two bedrooms and a bath. There were no quarters for Winnie, she rode the bus everyday to work, and the boys shared a bunk bed in one room, while Alice, Bill, and the baby slept in another.

Bill had refused to be quartered on the base but there were times when Alice wished she had insisted. (As if her insistence about anything ever did any good with Bill Whittington.) Surrounded by other army wives, she might have developed a few friendships. But stuck, as she was, in a neighborhood of older, grander homes she was an interloper in a town where everyone had known everyone else for generations (it was a lot like Chattanooga in that regard.) When Bill took her for drinks at the Officers' Club, the other wives who lived on the base were cordial but unwelcoming. They assumed it was Alice who had refused to live on the base, as if she was too good for army housing, but in reality it was Bill Whittington who felt that way.

She had known since her wedding night that her marriage was a mistake. She had been so nervous, afraid he would know that her air of inexperience was forced, nervous that she would give herself away through some inadvertent movement or sound. But she needn't have worried. He had unwrapped her like a gift, as greedy and disillusioned as a boy on Christmas morning who has been given the one thing he wants above all else, and possessing it, is now unsure of its value. Afterwards, he got up, dressed himself in a pair of silk pajamas, and then taking off his glasses, fell promptly into a deep sleep. She waited until his breathing was slow and regular, and then she crawled out of bed and into the bathroom, staring in the mirror at her blotched face and wild hair until black tears began to streak her face.

In the morning she rose and dressed herself carefully and went sightseeing with her new husband, walking hand in hand along the Battery, the low skyline of Old Charleston behind them. She became two Alices; the desperately unhappy, crying woman of the evenings, and the attractive, expensively dressed young wife of the daylight hours. Bill, after his initial infatuation with the physical act, settled down into the role of a genial but gruff older brother, taking Alice under his wing, instructing her in all the ways he found her lacking.

And because she was still intimidated by him and felt guilty that she did not love him enough, she allowed this instruction.

In the early days of their marriage, she played with the idea of ending her life. It was a taboo subject; she would never say the word "suicide", but in the quiet hours of early dawn she would sometimes imagine the cold metal of a revolver against her tongue, a fleeting sense of weightlessness as she took flight from the Walnut Street Bridge. What, she wondered, would the moment of death be like? A sudden extinguishment of all thought and emotion? Or a gradual dawning of something else?

But as the cold, hard light of early dawn crept into the room, she would put her wild nocturnal imaginings away. She wasn't a coward. She would never do that to her parents, would never visit upon them the grief of having to explain a child's desperate act to strangers, to hear the whispers, the pitying stares as they walked along the street. And when she felt the quickening of her first child deep in her belly, she banished such thoughts forever. Her life would never again be her own. She had been raised to accept the yoke of sacrifice and personal responsibility, and as each succeeding child was born, she submitted gracefully. She derived pleasure from her role as mother, and despite the lonely hours and sleepless nights, a feeling of self-worth she had not felt before. Her children promised hope, a feeling that she might transform her life, and in so doing, leave the past behind her forever. Her children would be her salvation.

Looking down into their sweet faces, she understood clearly now that her life would be one of atonement.

Seven

§§§

Josh and Macklin were sitting on the sofa playing Halo when Stella got home. She was tired; it was amazing how tiring a twelve hour shift could be, even one where you could read or nap a good part of the time.

"Hey," Macklin said as she walked in.

"Take that, asshole," Josh said, tapping his controller. Neither one looked at her. She threw her backpack down on a chair and walked into the kitchen.

"Bring me a beer," Josh shouted from the other room.

"Me, too," Macklin said.

The kitchen was a mess, dirty dishes stacked in the sink, a jar of mayonnaise with the lid off sitting on the counter along with a packet of bologna and a nearly-empty sleeve of white bread. There was no dishwasher and Stella was accustomed to washing everything by hand. She washed dishes as she used them, but Josh didn't, and on Wednesdays and Thursdays the sink filled quickly.

She pulled three beers out of the refrigerator and went back in and sat down, setting the beers down on the coffee table next to an empty pizza box.

"Was that dinner?" Stella said, looking at the pizza box.

Josh kept his eyes on the game. "Yep," he said.

"Thanks for saving me a piece."

His eyes slid to her, then back to the game. "You weren't here," he said.

She tugged on the beer, her eyes fixed on the flickering screen. If she had done that to him, eaten it all without leaving him a piece, he would have pouted for days. There was a double standard in this house. There had been since the beginning.

She stood up, too tired to think about it anymore, picked up her backpack, and headed for the stairs.

"Where are you going?" Josh said.

"To bed. I'm tired."

"You're always tired."

"I wonder why."

"Hey, try working an eight hour day, five days a week if you want to know what tired feels like."

"Yeah, dude," Macklin said. "Try dragging your ass out of bed every morning at seven-thirty."

She wanted to say, *Yeah? Well, try staying up until three a.m. doing homework while some asshole plays video games all night and drinks with his friends. Try working twelve fucking hours and then coming home to a trashed apartment and no food on the table, knowing you've got another three hours of studying ahead of you.* But it wouldn't do any good to get into a pissing match with Josh, especially with Macklin around. She would never win.

She was half-way up the stairs when Josh called to her, "I forgot to tell you, I need my car tomorrow."

She turned swiftly and came back to the bottom of the stairs. "How am I supposed to get to work?" she said.

He shrugged. "Isn't there a bus?"

"Not that I know of."

"Sorry but I'm meeting some friends after work and you don't get off until eight."

"If I don't show up, I'll get fired. Is that what you want?"

"I don't give a shit as long as you find something else."

Macklin chuckled. "Take that, bitch," he said to the screen.

Stella stood there, eyeing him stubbornly. "Can't you meet your friends Friday night?"

Josh's eyes slid to her. He let them rest on her a moment before going back to the game. There was a warning in his expression. "No," he said.

Because she didn't have the courage to stare at Josh, she stared at Macklin.

"Hey, don't look at me," he said. "My car needs a new tranny. Jessica's been taking me to work."

"Can she take me?"

"I doubt it. But you can call her."

She went upstairs and lay down on the bed with the beer resting on her stomach. She couldn't call Jessica; they weren't really friends. She only seemed to tolerate Stella because Josh and Macklin were friends. And she didn't know anyone else well enough to call them and ask them to drive her up Lookout Mountain at seven-thirty in the morning. She could call a cab but that would eat up a good portion of her earnings.

She should have considered this before she took the job. The distance, the lack of transportation up the mountain. Josh had been good about letting her use his car on Wednesdays and Thursdays, catching a ride to work with a co-worker who lived a couple of blocks over. It wasn't his fault she didn't have any friends.

She drank her beer, looking at the stains on the stippled ceiling. When she had finished, she leaned over and set the can on the floor, rummaging in her backpack for the small piece of paper Luke Morgan had given her.

"I wondered why you hadn't called me," he said. They were driving slowly up Lookout Mountain, the morning sun casting a rosy glow over the distant ridges.

"I've been busy," she said.

"I thought maybe it was because I'd asked too many personal questions the last time we met."

She turned her face to the glass, not saying anything. His car was a Jeep Cherokee, littered with bags of camera equipment and pieces of paper covered in lines of type. *Scripts*, she guessed.

"That coffee smells good," she said, embarrassed by the awkward silence between them.

"Oh, damn, where are my manners?" He grinned and leaned forward and picked up a plastic cup and handed it to her.

"You bought me coffee?" she said.

"Is that okay?" He glanced at her and then back at the road. "There's a cool little coffee house near where I live and I just picked up a couple of lattes to go. Nothing fancy, I'm afraid."

"No. It's really good. Thanks." She sipped her coffee, feeling guilty that she'd not called him for the class notes. Of course he'd wondered why she hadn't after that first time. It was no wonder she had no friends, always keeping herself aloof, drawing away whenever she felt someone coming too close. And what had he done, really, that was so terrible?

Nothing more than make a casual observation. A very astute, very troubling observation.

"Look, about that day we had coffee," she said.

"No. Don't explain. You don't have to. Sometimes I overstep my bounds. It's one of the qualities of being a documentary filmmaker - curiosity. What some people would call being a nosy asshole."

"I don't think you're a nosy asshole."

"Well, you don't know me very well yet."

She liked the way he said *yet*. As if he was certain that they would become friends, as if there was no hesitation on his part. She glanced at him, noting the strong jaw line, the way his hair curled softly around his ears. His face, in profile, was interesting, but not handsome. It was his eyes that gave his face its attractiveness. His eyes and his voice, pitched low and soothing like a stage hypnotist.

He swung his arm over the seat and picked up a faded messenger bag. "Here," he said, "look in that top pouch. I've been making you copies of Thursday's notes."

She didn't know what to say. She was not unaccustomed to the kindness of strangers. But she had forgotten how it comes over you when you least expect it; gratitude and surprise at the goodness of people. She took the copies from him.

"Thanks," she said.

"No worries."

She remembered Monica from the shelter in Birmingham. A young woman, a social worker not yet hardened to the troubles of others. She had taken Stella under her wing, had taken her in, given her a safe place to live and let her see how, with an education, she could make a good life for herself, independent of anyone else. It was Monica who had seen to it that Stella finished her GED, Monica who had taken her to sit for her SAT, Monica who had written reference letters and arranged for Stella to be accepted into a special program at the University of Tennessee at Chattanooga. Monica was the only true friend she'd had since she left home at sixteen, which explained why Stella had stopped taking her calls or answering her emails. If she failed, if she didn't make it, it would be easier if Monica didn't know. Stella spent a lot of time preparing herself for failure.

They had reached the top of the mountain and were driving slowly past columned mansions set back on wide sweeping lawns.

"Wow," Luke said. "Pretty high on the hog up here."

She laughed. "That's a Southern expression," she said.

He glanced at her, grinning. "Oh, I know quite a few Southern expressions now. *Mad as a bullfrog in a thumbtack factory. Crazy as a lizard with sunstroke. Stuffed like a Republican ballot box.*"

"It's only when I meet people who grew up some place else that I realize how crazy we talk."

"I wouldn't call it crazy. More like – descriptive. Creative, linguistically speaking."

"See, that's not something a Southerner would say. 'Linguistically speaking.' People would think you were stuck up as a dog with two tails."

"I like plain-spoken people."

The lawns of the large houses they passed sparkled with morning dew. The tall trees lining the street were beginning to leaf out and in several of the yards daffodils and snow drops raised their sunny heads.

"I can't wait to get out of the South," Stella said. "The minute I graduate, I'm out of here and I'm never coming back."

He glanced at her and she had the impression he was about to ask her something, but then thought better of it.

"Take a right here," she said, "and follow Brow Road."

The houses became increasingly grand as they followed the curving road. From time to time a space would clear, with the foggy valley spread out below them and the ridges of the mountains rising in the distance.

"Beautiful place," he said. "This view is better than anything I've ever seen in L.A. It reminds me a little of the Hudson Valley."

"Yeah, well rich folks always take the high ground." She hadn't meant it to come out the way it had, bitter and envious.

He glanced at her and again she had the impression that he was poised to ask her something, but thought better of it.

He said, "Do you like your job? You said you were a caregiver, right?"

"I like it all right. She's a pretty cool old lady. I didn't think I'd like her at first but she kind of grows on you. I don't know why. She has a lot of stories that she tells over and over again. She forgets she's already told me but that's okay, because I like hearing her stories. I'm guessing it drives some caregivers crazy, but I like it. Also, she's got this really dry sense of humor. I think she's hilarious."

"Sounds like someone I might like to film."

"Oh, no. She's very private. She'd never allow that." She pointed ahead through the windshield. "Do you see that speed limit sign? Take the first left after the sign. Don't pull up in the circular drive just let me out in front of the garage."

He did as she requested, leaving the car idling as she gathered her backpack and climbed out into the cool morning air.

"Hey, thanks," she said leaning over, the door resting on her hip. "I really appreciate this. And thanks for the notes, too."

"No problem," he said. "How are you getting home?"

"My boyfriend is picking me up," she said, feeling her face heat up at the lie. She had already decided to take a cab.

"You have a boyfriend?" His smile seemed to flatten at the corners.

"Didn't I mention that?"

"I don't think I asked."

"Oh. Well." She laughed nervously. She put her hand on the door. "Thanks again."

"I'll see you in class," he said, not looking at her, and she closed the door.

Alice was going out to lunch with Adeline, Ann, and Weesie and she was in a good mood. She rang the bell for exercise around nine-thirty and when Stella appeared in the doorway, Alice said, "Are you ready to walk?"

"Let's roll," Stella said.

As they passed the library, Alice stopped in the doorway, surveying the room. "Who's been moving my books around?" she said.

"I don't know, Alice. Has someone moved your books?"

"Of course they have! Look!" She pushed the walker ahead of her and Stella followed her into the library. Several piles of books were stacked on a low cabinet but the library looked much the way Stella remembered it always looking.

"These were not here before," Alice said indignantly, pointing at the stack of books. "Someone's been moving things around." Her hair, fine as a baby's, stood up in wispy curls around her face. "Why do people do that? Why don't they leave my things alone? I have everything the way I want it and someone comes in and decides my way is wrong."

"I'm sorry, Alice. I haven't moved anything."

"I didn't say you did. It was someone else."

Stella had no doubt that someone had moved things around. But it could have been done twenty years ago, and it could have been done at Alice's instruction and she had simply forgotten.

She said, "Do you want me to move everything back? Just tell me where you want this stack and I'll put it back."

Alice sighed. She shook her head. "No, don't do that," she said in a tired, discouraged tone. She stared at one of the framed photographs on the shelves. "I have no idea who those people are," she said.

They went on and did their five circuits. By the time they got to number five, Alice had forgotten about the library. She stopped in front of the French doors in the dining room, and stood looking down at the valley.

"Soon it'll be time for the kudzu to grow," she said.

"Do you get kudzu on top of the mountain?"

Alice chuckled. "Tell me where in the South we *don't* get kudzu," she said. "They say it grows up to two feet a day. Nothing kills it but frost."

"In East Rige, they've brought in goats to eat it."

Alice said, "Goats?"

"The city paid some guy last summer to bring in a herd of goats and stake them to the side of the ridge cut. Only after awhile the goats started disappearing and no one knew why."

Alice's eyes, in the slanting light, were a pale, milky blue. She snickered sofly at the idea of goats in East Ridge. "I remember when I was in the Garden Club," she said. She rolled her eyes and said "Gah-den" Club like a Southern aristocrat and it occurred to Stella that Alice did not see herself as an aristocrat. "The President of the Garden Club at the time was a very snooty woman. Very high and mighty. She liked to talk about her *great-great-grandfatha's slaves*. The woman was full of *happy darkie* stories."

"Now Alice," Stella said.

"Well, she was. Anyway, come to find out, it was her grandfather who first brought kudzu to Chattanooga. Can you believe someone actually thought kudzu would be a *good* idea? He went over to the Orient with a delegation of businessmen from Atlanta and they brought it back to use for soil erosion. Well, when it got out that Aurelia Hunt's grandfather was responsible for bringing kudzu to the South there was quite a scandal. The rest of the Garden Club mutinied. They nearly revoked her membership." Alice chuckled, shaking her head and rolling her eyes like a wicked child.

Stella grinned. "And you enjoyed that, didn't you?"

"Immensely."

They stood in the dining room, grinning at each other. Behind Alice's shoulder, Stella could see the portrait of the beautiful blonde woman. She had a slight smile on her lips as if she, too, was enjoying the Garden Club story.

Stella raised her hand and pointed at the portrait. "Alice, who is that woman?"

But Alice had already turned and started off across the wide dining room, and she obviously didn't hear her.

Alice's friends arrived promptly at eleven o'clock to pick her up for lunch. Stella and Alice were waiting for them in the foyer, and Stella opened the front door and said, "Hello!" She and Alice walked out onto the bricked stoop. Ann, the sister-in-law who was driving, jumped out of the car and came around to help Alice with her walker. She was a small woman with a dowager's hump and a brisk manner. Behind her, Adeline climbed stiffly out of the passenger's seat and stood beside the car, holding the door.

"Hello," Stella said again, trying to be friendly. "Alice is really looking forward to this."

Ann looked at Stella with the same expression of cold dismissal that Adeline had displayed earlier. Stella shut up. She tried not to let it bother her. She decided that from now on, she would ignore both Adeline and Ann. From the backseat of the car, Weesie leaned over and waved.

"Hello, I'm Weesie," she said.

"Hi, Weesie. I'm Stella."

She was unsure what she was supposed to do to get Alice to the car. She had seen a wheelchair in the guest bedroom but when she suggested using it, Alice had looked offended.

"I don't need a wheelchair!" she said. "I haven't needed a wheelchair since I got back from Cantor ten, five, oh I don't know how many, years ago."

Stella watched nervously as Alice navigated the steps with her walker. She put out her hand several times to steady her. "Are you sure you can do this? Do you need me to help you?"

Alice's face flushed a dull red. She was breathing heavily. "Young lady I've been walking by myself since long before you were born! No, I do not need your help."

The rebuke stung. Alice's expression was cold, contemptuous. Stella glanced at Adeline and saw a look of secret satisfaction pass swiftly across her face. Alice settled herself on the front seat, and pulled her legs in. Adeline closed the door and climbed into the backseat beside Weesie.

"Fold that walker up and put it in the trunk," Ann said to Stella, walking back around to the driver's side. "We'll be home in an hour and a half. Watch for us."

She got in and started the car, letting it idle while Stella folded the walker, placed it in the trunk, and closed the hood. As they drove off, everyone inside the car was laughing.

Stella walked back inside, slamming the door behind her. Her throat prickled; she felt bruised. Ridiculous to let her feelings be hurt by a group of old rich bitches. Stella walked an endless loop through the house, berating herself. Where was that tough exterior shell she had worked so hard to build? People couldn't hurt her because she wouldn't let them. She gave up before they did. She turned away before she could see the disapproval in their faces. She moved on. It had seemed a good enough plan up until now, but somehow, without being aware she was doing it, she had let her guard down with Alice. She had felt something growing between them, maybe not friendship exactly, but something intimate, personal. She had misjudged their relationship entirely and now she felt raw, wounded in a way she had not let herself feel in some time.

Inside the house she and Alice were one way with each other, but outside in the real world when Alice was with her own kind, it was something else completely. She saw that now. What she had mistaken for companionship and mutual respect was an illusion.

She was a paid servant, nothing more. She would do well to remember that.

She was in the fourth grade when Stella realized for the first time that she and her mother were poor. There was just the two of them in those days, traveling through Lower

Alabama (L.A., her mother laughingly called it.) Her mother's name was Candy. She was a Hamm from up around Maynardsville but she had not burdened Stella with this name, instead listing Stella's father's surname on the birth certificate. Earl Nightingale was a studio musician with *Dr. Hook & the Medicine Show* who came through Maynardsville on his way to Muscle Shoals to record an album. He would, no doubt, have been surprised to find that his night of tequila-hazed bliss with Candy had resulted in a daughter. Candy saw no reason to inform him, as he had no money, and everyone knew it was easier to squeeze blood out of a stone, than child support out of an itinerant musician.

Candy, in those days, weighed one hundred ten pounds and had a mane of thick red-gold hair, but over the years she put on weight, so that by the time Stella started fourth grade she weighed close to two hundred and fifty pounds.

Stella used to try to imagine her father. She saw him as a tall, stately man with a ready laugh and a loving, protective manner. Sometimes she imagined him with a guitar strapped to his chest, and sometimes she saw him as a fireman or an astronaut or a fighter pilot. She practiced saying, *My father says*, or *My father always lets me*, or *My father bought me a pony*. There were other children without fathers, she wasn't the only one, but they seemed a pathetic, slightly disreputable group and not one that Stella wanted to be part of. There was something precarious about her and Candy's rootless existence, their sad female undergarments hung out to dry in rented bathrooms, their old car always breaking down and requiring the kindness of strangers. Without a male presence in their lives they seemed diminished, vulnerable. There was a void at the center of their small world. And yet the men Candy brought home were dull and useless imitations; they did little to fill that void.

Stella knew what poor people were, she had lived among them all her life, but with the innocence of childhood, she had never actually considered herself to be one of them. She had no one else to compare herself to. Traveling around L.A., attending schools in small dusty towns, she was simply the smart girl who did her homework and didn't cause trouble in class. She never stopped to consider the socio-economic pecking order because L.A. was pretty much a level playing field – everyone subsisted on food stamps and welfare or, for the more fortunate, paycheck to paycheck.

Moving to Tuscaloosa in the fourth grade changed all of that. Stella attended a new elementary school in a high-achieving district she was not zoned for. Candy drove her every day to the edge of a prosperous-looking neighborhood and dropped her off, and Stella walked three blocks to catch the school bus. The school was large and bright and clean, and there were new textbooks and maps of the world in every classroom. The school library was a treasure trove and Stella immersed herself in *Mary, Queen of Scots* and *Black Beauty*, coming home every Friday with a backpack full of clean, shiny books so that Candy slapped her playfully on the rear end and said, *Lord, girl, you're going to wear your eyes out.* She met a dark-haired girl in her class named Donna Shelby, and they became good friends.

In October, Donna invited Stella to her birthday party. It was to be held on a Saturday afternoon at Donna's home. When Stella gave her the party invitation, Candy looked at the address, squinting her eyes against her drifting cigarette smoke, and said, "So you're friends with a rich girl, huh?" They were living at the time in an unpainted Victorian house that had been cut up into four apartments, the kind of sad, bedraggled-looking place that had Stella driven by, she would have thought, *Poor people live there.*

In honor of the prestigious address on the invitation, Candy took Stella to the Wal-Mart and allowed her to spend more than a few dollars on a birthday present. Then she walked next door and borrowed a party dress from their neighbor, a divorced mother of three whose daughter had been appearing in pageants since she was two. Their apartment was crammed with trophies and sequined tiaras and pink sashes that read, *Miss Celestial Queen* or *Miss Southern Belle Glitz.* The daughter, the current reigning *Miss Tallapoosa Depot Days*, was named Madalyn and she had a closet filled with over four thousand dollars worth of pageant dresses and it was one of these, a blue satin number with a frilled, sparkly underskirt that Candy procured for Stella.

On Saturday morning, Candy drove Stella to the party. The neighborhood was even more impressive than the one where Candy dropped Stella off to catch the school bus. Looking out the streaked window at the two-story houses set on perfectly manicured lawns, Stella felt a tremor in the pit of her stomach. Although imposing, the houses were alike in their facades so that after a few minutes of driving and turning, Candy became hopelessly lost.

Two women were walking down the street toward them, and Candy leaned out the window and flapped her hand. "Excuse me! Woo-hoo, excuse me!"

"No," Stella said. "Don't." She slid down in the seat. Her stomach hurt from the expansive quiet of the neighborhood and the realization that she and her mother didn't belong here. The two women approached cautiously. Stella was acutely aware of Candy's massive stomach swelling her *Redneck*

Woman t-shirt, and their multi-colored Chevy Chevette, shaking and panting against the curb like an old dog.

The two women approaching were thin. They wore tennis shoes and jogging clothes. "Can we help you?" one of the women said in a tone indicating that she would rather not.

"Hey, y'all, we're lost," Candy said cheerfully. She held the birthday party invitation out the window and waved it. "We're looking for 212 Persimmon Lane. The Shelby house. My daughter here, this is my daughter, Stella. Sit up and say hello, Stella. Well, anyway Stella's been invited to the little Shelby girl's birthday party and we're just trying to find the house. Y'all wouldn't happen to know the Shelby's would you?"

The woman pointed at the end of the street. "Last house on the left," she said.

Candy thanked them and they drove on. In the distance, the subdivision ended and Stella could see a series of wide, rolling fields and a lone chinaberry tree standing beside a small white house with a green barn out back.

Stella looked down at her blue satin encased lap. The frilled underskirt was beginning to raise a rash on her legs.

"I don't feel good," she said. "I want to go home."

"Oh, no you don't," Candy said. "I paid good money for that birthday present. I drove you all the way out here. You're going to the damn party."

The girl who opened the front door had long blonde hair and a vacant, bored expression on her pretty face. Her eyes traveled from Stella's shoes to her face and back down again. "Who are you?" she said.

"I'm friends with Donna. I'm here for the birthday." The girl looked a lot like Donna and Stella guessed she must be a sister. In the background Stella could hear the Spice Girls singing *Wannabe*. Several loud giggles and shouts of excitement told her the party was already in full swing.

The girl frowned, staring at Stella's dress. "You go to school with Donna?"

"Yes."

"That's weird."

Behind her, Stella could hear the high-pitched whine of her mother's car as it began its lumbering progress along the quiet street. Beneath the girl's sharply inquisitive stare, Stella was self-consciously aware of the car, the ridiculous party dress, the cheap, badly-wrapped present in her sweaty hands. It was as if she had gone her whole life with a blindfold over her eyes and now it had been suddenly and irrevocably ripped away. Standing in the bright slanting sunlight in the prosperous suburban neighborhood, Stella saw herself now through Donna's sister's coolly discriminating eyes. She had thought she was one person and now she realized she was someone else. She stared at her feet, deeply and hopelessly ashamed.

"Is that your mother?" Donna's sister said, her tone one of pitying amusement.

Stella shuffled her weight from one foot to the other. She didn't look up.

"No," she said.

Most of the other girls at the party were in her class at school. In the level democratic playing field of public school, Stella was friendly and popular. But here, with her new awareness of herself, she felt suddenly shy and awkward. The other girls crowded around her and said, not unkindly, "I love your dress."

"It's so shiny."

"Is that a slip underneath?"

They were all wearing jeans and sweaters. She was the only one in a dress.

"Thank you for coming," Donna said politely, smiling and taking the present from Stella. They were downstairs in the large walk-out basement that overlooked the sloping yard. A bank of white cabinets and bookshelves ran along one wall, faced by two leather sofas. Family photographs lined the creamy yellow walls. It was the kind of room you might see on a television show, and looking around at the rugs and the books and the clean upholstered furniture, Stella realized she could never bring Donna home with her, she could never ask her to spend the night. The idea of exposing Donna to the drab, dreary interior of their cramped apartment when she was used to all this light and airiness was unthinkable.

They listened to music and played games under the careless supervision of Donna's older sister, Cara. After awhile they went out into the yard and had pizza and soft drinks on a long table set up underneath the trees. Then they had cake and ice cream and Donna opened her presents. Stella waited in quiet anguish for Donna to paw through the stack of magnificently wrapped gifts to find her own meager offering – a book and a set of fizzy bath balls.

"Oh, I love *The Golden Compass*!" Donna said and hugged Stella. She made Stella sit next to her while she opened the rest of her gifts, including a watch, and a jewelry box with a tiny unicorn on its lid that twirled slowly to the haunting strains of *Wind Beneath My Wings*. Stella was fascinated by the unicorn and she turned the box over and rewound it several times as Donna continued to open her presents. On the last winding the mechanism stuck, and twisting the key hard, Stella was horrified to find that it had snapped off at the base. She looked up guiltily but Donna wasn't paying attention, she was exclaiming over another gift. Silently, Stella turned the jewelry case over and slid it back into its box.

She felt sick to her stomach the whole rest of the party. If she thought Candy would come and get her, she would have gone to the phone and called her. As it was, she sat quietly, smiling and red-faced, while Donna opened the rest of her gifts. She had amassed a mountain of presents and with any luck, she wouldn't notice the broken jewelry box until long after the party was over.

Cara came around with a black garbage bag and began to collect the paper plates and napkins. Stella jumped up to help her.

"Thanks," Cara said, thrusting the bag at Stella. She turned around and walked off. Late afternoon sun slanted through the tall trees shading the lawn. A breeze ruffled the leaves, lifting Stella's hair off her sweating face. She glanced anxiously at the house, hoping the party was almost over.

"Who broke this?"

Everyone stopped talking and stared at Donna who sat holding the jewelry box in one hand and the broken key in the other.

The girls looked at one another across the long table.

"Stella Nightingale broke it," Abby Reynolds said.

"No, she didn't," Donna said.

"Yes, she did. I saw her."

Donna looked at Stella. "Did you break this?" she said.

Stella shook her head. "No," she said.

Donna got up and left the table, followed by Abby and a clump of girls. They walked across the lawn and into the house. The few who were left looked at each other and giggled nervously. Faintly, in the distance, Hanson was singing *Thinking of You* and in the deep blue autumn sky, a faraway jet left a fleecy trail. Stella went around the table throwing away cans of soda and paper plates covered in half-eaten mounds of cake and melted ice cream. Some of the girls got up to help her. When they had finished, one of the girls took the garbage bag up to the garage. Stella hesitated, and then walked across the yard and into the house where Donna stood in the corner with a group of furiously whispering girls.

"I'm sorry," Stella said. "I have to go home early. I'm not feeling too good."

"Thanks for coming," Donna said. She leaned over and brushed Stella's cheek with cool, dry lips.

When she got to the basement stairs, Stella glanced behind her. Donna stood with her eyes down, listening as Abby hissed in her ear.

Stella went into the kitchen and called her mother and told her the party had ended early. She stood for awhile at the kitchen sink, looking down at the girls on the lawn. Donna's mother was having a drink in the soaring living room as she walked through. Stella thanked her and told her she had to go home early, and Donna's mother, glancing at her dress, murmured unconvincingly, "Oh, I'm so sorry."

"I'll wait outside," Stella said.

"Is your mother coming? I'd like to meet her. I've never met your mother."

"She has to work," Stella said. "My baby sitter is coming to pick me up."

"Oh?" Mrs. Shelby smiled coldly. She sipped her drink. "Where does she work? Your mother, I mean."

"In a dress shop."

"Which one?"

"I'm not sure." Stella began to back toward the foyer. "Goodbye," she said.

Mrs. Shelby got up and followed her. Stella opened the front door and stepped out onto the tall bricked stoop. Mrs. Shelby stood in the opened doorway behind her, her drink nestled in her hands. Faintly, in the distance, Stella could hear the squealing fan belt of the Chevette as it made its way through the maze-like subdivision.

"Where did you say you lived?"

"Thank you for having me," Stella said. "I had a very nice time."

The squealing was louder now. Mrs. Shelby's dark eyes left Stella's face and peered into the distance.

"Isn't that your mother now?"

"No," Stella said.

Mrs. Shelby gave her a cool, dejected look. A scent of ripe apples wafted across the lawn. Ludicrously, considering the time of the day and the urban splendor of the neighborhood, Stella could hear the distant crowing of a rooster.

Her friendship with Donna Shelby never recovered. Someone told the principal that Stella was illegally attending school in a district she didn't live in and Candy had no choice but to pull her out and switch schools. Three years later, Stella ran into Donna at a middle school football game. The small town where Stella currently lived was playing against Donna's school team. Donna was standing with a group of girls when Stella walked by and saw her.

"Donna!" she said, waving. "Hey."

Donna's eyes settled on her for a moment and then shifted indifferently to a point just beyond Stella's shoulder. Stella dropped her hand and walked on.

Behind Donna, one of the girls said loudly, "Oh my God. Who was *that*?"

"No one," Donna said.

Alice was in a jolly mood when she got back from lunch with her friends. She chattered on while Stella walked behind her, silent and brooding. Alice seemed to sense that she had offended Stella and she went out of her way to be charming and penitent. Or maybe it was just Stella's imagination. Maybe she wanted Alice to feel guilty for the way she had been treated in front of Alice's friends.

That night at supper, Alice turned to her and said, "Did you grow up here?"

"I'm from Alabama, Alice. You know that."

"Do I?" The old woman lifted a forkful of egg salad and chewed slowly, staring at the wall. She had awakened from her nap in a dazed, pensive mood and had spent the entire afternoon in her room watching the golf channel.

Stella picked up her peanut butter sandwich and then set it down again. "You told me when you hired me that you felt sorry for me, being from Alabama."

"That sounds like me." Alice continued to stare at the wall, chewing staunchly. She seemed lost in her own thoughts, lifting her fork from her plate to her mouth with almost mechanical precision. After awhile she glanced at Stella and said, "Do your parents live here?"

"My parents are dead. I'm an orphan." Stella wasn't sure why she had said this; it had just come tumbling out.

Alice put her fork down and turned her head slowly. She rested her faded blue eyes on Stella. "An orphan," she said. "How terrible."

She had said it because she wanted to give Alice a jolt. She was glad to see it had worked. "You get used to it," she said flatly.

"Did you tell me before that your parents were dead?"

"No."

"I think I would have remembered that." There was a long period of silence, during which they both stared at the wall, eating steadily. "Family life is complicated," Alice said finally. She had finished and she stacked her silverware on her plate. "It's wonderful to be loved but it can be confining, at times, too. You're never your own person; you constantly have to live up to someone else's expectations of who you should be."

Stella got up and took the dishes to the sink.

Alice said, "There's always an element of disappointment when someone you love let's you down. The deeper your love, the deeper your disappointment. I should know. I raised three sons. And I was the daughter of an overbearing mother."

"Do you want some ice cream?"

"No. Thank you."

Stella turned on the hot water and filled the sink.

"Holidays can be trying," Alice said. "All those past hurts and grievances bubbling to the surface. I used to dread Thanksgiving, all of us gathered around a long table, trying not to bring up anything painful. Trying not to air the family dirty linen." She continued to stare at the wall and then, without warning, she chuckled, her thin shoulders shaking. The overhead lights glinted off her scalp, pink and fragile as a baby's. "Adeline used to say her favorite Christmas lights were the tail lights of her children driving away." She pushed her chair back.

Stella went over and began to untie Alice's bib.

Alice said, "Do you have any brothers or sisters?"

"Two little brothers."

"But who raised you?"

"Foster parents," Stella said, feeling a grim satisfaction in saying it, not just in the lie itself but in the idea of the lie. She had often practiced using it; it carried a disturbing, undeniable weight that always brought people up short. How shocking to imagine what went on behind closed foster home doors. Shocking and terrible. But not nearly as terrible as what went on behind closed family home doors.

"How awful for you." Alice heaved herself up, grasping the handles of her walker. She blinked several times, the corners of her mouth drooping. She looked frail and helpless, and seeing this Stella was seized by an inexplicable desire to wound her.

"Life is hard for a lot of people," she said stoutly.

It was time someone shook the old woman out of her complacency, reminded her how the less-fortunate lived. There was something in Alice's self-satisfied demeanor, her naive belief in good fortune and fairness that made Stella want to tell her dreadful, shocking things. How do you live to be ninety-four and manage to avoid the unpleasantness of life? *By being fucking lucky*, she thought. *By being born to the right mother*. Life was nothing more than a crap shoot.

The phone rang suddenly, startling them both. Alice sat back down and leaned across the desk to answer it.

"Hello?" she said. "Hello?"

Stella turned around and went over to the sink to wash the dishes.

"Who is this?" Alice said irritably. "My grandson, Tim? Oh hi, Tim, how are you?" Her tone changed, became warm and friendly. "Well, you're a sweet boy to call. Yes, I'm sitting here with what's her name."

Stella squirted dish soap into the sink and foamed it with the sprayer attachment.

"Yes, I've got a new caretaker. That's right." She laughed. "Another one."

While Alice talked to her grandson, Stella washed and dried the dishes. Then she put them away and wiped down the counters and the stove.

Alice said, "You say hello to what's her name. Your wife. She's a real sweet girl and you need to be good to her." There was a moment's quiet and then Alice said,

"Okay, honey. 'Bye." She hung up the phone.

Stella walked across the room and stood in front of the walker, facing Alice. She folded the dishtowel carefully in her hands. "Why'd you call me *what's-her-name*?" she said.

Alice looked up at her in some confusion. "Did I?" she said.

"Yes. You did."

"Well, I don't know why."

"Don't you know my name?"

"Martha."

"No, Alice, not Martha. My name's Stella."

"Oh, Stella, I'm so sorry!" She put her hand to her mouth and her face changed, becoming pink and remorseful. She looked so distressed that Stella was instantly ashamed of bullying her, of trying to make Alice feel in some way responsible for her own unhappiness and insecurity.

She walked over and hung the dishtowel on the faucet. Then she stood staring at her somber reflection in the kitchen window.

"Sometimes I forget," Alice said.

"We all do, Alice. It's okay."

"I know you're Stella."

"It doesn't matter."

"And you're from Alabama."

"Don't worry about it, Alice. I don't know why I said anything." She turned around and went over to help Alice get up.

Alice stood, clinging to her walker. Her chin trembled and she looked crestfallen and ashamed. "Sometimes it just disappears," she said. "Everything that's in my head floats away and I can't remember."

"We're all like that."

Alice looked at her. "Are we?"

"Only the lucky ones," Stella said quietly.

The girl's face was filled with bitterness. She looked so lost and forlorn that Alice wanted to rescue her like she would a bedraggled puppy on a rain-swept street. She was just like the other girl. The one Alice could not, would not remember.

It was hard seeing a young face so filled with rancor. Only the elderly should express such defeat, such battering from the storms of life. The young should be immune from suffering. What was it the girl had said she was? An *orphan*. The word brought back childhood fears, a fear of loneliness, abandonment. When Alice was just a girl her mother had taken her to the Nashville School for the Blind and Deaf. It was Christmas and they had brought along baskets of fruit and Alice had gone down the rows of neatly made dormitory beds and given out oranges to the occupants. They sat at the ends of their beds, making unintelligible noises, their faces pressed to their oranges, which many of them had never smelled or tasted before. They were not all orphans, although some had been abandoned at the school door, but the rows of sterile beds, the faint scent of unwashed bodies and antiseptic, had made Alice think of orphanage asylums and surgical instruments.

She could hear the girl coming along behind her, her voice low and murmuring. She had forgotten to turn on the light and the hallway was dark, and as Alice walked, clinging to her walker, she saw Bill Whittington standing at the end of the hallway, as solid and substantial-looking as he had ever looked. She had seen him before, of course, but it had been awhile. He was dressed in his golf clothes.

Well, Old Girl, you'll have to face it sooner or later, he said.

Go away, she thought. *Don't bother me now.*

Best to get it over with, he said.

She ignored him, pushing the walker in front of her like a janitor sweeping trash. She could see his glasses glinting in the darkness. She thought, *Why do they keep sending you? Why don't they send the boy?*

He put his head back and laughed in that old way so that she felt a familiar tug at her heart. Twenty-six years she had lived without him; twenty-six long years of widowhood.

You don't get to choose, he said.

She pushed through him, feeling the chill of his presence against her breastbone.

Later, as she drifted off to sleep, he was there again, standing in the doorway and beckoning for her to come. She turned her face to the wall.

The dead are like that. Always leading you down paths you don't want to go.

Eight

§§§

At the end of March, a tornado struck Lookout Mountain. The day started out normally enough; the sky was slightly overcast as Stella drove up the mountain, but the dogwoods and azaleas were in bloom and the neighborhoods were filled with riotous color.

Elaine was in the kitchen writing notes in the binder when Stella arrived. She seemed in a worse mood than usual.

"Alice was restless last night," she said. "Once she sat up and said, *No, Bill, don't go*. It nearly scared me to death. And this morning she's in a foul mood."

"Poor thing. Bill was her husband."

Elaine gave her a long look. "Yes, I know." She scribbled a few more notes in the binder and then looked up again. "She's been really restless since you came. I've noticed that."

There was nothing Stella could say to this. She had the feeling that the more she liked Alice, the less Elaine liked her, although she couldn't say if it was jealousy on Elaine's part or something else.

Elaine grinned suddenly, showing a row of straight white teeth. "It's not the crazy, confused episodes you have to watch out for though. It's when they start having more and more lucid moments that you know they're going to die."

"Oh, don't say that," Stella said quickly, turning away and going to fill a glass of ice water for Alice's morning walk.

"That slip you picked out last night was too long," Elaine said, all business-like again. She tapped the pen on the counter, her expression brisk, irritable. "It hung down below her dress and she made me change the dress. She just stood there with her arms up and sighed, waiting for me to dress her. She doesn't blame you, of course, for picking out the wrong slip. She blames me. She always blames me."

"I picked the only slip that was in her drawer."

"Well, it was too long."

"How was I supposed to know that?"

"Next time you might try holding it up to the dress she's planning on wearing to make sure."

"Couldn't you just adjust the shoulder straps?"

"I suggested that but she wouldn't hear of it. She'd rather throw a big fit and have me change her. I think she likes finding fault with everything I do." Elaine turned and began to write something else in the binder, almost as an afterthought. Stella glanced over her shoulder and read; *Patient's dementia seems to be increasing.*

"Elaine, that's not true."

"It's just my opinion," Elaine said stoutly. "But I'm entitled to it. I'm entitled to make notes if I think they're relevant. I've been doing this for ten years. I sit with two other patients besides her. You only have her."

Stella went to put her purse and backpack away and didn't say anything else.

"And another thing," Elaine called after her. "She claims I broke her lamp, but I didn't. She likes the shade tilted up a certain way so she can read and today when I tried to do that, I noticed that the shade was sprung. It won't stay up. I tried to fix it but I couldn't, and now she's convinced I broke it. Which I didn't," she added fiercely to Stella, who had walked back into the kitchen. Elaine sniffed and rubbed her nose angrily. "I sit with two other patients who are very nice. They like me. Everyone likes me but her. She's been through twelve caregivers in the last year, including one who had a nervous breakdown and left in mid-shift. It's her, not me that's the problem. I won't give her the satisfaction of me leaving."

"I hope you won't leave," Stella murmured, not knowing what else to say.

Elaine went back to say goodbye to Alice, and Stella quickly wrote in the binder under Elaine's note, *I don't notice any change in Alice's cognitive abilities.* She could hear the two of them arguing on the monitor.

"Alice, I'm leaving."

"Well, all right then."

"I'll see you tonight."

"So you're not going to fix my lamp that you broke."

"Alice, I did not break that lamp."

"So you say."

"You know I didn't."

"Well, all right then. I'll make do as best I can."

There was a flurry of muffled activity and then the sound of the front door slamming. Stella stood at the kitchen window and watched Elaine walk by, her face pale with fury. She walked back to Alice's bedroom.

"Good morning," she said.

Alice looked up, smiling her most charming smile. "Oh, hello," she said. "The paper's there if you want to read it." She pointed to the other bed where the newspaper lay scattered.

She was dressed in a pink knit dress with a turquoise sweater. Her feet, clothed in pink socks and tennis shoes, were crossed demurely at the ankle.

Stella advanced into the room, leaning to gather the newspaper off the bed. "You've had an interesting morning, I hear."

Alice pointed at the crazily tilted lamp on the bedside table. "She broke my lamp," she said.

"Did she?"

Alice looked at her mischievously. "No, not really. I just like to get her riled. Sometimes I talk really low under my breath and when she asks me what I'm saying, I say *Nothing*. That drives her crazy."

Stella folded the newspaper against her chest. They stared at each other, grinning.

"Alice, you're terrible."

"I know, but it keeps life interesting."

"I'm glad you don't treat me that way."

"You don't act like she does. Besides, you're my favorite caregiver."

"I know you say that to all the caregivers."

Alice's smile widened. "I only say it to you," she said. "You are my favorite."

Stella, embarrassed by the pleasure she felt at this statement, glanced out the window at the steadily darkening sky. "It looks like it's going to storm," she said.

"Oh well," Alice said, going back to her puzzle book. "A little rain never hurt anyone."

Later that morning, Stella was sitting in the sunroom when the storm hit. She was trying, half-heartedly, to study for a biology test, wishing now that she had dropped the class when she dropped *Psychology of Gender*. When she had realized she wasn't going to be leaving Alice, she called Professor Dillard and explained her situation, promising that she would try to take the class in summer school. It was easier now, not having to see Luke Morgan, not having to rely on him for class notes. She hadn't seen him since that morning he drove her up Lookout to work.

She was bent over, reading, when the lamp began to flicker. At the same time she became aware of a strange whistling sound, like the noise an airplane engine makes when it's readying for take off. The glass of the windows rattled. Looking up, she saw the sky was black and the huge trees surrounding the house were bent nearly to the ground. Swirls of leaves and azalea blossoms swept across the verandah. Staring out the windows in alarm, she became gradually aware of a thundering sound in the distance, coming closer. At the same time a large limb fell from one of the swaying trees and she realized that the sunroom was the wrong place to be. She jumped up and walked through the house toward Alice's bedroom. As she walked down the long hallway, the lights flickered again, and went out.

Alice was sitting in the dark, trying to do her crossword puzzles. "The lights went out," she said to Stella.

"I know. The storm must have knocked down the power lines."

"What did you say?"

"The storm. Can't you hear the storm?"

"I'm sorry. I can't understand what you're saying."

Stella sat down on the opposite bed, staring out the window. Strange how Alice's hearing seemed to come and go, almost as if she heard what she wanted to hear, and not the rest. Gray clouds rolled in and rain began to fall, coming in at a slant and striking the windows like pebbles.

On the opposite bed, Alice said, "Ranting speeches. Starts with a T." She chewed on the end of her pencil. "I should know this one."

"Look at it come down," Stella said, watching the fierce rain rattle the windows.

"Tirade," Alice said gleefully.

"I thought tornadoes weren't supposed to hit mountains. I thought they only hit valleys."

They sat for awhile in the darkness, Stella watching the storm and Alice diligently working on her crossword puzzles. Far off to the east, the sky was clearing. The rain gradually lessened; it was falling now at a steady pace, straight down. Stella could see a roiling cloud of gray smoke billowing from the shrubs in front of Alice's house. She stared for a moment, thinking it was only fog, but then she saw a glow of red light, like embers. *Fire.*

"Clairvoyant one," Alice said. "Seer."

Stella stood up abruptly. "Excuse me, Alice, I need to make a phone call."

"Okay," Alice said. "I'm ready for snack. Bring it will you?"

Stella went into the kitchen, miraculously managed to get a dial tone, and called the Lookout Mountain fire department. Then she tried to call Sawyer but his phone was dead. She waited; staring out the kitchen window at the small fire that reflected now against the greenery and seemed to be throwing off sparks. Despite the steady rain, it sparked merrily. A pickup truck pulled up out front and two men in hard hats got out and walked cautiously toward the fire. They pointed and following their fingers, Stella could see a downed power line, snaking across the end of the drive and into the shrubbery. In the distance sirens wailed.

Stella fixed Alice's snack and took it back to her. Alice was sitting in the darkened room, peering at her puzzle book.

"I don't know when the power will be back on," Stella said loudly. She had no intention of worrying Alice by telling her about the downed power line. "There are sirens everywhere. It was a pretty bad storm."

"Storm?" Alice said. She put her book down and turned her head to stare out the window. "Is it raining?" she said. "The newspaper delivery man put plastic on the paper this morning and he's usually right. He always knows when it's going to rain."

"I tried to call Sawyer but his phone is dead."

"His phone goes dead when the power goes out but mine doesn't," Alice said, opening her packet of crackers. She slid one cracker out and popped it into her mouth, chewing thoughtfully. She pointed at the drawer of her bedside table. "There's a flashlight in there," she said.

Stella pulled it out and flicked it on to see if it worked. Outside the window, the two men in hardhats were setting up orange plastic cones around the downed power line. Stella set the flashlight down on the table. "Use this if you need it," she said to Alice who was blithely munching on her snack.

"I guess that means no TV," Alice said. "*No Wheel of Fortune* or *Jeopardy*."

"Well, maybe the power will come back on by then."

"Don't count on it. Last time it was out for days."

"We'll be pioneer women then. We'll live like they did in the good old days."

Alice hooted and shook her head. She picked up her coke, sipped it, and then set it down again. "The good old days weren't always so good," she said.

The kitchen had a gas stove but Stella wasn't sure how to light it, so she made a cold lunch of tuna salad, grapes, and coleslaw. Outside in the street a large power truck had arrived but Alice seemed unaware of the commotion in her driveway. Half-way through lunch Sawyer called on a cell phone to check on his mother.

"Oh, we're fine," Alice said. "We're just finishing lunch." She listened for a moment and then said, "Truck? What truck?"

Stella held out her hand to Alice. "Let me talk to him," she said.

She explained the downed power line and Sawyer said he wasn't too worried; he just wanted to make sure Al had plenty of canned goods because there were trees down across most of the roads and he wasn't sure when he'd get to the grocery store again. She checked the pantry and said there was enough to last several days and it wasn't until they'd hung up that she thought to ask him about lighting the stove. Well, perhaps Elaine would know how. She was sure Elaine would know.

She fixed Alice a scoop of Rum Raisin ice cream and then sat down beside her. The light falling through the windows was a dull gray and Stella had turned on the flashlight and left it sitting on the desk like a torch so Alice could see to eat. In the harsh light Alice's face seemed cavernous and ghostly.

We were snowed in once," she said, dipping her spoon in the ice cream. "In the big house over on Hammond. And when the men came to rescue us, to get the heat going and the water turned on, I went to the library and came out carrying a big bottle of whiskey to give to them. And Bill Whittington said, *Alice, where are you going with that?* And I told him and he said, *Not with my whiskey, you're not. Really, Alice, what's come over you?*"

She turned her head and looked at Stella. "Being stuck for a week in a cold house with three children, a guinea pig, and Bill Whittington. That's what had come over me."

Stella put her head back and laughed. It was something she could picture a youthful Alice doing, grabbing a bottle of whiskey and going forth to present it to her rescuers. "Well, hopefully, it won't take a week to get your power turned back on."

Alice chewed thoughtfully. "Well," she said finally. "It doesn't make any difference, we'll get through it one way or the other. I never have understood people running around getting upset by storms and such. You can't do anything about it, so why get upset?" She shrugged and popped the spoon into her mouth. Alice seemed almost cheerful, contemplating the destructive power of Mother Nature.

"Well, you'd probably feel differently if your house was one of the ones with a tree lying on top of it."

Alice chewed slowly, seeming to contemplate this. "I suppose you're right," she said finally. She turned her head and gave Stella a long, searching look. "Was your home damaged?"

It hadn't occurred to Stella to wonder. Not once had she thought of picking up her cell phone and calling Josh to see if he was okay. To see if her few belongings, a suitcase full of clothes, several boxes of books, had survived the storm.

"I don't know," she said. "I don't think so. I think my boyfriend would have called me if something bad had happened."

That afternoon they sat in the sunroom reading. It was the only room in the house with enough light falling through the windows to read by; Alice sat in a low chair with a pillow resting on her lap, her book, a history of the wives of King Henry VIII, resting atop the pillow. Stella had found a copy of Boswell's 1763 London Journal in the library and had instantly fallen under the spell of Boswell's prose, shocked by the sexual explicitness of his various accounts of his mistresses. It was hard to imagine that people of the eighteenth century, with their general lack of hygiene and access to contraceptive devices, would enjoy sex as much as her generation did. She turned to the frontispiece, where someone had written *Alice Montclair Whittington* in a flowing script. Hard, too, to imagine Alice reading this book; a youthful, blushing Alice. Hard to imagine that woman at all.

She shouldn't be reading Boswell, she should be reading *Brain and Biology*. She had put away her textbooks after the storm and hadn't reopened them. She was so far behind in her classes that it would be better if she dropped them all. And yet it was too far into the semester to get her money back; the school loans would have to be repaid regardless of whether or not she dropped the classes. She closed her eyes for a moment, letting the depressing facts of her present situation wash over her. If she quit school now, the debt hanging over her head would haunt her forever. And yet to continue on the path she was following, missing classes, turning papers in late, doing poorly on exams, would ensure that she was never accepted into graduate school. She would graduate with even more debt than she had now and she still would not be able to find a job as a counselor. Dr. Dillard had warned her that even social work would require a master's degree. She had started college with such promise, such hope for the future and now she found herself worn down by worry and fear that she would not be able to finish, that she would not have the stamina to do what had to be done in order to change her life. Perhaps she had been a fool to even think it possible.

Boswell wrote, *The truth is with regard to me, about the age of seventeen I had a very severe illness. I became very melancholy. I imagined that I was never to get rid of it. I gave myself up as devoted to misery. I entertained a most gloomy and odd way of thinking.* The book had obviously not been read in years; the pages were musty and brittle with age.

She wanted to believe that life would get better for her eventually. That she could wipe the slate clean and begin anew. She remembered her mother's insistence, all those years ago, that life would get better, *if only*. If only she could find a better job, if only a decent man would wander into their lives. Each time they moved Stella was promised a pink bedroom, a room of her own, a house with a yard and a white picket fence. Her whole childhood had been predicated on her mother's stolid, unchangeable belief that each new man who walked into their lives would bring these things.

Moody Bates had seemed a dream come true. With his steady job, his small, neat tract house in a neighborhood of small tract houses, his new Ford F-250 and riding lawnmower, he had swept them up like a genie and dropped them into a world they had hardly dared dream of. Stella had her own room with yellow dotted Swiss curtains. Candy quit her job and stayed home and cooked dinners that didn't come out of a box. When Candy found herself pregnant two months later, Moody married her, and the three of them settled down to a life that seemed, by all outward appearances, perfect.

Boswell was expounding on the "system" of mankind. *I can see that Great People, those who manage the fates of kingdoms, are just such beings as myself: have their hours of discontent and are not a bit happier.* Stella held the book up, fanning the pages back to the frontispiece. Without warning a letter slipped out and fell into her lap. It was frail and brown with age and picking it up and peering at the postmark, Stella could make out March 19, 1951. The letter was addressed to Mrs. William Whittington, care of the Commodore Hotel, New York City. She glanced at Alice, who was bent over her heavy novel and apparently had not seen the letter fall.

A sudden loud banging on the front door made them both jump.

"Goodness!" Alice said. "What was that?"

"Someone's at the front door," Stella said. She slid the letter back into the book.

"Well, go see who it is," Alice said.

It was Roddy, Alice's oldest son, and his wife, Hadley, dragging a cooler filled with ice behind them. Stella had never met either one but she'd seen photographs. He was a slight, attractive man with a full head of hair worn stylishly long, the kind of man who'd been irresistible to women his whole life and saw no reason to stop now that he was in his early seventies.

"Hey, I'm Rod," he said. His hair was still blonde and Stella wondered if he colored it.

"Stella," she said, smiling. "Your mom's back in the sunroom."

His wife, Hadley, was very pleasant and friendly, younger that he was by about fifteen years, Stella guessed. She introduced herself, glancing briefly, with an expression of detached curiosity, at Stella's lip ring and then going on into the sunroom to say hello to Alice. Stella followed Rod into the kitchen. He opened the refrigerator and began to toss things into the cooler. Stella had already moved most of the food into the freezer, but she could see now that the cartons of ice cream were beginning to melt.

"You'll need to throw all this ice cream out," he said, speaking in the same loud, overly-friendly voice Sawyer always used.

"Yes."

"I see from the cones in the driveway that the fire department has already been out here. Sawyer called me and told me there was a downed power line."

"That's right," she said.

He was wearing jeans and a sweater and Stella was struck again by how young he looked. Obviously, having money was like finding the Fountain of Youth. He had been married the first time around to the daughter of a man who showed up regularly on the Forbes list of billionaires, and he had worked for his father-in-law on various corporate boards until his divorce. Stella had learned all of this reading a book she had found in Alice's library written about the first families of Chattanooga. The Whittingtons and the Montclairs had figured prominently in the book.

"I'll do that," Stella said, indicating that she would throw away the ice cream. "You go on in and visit with your mom."

He turned and glanced at her, letting his eyes travel from her face to her chest and rest lightly on her hips.

"All right Stacey," he said in his forced jovial tone. "I'll leave you to it then."

Stella could hear the three of them talking in the sunroom as she cleaned out the refrigerator. Rod and Hadley had just returned from Italy and they spoke at great length about the Ponte Vecchio and the San Giovanni Square. Apparently, one of the family cousins had married an Italian Count several generations back and there was a lot of talk about the "Italian branch of the family."

"The Countess was very gracious," Hadley said. "Very welcoming and very gracious."

"She asked about you, Al," Rod said. "She remembered meeting you and dad at the Palazzo Vecchio. Of course, she was just a girl then, but she remembers you being very beautiful."

"Oh dear," Alice said. "Well, I hope you didn't show her any recent photographs then."

"Now, Al," Hadley said.

"Here are some photos of the villa," Rod said. "And here's our cousin, Rudolpho. You remember him, don't you? Cousin Rudolpho?" He used the same bullying tone with Alice that Sawyer did, only with him there was a slight edge of exasperation in his voice. He spoke in the same way to his wife, and it occurred to Stella, listening, that despite his charming demeanor, Rod was one of those men who found women stupid and vaguely annoying. He was the oldest son and yet he spent a great deal of his time traveling, leaving Sawyer to buy Alice's groceries, fill her pillbox, and write her checks. He lived only a few miles from his mother, and yet in the nearly three months that Stella had been sitting with Alice, this was the first time Rod had visited during one of her shifts.

"Oh, we forgot the lamp," Hadley said, in her slow, sweet drawl. "It's in the car."

"Well, go out and get it," Rod said.

"Lamp? What lamp?" Alice said.

"We brought you one of Billy's Boy Scout lamps."

"Why do I need a Boy Scout lamp? I've got lamps."

Roddy said, "Not any that work when the lights go out! The Boy Scout lamp is kind of like a big flashlight."

"Well, I've got flashlights, too."

Roddy gave her a stubborn, aggrieved look. "Are you saying you don't want it?"

Alice laughed. "Well, no. I guess I'll take it if you brought it."

"It's going to get pretty dark in here tonight."

"Well, all right then."

Hadley brought the lamp into the kitchen and showed Stella how to use it.

As they were leaving, Roddy said, "Nice to meet you, Sara."

Around five o'clock, the sky began to darken. Stella's cell phone rang and when she answered it, it was Charlotte. "There's another storm coming in and I'm going to send Elaine up early to relieve you. You need to get home before the next one hits."

"All right," Stella said. She walked back to the bedroom to tell Alice.

She was sitting up in bed with the flashlight shining directly onto her puzzle book. With her head bowed in serious concentration and her wispy curls standing out around her pink scalp, she looked almost childlike.

"Alice, Elaine is coming early tonight. There's another storm coming."

Alice jumped, startled, and put her hand on her chest. "I didn't hear you come in."

"I'm sorry. I should have warned you. I should have flicked the lights or something. Oh wait, I can't do that."

"You should have warned me," Alice said.

The temperature in the house was dropping, although it still felt pleasant enough to Stella. "Are you cold?" she said to Alice.

"Yes. Do you know how to turn on the gas fireplace?"

"I don't know. I don't think so."

"Roddy left some instructions in a bag on the kitchen desk. Last time the power was out, he turned on the gas fireplace so we would have some heat."

"Okay," Stella said. "I'll see what I can do."

She went into the kitchen and rummaged around for awhile but could find nothing that had to do with the living room fireplace. She checked the big chalkboard that listed the caregivers' phone numbers and names. Roddy's cell phone was not listed, of course, but Hadley's was. Stella hesitated a moment and then picked up her cell and called.

She explained to Hadley why she was calling.

"Oh, just a minute," Hadley said sweetly. "I'll get him." Stella could hear her telling Roddy why she had called. She could hear him in the background shouting, "Is there some reason why she can't read simple instructions?" There was a fumbling of the phone, a quick shushing sound from Hadley, and then Roddy came on.

"Hi, Mary Anna, how are *you*," he said with false cheerfulness.

"I'm fine, Rod. Thanks. Just wondering if you could tell me how to turn on the gas fireplace. Your mom is cold."

"Okay, let's start with the instructions, shall we?"

"Where are the instructions?"

"Oh. Well, they should be there by the fireplace."

"Okay. Alice seemed to think they were in the kitchen. That's where I've been looking."

Stella went into the living room and quickly scanned the mantle but didn't see anything.

"On the bookcase," he said. "Look there."

She found them.

"Okay. Now read them aloud. Let's start with number one, shall we?" He spoke slowly and loudly as if he was trying to communicate with a mentally-challenged child. The same way he had spoken to Alice. *Douche bag*. Stella felt a quick stab of pity for Alice.

She read the instructions aloud, feeling her face burn with humiliation. Faintly, in the distance, Alice began ringing her bell. Stella read through step 2. Alice's bell ringing became more frantic.

"I have to go," Stella said. "Your mother is ringing for me."

"Oh for…." He was so clearly perturbed that Stella smiled.

"I'll call you back," she said, and hung up.

When she got to the bedroom, Alice looked up and said, "Call Roddy. He might know where the instructions are."

"I already did that, Alice. I was on the phone with him when you started ringing the bell."

"Oh, you were? You were on the phone with Roddy? Okay, then. I won't bother you."

Stella went back into the living room and read through the instructions, the manufacturer's not his. Then she leaned over and turned on the fireplace. The gas logs lit up cheerfully.

She picked up her cell and punched Hadley's number. "Hello," she said. "Hello, Rod?"

"Hello?" he said after a short pause.

"This is Stella."

"Who?"

"I got it turned on."

"You got what turned on?"

"The gas logs."

"You did! All by yourself? Well, good for you!"

She grinned and raised her middle finger. She thought, *That's right, fucker.*

She went back to Alice's room and told her she'd managed to find the instructions and turn on the gas.

"Without Roddy's help?"

"That's right."

Alice chuckled. "I'll bet he didn't like that."

"I don't think he did."

Stella pulled a blanket out of the closet and followed Alice into the living room where the gas logs were flickering cheerfully in the grate. She settled Alice into one of the wingback chairs beside the fire and wrapped her in a blanket. Then she sat down in the other wingback chair.

"I may sleep in my clothes tonight," Alice said. "To keep warm."

"Good idea," Stella said.

They both sat quietly, staring at the flickering flames.

"Roddy has a bicycle," Alice said finally. "He rides all over the mountain. Once a year he goes up to New York with one of his sons and rides in that big race they have up there."

"Wow," Stella said. "That's impressive." She could imagine Roddy as a bicyclist. He had the lean, delicate build of a long-distance runner and she could picture him riding through the streets of New York in an aerodynamic skinsuit with a matching helmet.

"He's a character," Alice said, shaking her head. She had the blanket pulled up to her chin so that only her face was visible. "He comes sometimes and takes me to lunch at the

Sonic. And before we go he always says *Al, do you have your credit card?*" She chuckled, staring at the flames. "Last Christmas he took me out to dinner at the Mountain Grille. The whole family was there, a long table of Whittingtons. And when the bill came he leaned over and said, *Al, do you have your credit card? And I said, Oh, am I giving this dinner?*"

Alice chuckled again but Stella couldn't think of anything to say to this, so she kept quiet. It seemed wrong to her that a man with his own money would expect his mother to pay for everything but maybe that was just the way these trust fund families operated. Alice certainly didn't seem bothered by it; she seemed to find it amusing.

"This is what we used to do when I was a girl and the power went out," Alice said, staring at the flames. "When we lived up on Signal. We'd go next door to grandmother and grandfather's house and sit in front of a roaring fire and roast popcorn. Grandfather would tell his tall tales and we'd all listen, pretending to believe everything that he said."

"Why did you move to Lookout Mountain? Why didn't you stay on Signal? It's pretty nice up there." Stella had always heard that Lookout Mountain was a snooty place, closed and unwelcoming to strangers.

"I moved to Lookout because Bill Whittington was from here! There were lots of Whittingtons on Lookout. Oh, I felt like an interloper at first. But my grandmother had been a Jordan; she was from Lookout, so that made it easier. And over time I got used to it."

"Did you live with your husband's family?"

Alice looked at her in horror. "Oh no," she said. "That would never have worked. Bill was an only son. He had two sisters but he was the only boy. He was his mother's special child. Mrs. Whittington wouldn't have liked having me in her house."

Stella had seen a photograph of Mrs. Whittington. Dour and horse-faced like her son, they looked so much alike Stella had known instantly who the old woman was. In the photograph she was wearing a pearl choker and a padded suit and her white hair was swept back from her face in a severe style. A terrifying woman. Although, Alice, no doubt had given as good as she got. Stella smiled, thinking of this.

"We lived in an apartment on the side of the mountain when we were first married," Alice said. "It was a big old house divided up into four apartments and there were three other young couples, all friends of Bill's living there. So we had a gay old time."

Stella stared at one of the photographs of Bill Whittington on the bookcase, trying to imagine him as a young man intent on having a good time, trying to imagine Alice as a blushing bride. It would help if there were photographs of Alice as a young woman in the room, but there were none. Stella had checked. The few photos of her were of an indulgent grandmother, gazing down at a crowd of blond-haired grandchildren. Most of the silver-framed photographs were of a dapper Bill Whittington posed in front of a train, standing beside an ivy-covered wall, carving a Thanksgiving turkey on a silver tray. In all the photographs, he was dressed in a suit and tie.

Alice laughed suddenly and said, "My grandfather. Now he was a character! When I was a girl, he took Dob and me with him on a business trip to Chicago." She was already off on another tangent, which happened frequently; her memories seemed to come in strands that rolled in and out of her consciousness like balls of yarn. Follow this strand and it might lead here; but then another ball rolled into view and took her off on a completely different path. Sometimes she would be talking about one person and Stella would realize that she had already heard the story, and Alice had confused the characters. People melded in her mind, characters formed out of bits and pieces of other characters, stories became intertwined. And then, oddly, there were flashes of clarity, scenes remembered down to the most minute and telling detail.

"On the way up to Chicago, Grandfather told Dob not to drink any RC Cola, so the first thing Dob did was to buy two RC Cola's and then drink them in quick succession. He proceeded to throw up in the street and grandfather said, *You drank RC Cola didn't you?* And Dob said, *Yes, sir, I did.* And grandfather said, *Boy, you are as stubborn as a mule. You are just like your grandmother.*" Alice made a wry face, remembering.

"Well, that night grandfather took us to see a show. *Now children*, he said. *You must close your eyes when I tell you to and you mustn't peek.* He was going to see that famous lady who danced behind the fans and took her clothes off on stage."

Stella was quiet for a moment, considering this. "Gypsy Rose Lee?" she said, blinking. "He was taking you to see *Gypsy Rose Lee?*"

"That's the one," Alice said. "Well, anyway, the time came when he told us to close our eyes, and of course neither one of us did. We stared through our fingers and saw the whole show. And as we were leaving grandfather said, *Now, don't tell your grandmother.* Of course, the first thing Dob does when we get home is to tell grandmother."

Stella laughed. She put her head in her hands and wiped her eyes. "Oh my God, I can't believe your grandfather took you to see a stripper."

"She wasn't a stripper," Alice said staunchly. "She was a fan dancer."

"I can't believe you saw the real Gypsy Rose Lee in Chicago."

"Well, we did."

"What did your grandmother say?"

"She said, *Mr. Montclair have you lost your ever-loving mind?* They were very formal in those days. *Mr. Montclair this*, and *Mrs. Montclair that.*"

"I'll bet she made him suffer. I'll bet she fed him cold suppers for a week."

Alice looked at her blankly. "Grandmother had a cook," she said mildly. "She wouldn't have known the first thing about fixing supper. She didn't even like to set foot in the kitchen. I guess I get that from her."

"Still she must have found some way to punish him."

"Things were different in those days. Wives were obedient to their husband's wishes."

They were both quiet, staring into the fire, each lost in her own thoughts. After awhile Alice stirred and said, "Mother couldn't cook either. I remember when I was a girl she took cooking classes down in Riverview with a group of other women. Thursday night was the cook's night off, so one Thursday night mother comes in and says, *Children, you're in for a special treat. I'm going to cook dinner for you tonight.* She was so excited that even my father kept quiet, although we were all nervous sitting at the dining room table and listening to my mother bang around in the kitchen. So finally she calls to me and I go in to help her. *Get that big can of pears down for me,* she says, pointing to the top shelf of the pantry. I get it down and open it for her and she points to five plates that she's got lined up on the counter with lettuce leaves lying on them. *Take a half of a pear and put it on the lettuce with the scooped side up,* she tells me. So I do what she says and when I'm finished she takes a jar of mayonnaise out of the icebox and puts a spoonful on each of the pears. Then she sprinkles them with nutmeg and holds them up and says, *There! Supper*!

I helped her carry the plates out and set them on the table and no one said anything, we just ate those pears and went to bed hungry that night."

Stella grinned. "Well, that was the right thing to do, I guess."

"Of course it was."

"You've had a very interesting life, Alice."

"Well, I don't know about that."

"There's not many people alive today who can say they once saw Gypsy Rose Lee perform."

Alice looked at her. "Who?" she said.

The girl was talking again but Alice had no idea what she was saying. Her face was turned toward the fire so Alice couldn't read her lips. Her black hair, obviously dyed, had begun to grow out and the roots were showing a pale blonde so that, from a distance, she looked like she had a bald patch on top. With her head tilted toward the fire, her scalp looked pale and fragile, like the crown of an egg.

She worried about the girl, worried that she was too thin, that she seemed bowed down by some secret tragedy. Alice knew all about secret tragedies, how they could crush you over the years. What was it the girl had said? She was an *orphan*. Hard enough to get through this life as it was; Alice could not imagine doing it without family. She could not have borne what she had to bear without Adeline. As contentious and prickly as Adeline had been as a girl, there had been two of them and they had closed ranks and presented a united front when it came time to face what they'd had to face. Mother and father and grandmother and grandfather, too.

She was getting close to something here. Some memory she'd long ago put away. Alice could feel it slithering around in her bowels.

The girl looked up at her, still talking, and smiled, and Alice smiled back. The cat had been at work again along her arms; Alice could see fresh wounds along the tender skin above the girl's wrists. Why didn't she get rid of the contentious animal? Why keep something that was so intent on causing pain?

With any luck the girl would make a family of her own. A clan, a bulwark against the tragedies of life. That was what she had done; putting the past behind her, accepting what had to be accepted and immersing herself in all the mundane details of family life until everything else got crowded out. Finding a purpose where before there had been only chaos and pain.

Alice said abruptly, "Don't settle for a life you don't want."

The girl stopped talking. She gazed at her in confusion. "What?" she said.

Alice looked down, embarrassed that she'd spoken aloud. But then she thought better of it and she raised her chin and said fiercely, "Women don't have to settle these days."

The girl turned her face to the fire, thinking about this. "Did you settle?" she said.

Alice stared at the flames and said nothing. It was easier sometimes just to pretend she hadn't heard.

Outside the French doors the sky was darkening ominously. Huge trees swayed in the wind.

"There's another storm coming in," the girl said.

"I'm not worried."

"Storms don't frighten you?"

"No. You get to be ninety-four and death loses its sting."

That wasn't true, exactly. You never got over your fear of death; you just became more accepting of its inevitability. Religion helped some. As a child, Alice had felt herself protected from death and all its tragedy. She had thought of God as a grandfatherly figure, cheerful and benign, but as she grew older she had imagined him stern and judgmental, prone to pick favorites. After Sam's death she saw him as cold and distant, more enthralled with creating the world than with actually governing it. Lately she was coming around again to the idea of a kindly, St. Nicklaus-type figure, a benevolent God who looked down on the world and all its follies with humor and patient sadness.

"We have so many tornadoes in Alabama." Stella put her head back against the chair, drawing her feet up under her. "I used to dread them as a child. I used to have this recurring nightmare where I was crouching in a ditch in a field and far off in the distance, I could see a tornado coming. It was a big black shape coming steadily toward me. I was filled with this intense fear, and yet paralyzed too, knowing there was no place I could run, no place I could hide to be safe."

"You never know when tragedy will turn to good fortune," Alice said unexpectedly. Sometimes what came out of her mouth surprised her.

The girl stared at Alice, a slight smile on her lips. "No, I suppose not."

"After all, infirmity brought you into my life."

The girl's face crumpled suddenly like a box left out in the rain, and she dropped her eyes and turned toward the fire. Despite her reaction, Alice could see that she was pleased.

Elaine arrived a short time later and the feeling of warm companionship in the room instantly evaporated.

"There are trees down everywhere," Elaine said, sliding out of her rain coat. "And even reports of a few fatalities." Her eyes were bright, her face flushed. Elaine was thirty-seven years old and she lived with her Evangelical Christian parents in a trailer on the back side of Signal Mountain. A tornado with fatalities was the most excitement she could hope for.

"There have been storms in the past and there'll be storms in the future," Alice said flatly. Her whole attitude had changed the minute Elaine walked into the room.

"Not like this one," Elaine said.

"Just like this one," Alice said stoutly.

Elaine shook her head. She paused, as if checking a mental list of recent catastrophes. "I don't remember one with fatalities."

"Oh? How about the storm of 1974? How about the flood of 1973?"

"We're talking about tornadoes, not floods."

"We were talking about storms."

"Well, I better get going," Stella said, rising. If this went on much longer, she'd wind up refereeing a catfight. And she had a pretty good idea who would win. She turned to face Elaine. "You say there are trees down. Can I get down the front of the mountain?"

"Yes, they've got the main roads open. But the side streets are covered in debris. You'll need to take a left out of the driveway, take a right, and then follow it down past the water tower to Bragg. Then take a right on Bragg to Scenic Highway."

"Okay, thanks."

"The expressways are clear. I don't know about the rest of town."

"All right." Stella turned to Alice. "I'll see you tomorrow."

Alice gave her a wry look. "Are you leaving me?"

"Sorry."

"Oh, all right then." Alice's blanket slid down, revealing her dress and sweater.

"We should go ahead and get you ready for bed," Elaine said. "And then I'll see what I can fix for dinner."

Alice jutted her lower lip and dipped her head like a child readying herself for a tantrum. Stella said quickly, "Alice was just saying that she thought she'd sleep in her clothes tonight so she can stay warm."

Elaine said doubtfully, "Well, we'll have to see about that."

"There's nothing to see about," Alice said stubbornly. "I'll decide what I'm going to wear."

"Those clothes are dirty."

"They're not dirty! I've only worn them twice."

"Exactly."

"I'll wear what I want."

"We'll see about that."

"Don't tell me what to do!" Alice said. "I've been dressing myself for ninety years. I've been dressing myself since before you were even born. If I want to wear my clothes to bed, then I'll wear my clothes to bed!"

They were still arguing when Stella left.

Coming down into the valley, Stella could see that half of Chattanooga was dark. She took the expressway as far as she could and then got off at Manufacturers Road, following Cherokee into the neighborhood in North Chattanooga where she lived. Trees were down everywhere; lying in yards, across automobiles or houses, their roots upended. Twisted sheet metal and debris clogged the glistening streets. It had begun to rain again, drumming against the roof of the car. Stella drove slowly, curiously elated by the devastation she saw around her. She turned left on Unadilla and saw that the lights in the houses on the left side of the street were off, but those on the right side were on.

Josh was watching a movie when she got home.

"The cable's off," he said morosely.

She walked past him and then stopped and turned around, dropping her backpack at her feet. "Do you realize that half the city's without power? My God, Josh, there was a tornado. People were killed." She didn't ask him why he hadn't bothered to call and check on her. To see if she was all right. They were beyond that.

He let his eyes rest on her a beat and then went back to the movie. "What's for dinner?" he said.

She gave him a long, studied look. She slung her backpack over one shoulder and then turned and walked toward the stairs.

"What's for dinner?" he called after her.

"Whatever you want to make," she said.

She let the water run and then lit a few scented candles and set them around the edge of the tub. Far off in the distance she could hear the whirring of chain saws and above that, the whistling of the rising wind. It was insanity, of course, to lie in a bathtub while a storm raged around her, but Stella was feeling reckless. Besides, she had read somewhere that a bathtub was one of the safest places to hide during a tornado.

She pulled Boswell out of her backpack and slid into the tub, letting the hot water rise around her shoulders. After a minute she laid the book down on the edge of the tub and dried her hands on a towel. Then she opened the book and carefully pulled out the letter. She felt guilty, holding it. She stared again at the spidery handwriting, the faded brown paper, delicate and crackled with age. *Mrs. William Whittington.* Stella felt ashamed. She felt as if, by reading the letter, she would be betraying a great trust. And yet she was curious, too. She stared at the postmark. *March 19, 1951.* Almost fifty-eight years ago. She opened the flap and with trembling fingers, pulled out the letter.

The handwriting was small and cramped, written at a slant and difficult to follow. Stella quickly scanned to the bottom of the second page to see who had written it. *Mother.*

March 19, 1951

My Dearest Al –

Well, I drove up Lookout today to check on the Whittington family. Found everyone fine. Leta had mopped the kitchen floor and was ironing. Sawyer and Sam had just walked home from school. Rod joined us a short time later, getting off the bus. Sawyer had drawn a picture of you and Bill in New York and it was so sweet. I offered to take them to the drugstore for a soda and they said "fine." Rod stayed home listening to some melodrama on the radio. We had sodas and then I bought some fudge to bring home for later. Sam bought a book that he put his name in to send to the Baptist Boy's Home.

I don't know if you heard but Agnes Kemp had a heart attack. It was at the dinner table on Sunday. Dr. Kemp gave her a hypodermic and then took her on to the hospital and they say she'll survive but she'll have a long recovery. She won't be sailing to Europe. They've had to postpone their trip.

The papers are full of the terrible train accident up in New York. Sawyer says he's glad you and Bill flew to New York and didn't take the train. Life can be tragic sometimes. I guess we all know that.

I'm glad you went with Bill on his business trip to New York. Sometimes I think you push yourself too hard, Al. I hope you won't mind me saying this but I worry about you. You mustn't blame yourself. I feel sometimes that she's close. I had a dream last night that I could hear her walking in the hallway outside my door, her little feet pattering, and it made me so happy. It was a happy dream in spite of everything that's happened.

My love to you both.

Mother

Nine

§§§

After that night on the river, Alice didn't see Brendan Burke again for two months.

She had already put off two dates with Bill Whittington but she couldn't put off a third. She'd allowed him to bring her home that night from the dive on the river so she owed him at least one date. He took her to dinner and a movie, *The Gay Divorcee*. As far as Alice was concerned, that was it. She spent two weeks visiting a friend in Birmingham and when she returned to Ash Hill, she was angry to discover that her mother had accepted a date for her with Bill Whittington to go dancing at the Country Club.

"You shouldn't have done that," Alice said.

"He called when you were away. I thought you'd be fine with it," her mother said, avoiding her eyes. "You'd already accepted one date with him."

There was nothing she could do but go. The thought of coming up with an excuse and calling him back was worse than just going. She was quiet on the way to the dance, politely answering his questions about Birmingham, but not giving him much more encouragement than that. It was best that she let him know tonight that she had no intention of accepting anymore dates with him. Most girls would have jumped at the chance to date a wealthy bachelor from a good family, but Alice saw no reason to string him along. The life he offered was a life she could never possibly accept, and it was best that she make that clear to him so that he could go back to dating girls like Isabelle Aubrey.

It was a warm spring evening; the dogwoods were in bloom as they wound their way down the road from Ash Hill to the Country Club on the river. A long line of cars waited in the circular drive and as they reached the front entrance, Bill got out and handed his keys to the valet, going around to open Alice's door. She took his arm and they walked up the carpeted steps.

The room was crowded with dancers. A dais had been set up at one end of the large ballroom and a band played *Delta Serenade*. The long windows overlooking the river had been thrown open to catch the evening breeze. Squeezed along the edge of the dance floor were a jumble of round tables covered in white tablecloths where spectators sat sipping their cocktails and watching the dancers. Bill and Alice made their way slowly through the crowd, stopping to speak to those they knew, to a large table of Bill's friends and their dates. They were all drinking Old Fashions and Bill, without asking her, ordered two from the waiter.

The band was playing *Moon Glow* and they got up and danced. They danced to *April in Paris* and *I Only Have Eyes for You* and then the waiter brought their drinks and they sat down again. The conversation at the table was much like the last dance they'd attended; golf, stock market forecasts, who had better legs, Betty Grable or Ginger Rogers. They were like a group of fraternity boys trying to outdo each other and Alice had a feeling their conversations would always be like this, boring, one-dimensional, self-indulgent, even into advancing age and infirmity. They would always call each other nicknames like *Wedgehead*, *Wimpy*, and *Cheese*. They would laugh at the same jokes, keep the same safe friendships, marry the same type of women and breed the same kind of children. The monotony of their comfortable lives filled Alice with a dull creeping dread.

She thought of New York, the bright lights of Broadway, the noise, the dirt, the crowded anonymity of the streets. She imagined a Brownstone walk-up with a geranium pot on the windowsill, a clean, tidy space filled with her things. An orderly existence, a quiet, contemplative life.

"May I have this dance?"

Brendan Burke leaned over with his hand on the back of her chair, his fingers just inches from her bare shoulder. She looked up at him.

"Yes," she said.

"Now just a minute," Bill said.

"You don't mind, Old Sport, do you?" But he had his hand on her elbow and he was already leading her away before Bill Whittington could say anything else.

They walked out onto the dance floor. The band struck up a lively rendition of *Let's Fall in Love* and Brendan pulled her into his arms.

"Good evening, Miss Montclair."

"Good evening, Mr. Burke."

He was dressed in a well-tailored evening suit that had obviously been made for him. An expensive suit. His dark hair, swept back from his forehead, glittered under the lights.

"I'm surprised to see you here."

"Oh?" He smiled pleasantly but his eyes stayed fixed, unwavering. "Are you surprised I was able to join?"

"Well, no." Beneath his steady gaze, she felt flustered. She was surprised he had been offered membership; that was exactly what she had been thinking. In the old days he would never have been accepted but the world was changing. The Depression had made paupers out of wealthy men and rich men out of clever ones.

"Perhaps you don't see me as country club material."

She met his eyes boldly. "It really doesn't matter how I see you."

"I had no choice."

"Oh?"

"I couldn't figure out any other way to see you."

He said it with such sincerity that she could do nothing but look away, blushing furiously. At the table behind his shoulder, she could see Bill Whittington watching them closely. The song ended and they stepped apart, clapping politely. Bill rose and began to make his way through the crowd.

Brendan leaned close and said to her, "I want you to go out with me."

"I can't," she said.

"Why?"

"Oh, Mr. Burke, there are so many reasons."

"Name one."

Someone had stopped Bill Whittington at the edge of the dance floor. He stood chatting in a friendly manner, glancing at them from time to time.

"My sister, for one," she said.

"I don't date your sister."

"Yes, but I don't think she would be happy about me seeing you."

"She's young. She'll get over it."

"So you say."

"I warn you. I'm persistent."

"Yes. I can see that." Bill Whittington had disengaged himself and was doggedly making his way through the crowd toward them. Behind her the band was warming up for another number.

"Here comes my date," she said.

He didn't look around. "Say yes or there'll be a scene."

Their eyes met, held.

In a low, fierce voice she said, "Are you blackmailing me, Mr. Burke?"

"Call me Brendan."

"Are you blackmailing me, Brendan?"

"Yes."

The couple next to them was listening to their conversation. Alice was suddenly aware of this, and of the approach of her date, who had a sullen, determined expression on his face.

"All right," she said. "I'll meet you."

"Tomorrow night."

"Don't be ridiculous."

"Tomorrow night at the Blue Bird Café."

"I don't know where that is."

"Corner of 8th and Main. 7:00."

Bill Whittington had his hand out, reaching to tap his shoulder.

"All right," she said.

Brendan swung around. "There you are," he said pleasantly to Bill and stepped back, relinquishing his claim to Alice. He nodded slightly in both their directions and, without another word, swung around and walked off into the crowd, his dark hair glistening like a crow's wing.

That night she couldn't sleep, thinking about him. It was foolish, she knew, agreeing to meet him. It would end badly. Yet she couldn't stop thinking about his face as he bent above her on the dance floor, his expression calm, reticent, and yet certain, too. It was that certainty that bothered her, as if he had known all along that she wouldn't deny him.

And then there was the problem of Laura. Her sister had ceased her midnight ramblings and now lay entombed behind her bedroom door, her face turned toward the wall. Alice had gone to school and collected her books and assignments, but Laura would not look at them, and finally, in desperation, Alice had finished the assignments herself. Laura would not walk across the stage with the rest of her class but at least she would graduate. Mother sent a note explaining her absence at the coming graduation ceremony due to illness.

If anyone saw Alice with Brendan Burke and reported it to Mother or Father, she would tell them that she was intervening in her sister's unfortunate love affair. They would believe that readily enough; they would even be grateful for it. The more she thought about it, the more Alice convinced herself that this was the actual reason she was meeting Burke. To put a definitive end to his connection with her family. She would tell him the same thing she had told Bill Whittington when he brought her home from the Country Club dance. She was leaving for New York in the fall. Clarice was graduating from Sweet Briar and going up over the summer to find them an apartment.

Bill had stared at her, his eyes unreadable behind the glint of his glasses.

"Do your parents know about this?" he said finally.

"Of course," she lied.

"And what will you do in New York?"

"Live."

It sounded trite, childish. She avoided his eyes, turning to go in.

"Will I see you again over the summer? Before you leave to begin your new life in New York?" There was a hint of something in his voice, not sarcasm exactly, but derision, disbelief.

"We're bound to run into one another," she said mildly. "After all, it's a small town."

"That isn't what I meant and you know it."

"No," she said. "I don't see the point."

"Goodnight then."

"Goodnight."

She felt a sense of relief, watching him drive off and yet a faint sense of unease, too. Now that she had spoken the words aloud, New York was no longer a dream; it was a reality. There was no turning back now.

She wondered if Brendan Burke would be so easily discouraged.

He was waiting for her outside The Blue Bird Café. As she emerged from the alley behind the building where she had parked, he saw her and took off his hat, walking slowly toward her. It was a beautiful evening, warm and balmy. Above the roof of the Chattanooga Hotel the sky was a pale blue, tinged with pink clouds.

"Good evening, Miss Montclair."

"Good evening, Mr. Burke."

His manner was jovial, slightly teasing. He did not take her arm but walked beside her, matching his stride to hers. The café was crowded but she didn't see anyone she knew, and she saw now why he had picked the place. They chose a small table in the corner near a window. The waitress came and brought them menus, smiling at Brendan, and Alice took her gloves off and laid them across the table.

"She seems to know you well," she said, looking at the menu.

"I eat here a lot. My shop is just around the corner."

She looked at him. "I thought your shop was in Brainerd."

"I have one there, too."

"So you have two service stations?"

"Three, actually."

She looked down again at the menu, reading carefully. "Is there money to be made servicing automobiles?" she said rather casually, and then instantly regretted it. He would see her as one of those women who cared only for money. He probably already saw her that way.

"Automobiles will change everything about this country. Look at all the state highways being built. And there's even talk of a national interstate system crossing the country at sometime in the future. People will move freely from place to place, they'll no longer be tied to the small patch of land where they were born. Goods will be shipped from one end of the country to the other."

"But isn't that why we have trains?"

"Trains were the past. The automobile is the future. There'll come a time when every family will own one."

She glanced up at him, her light-colored eyes resting for a moment on his face. "You have a rosy view of the future considering we're still recovering from one of the worst Depressions in history."

He stared at her, his face darkly handsome, his expression bold but wary. "I'm an optimist," he said.

She felt the comment was directed at her and, despite her reservations, she smiled.

"You have a lovely smile," he said.

She read the menu and said nothing.

He leaned toward her, lowering his voice. "You really are quite pretty. But I suppose you hear that all the time."

"I think I'll have the catfish," Alice said.

"I'll bet you hear it all the time from pompous fools like Bill Whittington."

She closed the menu and laid it on the table, sitting back in her chair with her hands crossed in her lap. "You don't know Bill," she said. "You shouldn't pass judgment on people you don't know."

"I know he and his friends tried to have me blackballed from the Country Club. Luckily I know several of the membership committee and I was able to call in a few favors."

"Why would you do that?" she said sharply. She meant, *Why would you want to belong to a club where people will constantly slight you?*

"You know why," he said, his expression bold, unwavering.

She ordered the catfish. The waitress brought them tall glasses of iced tea and a basket of golden brown hushpuppies, just out of the fryer. He told her about his childhood in Kansas, the long flat prairie, the grasshoppers that dropped out of the sky like a biblical plague, eating everything in sight. She listened, smiling slightly, imagining the dug out homes with their earthen walls and ceilings, imagining him as a boy, curious and self-possessed. He had a way of telling a story that made you feel as if you were there.

When he had finished, he shook his head and said carelessly, "Enough about my dreary childhood. Tell me about you."

"Compared to yours, it was very – tame."

He laughed. "You don't strike me as the kind of woman who had a tame childhood."

"I'm not sure that's a compliment."

"Trust me, it is. I like spirited women."

She ignored the overt familiarity of this remark and told him about Charlie Gaskins, how he'd thrown rocks at her and how her mother wouldn't let her retaliate because he had a stutter.

"You must have been itching to toss a few rocks."

She grinned. "Yes, I suppose I was."

"I can't imagine you as the kind of person who lets others take advantage of you."

She said nothing, turning her face to the window. Dusk was falling and the lights of the city had begun to glimmer. The waitress brought their meals.

"What about now?" he asked her.

"Now?" She chewed slowly, looking at him.

"What's in your future? Marriage, motherhood, a life of comfort and ease?"

She looked down at her plate, carefully removing the bones from her fish. "Isn't that what most women want?"

"Yes, I suppose it is."

Now was the time to tell him about New York and yet his expression, intense, expectant, kept her silent. She was afraid she'd sound like a boastful child. What did she know, really, about New York? How would she make a living? Her father would be happy enough to pay for a summer vacation with the understanding that she would return in the fall; he'd be far less likely to support her if she chose to stay in the city. She had always been comfortably well off, had never worried where her next meal was coming from. All her life she had taken money for granted; but she could imagine that living without it would be a very difficult thing indeed. She would somehow have to make her own way. The usual understanding was that educated women who wanted careers had three to pick from – teacher, nurse, or secretary. Alice wanted none of those. She wanted something challenging, glamorous, slightly dangerous. Everyone said there would be another war and, if so, men would be called up to fight and jobs would be opened up to women. She had only to wait until the right one presented itself.

In the meantime, perhaps she and Clarice could waitress for awhile. Or get a job as hat-check girls in some nightclub frequented by artists and musicians and gangsters. Or better yet, land a job as a magazine or newspaper writer. They hired women writers nowadays. Look at Martha Gellhorn. Alice had always been a reader, a storyteller, and there was no reason why she shouldn't get paid for it. She imagined herself at a typewriter, a cigarette dangling from her lips. She would walk to the park, the library, have dinner in small cafes with other women like her (surely in New York there would be other women like her, women who liked a good argument and read Mary Wollstonecraft and Charlotte Perkins Gilman.)

They finished eating and he lit two cigarettes and gave one to her. She felt awkward, mildly disreputable smoking in public. It was a giddy feeling.

"There's a jazz club I want to take you to," he said, exhaling.

"I can't." She glanced around the cafe again, making sure she didn't see anyone she knew.

"It's Saturday night. Live a little."

"I have to help mother with the flowers for church." It was a lie; she avoided his eyes, resting her elbows on the table and leaning forward slightly.

"Is that the best you can do?" he said.

He raised his hand and motioned for the waitress.

She colored lightly at his implication but shook her head stubbornly. "I can't."

His expression changed, becoming detached, coldly polite. "You won't see anyone you know. I can promise you that."

"I don't care about that."

"Don't you?" He looked up at the waitress, smiling in a subtly contemptuous way. "You can bring the check," he said.

He was quiet on the ride out to the jazz club and Alice was amazed to find herself sitting beside him, the darkened countryside rolling away on either side of the car. The mountains were black against the moonless sky. Here and there the lights of a lone house twinkled along the ridge.

Crazy to have left her car in the alley and ridden with him. Crazy to have come at all.

And yet, after his comment in the café, how could she not? There had been a challenge in his invitation, a subtle avowal that he might have been wrong about her after all. The truth was, she didn't want to be seen with him, and yet to acknowledge that would make her seem cowardly and pretentious. Laura had more courage than she did.

"Do you like jazz?"

Startled out of her thoughts, she turned her face from the window.

"I suppose I do," she said.

"Have you ever been to the River Rat Club?"

"No."

They were speeding along the road toward Nashville. Through the trees, the black river glinted. "It was supposedly built as a hideaway by Al Capone for his Tennessee mistress. They say there are tunnels that run from the cellar to the river where the bootleggers used to bring the liquor in."

"I've never heard of it."

He laughed, his face gleaming in the dashboard lights. "Stick with me, kid. You'll learn all kinds of things."

They got off the blacktop and followed a sandy road for about a quarter of a mile before turning into a narrow lane. A metal cattle gate with a chain and a padlock stood open as they passed slowly down the sandy track, thick underbrush crowding in on either side of the car. They drove for nearly a quarter of a mile before Alice began to see light through the trees. The road widened and the trees on either side gave way, and they were suddenly in an open field, crowded with automobiles. An ordinary-looking house with all its windows lit up sat on a bluff overlooking the river. Alice could hear the distant wail of a clarinet.

They parked the car and got out and walked up the sandy drive to the house.

He pushed his way in ahead of her, taking her hand. The music was an assault to the ears, the smoke, the closely packed bodies reeking of whiskey and tobacco and sweat was almost too much for her. She had to breathe through her mouth, looking down at her feet as he pulled her along. There were no tables but he managed to find them a couple of spaces at the bar, and he made room for her beside him and ordered two Highballs.

He leaned over and said into her ear, "See anyone you know?"

She shook her head, looking around the smoky club.

"Not your usual crowd."

"No," she said, hoping her relief wasn't too apparent.

The band was playing *I'll Get By* and the dance floor was packed. Beside them at the bar, a couple of young women wearing too much rouge laughed loudly. Their dates eyed Alice boldly.

"Do you come here often?" She had to lean in to talk to him, so close she could smell the faint scent of his cologne.

"I come for the music," he said. He leaned his elbows on the bar behind him, regarding her with a grave expression. Beneath his steady appraisal, Alice found herself wondering if her lipstick was applied correctly, if her hair had lost its carefully-constructed wave and gone wild and curly in the heat.

"The Jazz Age is dead Up East," he said, "but down here everyone's still dancing the shimmy."

"So you're saying we're provincial hicks."

"Compared to New York, yes."

She eyed him above the rim of her drink. "Spend a lot of time in New York, do you?"

He frowned, looking down into his glass. The part in his carefully combed dark hair was as white and straight as if drawn with a ruler. He was wearing a navy blazer and a pair of wide-bottomed trousers, and Alice was struck again by the quality of the cloth and the fit of his clothes. So different from the first night she'd met him, in his greasy jumpsuit with his hair combed carelessly and breaking over his forehead.

"I go up a couple of times a year on business." He swirled his drink, and looked at her. "Have you ever been?"

"Many times. A number of the girls I go to Sweet Briar with are from the city. We'd ride the train up on the weekends to go to house parties."

He looked at the dance floor, watching the sweating couples who were dancing with vigorous abandon. "Sweet Briar," he said distantly. "Where's that?"

"Virginia." She hesitated a moment and then added, "Didn't my sister tell you where I was in school."

He stared at the crowd. The music crescendoed and then stopped. The musicians shuffled around on the stage and set their instruments down to take a break. "Your sister rarely mentions you at all," he said, grimacing, and tossed back his drink.

Ridiculous that his comment should bother her, but it did. She had been the one to bring Laura up, not him. But mentioning her seemed to set up a chill between them, an uneasy distance, so that they both stared at the dance floor for some time without speaking.

It was easy to tell herself that she was here to rescue her sister, to see to it that she didn't risk her reputation on a man like Brendan Burke. And even her promise to see him tonight, extracted from her on the Country Club dance floor, had been more about preventing a scene with Bill Whittington than anything else. Or so she had told herself earlier, as she carefully dressed to meet Brendan. But why then, had she agreed to come with him to the jazz club? Why had she been so hesitant to let the evening end? What excuse could she possibly find for that?

She found him attractive; there was no denying it. He was different from the men she usually dated. They were polished and self-assured but he had his rough edges, a feeling of containment that seemed at times, forced. She felt that by hiding parts of himself away, by keeping secrets, he made himself more interesting. She imagined him a man capable of great passion. She had seen it in his face earlier when he spoke of jazz, when he listened to the five-man negro band build to the pumping crescendo of *I'll Get By*, the *ride-out* he called it, his lips parted, eyes narrowed with pleasure. His hands, with their long blunt fingers, rapped the bar in time to the music. It was easy to imagine those hands, strong, capable, cupping a breast or stroking a thigh.

"A penny for your thoughts," he said and she looked up to see him regarding her with a look of curious amusement.

Her face flushed with a sudden heat and she turned her shoulders, leaning back against the bar.

"Are you all right?" he said.

"It's rather warm in here."

"Let's finish our drinks and then we'll leave."

The band climbed back onto the stage, swinging into a spirited rendition of *Nagasaki*, and the crowd reacted enthusiastically. A young man in a Glen plaid suit came up and tapped Alice on the shoulder.

"Would you like to dance?" he said.

"No, she wouldn't," Brendan said. He took her hand and led her toward the dance floor.

"That was rude," Alice said.

"Was it?"

"You know it was."

"I'm not as generous as Bill Whittington," he said, pulling her smoothly into his arms.

It was after midnight when they finally left. Walking out into the cool night air was like diving into icy water. Alice stopped for a moment, breathing deeply, filling her lungs hungrily. He still held her hand. She didn't pull away.

They walked quietly down the sandy lane toward the field where they'd parked the car. The field was less crowded now; only a few dozen cars remained. The grass glistened wetly in the slanting light from the club windows. He leaned and opened her door and then held it, slightly askew, so she couldn't step inside.

"I want to see you again," he said. His face in the dim light was pale but determined.

"I don't think that's a good idea."

"Are you engaged to Whittington?"

"No."

"Then I want to see you again."

"Look," she began reasonably but, without asking, he leaned over and kissed her. The move was so unexpected, so smooth and practiced, the weight of his mouth so pleasurable, that she gave herself up to him almost immediately, leaning with her back against the warm car while he kissed her hungrily.

The music began again, faintly, the beginning strains of *Summertime* rising along the ridge tops into the starry sky. Far off across the river, the distant sound of a passing train echoed, low and mournful.

Laura was sitting up in bed reading *Anna Karenina* when she came in. She called softly to Alice as she walked by.

"Have you been out with Bill Whittington?" Her face in the lamp light was thin and hauntingly beautiful.

"No," Alice said. "With some friends."

"Ah." She smiled faintly and looked down at her book, a delicate color rising in her face. "Mother said you had broken it off with Bill."

"Mother seems to keep her ear to the ground when it comes to my affairs."

"You know how she is."

"Yes."

"Well, goodnight then."

"Goodnight, Laura."

Ten

§§§

Alice's power was back on when Stella arrived on the following Wednesday and the orange cones across the end of her driveway were gone. Elaine was busy writing in the binder when she walked into the kitchen.

"When did the power come back on?" Stella asked, setting her backpack down on the counter.

"Sunday night. The second storm that came in Thursday night was awful. It hit not long after you left. I made Alice get in the hallway and we huddled there until it passed."

"I'll bet she liked that."

Elaine gave her a faint, practiced smile. "How about you?" she said. "Did you lose power?"

"No, believe it or not, we were one of the few houses in the whole valley that didn't."

"Lucky you. It's still out on Signal."

"Sorry."

Elaine began to collect her knitting, stuffing it into a long embroidered bag. "Oh, one other thing. The cable's out. So Alice can't watch *Family Feud* or *Wheel of Fortune*. It's made for a couple of tense nights."

"Well, we don't watch a lot of TV anyway."

Elaine straightened, an expression of curious disbelief on her face. "Really? What do you do then?"

"Mainly Alice tells me stories and I listen."

Elaine stared at her as if she couldn't quite comprehend this. She gathered her embroidered bag and her laptop. "I'll see you tonight," she said.

Stella waited until she heard the front door slam and then she opened the binder and read what Elaine had written.

Restless last night. She dreamed about someone named Brendan. When I asked her this morning, she said she didn't know who I was talking about. She was breathless this morning when I woke her.

Stella walked down the long hallway to the bedroom to say good morning.

"Oh, hello," Alice said. "You're back."

"Did you think I wouldn't be?"

"Sometimes I wonder."

"So the power came back on Sunday night?"

"Yes. And not a minute too soon. She had me get in the hallway while she was on the phone to her mother, hysterical, that we were going to get killed by a tornado."

"Sorry, Alice. I probably should have stayed."

"I kept telling her, *If we get hit by a tornado, so what? If it's our time to go, it's our time to go.*"

"I'm sure that made her feel a whole lot better."

"Do you know what she said to me last time we were sitting in the dark? She said, *Alice, I'm going to sing you some hymns.*" Alice rolled her eyes and her expression was so droll that Stella laughed.

"And what did you say?"

"I said, *Oh, yes please.*"

"And how long did this go on?"

"Too long."

"Well, don't worry. I'm not going to sing you any hymns."

"Thank you," Alice said.

That morning as they walked through the living room, Stella looked down at the hazy valley and said, "Alice, can you see the Incline from here?"

"What?"

"The Incline."

"The what?"

"The Incline Railroad," Stella said loudly. "Can you see it from here?"

"You can't see the Incline from here. It's on the other side. Although the view on this side is better than on East Brow. Over there all you can see is the cemetery and the cement factory." She chuckled maliciously when she said this, sliding her walker out in front of her.

The Incline was the steepest passenger railway in the world. It ran up the side of Lookout Mountain and in places boasted a vertical incline of over seventy percent. Stella had ridden it once when she first moved to Chattanooga. It began in a little town at the foot of Lookout Mountain named St. Elmo, an old suburb of Victorian cottages fallen on lean times, and ended at the top of the mountain near Point Park, a world famous tourist attraction.

Later, as they where having lunch, Alice said, "You know, I went one day to pick up my son, Roddy, at the Incline and he wasn't there. My children all went down to Miss Fenimore's School and the teacher was supposed to put them on the Incline after school and I'd pick them up at the station. Anyway, one day Roddy wasn't on the train. His cousins,

Spears and Barrett, were there but Roddy wasn't. So I drove down to Miss Fenimore's School and I said, *Where's Roddy? You didn't put him on the Incline.* And the teacher, Ann Ricks, said *Oh, did I forget one of the Whittingtons? There's just too many of them to keep track of!* And she and the headmistress acted like it was just a big joke. So I lit into them. I mean, I really let them have it."

Stella laughed, imagining Alice in her prime doing battle with a couple of prim school teachers.

"Now see," Alice said in a querulous voice. "You're laughing just like they did. I didn't think it was funny."

"Sorry, Alice." Stella coughed and put her fist to her mouth. She looked down at her plate. After a moment of quiet chewing, she swallowed and said, "Was he okay?"

"Who?"

"Roddy."

"Oh, Roddy was fine. He was waiting for me up at the Incline station. When Ann Ricks drove off without him he just took the bus down to the station in St. Elmo and took the train up."

Alice finished her lunch and pushed the plate away. She wiped the front of her bib with a napkin. "Well, that was very nice," she said.

"I'm glad you liked it," Stella said.

"You're a very good putter-together person."

"Well, Sawyer keeps the refrigerator pretty well stocked so I don't have to think too much about it."

"He's a very good shopper. And griller. He loves to cook things on his shiny new grill."

"Lucky for his wife," Stella said. She was still thinking about Alice doing battle with the school teachers and trying to imagine her as a young mother. Had she been the nurturing type, the kind who played games with her children and helped them with their homework? She couldn't imagine Alice as a nurturer. There was something aloof and distant about Alice; and her sarcastic tongue would have been sharp in those days, too. She had seen the way Alice's friends treated her, how afraid they were to call and cancel luncheon appointments, how they seemed to cower in the face of her changing moods. There was no doubt in Stella's mind that in school Alice had been one of the Mean Girls. The girl, who, with her sullen, bored demeanor and wicked tongue, would have been the leader of all the others. She said, "Did you like to cook when your children were younger?"

Alice gave her a droll look. "I don't cook," she said. "I thaw."

Stella grinned. "I've never heard it put that way but I like it."

"The first time I saw frozen dinners in the supermarket I thought they were the most marvelous creation."

Still grinning, Stella rose to collect the plates. "Would you like some ice cream?"

"What have we got?"

"You name it, we've got it."

"Okay. Surprise me then."

Stella fixed a scoop of Banana Split and set it in front of Alice, and then sat back down. *No*, she decided, Alice would have been a detached mother. Perhaps not as detached as Stella's own mother had been once she married Moody Bates, but Alice would have allowed a series of nurses to raise her children. She would have been busy with board meetings and bridge groups and fund raisers, all the standard activities women in her socio-economic group were expected to participate in. Stella thought, guiltily, of the letter she'd read written by Alice's mother, the reference to the woman in the kitchen ironing – now what had her name been – *Leta*? Alice's children would have been raised by a series of Letas.

"Did you like having children, Alice?"

Alice turned her head and stared, her eyes fixed and colorless. Her skin, in the slanting light from the kitchen window, was crisscrossed with fine wrinkles like old parchment. "What do you mean, *did I like it?* It wasn't something I thought about. You just did it because it was expected of you in those days. You got married and you had children. There weren't a lot of choices back then."

"No, I suppose not."

Alice turned back to her ice cream. "Oh, that looks lovely," she said, dipping her spoon. "What is it?"

"Banana Split."

"Do you want some?"

"No thanks."

Alice took a spoonful and stared at the wall, her mouth moving soundlessly. "Do you have children?" she said finally.

"No, Alice."

"Oh, that's right." She jerked her head impatiently, as if she had just remembered their prior conversation. She pointed at the ice cream with her spoon. "What's that red stuff on the top?"

"Cherries? Don't banana splits have cherries on top?"

"I guess they do," Alice said. "Do you have a husband?"

"A boyfriend."

"Does he make you happy?"

"Well," Stella said.

"Don't answer that," Alice said. "It's none of my business."

Outside in the street a truck chugged by. Stella cast about for something to say to change the subject. "Sawyer is a very good shopper," she repeated lamely.

"He's a good kid, as Bill used to say." Alice stuck another spoonful of ice cream into her mouth and chewed slowly, staring at the wall with an expression of rapt attention. "He does a lot of good work for The Salvation Army. He took over his place on the board from me."

Stella had seen the various crystal bowls and plaques scattered throughout the house from both The Salvation Army and Big Brothers/Big Sisters, thanking Alice for her tireless efforts on their behalf.

Alice chuckled, her white curls trembling faintly. "At Christmas time, Sawyer likes to stand outside the Walmart at the foot of Signal Mountain ringing the bell."

"Really?" Stella said. It was comical, the idea of this trust fund scion haranguing the upper-middle class suburbanites for change. Stella decided once and for all that she liked Sawyer.

"That's really nice of him," she said.

"He learned it from me," Alice said. "When the children were little we used to stand outside Goldman's Department Store ringing the bell at Christmas time. Do you remember Goldman's? No? Well, it was the fanciest store in town and everybody shopped there. People will act funny when you're trying to get money out of them. We'd stand out there and I'd see someone I knew trying to duck into a side entrance and I'd send one of the children around to block their way. *'Hello, Mrs. Jones'* they'd say sweetly. *'And how are you today?'*"

Stella snorted. "Alice, you were awful!"

"Terrible," Alice said.

"I wouldn't want to owe you money."

"No, you would not."

"You're worse than Tony Soprano."

"Who?"

"Never mind. At least it was for a good cause."

"Amen to that," Alice said serenely.

Stella put Alice down for her nap and then she lay down, too. She fell instantly into a restless sleep, and dreamed about her mother. They were in a car going somewhere and Candy was driving; only as they drove down a country road shaded by tall trees, Stella became gradually aware that it wasn't her mother at all behind the wheel. It was someone else, a person in a hood whose face she couldn't see. The dream took on an ominous tone at this point and the landscape began to darken. Stella knew she should turn to look at the figure but she was too terrified to move, afraid that she might draw attention to herself. She made herself as small as she could in the corner but she heard a loud whooshing sound outside the window, and turning she saw a great owl flying beside the car, fixing her with its savage, golden eye.

She awoke with a start. She was in the sunroom, lying on the hard, dilapidated sofa. Alice's furniture looked as if it hadn't been replaced for forty years; the fabrics faded, seats hard and devoid of any springs or padding. Outside the long windows the sun shone brightly and a line of pale clouds drifted across the deep blue sky.

She lay for a long time watching a pair of starlings build a nest in the top of a tall white oak on Sawyer's front lawn. The birds flittered about, carrying twigs in their tiny beaks, and Stella watched, amazed at their tireless energy and sense of shared purpose. Who had taught them to work like that? Did they know chicks were coming, were they capable of looking into the future and assessing the needs of their brood, or were they operating solely on instinct?

A sudden childhood memory. She was in the driveway with her little brothers. Her step dad was cleaning out the garage and he had hauled an old chest freezer to the end of the short driveway to make room for an assortment of tools, bicycles, bins, and metal shelving. He had gone inside to get a cold beer and he'd told her to watch her little brothers, who were racing their skateboards through the scattered debris on the driveway like a couple of demolition derby drivers.

She said quietly, "Yes, sir," watching him disappear into the shadowy depths of the garage. When he first married her mother, Moody Bates had been a generous, tolerant stepfather. But as the boys were born, and especially since she'd reached puberty, his attitude toward her had changed. He was cold and distant now, and Stella had the feeling that no matter what she did to please him, it would never be enough.

She sat down on a metal stool, listlessly tapping the concrete drive with a yardstick. Far off in the distance, a dog barked incessantly. Stella slumped on the stool, watching the *tap-tap-tap* of the yardstick, listening to the roar and clatter of her brothers' skateboards.

Without warning, a pick-up truck pulled to the curb and screeched to a halt, and two guys in cowboy hats jumped out and began to maneuver the freezer toward the bed of the truck. Before she could say anything, the screened door swung open behind her and Moody rushed out shouting, "Hey, what the fuck do you think you're doing? Get away from there!"

The two men looked at him. He tossed his beer can like a grenade and it bounced against one of the men's chests and exploded on the ground at his feet. Moody rounded his shoulders and came on, and without a word, the two turned around, jumped back into their truck, and drove off.

He seemed heroic to her, standing there with his plaid shirt flapping against his thighs and his shoulders rounded for battle, shaking his fist at the retreating truck. Like something out of one of her history books. King Leonidas facing the Persians at Thermopylae. William Wallace exhorting the Scots at the Battle of Sterling Bridge. Wanting to express her appreciation for his courage, she said instead, quite unexpectedly, "I saw them coming. I knew they were going to steal something." The words just fell out of her mouth.

"Well, then why didn't you say something?" Moody said, rounding on her. "Why didn't you yell?"

She wasn't sure why she had lied. She hadn't seen them coming. She had wanted to impress him, she had wanted him to notice her, but instead she could see from his pained, disgusted expression that he was not impressed at all.

"If you saw them coming, you should have said something! Now get that shit picked up and start stacking those shelves in the garage in case they come back."

"Yes sir." His disdain was like cold water thrown in her face. She kept her expression blank; she wouldn't cry until later, when she was alone. He didn't like it when she cried. Her little brothers watched her gravely, and then they, too, began to carry items back into the garage.

Later that night after a few beers, Moody entertained Candy at the dinner table with his tale of saving the freezer. "Those old boys didn't know what hit them! I lobbed a beer can at one of the sumbitches and he just stood there, staring at me like he was looking at a crazy man, and then I rushed them.

They ran like pussies. Didn't they boys?" he said, grinning at Anthony and nudging George on the shoulder.

"Yes sir," George said. "Like pussies."

Candy giggled and looked at Moody in loving admiration. Stella pushed her black-eyed peas around on her plate with a fork, listening to them.

"We showed them a thing or two, didn't we boys?" Moody said, slapping his sons on their frail backs.

And George, who as the middle child was the peace maker, who always tried to put broken things back together again, whether they were crockery or electronic devices or family bonds, took Moody's hand and laid it down on top of Stella's.

"Stella was there, too," George said. "She helped run off those old boys, too."

Stella said nothing but smiled at George, not looking at anyone else, not even Moody. Least of all Moody.

As his hand touched hers, she had distinctly and unmistakably, felt him flinch.

After she and Alice finished their afternoon walk, Sawyer called to tell them the cable was back on. He had called the cable company's headquarters in Knoxville and complained to the CEO that everyone a street over had cable, and there was no reason why Brow Road should not have it, too. He had explained all this to Alice and Stella that morning when he came to fill Alice's pill box. Whatever he said had obviously worked, because when Stella looked out the kitchen window at lunch time, she saw a cable truck with a guy climbing a pole in front of Sawyer's house.

Alice's televisions were high-def with more electronic equipment attached than Stella could possibly understand and she was unable to get the game show channel back on. Alice called Sawyer and he agreed to come over and reset the channels.

He was in a good mood when he arrived.

"Thanks for calling the cable company CEO," Stella said. "I never would have thought of that."

"I may have been a bit rough on him. I sent him flowers this afternoon."

"I never would have thought of that either."

He sat down and began to fiddle with the television. They were sitting out in the sunroom, Alice and Stella in their worn club chairs and Sawyer in a straight backed wooden chair pushed close to the set.

Behind him Alice said, "See how handy he is? His father was never like that. He couldn't even change a light bulb."

"He could, too!" Sawyer said, swiveling his head and giving his mother a reproachful look.

Stella could imagine him as a boy, blonde and sweet-natured, always trying to shore up the family façade. To convince himself that everyone was loyal and light-hearted and loving. Just like George.

Alice laughed at his expression. "I don't even think Bill knew where the light bulbs were kept," she said.

"Yes he did! Stop it, Al." He picked up the remote and began to punch buttons, looking at the blank screen.

Alice giggled. "I don't know where he gets his height either," she said to Stella, talking about Sawyer as if he wasn't even there. She grinned at Stella and then swung her head back to her son. "How tall are you?"

"Seven foot six," Sawyer said.

Alice giggled.

The blank TV screen bloomed suddenly with images. Sawyer began to scroll through the channels.

"See if you can get *Family Feud*," Alice said. "I think it comes on now."

"Take it easy, Al. I've got to get it programmed first."

They were still arguing good-naturedly when Adeline swept in. She hadn't rung the bell or anything; she just walked in like she owned the place. Stella got up so Adeline could take her chair, and went into the kitchen. She stood at the kitchen window, looking out at the neatly landscaped lawn and listening to the three of them. Alice was in a fine mood, and they were all laughing and gossiping about a neighbor who was building a monstrous house at the other end of the brow.

"You know he petitioned the city council to put in his own private Incline up the mountain," Adeline said.

"Oh good Lord," Sawyer said. "Some people have more money than sense."

"The house looks like a country club," Adeline said. "It's obscene."

"I hope they turned him down on the private Incline," Alice said.

"That's exactly what they did," Adeline said. "After they finished laughing."

"What's his name?"

"Petrakis."

"What kind of name is that?"

"Greek. I think."

"He's from Birmingham."

"Well that figures," Alice said.

"Made his money in the pest control business."

"The what?"

"Pest control. You know. Bugs. Rodents. Things like that."

The theme song from *Family Feud* blared suddenly.

"Oh, goody," Alice said. "You fixed it."

Sawyer hit the mute button. "Well, I don't know about that but I got it programmed."

"You're a good kid, as your father always used to say."

"Stop it, Al."

After he left, Alice called to Stella to come in and sit with her and Adeline. Adeline wore a tailored skirt and a blouse that tied around the throat and a pair of high-heeled pumps. Her hair, unlike Alice's, which was curly, was straight and cut stylishly just below her jaw.

"Would you like something to drink?" Stella asked, standing in the doorway.

"A glass of water please," Adeline said.

"Alice?"

"I guess so. I might as well hydrate while I'm sitting here."

She and Stella grinned at each other.

Stella brought their glasses of water and then sat down in the chair vacated by Sawyer. She was nervous still, in front of Adeline, but not as nervous as she had once been.

Adeline sipped her water and then sighed, staring out the long windows overlooking Sawyer's beautiful lawn. Her expression was distant, pensive. She set her glass down on a small table near her chair.

"We've lost Brooks," she said in a deep, somber voice.

Alice stared at her a beat. "What do you mean, we've lost Brooks?"

"He's gone."

"Adeline, Brooks has been gone since 1979."

"I had him in that urn on the mantel and when the new cleaning girl left, the urn was gone. I could see little pieces of broken pottery near the wingback chair, you know the one Mother gave me, and there was ash on the bricks. I think she knocked Brooks over and was afraid to tell me."

"Who, Mother?"

"No, Alice, not Mother! The cleaning girl."

"Weren't you supposed to sprinkle his ashes over Augusta National thirty years ago?"

"Don't start with me, Alice," Adeline said, giving her a sullen look. "You know I never liked golf."

They were all quiet for a few minutes, sipping their water.

"Well," Alice said finally. "Well."

Stella stared at the bricked circular drive in front of Sawyer's house. His wife's Nissan was parked in front, with Sawyer's ten-year-old Lincoln parked behind it. It was one of the things about the old-moneyed rich that Stella found amusing, the fact that they drove ordinary cars. Not a Mercedes or Lexus in the bunch.

Adeline sighed again, putting one hand to her throat. "Poor Brooks," she said. "Swept out with the rubbish."

Alice snorted and looked at Stella. Stella put one hand to her mouth, stood up quickly, and walked out.

"What's wrong with her?" Adeline said.

"I wouldn't know," Alice said, pulling a Kleenex out of the box and covering her face.

Later that night, as Stella was getting Alice ready for bed, Alice looked up and said, "Did I ever tell you about the time Roddy was supposed to ride the Incline and the teacher forgot to put him on? I was waiting at the top and his cousins were there, but no Roddy. So I went down to the school and Ann Ricks, his teacher, said, *"Oh, did I forget Roddy? I'm sorry there are just too many little Whittingtons to keep up with."*

Stella, remembering their exchange that morning and not wanting to piss the old lady off again by laughing, widened her eyes and said, "Oh, Alice that's terrible."

"You're darn right it was terrible! I let both Ann Ricks and the headmistress have it. I mean, I really lit into them."

Stella rearranged the pillows behind Alice's head and then began to smooth baby oil on her legs. Her skin was blue and mottled and thin as wax paper. The baby oil wasn't even absorbed; it just sat on top of the skin, slick and shiny.

"And later when Dob said he was going to marry Ann Ricks, I said, *Oh, no you're not.* I still had not gotten over the Roddy incident."

Stella stopped rubbing. "Your cousin Dob?"

"He was married to Ann Ricks. She was his first wife. He married her when he got back from the War. Old lady Ricks, her mother, was the richest woman in St. Elmo. She owned real estate all over town and she'd go out every month and personally collect every rent dollar that was owed her. She was rich as Croesus but she still had the first penny she'd ever made. That woman did not believe in spending money.

Anyway, she wasn't happy about the marriage either. She had two other daughters who had married and she'd told Ann, *You can't marry. You have to take care of me in my old age.* She had Ann's whole life planned and it didn't include marriage to Dob Montclair. She wouldn't even speak to Ann after the wedding. She disinherited her, wouldn't give her a cent, and Ann and Dob could have used the money because Dob was a poor law school student and they had five children in quick succession."

Stella put the cap back on the baby oil. "She sounds like a character, that old lady Ricks."

"Oh, she was a character all right. She lived in a big house next to the Incline. A huge old house that hadn't been painted in fifty years. The city got tired of looking at that eyesore so they told her she was going to have to paint it. They wrangled back and forth for awhile but finally the city threatened to condemn the property. So she complied. She had the front painted. The other three sides she left as they were."

"I'll bet the city didn't let her get away with that."

"Oh, she got the last word."

"How's that?"

"She died before they could cite her."

Stella went into the bathroom to wash her hands. When she came out, Alice was staring at the TV screen with a faraway expression on her face. Stella pulled the covers up to her chest, plumped the pillows behind her head. "Did she ever forgive Ann for marrying Dob?"

"Old lady Ricks? Oh no," Alice said. "When she died she was worth millions but do you know how much she left each of Ann and Dob's children? Her own grandchildren? One dollar each."

"That's terrible."

"I thought so."

"How could you do that to your own daughter? Your own grandchildren?"

"Funny what some people will do for money," Alice said.

On the drive home, Stella thought about Ann Ricks. What was worse; to be raised in poverty knowing you had no choice, or to live in poverty knowing your mother could do something about it if she wanted to? She decided that poverty without choice was worse. There were no delusions there, no glimpses of a hopeful future.

Her cell phone beeped. She checked and it was a text from her carrier, saying that she was to call immediately on an important matter. Meaning that once again she was being threatened with disconnection if she didn't pay her bill.

"Get in line," she said to the phone and tossed it down on the passenger's seat. She had so many bills to pay now it was not even worth opening the stack on the coffee table. Mostly medical bills from when she'd had to go to the emergency room last fall for a broken ankle that still bothered her on cold, rainy days. It would be better if they did disconnect her cell because then she wouldn't be hounded by creditors calling at all times of the day or night.

And to make matters worse, Josh was loosing his patience with her. Last night he had pounded on the bathroom door and demanded that she pony up her share of the rent.

"What are you doing in there?" he said suspiciously. "You've been in there for hours."

She stood and quickly cleaned herself up. "I'm going to be a little late this month," she called to him, running the water in the sink to distract him. She put the razor away in its little case and tucked it behind the toilet.

"So what else is new?" he said.

"I'm looking for another part-time job," she lied.

He gave a quick thump on the door with his fist and then walked away. It was the only way they talked to each other these days. He on one side of a door and she on the other. Whatever small feeling she had felt for him was gone and she was left now with only resentment and bitterness. She would leave him tomorrow if she had anywhere else to go. She would start over, if she could.

The sun was setting as she drove down the mountain, a glorious display of red and purple clouds above the city skyline. She drove with her window down, one arm resting on the sill. The air was balmy and fragrant with spring. Days like this reminded her of her earliest childhood, when it was just her and Candy traveling through the Deep South. Late spring was when they always moved, when Candy tired of her job or the man in her life, and got itchy to move on. There was a gypsy-like feel to spring, a sense of hope that things would get better, that a new life waited for them just over the next green hill.

Stella propped her elbow on the sill and leaned her head against her hand. She felt listless, depressed. Cell phone texts from collection agencies, moments of introspection could do that to her. She felt as if her life was slipping away and she was powerless to stop its inevitable slide. She had read case histories where children, even those who had been horribly abused by a parent, will choose to be returned to that parent. Fedderson had written considerably on the subject.

It seemed sad to Stella that with all her experience and education, she still had days when all she wanted was her mother.

Eleven

§§§

Bill Whittington was becoming more and more visible. He no longer shimmered at the edges with diffused light but came through clear and solid. And he came more frequently, too, standing in her bedroom doorway with one shoulder pressed to the jamb. Sometimes he was in a suit but usually he was dressed in his golf clothes.

"We had a good life, Old Girl," he said to Alice one night as she was drifting off to sleep.

She opened one eye and stared at him. "Can't you see I'm trying to sleep?" she said.

"All things considered."

She readjusted her pillow behind her head and lay back down. She could see him between her feet, hovering several inches off the ground.

"I'm not saying it was perfect. I had my," he hesitated here. *"My indiscretion,"* he continued. *"And you, of course, had yours."*

She sighed. It seemed unfair that the dead were privy to the secrets of the living. She wondered what she would learn about Bill Whittington once she passed over.

"Nothing you don't already know," he answered.

"Hush," she said. "I'm trying to sleep."

"All in all, I'd have to say it was a good life."

"I suppose so."

"Not everyone can say that."

"No."

"I knew from the first time I saw you that you were the girl for me."

"Oh, for goodness sakes."

"You have to admit, Al, there aren't many who've had the chances we had."

She was quiet for a moment. "I suppose not," she said in a quiet voice. She could hear footsteps coming along the hallway. He shimmered in the doorway, beginning to fade.

"Leave the regret behind you. Let it go."

"That's easy for you to say."

The hall light clicked on suddenly and Alice raised her head from the pillow, blinking. Elaine's thin, startled face came into focus.

"Who are you talking to?" she asked Alice, her tone wary, suspicious. "I heard you on the monitor."

Alice closed her eyes and lay back down, turning her face to the wall.

"No one," she said.

Bill had made Alice pack his leather-cased traveling bar so they could stop for highballs at cocktail hour. He was a man of custom and ritual and he refused to leave the trappings of polite society behind him when he traveled. They were driving up to Charlottesville to see Roddy graduate. Sawyer was still in prep school and he couldn't come, so it was just the two of them setting out on a lovely May morning. The azaleas were in bloom and everywhere the city was ablaze with riotous color. Alice, who, as a good Presbyterian, often made do with a splash of ginger ale and lime, would have been happy to leave the bar behind. But after twenty-five years of marriage, she had learned that it was easier to simply give in to Bill's demands.

"Damn it, I wish we hadn't told Froggy we'd stay with them," Bill said. His snowy white shirt was spotless, ironed and starched. His cufflinks glittered in the sunlight.

"Well, we couldn't very well tell them 'no' when we've stayed with them every time before."

"Guest beds are always so wretched."

"He's your fraternity brother," Alice reminded him.

They drove for awhile in silence, lost in their own thoughts.

"Never thought I'd see this day," Bill said, smoothing his school tie against his narrow starched chest.

"Nor I," Alice said.

Roddy had taken six years to graduate, not because he wasn't as smart as Sam, but because he was less willing to apply himself.

"I swear, if Sam hadn't come up and done so well, I don't think Roddy would have ever finished. He couldn't bear the idea of his younger brother doing better than he did."

"Oh, I don't think that's it at all." *Alice was a fiercely protective mother. When the children were small they had been cared for by a colored woman named Leta while Alice volunteered at her various charity organizations. Working with underprivileged children she had seen first-hand the damage visited on children by irresponsible, uncaring parents.* "It just took Roddy a little longer to find himself, is all."

Bill sighed. "Well, it takes some longer to get over fool's hill than others."

"There's nothing wrong with Roddy's intelligence," she said quickly.

He looked at her and grinned. "Now, now, calm down, Mother." *He patted her fondly on the knee.* "They're all fine boys."

"Yes, they are."

"And I'm proud of all of them."

"Of course we are."

"I'm especially proud of Sam for being chosen to live on the Lawn. That's quite an honor."

"Yes," Alice said.

Sam was a rising senior and had been chosen to live on the Lawn next year. Roddy had applied but had never been accepted. They were both tall and good-looking but their temperaments were very different. Sam had an easy, carefree manner that made him popular with students and faculty alike, and assured him entrance into one of the best secret societies, The Raven Society. Roddy tried too hard and inevitably rubbed people the wrong way. He had a tendency to brag about the branch of the family who had married into European nobility, and Sam would never have done such a thing. Sam wrote and performed in a skit held during Easters, a hilarious spoof that made him a legend on campus. He had effortlessly pledged Delta Kappa Epsilon while Roddy had had to make do with SAE, Bill's old fraternity.

"And don't forget, this is Roddy's day. Make sure you congratulate him."

"Well, of course I will, honey."

Alice loved all her sons. But she was the first to admit that her love had different qualities for each; it was something she hadn't realized before she had children. That you could love each one in a different way.

"They're fine-looking boys. I'm glad they got your looks."

It was true, they were all tall and blonde and blue-eyed. They took after the Sawyers. Bill was constantly having photographs of himself taken with his handsome sons who towered over him. Alice avoided having her photograph made whenever she could. She had begun to put on a middle-age plumpness that bothered her, and she was self-conscious now about seeing herself through the unforgiving lens of a camera.

"My mother told me I should marry you because you'd produce good-looking children."

"Oh, she did, did she?" Alice gave him a cynical look.

"She said the bloodlines would tell."

"That sounds like something your mother would say."

"She was a Grand Old Gal."

"She was a GOG, all right."

"Now, honey."

Growing up, as he did, in an all-female house, Bill had been the darling of his mother and sisters. His father had died when he was only ten and he'd been spoiled and pampered. Alice had not been fond of her mother-in-law. They'd been wary adversaries, competitors for Bill's affection. It was her mother-in-law's constant interference that Alice felt had so spoiled the early years of her marriage. She had finally put her foot down and the old woman, as if to spite her, had promptly sickened and died.

Bill's sisters were vain, silly creatures who made Alice glad she'd only had sons. Madeline, the eldest, was so stupid she had barely passed through school. It was only her grandfather's position as head of the county school board that had insured her graduation. Louisa, the youngest, had been married four times, to four different scoundrels who had to be bought off each time in order to keep the divorce proceedings quiet. She lived now in Sea Island, Georgia with her "yard boy," Antonio, a former golden gloves boxer who did odd jobs around the house and kept her pool clean.

"You were a real thoroughbred," Bill said, giving her an appreciative look.

"Watch the road please," she said primly.

"Legs like a goddamned show girl."

"Oh? How many show girls do you know?"

He laughed and patted her knee. Pleased, she turned her face to the window so he couldn't see her smile.

At five o'clock they stopped for cocktails. It was in a little town called Orangeville at a city park overlooking a small duck pond. The park was deserted except for two young boys who ran along the edge of the pond throwing bread to the ducks. Their mother sat at a picnic table, reading, occasionally glancing up to check on them.

Alice opened the bar on the seat between them and Bill did the mixing honors. They had stopped at a local drive thru and picked up cups of ice. She took a package of crackers and a container of olives out of a paper sack and set them on the dash.

Bill handed her a drink and touched his glass to the edge of hers.

"Mud," he said.

"Mud."

Alice drank her highball in silence, watching the boys. The alcohol relaxed her; she felt a pleasant warmth seeping through her limbs, a sense of contentment and ease. She knew women who drank alone in the afternoons while the husband was at work and the children were at school, but she had never been one of them. Not that she hadn't been tempted. The long slow days of summer were the worst, when the children were home from school, and she had too much time to sit and think. Increments of time were built up like wooden blocks, one atop the other; breakfast, a walk in the park, lunch, nap, all carefully constructed to make up a day. The memory of her past was like a raw wound then; she had not yet learned the trick of packing her memories away like so much well-worn baggage.

She had known, instinctively, how easy it would be to surrender to the habit of drinking alone, to sink into the pleasant oblivion of intoxication, and so she had denied herself. She kept her feet firmly planted on the straight and narrow path laid down by her staunch, self-denying Presbyterian ancestors.

It was only now, when the children were grown and the painful memories of her youth had subsided to a dull insistent ache that she sometimes allowed herself the pleasure of drinking with Bill. Never alone.

"Congratulations," he said, touching his glass to hers again.

"For what?"

"For getting our first child through college. One down, two to go."

She smiled and sipped her drink.

"I thought we'd stop for dinner at that little café in Waynesboro."

"All right."

It was a good place to eat. Warmed by the alcohol, she felt a stir of anticipation. She felt peaceful, oddly disconnected from her normal life. It was as if she was viewing the two of them from a distance, as a stranger might; a middle-aged but still attractive couple, prosperous, content, safely optimistic. She had a sudden vision of her life opening up to infinite possibilities; travel to exotic places, meals in foreign cafes with unpronounceable names. Her youth had been spent in the rigors of raising a family but surely now she and Bill could lead their own lives. Surely they were entitled to that golden period she had heard slyly referred to as the "Second Honeymoon."

Bill leaned over and touched her on the knee. "Do me a favor and get that map out of the glove box, will you?"

Alice took it out and handed it to him and he set his drink on the dash and opened the map on his lap, smoothing the edges. "Now, Froggy says we're to ignore the road construction signs coming into Charlottesville. He says to proceed as usual."

"Do you really think that's a good idea?"

"He says the signs are only for the tourists. And if we have to go around the city and come in the other way, then we'll have to drive all the way through town to get to Froggy's."

They had another cocktail when they stopped for dinner. The restaurant was crowded with well-dressed, middle-aged couples who, like them no doubt, were on a pilgrimage to Charlottesville to watch their children graduate. Looking around the crowded room, Alice had the pleasant sensation of feeling herself intimately connected to things outside herself; the jolly crowd, the hum of conversation, the flickering candle light. She was not drunk but she was mildly relaxed. Twice she giggled at Bill's off color jokes.

When they set out again, evening was falling. Faint stars shone above the dark ridges of the distant mountains. The traffic was heavier now than when they first started out, and Bill was quiet, concentrating on the road. When they came to the turn off they usually took, he slowed the car and pulled to the shoulder. A large detour sign straddled the two-laned road in front of them. Cars hurtled by on the highway, their headlights illuminating the detour sign like a spotlight.

"I don't know," Alice said hesitantly. "I almost think we should go around."

"Froggy says we'll be fine."

"If there's a detour sign, there must be a problem. We don't know this road well enough to chance it. What if there's a bridge out?"

"Well, Froggy lives here," he said stubbornly. "He should know."

Alice sighed, knowing that further argument was fruitless. He always became more certain and insistent when he drank.

"You get out, Al, and walk ahead of me."

She looked at him. "Are you crazy?" she said. "I have my good pumps on."

"I'll drive slowly and keep you in the headlights."

"I know that must be the whiskey talking because no sane man would suggest such a thing."

"Go on now." He leaned across her and opened the door. "Out you go."

She got out and began to walk purposefully down the center of the road. He followed slowly behind, brakes squealing, headlights casting a half-moon of light around her feet.

"See anything, Al?" He leaned out the window, resting on one elbow. Insects swarmed the blacktop. Tall trees rose on either side of the road, blocking the starry sky.

"I can't see a thing. It's pitch black."

"Damn it, Al. Walk out ahead a bit so I don't hit you with the bumper."

"There are bugs out here I don't even know the name of."

"Your comment about the bridge being out has got me thinking. I'm pretty sure there is a bridge on this road."

She turned around and faced him, her hands on her hips, and he put his foot on the brake. "Then why am I out here?" she said. "This is crazy. Let's go back to the highway and drive around." She was certain now that she heard the faint sound of rushing water.

"Froggy would have told us if there was a bridge out. He would have remembered that."

"Then you get out and walk ahead."

"Aw, come on Al. Be a sport."

She crossed her arms on her chest. "Who do you think I am? Sacajawea?"

"Sacajawea would have done as she was told."

"Well, there you go then."

"Aw, hon."

She stood in the middle of the road facing him, her white-gloved hands resting just beneath her breasts, her hat tilted at a jaunty angle. He leaned out the window, regarding her mildly.

"You do look a bit overdressed for trailblazing."

"I suppose you think that's funny."

The comic aspect of their situation struck them both at the same time. Alice snorted suddenly and put her hand to her mouth. Bill put his head back and laughed. She walked to the car and climbed in.

"You," she said.

"Aw, you."

She giggled. "Sacajawea," she said.

Bill put the car in reverse and began to back slowly along the deserted road. "Wait until I tell Froggy," he said.

After they arrived, Froggy Murch mixed a batch of highballs. His wife, Mona, pulled out a tray of hors d'oeuvres and set it down on the coffee table. They sat in the Murches' big pine-paneled den and laughed about Alice trying to find her way in the dark.

"You know, now that you mention it, I think that bridge might be out!" Froggy said.

"They could have been killed!" Mona shrieked.

This comment brought another round of raucous laughter.

Alice had always liked Froggy and Mona. Froggy and Bill had played on the UVA golf team together and they had been fraternity brothers and good friends ever since. When Alice and Bill came up for UVA football games, they always stayed with the Murches. Froggy and Mona had two children; a son Roddy's age and a daughter a year younger than Sawyer.

Froggy mixed another batch of highballs and they laughed and told stories about their college days. Mona had been at Hollins when Alice was at Sweet Briar. The boys from UVA would come up for weekend parties and dances, although Froggy and Bill had already graduated by then; Mona met Froggy at a Country Club dance in Richmond.

While they laughed and told stories about their fraternity days, Alice watched Bill. In the soft glow of the lamp light, his face was angular, darkly shadowed along his jaw and lower cheeks. He was not handsome but he was attractive, as middle-aged men so often are; self-assured, alert, vigorous. He had a small man's taut physique, and his sense of humor gave his face a lively appeal. More and more in the past few years, Alice had been surprised, catching a glimpse of her husband across a crowded room or dance floor, to feel a certain stir. An awareness of him, not so much as a husband, but as a stranger, someone she might be seeing for the first time. She wondered if other women saw him as she did. She knew they did.

There had been that unpleasantness a few years back with a young woman in the secretarial pool of the insurance company where he worked. Nothing had ever been openly discussed or acknowledged, no accusations, no dramatic confessions of guilt. Both Alice and Bill had had too much pride for that. But there had been a change in him that she had noted; an extra attention to his dress, a jaunty bounce to his step, long unexplained evenings at the office. Most disturbingly, he had given up his Saturday golf game. Twice she had called the club on days when he left the house dressed in his golf clothes, only to be told that he wasn't scheduled for a tee time. And when she asked him later, "How was your golf game?" he replied cheerfully, "Fine. Oh, fine."

She had been warned by Sally Vincent, the wife of one of Bill's partners. The wives protected one another from the depredations of the secretarial pool, circling the wagons around their homes and children and husbands, presenting a sharp-eyed, united front. Divorce was rare, but it was not unheard of, in those days. Alice, *warned, was paralyzed with humiliation. She did nothing. In the end it was Sally Vincent who saw to it that the young woman was fired.*

Bill moped around for a bit, drank too much, was short-tempered with Alice and the children. But in the end, he seemed to come out of it thankful and relieved, as if he realized how close to financial and social ruin he had come.

Bill and Froggy, arm in arm, were singing The Good Old Song. Alice looked at her husband, his face animated and youthful, and thought suddenly of the way he looked in bed; determined, attentive in a hearty and businesslike way. The young secretary had had her uses after all. Bill was better in the bedroom after her than he was before.

Even now, she could feel her face warming. Alice looked down at her empty glass, rattling the ice cubes. Remarkable, that after all these years she had begun to welcome his attentions.

"Come on, Al! Join in!" he said motioning for her with the hand that held his highball.

"I can't," she said. "You know I can't sing."

Was this what happened after years of routine and sacrifice and raising children? Did you begin, once more, to slip back into the dreamy world of adolescent fantasies?

"Stop that excruciating racket and mix us some more drinks," Mona said to her husband. "Al and I are parched."

Bill crossed the room and took Alice's empty glass.

She wondered if she would have been happier if she'd accepted from the very beginning that part of her that could have been content with a man like Bill Whittington, and simply let the rest go.

It was long after midnight when they finally stumbled up the stairs to bed.

"Night, night you lovebirds," Froggy said. Mona pulled him into the bedroom and closed the door.

They went on down the hall to the guest room, which had twin beds and an adjoining bath. Bill brushed his teeth and dressed in his favorite pajamas. Alice washed her face and stripped down to her slip and threw herself across one of the beds.

"Do you join me in my little bed, or do I join you in yours?" Bill said.

"Don't be ridiculous. They'll hear us."

"Right," Bill said, throwing back the covers and rising. "Yours it is then."

"Get back in your bed," she said.

"Aw, come on Sacajewa. Be a sport."

"I'm tired." Perhaps it was the effect of the alcohol or of Bill rubbing his bristled chin against her neck, but Alice began to giggle.

"That's my girl," Bill said, and rolling on top of her, lightly bit her earlobe.

Graduation day dawned foggy and overcast. They met Roddy and Sam at an inn near the campus for an early breakfast. Roddy was in a sullen mood, glancing from time to time out the windows at the overcast skies.

"Wouldn't you know it would rain today," he said.

"Don't worry about it," Alice said. "If it rains, it rains. This is your graduation day and you should be enjoying it, not worrying about the weather."

"I can tell you right now, if they move the Final Exercises from the Lawn to Memorial Gym, I'm not attending."

Bill looked at him. "Oh, you'll attend all right."

"No, I won't."

A vein rose in Bill's temple. He smiled, showing his teeth. "Your mother and I didn't drive five hundred miles for the fun of it. We're here to see you graduate."

"Well, if the ceremonies are held on the Lawn then your drive wasn't in vain," Roddy said arrogantly. "If not, forget it."

"Now you listen here," Bill said, and Alice laid a warning hand on his arm.

"Not here, please," she said in a low, smooth voice.

Bill stopped and leaned back in his chair, looking around the crowded restaurant.

"Hey, pops, I like those cufflinks," Sam said, picking up one of Bill's wrists and pulling it closer.

Bill, pleased, allowed himself to be distracted from assaulting Roddy. He was a polished dresser and always took compliments on his appearance seriously. He cleared his throat and said evenly, "They were my grandfather's. He had the same initials as me."

Roddy scowled and leaned back insolently in his chair, his legs stretched in front of him. Alice sighed and sipped her coffee, listening half-heartedly to Bill and Sam talking about Bill's grandfather. Roddy was the most like Bill in temperament, and as a child he had been encouraged by Bill in his behavior. The Little Prince, Bill had called him, chuckling. But now that Roddy was grown he and Bill butted heads over everything; Roddy's career choice (he had decided to become a teacher rather than join the family insurance company), his choice in women (Roddy had been briefly engaged last year to an unsuitable Italian girl from New Jersey), his refusal to settle down in college and finish in four years. All these things Bill seemed to take as a personal attack.

Which perhaps they were.

Sam had his father fully engaged now in telling stories about his grandfather. The waitress came by and discreetly refilled their coffee cups.

"At one time he was the richest man in Chattanooga but he died nearly penniless," Bill said. "He had too many irons in the fire, my father always said. And he died before any of them could pan out."

Sam looked at Alice and smiled. He was dressed in blue seersucker pants and a white oxford cloth shirt with a yellow sweater tied around his shoulders. He was beautiful, almost feminine in the perfection of his features. His hair, worn longer than was fashionable, swept his forehead, ending just above his eyebrows.

"And your great-grandfather was the one who came down with the Union army and never went back to Ohio," Sam added encouragingly to his father, and Bill launched into a story they had all heard many times before. Sam, the eternal peacemaker, smiled serenely at his mother.

There was something fragile about him. He was the most charming of her children, the most popular, and yet Alice had always felt a nagging uneasiness for him. His cheerful exterior hid a sensitive nature. She never worried about Roddy and Sawyer; they both had a selfish streak in their natures, an ability to come out on top no matter what. But Sam seemed soft, vulnerable.

When he was a child she had had a recurring nightmare about him. He had drowned in the river and she had been called to come down to the morgue and identify his body. He was lying on a slab, stiff and pale, and in her grief, she couldn't look at the rest of him, only his feet which were narrow and shapely as a girl's. It was always the same dream. He was a small child, she was unable to look at anything except his slender feet; her anguish was always fresh and unendurable.

Unable to believe the dream wasn't a premonition, she had shuddered each time he went swimming, had refused to let him go on vacations with friends to the beach. It was only as he reached adulthood that the nightmare began to fade.

The waitress brought their breakfast and they ate quickly. The sun began to break through the clouds, falling in cheerful bands across the table and the dark, polished floor. Roddy's mood began to lighten.

He looked at his watch, gulping his coffee. "I'll have to hurry," he said. "We're supposed to be on the Lawn by ten o'clock."

"Well, before you go, I want you to have this." Bill took an envelope out of his pocket and laid it on the table beside Roddy's plate.

Roddy wiped his hands on his napkin and then opened the envelope, carefully reading the card inside before he unfolded the check and bank statement.

"The trust fund, of course, was set up by your grandfather Jordan before he died. You can access it now, but I advise you to leave the money alone and let it grow. The check is from your mother and me."

Roddy stood and came over to his father's chair and Bill stood, too. They shook hands formally.

"Thank you, sir. That's very generous of you."

"We're proud of you, son," Bill said. "Very proud."

Roddy leaned over and kissed Alice's cheek. "Thank you, mother."

"We're so proud of you, honey, and I know your grandparents would be, too, if they were here."

"Good show, old man," Sam said in his best British accent, and Roddy bopped him on the head with his fist as he slid back into his chair. Sam said, "So how are you going to spend the loot?"

"I'm going to use part of it to buy a bicycle."

"What?" Alice said.

"An Italian racing bike."

Bill sat down. He stared at his son, a puzzled expression on his face. "Why?" he said mildly.

"You know why," Roddy said, glancing at his father as he tucked the envelope into his pocket.

As children, Bill had refused to allow the boys to have bicycles. They had lived on a long hill and another boy, a neighbor, had been killed riding his bike down the hill and into the path of an oncoming car.

Outside the window a family group stood in the parking lot taking photographs.

Bill tapped the table with his fingers, his lips pursed, considering his oldest son with a cool, speculative look. "Aren't you a little old for a bicycle?" he said finally.

The color rose in Roddy's face. "It's an Italian racing bike. I'm going to use it to get in shape and then I'm going to enter a few races."

"I see," Bill said.

Alice could feel her husband's agitation building; she could hear it in his voice, see it in the way he was sitting. Roddy had always had an explosive temper and this day, of all days, he seemed primed and ready to go off. A scene in a restaurant would ruin the day, would forever mar what she had hoped would be a happy family occasion. She glanced from her husband to her son, giving them both a pleading, warning look, but neither one noticed her.

Roddy finished his coffee and wiped his mouth with a napkin. He punched his brother on the arm. "I've got to get to the Lawn, squirt. You coming?" He ignored his father, adopting a sly, careless manner.

Sam pushed himself back from the table, stretching his long legs. "I suppose so."

Bill continued to stare at Roddy, a pleasant smile curving his mouth. "Are you asking me to apologize for something?" he said to Roddy. "Because you'll get no apology from me. I did what I had to do to keep you safe."

"Hush," Alice said.

"Sure, pops, we know you did," Sam said, rising. "No one's blaming you."

Roddy stood more slowly, leaning against the table. "You can't keep people safe by being fearful and overprotective."

Bill stared at him, smiling grimly. "Well," he said. "You're still here, aren't you?"

Alice picked up her gloves and began to put them on carefully. "Do you boys need us to drive you back?" she said.

"No," Roddy said, turning to her. "Stay and finish your coffee. The squirt and I can walk." Roddy gave his brother a playful shove. He looked at his father. "Thanks again," he said. "For everything."

"You're welcome," Bill said.

"I'll see you out there."

"Yes, darling. We'll see you there," Alice said. She watched her two tall sons walk across the crowded room. At the door, Sam turned and came back. He leaned and clapped his father on the shoulder.

"Don't worry, pops," he said. "He's just nervous is all."

"Is he?"

"Sure. Big day and all that." He kissed Alice on the cheek and then turned and hurried after his brother.

Through the big plate glass window, Alice could see the two of them in the parking lot. They stood facing each other, talking earnestly, and then Roddy turned and Sam followed him, walking across the lot toward the campus. She watched them go, the sun glinting along their blonde heads. Her boys. Her beautiful boys.

"Do you think they have any idea how difficult it is to raise a child to maturity?" Bill said.

"Of course they don't," Alice said. "They won't know until they have children of their own."

"No, I suppose not." Bill lit a cigarette and motioned for the waitress to clear the table.

Alice watched them go until they were nothing more than small disappearing dots, and it was then that she felt, quite unexpectedly, a memory of that old chilling dream of death, a shiver of uneasy premonition.

Twelve

§§§

Arriving at Alice's on a warm Wednesday morning in early May, Stella was surprised to find Elaine in a cheerful, talkative mood. Stella waited until she had left and then she went and checked the notebook. *Alice was restless last night*, Elaine had written. *She got up confused and didn't seem to know where she was or what day it was. Said she dreamed about people from "way back."*

Despite Elaine's notes, Alice seemed in fine spirits. She was supposed to go to the doctor this morning for an eye exam and Stella was to drive her, the first time she'd ever driven Alice anywhere. Janice had left detailed notes of where Stella was to park, and how she was to go in through the sliding doors on the lower level to get to the doctor's office.

Miss Alice likes going down Broad Street, she had written. *It's a route she recognizes. If you drive the expressway she might get confused and think you don't know where you're going and this will upset her. And don't forget to get your parking ticket validated when you go in. Please make sure you have plenty of gas in your car because Miss Alice doesn't like to stop for gas.*

Stella had to throw a stack of magazines, books, and empty Styrofoam coffee cups into the backseat to make room for Alice. She helped Alice climb in and fasten her seatbelt, and then she folded up the walker and stowed it in the back.

"What kind of car is this?" Alice said, looking around.

"Honda Civic."

"I like it. The seats are comfortable."

It was a beautiful morning, warm and sunny. As they left the mountain, Alice looked around like a bright-eyed little bird, commenting on several houses where people she knew used to live. She seemed clear-headed and sharp this morning, and it occurred to Stella that Alice didn't get out much and driving anywhere in a car was probably a real treat. Except for the occasional trip down to the Sonic Drive In for a chili-dog meal with one of her sons, or her Friday evening excursions with Adeline to The Mount Vernon Restaurant for Coconut Cream Pie Night, Alice was pretty much housebound.

"When did you stop driving, Alice?"

"Oh, I don't know. How old am I? I really can't remember when I stopped driving."

"So you're getting your eyes checked today?"

"I've been going to Dr. Monroe for years. Bill went to him and liked him so I just started coming, too, when my eyes got bad. Back before they took the car away from me I used to drive myself. They put these drops in your eyes that make everything all blurry."

"I don't think you're supposed to drive after they dilate your pupils."

Alice waved her hand dismissively. "I could find my way home blindfolded in those days," she said. "Back before my mind went."

"Your mind is fine."

"Some days," Alice said. She was quiet for a moment. "Roddy goes to Dr. Wallis up on the mountain. You know they don't make house calls anymore? Doctors. So it'd be real convenient to go to Dr. Wallis. I tried to get in with him a few years ago but he wasn't taking any new patients. And Potter, the doctor I see for my heart, moved his office way out to the new mall which I don't understand because it's a smaller place and much too busy. People coming and going all times of the day. So I started looking around for another doctor and then I realized it'd be far less trouble to just die."

Chattanooga was spread out below them, glistening in the sunlight, the distant mountains wreathed in clouds. As they snaked their way down Lookout, Alice pointed out a road on the left.

"That's where Bill and I used to live when we were first married," she said. "Down that road."

Stella turned her head but could see nothing but a high-pitched roof rising out of a stand of trees.

"In those days it was cut up into four apartments but someone has bought it and is turning it back into a family home." Alice shook her head, chuckling. "I'll have to tell Weesie I found it. I couldn't remember where it was the last time I saw her. She came to get me and took me for a ride around the mountain."

"Weesie can still drive?"

"We used to live next door to each other on Hammond Road and I had this dogwood tree that had come from my grandmother's yard that I wanted to see in bloom. So Weesie said she'd come up and get me and we'd drive over and see it. Well, we must have driven around for about an hour but neither one of us could remember how to get to Hammond Road. Can you believe that? We lived next door to each other for twenty years but neither one of us could find the street.'

"Well, I bet you had a good time anyway.'

"After awhile it got to be kind of funny. Weesie said, *Well, I guess it's official, Al. We've both lost our ever-loving minds.*"

They drove past The Mount Vernon Restaurant, the new grocery store, and the CVS drug store. Stella stayed on Broad Street just like Janice had instructed. They drove past store fronts, some dilapidated and empty, some renovated into charming shops. As they drove, Alice turned her head from side to side, remarking on the changes she saw.

"That used to be Tanner's Butcher Shop," she said. "And that's where the old grocery store was. The A&P, I think it was."

The downtown area was crowded with office workers and tourists hurrying along sidewalks framed by tall gray buildings. The city's electric buses whirred along quietly, headed for the riverfront and the new aquarium.

"This is where the street car used to run," Alice said.

They turned right on Fourth Street, heading up the ridge past the university toward the Arts District.

"Oh, there's the Junior League Office," Alice said, pointing. It was a small, squat building with a large sign out front. "Adeline and I were both Junior League presidents. We had our pictures taken and later they hung them up in the hallway. We heard about the display and Adeline and I decided to go down there a few years ago and look at the photographs. Anyway, we walked in and there was this young woman and we told her who we were and that we had come to see our photographs.

She looks at us and says, 'Black or white?'

Adeline and I just stared at each other. 'Why, we're *white*,' I said.

'Yes, I *know* that,' the woman said. 'What I meant is, is your photograph black and white or color? The black and white ones are hanging at the end of the hallway there.'"

Fourth Street became Third. They passed the hospital on the left and turned right at the next street, past a nondescript building with tinted windows, one of those square cement monstrosities put up during urban renewal to replace some charming Victorian.

"Turn here," Alice said, and they pulled into a parking lot behind the building. The parking lot was nearly empty. A long ramp with metal guide rails led down a slight incline to a pair of sliding doors. Stella retrieved the walker from the trunk and helped Alice climb out. They walked slowly across the parking lot toward the sliding doors. As Alice approached the ramp, her speed picked up and Stella had to grab the frame to keep her from hurtling forward like a luge.

There were only three patients in the waiting room, a bearded man and a well-dressed older couple watching Fox News. The office looked like a set from a nineteen sixties television show; shag carpeting, low squat Naugahyde furniture, big orange lamps with oversized shades. Alice sat down in one of the chairs while Stella went up to sign her in. When she got back, Alice had picked up a *Ladies Home Journal* with a headline that read, *How to Love Your Job!*

"Here's an article you might want to read," Alice said.

"I don't need to read that," Stella said. "I love my job."

"Ha, ha," Alice said.

Stella sat down and began to leaf through a *People Magazine*.

After a few minutes, Alice said in a loud voice, as if they were the only two in the room, "Here's an article about a middle-aged woman who decided to get a raven tattoo. I think

I'll get a raven tattoo. Right here on my wrist." She held up one heavily-veined arm for Stella's appraisal.

"Actually, I could see you with a raven tattoo," Stella said.

Alice continued to leaf through the magazine. "And here's one about a woman who only had sex three times and still got HIV. She says, *I only had unprotected sex one time and it turned out to be a disaster."*

The well-dressed couple watching *Fox News* turned their heads and stared.

"Keep it up," Stella said. "And I'll take that magazine away from you."

A bored-looking nurse stepped into the waiting room carrying a clipboard. "Matlock," she said loudly. "Shirley Matlock."

The couple rose. As they walked past the woman slanted her eyes at Stella in a look of stern disapproval. It was obvious she felt Stella should do a better job of keeping Alice under control. Her husband, a portly, florid-faced gentleman, followed her, vainly attempting to button the top button of his sports coat. Alice looked up from her magazine.

"Lord," she said loudly. "I'd hate to have to feed *him*."

Stella stayed in the waiting room reading magazines while Alice was hurried off to the examining room. She was back there for quite awhile, until a harried-looking nurse came out and said brightly and with some relief, "Miss Alice is ready to go."

Stella followed her down a long hallway to a small examining room where Alice sat chatting with the doctor.

"Dr. this is Stella," Alice said.

"I've been telling this young lady about my last vacation," Dr. Monroe said. He was a pleasant-looking man in his mid-fifties.

Alice chuckled and said in a sly, flirtatious manner, "He goes to Disney World with his wife and leaves the children at home. Have you ever heard of such a thing?" She obviously liked the doctor very much. Her behavior around him was sweet and simpering, unlike the belligerence she displayed toward his patients and staff.

Stella helped Alice rise and go back out front to the payment desk.

"Okay, Miss Alice," the nurse shouted nervously. Her hair rose up over her forehead in an explosion of blonde curls.

"You don't have to shout," Alice said.

"Do you have your credit card?"

"I wish I had a nickel for everytime someone's asked me that."

"Ha, ha," the nurse said, taking the card. She read over the doctor's notes. "Okay, now it says here, your glasses prescription has changed and you need to step across the waiting room to the fitting room and we'll get you fitted for a new pair."

"I don't want a new pair," Alice said. "I want the ones I'm wearing."

The nurse looked confused. She was obviously terrified of Alice. "Oh," she said. "Do you want me to send those frames off and have new lenses put in?"

"No, I do *not* want you to send them off," Alice said. "How will I watch *Wheel of Fortune* without my glasses?"

Stella stepped up beside her, smiling pleasantly at the nurse. "Look," she said reasonably. "Just go across to the fitting room and pick out frames exactly like the ones she's wearing and send them off."

"Oh, she'll have to be fitted," the nurse said. "We can't just pick new frames and not fit her."

Alice stared at her with an expression of growing displeasure. "I am ninety-five years old," she said.

"Ninety-four," Stella said.

"I am ninety-four years old and I do not intend to stand here while you dither around."

Stella smiled sweetly at the nurse. "You sure you don't want to pick those out yourself?"

The nurse hurried off. Alice said loudly, "I hope she lives to be one hundred and two and goes blind."

"Behave," Stella said.

"Well, it's ridiculous," Alice said. She looked around for a clock. "How long have we been here?"

The nurse came back a few minutes later carrying a set of frames that was a close match to Alice's glasses. "How about these, hon?" she said. Her smile had a fixed, shiny look, as if it had been molded in plastic. Stella had to admire her stamina.

"Oh, I don't care," Alice said. She sighed dramatically, and then sighed again. She looked at the nurse suspiciously. "What did you do with my credit card?"

"It's here," the nurse said brightly. "I have it right here."

"I don't want you to get it mixed up with somebody else's."

"Oh, I've been doing this job for fifteen years and I've never gotten credit cards mixed up!"

"Well, there's a first time for everything," Alice said.

The nurse ran the card through the reader and brought it back to Alice for her signature.

"Okay, hon, you done real good!" she said, avoiding eye contact and handing the receipt to Stella.

"Can we get out of here now?" Alice said.

"Oh Miss Alice, you're a pistol!" the nurse said.

"I wish I had a pistol," Alice said.

"Now Miss Alice, do you want to go ahead and make an appointment for next time?"

"Who says there'll be a next time," Alice said grimly.

As they came out into the bright sunshine, Stella said, "Well, he seems like a nice enough doctor." Dark clouds rode the horizon and there was a smell of rain in the air.

"Yes, he's pleasant enough. But that saucy little number he's got working for him is something else." In a high falsetto voice, Alice mimicked, "Why, Miz Whittington is that your good ear or your bad ear? Can you hear me? 'Cause what I want you to do is put your chin down right here so I can check your eyes with this machine."

"Why would I put my chin down there?" Alice said indignantly, stopping to look at Stella. She was breathing heavily, her chest rising and falling. They were half-way up the ramp. "There's no telling how many others have laid their chins down there."

"Maybe they clean it in between patients."

Alice shook her head and began to push her walker slowly up the incline. "I doubt it," she said.

"Yeah. You're probably right."

They walked up the slope to the rusty car sitting forlornly in the middle of the empty lot. One of the hubcaps was gone and the passenger door had a long, jagged streak where the paint had been scraped off. Stella helped Alice inside and then shut the door, putting the walker in the back and going around to the driver's door.

She slid in and fastened her seatbelt. "Shoot," she said. "I forgot to get the ticket validated."

"Oh for crying out loud, don't go back in there," Alice said sharply, opening her purse and taking out a few coins. "Let's get out of here."

Stella dropped the coins in the box and the parking barrier rose with a slow lurching motion. She pulled out into the sparse traffic, and then took a right, not realizing that she was taking a different route home. They passed the old baseball stadium on the left. Rows of tall Victorian houses, once prosperous but converted now into dilapidated apartments, rose on both sides of the street. Alice sat with her purse on her lap, staring out the window.

"Well, look at the bright side," Stella said. "At least you don't have to come back again for another year."

"With any luck," Alice said. "I'll be dead."

They drove down Central Avenue past the edge of campus and the Fortwood Historical District. Stella took a right on a side street, thinking it would lead them back to Third, the way they had come, but she realized almost immediately that she'd taken a wrong turn. She didn't know this street at all.

"Do you know where we are, Alice? Because I don't."

"Oh Lord. Are you saying we're lost?"

"No. I can turn around." Stella pulled to the side of the narrow street so she'd have room to make a U-turn.

The neighborhood was run down, a series of overgrown vacant lots and big trees and rambling, unpainted houses that had been converted into apartments. Alice lifted her hand and pointed to a large brick house with a maze of fire escapes running down one side.

"Do you see that place? That was my great-grandmother Jordan's house."

"No, Alice. Really?" It took up nearly the whole block but was as sad and dilapidated as its neighbors.

"And there," Alice said, pointing to a vacant lot across the street where a series of weed-choked brick steps ran up the slope from the sidewalk. "That's the house where I was born. Or at least that's where it used to stand."

They sat with the car idling against the curb, staring up at the old steps.

"Are you sure?" Stella said.

"Of course I'm sure."

"I thought you grew up on Signal Mountain."

"My parents had a summer home on Signal Mountain. During the school year we lived downtown. And later, after I was grown, my father bought a house in Riverview. Ash Hill, it was called."

"See," Stella said. "Your mind is as clear as a bell."

"It comes and goes," Alice said.

Stella pulled away from the curb, driving slowly down the street. Now that Alice had recognized where they were, she saw no reason to turn around.

She said, "How old were you when you moved away from here?"

"Oh, I don't know. I can't remember that."

A large, square house with a porte-cochère covered in trailing vines, stood on the corner.

"That's where the Bakers used to live," Alice said, beginning to show some enthusiasm. She put one hand up on the window glass. "They had a daughter my age. Sarah. When she moved here and started at Miss Fenimore's School, all the boys thought she was so pretty. All the girls hated her."

"That sounds about right."

"Later, she became one of my best friends." She tapped on the glass, pointing out a tall stone wall. The memories seemed to be coming fast and furiously now. "Do you see that stone wall? We used to sit there and wait for the ice man to come around. He had a mule that pulled a wagon with a big block of ice in the back packed in sawdust. If you wanted ice for your icebox, he'd stop at your house and chip off a block for you. We children used to follow him around because sometimes he'd chip off smaller pieces for us. It was a wonderful summer treat."

"So you lived down here for awhile then?"

"Until we built the summer house on Signal." She spread her fingers on the glass, leaving a faint imprint. "Mr. O'Leary was the vegetable man. He used to ride through the streets in his wagon and we'd run out and buy tomatoes and corn and okra. *Okrie* my little sister called it."

She paused. Her hand slid down the glass and dropped into her lap.

"Your little sister?" Stella said. "Adeline?"

"No," she said. "The other one."

Stella slowed down and glanced at her. "You had another sister besides Adeline?"

Alice nodded her head. "Yes," she said.

"What was her name?"

Alice turned her head and stared at her with a stubborn, affronted expression. "Why are you asking me that?" she said in a thin, querulous voice.

Stella, taken aback by her reaction, said, "I don't know. I don't know why I asked."

"I don't know either," Alice said, turning again to the window.

They drove down the street until they reached the campus and then they turned left. Alice was silent for a long time. Later, as they started up the mountain, she said quietly, "Isn't it the most ridiculous thing?"

Stella, lost in her own thoughts, said, "What? What's ridiculous?"

"I can remember the name of Mr. O'Leary the vegetable man. But I cannot remember the name of my own dear sister."

Driving toward the mountain, Alice felt herself awash in memories. Scenes from the past flashed through her mind like a magic lantern show, one fading into another and then materializing as something else. Watching them, Alice was filled with a sense of delight and vague but insistent foreboding.

She saw herself as a girl lying in the grass on a summer day, reading. She had brought a quilt to lie on, and a pillow, and a pitcher of ice cold lemonade. She spread the quilt in the shade of an oak tree, at the edge of a forsythia bush. Cicadas sang in the heat and from time to time, a warm breeze stirred the tops of the tall trees.

In those days the world had felt safe and full of wonder, both infinite and knowable. She had felt in her life a kind of divine presence, a shimmering state of grace that seemed to surround her like a shining light, guiding her, protecting her from harm.

But all of that had changed. She had changed. She no longer believed in fairy tales.

She had always been a person who lived inside her own head. Even now she knew that her visions of Bill Whittington were simply her own lonely imaginings. They weren't real. She never told any of the caregivers about his visits; she didn't want them to think she was crazy in addition to being senile. *Crazy old Alice talking to herself in the dark like a Norse witch.* She wouldn't give Elaine the satisfaction of recording such a thing in the book.

Beside her the girl sat quietly, lost in her own thoughts. Her profile was strong and self-contained, but her arms and shoulders seemed frail; at the end of one sleeve a raw, ugly wound marked her wrist. She had grown so thin, insubstantial, as if she might be slowly fading away. The girl's troubles pained her although Alice was unsure what they might be. The girl never complained; she was humorous and attentive, and yet there was some hidden sorrow that passed between the two of them, a connection that could not be explained, but was simply acknowledged and accepted.

Alice's memories flowed around her like a warm current while she drifted lazily, letting herself be drawn along. A Christmas morning blizzard, swimming in the cool waters of Rainbow Lake, Sawyer's sweet freckled face as she bent to wipe his nose.

A pale angelic face swam suddenly into view and she started in panic and kicked hard against the current, skimming away. Fear prickled her chest, a sense of being swept toward something she could not, would not face. She closed her eyes, willing it away, and then opened them again.

It had begun to rain, falling in soft patters against the roof and the hood of the car. The brightly-lit stores of Broad Street glistened in the rain. Above them the eastern brow of Lookout Mountain loomed, as proud and jutting as the prow of a great ship.

Alice opened her purse to search for a Kleenex. Growing old was not the peaceful letting-go she had once thought it would be.

On the long drive home Stella thought about Alice's mysterious sister, the one whose name she could not, or would not, remember. There was something willful in Alice's forgetting. Weighed down by her own secrets, Stella recognized furtiveness in others, the turning away of the eyes, the deliberate and artful misunderstanding of questions. For no reason other than her own unsatisfied curiosity, it occurred to her suddenly that the portrait of the lovely blonde woman in Alice's dining room might be this forgotten sister. Someone whose life had taken on tragic meaning; someone Alice no longer wished to think about or acknowledge.

Laura.

She felt a cold prickle at the nape of her neck, an odd shiver of recognition. That was the name Alice had whispered on the monitor that first day, her voice hoarse with sorrow and regret. Stella remembered Adeline's expression when she mentioned the experience, the way her face had changed and she had drawn herself up warily. *You must be mistaken.*

Alice was quiet for most of the drive but by the time they returned home she seemed to have recovered some of her earlier talkative mood.

"We'll do our exercises now and get them over with," she said to Stella. "You be the counter."

"I'll be the counter."

She followed Alice through the butler's pantry as they began their loop, turning on lights so Alice could see. It had not occurred to Stella that the wealthy could suffer from despair and adversity. She had believed money to be a protection against tragedy and she was amazed now that she had ever been so naïve as to accept this. The rich, despite their advantages, were no different from the poor when it came to human suffering.

"On our way rejoicing," Alice said, pushing the walker ahead of her. Her curly hair was parted in back and the pink scalp showed through, tender and fragile as an infant's.

As they walked through the dining room, the eyes of the beautiful young woman seemed to follow them. Her lips curved in a sly, reticent smile. Looking at her, Stella felt again that strange feeling of recognition, as if something inside her might be swinging open, revealing itself. She hesitated, staring at the woman, wanting to ask Alice who she was, yet not wanting to hurt her, to bring back the painful past.

The wheels of the walker whined softly. As they crept past the living room coffee table, one of the waxy leaves of a tall white orchid dropped to the table.

It was just as likely that Alice would not remember the woman in the portrait at all, would have no idea who she was.

"Okay," Stella said as they reentered the pantry and she began her counting of their laps. "That's one."

"Just begun," Alice said, snagging one of the wheels of the walker on the door frame. She extricated herself, muttering, "Now who moved that door?" and went on.

They walked again through the kitchen and out into the dining room. Stella glanced at the portrait and then down at the carpet, following Alice's slow, shuffling footsteps. "I saw on the calendar that someone named Harry Rosser is visiting you today at 3:00."

"Who?" Alice said.

"Harry Rosser."

"Oh, Harry Rosser." Alice lifted the walker and put it down again on top of the faded Oriental carpet in the living room.

"Who's he?" Stella said.

"He's a boy I helped get through Smithson School. He lived with his grandmother, she was a schoolteacher, and she wanted him to have a good education. I guess that's how I got involved." Alice, slightly breathless, thrust the walker ahead of her. She shook her head slowly. "Little Harry Rosser," she said.

"How long since you saw him?"

"Oh I don't know. He was at Sam's funeral. I don't remember when that was."

Sam. The son who had died. The one who Alice never spoke of. They entered the foyer and walked down the long hall to the butler's pantry.

"Okay, that's two," Stella said loudly.

"Woo hoo hoo," Alice said.

She stopped in the kitchen at the desk where Stella had set a tall glass of ice water. Alice leaned and picked it up, her hand cupped and twisted with arthritis. Stella turned her head and stared out the kitchen window while she drank.

"Very good," Alice said, setting the glass down carefully. "Very nice indeed."

They walked on into the dining room. The sky was overcast and the light falling through the long windows was gray and oppressive.

"Well, that's nice of him to come for a visit," Stella said, wondering if she should turn on a few of the lamps for Alice. "Harry Rosser. Does he live here in town?"

"Oh I don't know. No, I guess he doesn't. I don't know where he lives."

Beyond the living room French doors, the valley was shrouded in low-lying clouds. The mountains rose like islands in a foamy sea. Alice picked up the walker and set it down on the Oriental rug. She was breathing heavily now.

As they reached the pantry again, Stella said, "Okay, that's three."

"Tee hee hee," Alice said.

It was their last full circuit through the dining room past the portrait of the Woman in Blue. The last loop would be a short cut through the pantry door and across only one end of the long dining room. They would not pass the portrait again.

Stella flicked on the wall switch. As they reached the long wall she pointed at the portrait and said, "Alice, who is that woman?"

Alice stopped walking and stared at the painting. Her expression was odd, dreamy and reflective and filled with sadness, too. They both stood gazing at the young woman whose face was turned slightly away from them as if she was coyly avoiding their inquisitive stares.

"Why," Alice said. "That's me."

"That's you?" Stunned, Stella stood trying to see the resemblance. "Oh my God, you were beautiful."

"The artist was generous," Alice said wryly.

She began moving again, pushing the walker out in front of her and shuffling along behind. Stella followed her, leaning to switch on lamps. She couldn't help but feel disappointment over the portrait; she had been so sure she was onto something. She felt certain the forgotten sister was named Laura, and she had hoped that this might be a portrait of her, a key to unlocking Alice's forgotten memories. She wanted to know what had happened to Laura. She was like a child, wanting to know what had happened, wanting Alice to tell her a story.

Alice said, "My mother dragged Adeline and me up to New York to have our portraits done. I had already married Bill; I was really too old for such foolishness, but my mother was a formidable woman when she set her mind to something.

There was no arguing with her. She insisted on being shown into the studio of one of the celebrated New York portraitists, and would not allow herself to be cowed by the other grand dames who were waiting there ahead of her. After all, her grandfather had started the First National Bank of Chickamauga. He had been one of the first millionaires in Chattanooga. *She* had nothing to apologize for.

Anyway, she breezed into this well-known photographer's studio dragging Adeline and me in her wake. In the middle of his crowded waiting room she raised her arms like a stage actress and said grandly, '*I've come to have portraits of my two beautiful daughters painted.*'"

"Wow," Stella said. "And what did you do?"

"My sister and I looked around to see who the two beautiful daughters might be."

Stella laughed. She could picture the scene, the mother heavy and dowdy in the way middle-aged women of those days always were, dressed in clothes that would have been considered chic in Chattanooga, but not in New York. The two humiliated daughters. "Well, it's a lovely portrait," she said.

"Adeline hated hers so badly she hung it in the garage."

Stella had no problem imagining Adeline doing this. Adeline, the perfectionist, couldn't help but be disappointed in any portrait painted of her. Still, if Alice's painting was even close to being realistic, she had once been a beautiful woman. Looking at the frail, stooped woman who moved slowly across the living room in front of her, it was hard to imagine the young woman, so blonde, so slim and graceful, her shoulders bare, draped in the blue dress that so admirably matched her eyes.

They had reached the pantry for the last, short leg of their walk. "Okay, Alice, that's four. Last one."

"Oh, goody. Can I go through the door?"

"Yes, you may. And I'll get your water so you can hydrate."

"Okay. I'll wait for you," Alice said, stopping.

It was something Stella had never seriously contemplated; old age, infirmity, being locked up inside her own head with nothing but illusive memories of the past. Odd, how she could not picture herself this way. When she tried to look into her own future all she saw was drifting clouds and snatches of a moonlit sky.

Alice stood in the doorway of the butler's pantry, breathing heavily. Stella walked into the kitchen and picked up the glass of ice water and hurried back.

"I'm here," she said.

"I'll go back to my room and work on puzzles until lunch," Alice said, beginning to move off. Stella followed her, turning off the lamps. Alice didn't like the lights left on, anymore that she liked to see food wasted or restaurant meals bought without the use of coupons.

"You might want to take your nap a little early today," Stella said, following her. "Since Harry Rosser is coming at three."

"Who?" Alice said.

"Harry Rosser," Stella repeated loudly.

"Oh, Harry Rosser."

"The boy you sponsored at Smithson."

"Oh, that one."

"It's awfully nice he's coming to visit you."

"I hope he's not going to ask for money," Alice said.

They arrived promptly at three o'clock, two well-dressed gentlemen in a white Lexus. When Stella opened the door, the shorter of the two said in a loud, animated voice, "Hello. Would you like to buy some encyclopedias?" The tall one with the shock of gray hair let his eyes roam over Stella, coming to rest, pointedly, on her chest and t-shirt that read *Ladies' Sewing Circle and Terrorist Society*. They looked a little like car salesmen with their smiling, predatory manner and their suits and ties and dark shiny shoes. Stella guessed them to be in their mid-sixties.

"Please come in," she said. "We've been expecting you." She walked ahead of them into the living room and indicated the long sofa. "If you'd like to have a seat, I'll tell Alice you're here." The taller one was staring at her ass. Stella turned around and faced him, putting her hands on her hips and eyeing him boldly. Neither one seemed inclined to sit down on the sofa, and ignoring her, they walked over to the French doors overlooking the valley. They stood looking down at the river, chatting in the manner of men who are nervous and ill-at-ease while trying not to show it.

Stella went back to the bedroom to get Alice.

"Is he here?" Alice said, looking up from her puzzle book.

"There's two of them."

"Two of them?"

"Yes. I didn't catch the other one's name."

"Oh, Lord. They're definitely here to ask for money then."

"Should I call Sawyer?"

"I told him Harry Rosser was coming at three today and he said he'd come over." She rose slowly from the bed and reached for her walker. "Here, look in that top drawer over there and see if you can find me a scarf to wear." Stella did as she was told, pulling out a multi-colored scarf that matched Alice's green dress.

"Don't you know how to tie it?" Alice said, watching helplessly as Stella, flustered, attempted to loop the scarf around her neck.

"I have no idea."

"Sling it around this way until it's just a narrow strip and then tie it on the side."

"There," Stella said when she was done. "That looks good."

"Does it?" Alice stared at herself critically in the mirror above the dresser.

"Yes," Stella said. She was afraid Alice would make her retie it.

"Okay, bring me my gold earrings from that drawer over there and brush my hair will you? I look a sight."

As she entered the living room, both men turned. The shorter one walked toward her with outstretched arms.

"Hello, Alice dear," he said, embracing her gently.

"Hello," Alice said. "Who are you?"

"Don't you remember me?" he said, pulling away. He patted her awkwardly on the shoulder. "I'm Charlie Connor." He had a spiral-bound book clamped under one arm.

"Oh," Alice said. "Charlie Connor."

Stella could see that she had no idea who he was. Alice lifted her face to the taller man who leaned over and put his arms around her.

"Hello, Little Mother," he said, patting her gently on the back. Stella could see his face, sly, obsequious, as it rested on Alice's shoulder. *A handsome man used to having his own way,* Stella thought, *with just a touch of self-conscious arrogance about him.*

"Sit down, sit down," Alice said.

The tall man let her go. "You remember me, don't you, Little Mother? I'm Harry Rosser. I used to come up and spend the night with Sam when I was at Smithson. You were like a second mother to me."

"Little Harry Rosser," Alice said.

"I remember Sam's bedroom had stars painted on the ceiling. I thought that was the most wonderful thing." He looked at Charlie Connor as if for confirmation of this miracle. "Stars painted on the ceiling."

"I don't remember that," Alice said.

"And this chair," Harry Rosser said, pointing to one of the wingback chairs flanking Alice's fireplace. "I remember this very chair. I used to sit on it and Sam would lie on the sofa in your big house over on Hammond and we would listen to the radio."

"Speaking of chairs," Alice said. "Why don't you have a seat?"

"Oh no," the smaller man said, moving up closer to Alice. They both faced her, towering over her so that she had to look up to see them. "We've brought you something, Miss Alice. Something we'd like to present to you if the lighting was better. It's pretty dark in here." He looked anxious and flustered and it occurred to Stella that they'd rehearsed this speech, and that it wasn't going well. She went around the room and began to switch on the lamps.

Both men moved up on either side of Alice and the short one held out the spiral bound book formally. He cleared his throat and said, "As you may or may not know, Miss Alice, it's the fiftieth reunion of our class at Smithson."

Alice broke in and proceeded to tell them that her people had always been "Westover people", and that she'd only sent her sons to Smithson because Bill's family were "Smithson people."

Both men smiled politely while she rambled on. When she had finished, Charlie cleared his throat and began again. "It's the fiftieth reunion of our graduating class and we've put together this book on the class members especially for you. There are some pictures of Sam in here, too."

Alice said, "What was the name of the headmaster at Smithson?"

"Dallas," Harry said helpfully. "Dallas Calhoun."

"That's him," Alice said. "I always told Bill it was a good thing Dallas Calhoun's great-grandfather had started the school because otherwise he might have been out of a job. He wasn't exactly the sharpest crayon in the box."

The two men stared at each other above Alice's head. The shorter one colored and began to smooth his tie on his chest. "Well," he said. "Well."

Through the sunroom windows, Stella could see Sawyer come out of his front door and start across the lawn toward his mother's.

Harry Rosser put his arm around Alice's shoulders. "Would you like to see some of the photos of Sam, Little Mother?"

"No, I think we should do the presentation first," Charlie said.

"I don't think it matters," Harry said.

"You two aren't here asking for money, are you?" Alice said, peering up at them.

There was a moment of stunned silence. Then they both laughed.

"Little Mother," Harry said mildly.

"Of course not," Charlie said.

"Well, that's good," Alice said. "Because Sawyer keeps my checkbook. I couldn't write a check now even if I wanted to."

On the mantle behind them, the clock ticked steadily. Harry dropped his arm from Alice's shoulders.

"Do you think Sawyer might be home?" he asked politely.

"He's on his way over," Stella said. "He should be here any minute."

Harry turned his head and gave her a cool, appraising look.

"Well, we might as well sit down to wait then," he said, his tone distant, reserved. Alice sat down in one of the wingback chairs and Charlie sat down in the other. Harry pulled a chair up close to Alice's and opened the book. "Here," he said. "Here's a photograph of Sam at homecoming."

"Remember when the girls at Marymount voted him Mr. Personality our senior year?" Charlie said.

"Well, he was Mr. Personality," Harry said. "What was the name of that girl he dated all through prep school? The tall, plain one."

"Leonora Ferguson," Charlie said.

"That's the one! Funny, he could have dated anyone but he stuck with her. She had big hands and was flat-chested like a man. They were always laughing and having such a jolly time together. I wonder what ever happened to her?"

"She married someone else," Alice said shortly.

"I mean, Sam could have dated anyone," Harry said quickly, picking up on Alice's tone. "He was always popular with the girls. They were crazy for him. That's why it's so funny he never married."

"Too many choices, I suppose," Charlie said. "He was having too much fun being a swinging single."

The front door opened and Sawyer walked in. "Well, look who's here," he said, shaking hands with both men.

"They aren't here to ask for money," Alice said to Sawyer.

"Well, that's good," Sawyer said.

"Can you believe this is little Harry Rosser?" Alice said. "I would never have recognized him."

"We brought your mother a copy of our fiftieth reunion book," Charlie said to Sawyer, sitting down again.

"Wonderful," Sawyer said. His manner was guarded, vigilant, and it occurred to Stella that people like the Whittingtons were always having to erect barricades against money seekers and scam artists. Sawyer sat down on the sofa across from them. Stella turned and walked across the living room and dining room into the sunroom. She sat at the table where she could observe them quietly.

"It has updates on all the class members," Charlie said, pointing. "There's a memoriam to your brother."

Harry opened the book to another page and held it up to Alice. "Here's another picture of Sam. We were on our way to the tennis courts."

They sat around making small talk for another ten minutes but Stella could see their hearts weren't in it. Alice sat with the book open on her lap, staring out the French doors at the distant mountains. The storm had cleared and a weak sun shone sporadically from a veil of swiftly moving clouds.

When it was time to go, Harry stood and leaned to hug Alice.

"Goodbye, Little Mother," he said.

Alice looked up at him. Her light-colored eyes flickered over his chest and shoulders, came to rest stolidly on his face. "Who are you?" she said.

"Al, that's Harry Rosser," Sawyer said loudly.

Alice frowned, still looking up at him. "Little Harry Rosser?"

"That's right."

"I never would have recognized you," Alice said.

Sawyer showed them out. Stella walked over to Alice, who was staring down at the opened book on her lap as if she was seeing it for the first time. She seemed distracted, and Stella leaned over and touched her gently on the shoulder. A photograph of a handsome young man in tennis clothes stared up at them from Alice's lap. *Sam.*

"Alice, would you like to watch some TV out in the sunroom."

"That was Harry Rosser," Alice said vaguely.

"Yes, I know."

Alice stared down at the photograph, her thin neck bowed. Her hair stood up around her delicate scalp like cotton fluff. "He brought back so many memories," she said. "They all came flooding back." She glanced up at Stella and then down again, smiling in a queer, tight way. Her chin trembled and without any warning, she began to cry. Oily tears rolled down her cheeks and plopped onto the open book

Stella didn't know what to say. She had thought Alice was one of the lucky ones who got through life relatively untouched by suffering, but she could see now that this wasn't true.

She knelt beside Alice and, without a word, put her arms around her.

Adeline called around five o'clock that afternoon and said she and Weesie were coming for a visit tomorrow. Stella and Alice were sitting in the sunroom reading when she called.

Alice had recovered from her short crying jag and seemed herself again. Sawyer had come back in after the men left and teased her about breaking Harry and Charlie's hearts and she had responded with a sly grin.

"I told them you keep my checkbook," she said. "And the starch seemed to go out of them." She held up the spiral-bound book. "Here," she said. "You can have it."

"Al, they brought it for you!"

"I don't want it," she said.

Adeline talked for awhile on the phone and Alice listened. Right before they hung up, Alice shouted into the mouthpiece, "Guess who was here today?"

"Who?" Adeline said loudly. Alice had the volume turned up high and Stella could hear her clearly.

"Little Harry Rosser. Do you remember him?"

"Oh, yes. I remember Harry."

"Only he's not so little anymore. He's over six feet tall."

"Really?"

"I didn't even recognize him. He was talking about coming up to spend the night at my house and there being stars on the ceiling. I had no idea what he was talking about."

"In Sam's room. Don't you remember? We painted stars on the ceiling because he was so into the constellations."

"I don't remember," Alice said.

"You'll have to tell us all about Harry Rosser tomorrow. We'll have a gossip fest."

"Well, I'll save it for tomorrow then," Alice said, and hung up.

Thirteen

§§§

On the way home that evening, Stella's cell rang. It was Professor Dillard, her advisor.

"I'm worried about you," she said. "I heard from two of your professors today that you haven't been coming to class."

"Yeah, I meant to talk to you about that. I've been sick."

"Sick? For three weeks?"

Stella said nothing. She had been crazy to think she could put herself through college. She was so far behind, she'd never catch up. She'd never be able to pay off the school loans she had now, much less the ones she'd have to take out for grad school. Assuming she'd even be able to get into grad school, which seemed highly unlikely at this point.

Professor Dillard sighed loudly and then began again more reasonably. "I'm worried about you getting into grad school. We've talked about this. Your grades are really important if you want to get into a top notch university and, honestly, with what I'm seeing this semester, I don't think you can get in at all."

"I've been thinking about dropping out."

There was a sharp intake of breath, a pause. "Oh, Stella, no. You've worked so hard. You've come so far."

She steeled herself to the disappointment in Professor Dillard's voice, the tone of strident sympathy and concern. Ridiculous that she should feel a swelling in her throat, a hint of impending tears.

She took a long, deep breath and calmed herself. She said carefully, "I've been thinking about dropping out and working for awhile to save some money before going back." It was true. She had been thinking about this for some time. She had thought she might pick up another shift or two with Alice, maybe find a waitressing job for the weekends.

"If you drop out, you won't go back," Professor Dillard said flatly. "Besides, with this semester's grades you might not be able to get back in anyway."

Stella passed the rock cave at the foot of the mountain where they had locked up the Cherokees before moving them west on the Trail of Tears. Dusk was falling and the sky was a deep purple. Bats flitted in the soft, warm air.

"Okay, let's try this." Professor Dillard's voice had taken on a bold, determined tone. "I'll put in for a medical leave of absence for you for this semester. That way you'll get to drop all your classes instead of having to take an F or incomplete."

"Will I get my tuition back?"

"Unfortunately, no. It's too late for that."

Stella was quiet, considering this. "Don't I need a doctor's note or something?"

"No. You come see me and I'll fill out a form saying you've been under a great deal of mental stress and anxiety."

"You mean, like a nervous breakdown?"

"We'll make it sound a little more convincing than that." She was quiet for a moment and Stella, feeling her hesitation and knowing there was something else, stiffened. "But I'll only do this, Stella, on one condition."

Stella stared at the distant rim of mountains. "And what condition would that be?" she said slowly.

"That you agree to come in for counseling."

"That's not necessary."

"You can see me, or I can refer you to one of my colleagues."

"I don't need counseling. I'm fine."

"We're going to address issues that should have been addressed a long time ago."

"There are no issues."

"Your arms for instance," Professor Dillard said.

Stella felt a sharp pain between her shoulder blades. As always, when cornered, she felt herself go limp, begin to drift.

Professor Dillard said, "I'm going to take your silence as acquiescence." She waited for Stella to protest, and when she didn't, she said, "Friday morning at ten."

"I can't. I have class."

"No, you don't. Not anymore."

The pain had begun to throb, spreading out across her shoulders and down her arms. She could see the railroad tracks ahead and she slowed down. Her mouth felt dry, grainy.

"We can do it at my house if you'd rather not show up at the counseling office at school. It would be more private there."

Stella slowed at the crossing and looked both ways. She stared warily through the windshield, feeling the pain now beneath her breastbone, sharp and insistent. It swelled, pushing against her ribs. Her whole body was trembling. She wondered if this was what a heart attack felt like.

"All right," she said.

"I'll send you an email," Dr. Dillard said, and hung up.

What had she done?

She left the tracks behind and thumped the accelerator, cruising steadily up the overpass that crossed the train yard. Ahead, the lights of downtown were coming on, gleaming against the velvety background of the evening sky. She passed a well-lit restaurant with its patrons illuminated behind a plate glass window. An old man in a motorized wheelchair trundled along the sidewalk.

The pain had begun to throb in time with her heartbeat. It spread through her like a warm tide. She felt disconnected, lightheaded. It was if she was watching herself from a great distance, waiting to see how it would end. She had had this feeling before, in the bathroom as she did her careful work. Her secret work. She sensed sometimes as she watched the blade make its delicate cut, how close to death she was; a subtle pressure here, a deeper cut, and it would all be over. On her bleakest days, she knew she could do it.

Oblivion; a terrible and wondrous thought.

But what if she was wrong? What if the Buddhists had it right? What if there was no oblivion, no way out; only the wheel of Samsara, turning endlessly until she faced what she had to face, got it right finally? What if, by her desperate act, she was forced to wander aimlessly through the spirit world, trapped forever in a Purgatory of her own making?

It was fear that kept her from taking the final step. Fear of the unknown. Fear of the consequences of her actions.

Adeline and Weesie arrived around five o'clock the following afternoon for their visit with Alice. Alice and Stella were sitting in the sunroom watching *Family Feud*.

"Oh, I love this show!" Weesie said, clapping her hands with a shy, tender smile. Despite her age, she had a girlish, coquettish manner.

"There's too much jumping up and down and screaming," Alice said. She complained incessantly about *Family Feud* but it was one of the shows she insisted on watching, mainly so she could criticize the contestants' dress. She pointed at the TV screen. "Look at her hair, hanging down around her face like that. It just looks terrible." Alice wore a yellow knit dress and a purple cashmere sweater and a pair of tennis shoes. Her socks were yellow with white pom-poms.

"Schempf?" Adeline said, reading the family name on the display board. "What kind of name is that?" She looked very tall and very elegant, dressed in a tailored gray pantsuit with heeled pumps.

Stella went into the kitchen and poured them all glasses of ice water. When she came back in, they were gossiping about someone she didn't know while the theme song from *Family Feud* blared in the background.

Alice pointed at the TV and said, "Turn that off, will you?"

Stella clicked it off and turned to leave.

"You don't have to go," Alice said to Stella. "Sit down and join us."

Stella sat down. Adeline glanced at Weesie but said nothing. She turned to Alice and said, "So you saw Harry Rosser yesterday?"

"I wouldn't have known him," Alice said. "He must be six foot six."

Adeline tapped one finger against the rim of her glass, looking down thoughtfully. "You know he made a pass at me once at a Smithson Christmas Tea. He couldn't have been more than fourteen years old. I was bending over ladling punch into glasses and he came up behind me and said, *Hey, Doll, how about a kiss?"*

"Oh Adeline," Alice said.

Weesie giggled.

"I turned around and he was holding a sprig of mistletoe over his head and grinning like a Cheshire cat. He always was a fresh kid."

Alice gave her a disparaging look. "He was always very polite to me."

"Well, Al, of course he was. You practically paid his tuition. When he found out I was your sister, I thought he was going to be sick all over the Christmas cookies. The color went out of his face and he rushed out and didn't come back."

"I don't know about any of that," Alice said doubtfully.

"Well, Al, I'm telling you about it. It happened just like I said it did."

"You were always so vain. Maybe you just imagined it."

"I was vain?" Adeline said, looking at her sister coolly. "Look who's talking."

The two began arguing in loud, strident voices.

Weesie looked at Stella and smiled apologetically. "Do you go to college?" she asked politely. She wore a silk scarf knotted stylishly around her neck and a pair of white slacks and a pale pink sweater set. Her shoes were sensible flats.

"Yes," Stella said. *Technically anyway*.

"And what do you study?"

"Psychology."

Weesie's carefully made up face registered her surprise. "Oh, how interesting!" she said, setting her glass down. "What will you do after college?"

"Well, a lot will depend on whether or not I'm able to afford grad school. I'd like to work as a mental health counselor."

Adeline, who had tired of arguing with Alice, said, "I hope you're not going to be one of those therapists who tells people all their problems are because of their childhoods."

"Most people's problems are because of their childhoods," Stella said.

Adeline wasn't having any of it. "I get so tired of hearing people whine about having bad parents. It's ridiculous. I'm sure my kids whine about me to their therapists."

"I'm sure they do," Alice said.

Stella said to Weesie, "I'd like to work with young girls with self-esteem issues."

"Oh, how wonderful!" Weesie clapped her hands and flashed her tender smile. "You young girls are so lucky to be able to have such wonderful careers. I had five children and a husband. That was my career."

"It's better to have a choice," Stella agreed. She supposed that to these women she must seem like a young woman with unimaginable freedom. Here she was envying them their wealth and sheltered lives while they were, no doubt, envying her her youth and freedom to do as she pleased.

Adeline waved one hand dismissively. "Oh, we had choices. You could be a secretary or a nurse or a teacher. Or, if you were really, really lucky, you could be a housewife. That was considered the pinnacle of success." She sipped her water and set it down again, glancing at Alice. "Remember, Al, when you used to talk about running off to live in New York? How you used to brag you were never going to get married?"

"No," Alice said.

"It used to drive Mother crazy."

"Well, that's probably why I did it then."

"I can't even imagine being a housewife back in the fifties and sixties," Stella said. "It must have been really boring." She looked around, giving them a reckless grin. "No offense," she said.

"None taken," Weesie said, lifting her glass.

"I mean, most of you had other women who watched your children and cleaned your houses, so what did you *do* all day?"

"Oh you'd be surprised," Adeline said.

"There was always the charity work," Weesie said. "There was a lot of that. And there were school committees, and ladies luncheons, and bridge groups. Our days were a lot busier than you think. And of course we had to keep our husbands happy. Wives were a lot more concerned in those days about keeping their husbands happy."

"I guess *The Feminine Mystique* ruined all that," Stella said.

"The what?" Weesie said.

"Being a housewife was more exciting than you might think," Adeline said. She looked at Alice. "Remember that time Boofie Lloyd outran the police on her way home from The Girls Cotillion board meeting?"

Weesie giggled. "I had forgotten that," she said.

Stella looked from one to the other. "She outran the police?" she said.

"It was meatloaf night," Alice said, settling down to the story. She was always confident when a memory came back to her, clear and indisputable. "The maid's day off and the only thing Boofie knew how to cook was meatloaf. Charles Lloyd was awfully partial to Boofie's meatloaf and she knew he'd be angry to come home to a dark house with no supper made."

"She did make a good meat loaf," Weesie said.

"So she was in a big hurry coming home late and she was driving a little too fast," Alice said.

Adeline made a wry face. "And the cop was waiting for her there at the foot of Lookout."

"Did he have his lights on?" Stella said.

"Oh, yes," Alice said. "Boofie looked in the rearview mirror and she saw the flashing lights and she knew how mad Charles would be if she came home late *and* with a speeding ticket. So she just stomped on it."

"Stomped on what?" Weesie said.

"The gas pedal."

"Oh."

Stella said doubtfully, "But how could you outrun the police coming up a mountain?"

"You'd have to want to do it bad," Adeline said.

"What was she driving, a Maserati?" Stella said.

"Buick Estate Wagon."

"Oh come on!"

"You'd have to know Boofie," Alice said.

"She had one of the first electric door openers on the mountain. So as she came screeching around that last corner onto her street, she hit the button and the door went up and she pulled in and shut off the car. The door was almost down again when the cops went by with their sirens flashing."

They all chuckled, remembering. Stella looked from one to the other.

"I remember when she got that garage door opener," Adeline said. "She didn't even want it but Charles made her take it."

"Good thing," Alice said.

Across the lawn a pair of squirrels chased each other along Sawyer's steeply pitched roof.

"Wow," Stella said. "She sounds crazy."

"She was a character," Alice said.

"I liked her better when she was younger," Adeline said. "She got to be a real complainer later on."

Alice said to Stella, "She was one of those people who always had something wrong with her. Always complaining about some operation she was going to have."

"It got so bad after awhile that even her daughter, Rose, didn't like going over to see her. *I'm going to die, she'd say. There's something wrong with me and I'm going to die.*"

They were all quiet for a moment and Stella waited patiently, looking around the room. "So what happened to her?"

"She died," Alice said.

"Rose came in one morning and she was lying in her bed. Dead."

No one said anything. Outside the long windows, the late afternoon sun fell through the arching branches of the trees, dappling the lawn with shade.

"So maybe there was something wrong with her after all," Stella said.

Weesie sighed.   Adeline shrugged her shoulders. "Maybe," she said.

"You have to understand this went on for over thirty years," Alice said to Stella. "She could have died from anything."

Stella got up and began to collect the empty glasses.

"I think she did it out of spite," Adeline said. "Because no one believed her and she wanted to prove them wrong."

"Laura, see if there are any of those macaroons in the refrigerator," Alice said.

"I'll see what I can find." Stella turned and walked out.

Weesie slowly swiveled her head. She stared at Adeline and then at Alice. "You called her Laura," she said.

"Did I?"

"Yes," Adeline said. "You did."

"Who's Laura?" Alice said mildly.

Alice was tired after they left and Stella made an early supper. They usually ate around six-thirty so Alice could watch *Wheel of Fortune* at seven, but tonight she looked so tired, Stella didn't think she'd be able to stay awake until then.

They ate quietly, staring at the wall calendar marked with the caregivers' schedules.

"That new girl, Rita, comes on Friday," Alice said, finishing her barbecue pork.

"Is she nice?"

"Very nice. She has a granddaughter that she takes care of. Her son is divorced and he lives with her. He has the granddaughter and Rita is always taking her out and buying her prom dresses. I guess the girl expects that."

"Girls can be expensive."

"They always want you to buy them things," Alice said, starting in on the rest of her coleslaw. "When I was a girl, if my mother wouldn't buy it for me, I'd call grandmother."

"And did that work for you?"

"Always."

In the distance, a train whistle blew, deep and mournful. Stella had always hated the forlorn sound of a passing train; it depressed her, made her think of grief and loneliness and lost opportunities. Perhaps it was because her father had taken a train when he left her mother, bound for New Orleans. She pulled the crusts off the rest of her peanut butter sandwich and pushed them to the side of her plate.

Alice said, "When I first married Bill, he asked me did I want him to open up a charge account for me down at Louella's. Have you ever heard of Louella's?" She turned her head slowly, her opaque eyes resting on Stella.

"No."

"Well, it's gone now. But in my day it was where all the young wives went to shop. I'd never heard of a charge account but when he explained to me how it worked and asked me did I want one, I said, *Yes, please.*" She finished the last of her okra and stared at the wall, her jaw moving slowly. Stella got up and began to clear the dishes.

"What's happened to Dob?" she said, trying to move Alice away from the melancholy memory of her dead husband. "We haven't seen him for awhile."

"He's been up visiting his son in North Carolina. You know the son and his wife have seven children."

"Seven?"

Alice chuckled. "That's what I said. Anyway, he's back so I expect we'll hear from him shortly."

Stella fixed Alice a scoop of mango ice cream and set it down in front of her.

"Oh, goody," Alice said. "Mango." She ate for awhile in silence, staring straight ahead and bringing the spoon slowly to her mouth. After awhile she stirred and said, "They're having a birthday party tonight for Charles Gaskins. Dob's going to that. He and Dob used to play together as boys."

Stella rolled her paper placemat into a thin cone. "Is that the Charlie who used to throw rocks at you when you were a girl? The one with the stammer?"

"He used to hit me on the backside with his slingshot."

"I'll bet you were fond of him."

"Oh yes," Alice said, setting her spoon down. She dabbed her mouth with her napkin. "I never much cared for him when we were younger. Funny thing, though. He grew up to be a war hero. Stormed a German machine gun nest on Omaha Beach, I think it was."

"Really?"

"No one was more surprised than me." She pushed her ice cream bowl away. "Still," she said. "I guess you never know how people will turn out."

After she put Alice to bed, Stella went into the library to wait for the night caregiver to arrive. It was a warm, balmy evening. Outside in the street, couples strolled in the gathering dusk with their dogs. Late spring had always been one of Stella's favorite times of year. As a child she had counted down the days until the end of school, imagining herself splashing barefoot in the creek, riding her bicycle to the municipal pool, lying in the grassy shade beneath the branches of a spreading tree. Those were the summers Stella had imagined and yet the reality was always much different. They were always traveling in the summer, staying with family members or one of Candy's friends in some hot, dusty town while Candy looked for work. Always striking out in search of a new life in a place where no one knew them.

Stella put her head against the back of the wingback chair and stared through the long windows. She didn't want to think about her mother. She felt depressed enough remembering Professor Dillard's phone call. And yet a huge weight had been lifted from her, too. She had been dreading final exams, knowing it was too late to bring her grades up. She had been contemplating dropping out and yet that option had seemed so final, so cowardly, the act of a desperate woman who would not, could not think clearly. Despite making it easier for her in the short term, the medical leave suggested by Professor Dillard did little to reassure her that things would turn out well. She had known for some time that they would not. She had the feeling a reckoning was coming; she would have to pay, sooner or later, for her mistakes. Everyone did.

Across the street, the gas lamps on the stuccoed gate posts of the white mansion came on, beginning to flicker. The lights were on in all the downstairs rooms of the house, glowing cheerfully in the gathering dusk.

Odd, how it had all begun to unravel this spring. She had been in control up until then; she had managed to keep it all tamped down. She had overheard one of her professors say to another, *She's a strong-willed, determined girl. She'll go far in life.* How easily people were fooled. Pretend you are in control and you can convince anyone. Even the cutting had seemed a small thing, restrained and disciplined. Fragile incisions made to release that which couldn't be acknowledged, like holes in an earthen dam, letting just enough trickle out to keep the dam from bursting.

And now she had agreed, in a moment of desperation, to let Professor Dillard counsel her, to poke her fingers in among all the dark crevices where Stella had carefully hidden herself away. To breach those barricades she had so vigorously and painstakingly erected. The idea was excruciating. Humiliating and excruciating.

She closed her eyes. It occurred to Stella that her education in psychology had been less about uncovering the psychic wounds of others, and more about hiding her own. She thought of Alice's comment, *You never know how people will turn out.* But that wasn't exactly true. Who was it who had said, *Character is destiny?*

What a dismal future awaited her, if that was true.

She opened her eyes, staring bleakly at the wall of books. On the top shelf a title caught her eye. *Anna Karenina.* She had never read Tolstoy. She rose and walked over to the bookshelves, and standing on a small step stool to reach the top shelf, she pulled the book toward her. It was a red leather-bound volume with gilt lettering. She opened it, inhaling the musty scent of old paper. An inscription in the front read, *To Alice from her sister, Laura. Summer of 1935.*

Stella stared at the inscription until her vision shimmered and went dark at the center. She held the book to her chest and stepped down, walking carefully across the room to the wingback chair. She opened the book on her lap, fanning the brittle pages with her fingers. The musty scent rose again, reminding her vaguely of something not altogether pleasant, but compelling, and lifting the book she set her face against an open page and breathed deeply. Two fragile, faded pieces of paper fluttered to her lap. The first was a yellowed newspaper clipping showing a photograph of three lovely girls dressed in flowing white gowns, their faces turned in profile. The caption read, *The Sisters Montclair as the Three Graces.* Stella recognized Alice and Adeline. The third, and most beautiful, must be Laura. The lost sister.

She picked up the other scrap and stared down at it, feeling a faint prickling along her scalp. Written in a childish scrawl so faded with age as to be nearly illegible were two lines.

We forgive you.

Please forgive me.

There was a strange humming in her ears. Holding the translucent scrap up to the fading summer light, Stella noticed that her hand was trembling.

Fourteen

§§§

Stella had been to Professor Dillard's house once before for a departmental party.

It was in North Chattanooga, in a neighborhood of small, charming nineteen-twenty bungalows. On the morning after she found the odd scrap of paper in *Anna Karenina,* Stella parked in the street in front of Professor Dillard's house and walked across the lawn. She stumbled once in the neatly-mown grass, catching her toe on a barely-submerged tree root. She had slept poorly the night before, awakened several times by a series of menacing dreams that left her groggy and irritable.

She followed a bricked path around the side of the house to a large wooden gate set in a tall hedge. A sign on the gate read, *Please Come In.*

The back yard was shady and pleasant, a small patch of lawn surrounded by shrubs and trees of varying heights and shades of green. Across the lawn was a small carriage house painted yellow, like the house, with dark green shutters. Professor Dillard's office was on the bottom floor, Stella remembered. An outdoor stairway ran up the side of the carriage house to the floor above. Luke Morgan's apartment.

Professor Dillard had told her Luke was away, spending the summer in New York with his parents.

She knocked on the door of the office and a voice called loudly, "Come in."

Professor Dillard was standing with her back to the door, going through a large gray filing cabinet. "Hello," she said to Stella, turning and indicating two chairs in front of the narrow desk. "Would you like some tea?"

"No. Thanks." Stella was nervous; she could hear it in her voice which had a slight tremor and a touch of hoarseness.

The desk was very sleek and modern. It looked like a door laid over a pair of black trestles, open and small in scale. The two chairs facing the desk were closest to the door, Stella noted, a classic clinical setting. Subtly implying to the patient that should she or he have a freak-out and need to escape, the flight path was clear. A series of built in bookcases covered three walls of the office and on the fourth was a sofa with an Edward Hopper print hanging on the wall above.

"*Morning Sun,*" Stella said.

"Oh?" Professor Dillard said, closing the filing cabinet with her hip. "Do you like Hopper?"

"I think it's interesting that so many of his women seem to be gazing wistfully out an opened window, as if they're looking at something only they can see."

"An interesting observation."

Stella colored, aware that everything she said in this office would be construed in psychological terms. "Have we started already?"

Professor Dillard laughed. "Are you sure I can't get you anything to drink? Water? Coke?"

"No. Thank you." Stella sat down in one of the chairs facing the desk.

Professor Dillard smiled, letting her eyes rest on Stella. She sat down, leaning forward with her arms resting on the desk, her hands clasped in front of her. "I want to reiterate what I said earlier, Stella. If you're not comfortable talking to me, I'm happy to recommend a colleague."

"I'd rather not talk to anyone," Stella said quickly. Professor Dillard continued to smile but said nothing. Stella sighed. "I know. A deal's a deal. And I'd rather talk to you than anyone else."

Professor Dillard opened a file on her desk and made a few notes on a notepad. Outside the window a hummingbird hung motionless above a box of red geraniums.

"You were very courageous to agree to this, Stella," she said. "You seem to be a very confident, self-assured person. Tell me, have you ever seen a counselor before?"

"No."

"We spoke briefly yesterday about you failing some of your classes. You've been a good student up until now. Can you tell me, from your point of view, what the problem might be?"

"You mean, why my grades have slipped?"

"Yes."

"I don't have any money. I have to work to put myself through school."

"And how many hours do you work?"

"I don't know. Twenty-four or so a week."

"And where do you work? What kind of work do you do?"

Stella told her, embellishing the details of caring for Alice so that it sounded like a more demanding job.

"I see," Professor Dillard said. "So you work one job?" She looked at Stella, who nodded in agreement. She glanced down at the file which Stella realized now was her school file. "And last semester you worked for awhile at a work study job and also at a coffee shop, is that right?"

"Yes."

"And how many hours a week did those two jobs total?"

"I don't know. Thirty or forty, I guess."

"So you actually worked more hours last semester and still managed to keep your grades up."

"I didn't work two jobs the whole semester. I had to drop the coffee shop job." Stella shifted uncomfortably in her chair. "Look, I'm under a lot of pressure," she said. "You don't know what it's like always having to worry whether you'll have enough money to pay the rent or buy groceries."

Professor Dillard glanced up at her and then back down at the file. "Actually I do know," she said. She made a few notes on the pad. "But you've always had to work. It's been like that for you from the beginning, hasn't it?"

Stella stared at her. "Yes, I see what you're implying. I've done it all in the past so I should be able to do it all now. I guess I'm just a fuck up."

Again that slight, evasive smile. The professor put the pen down and looked up. "How would you describe yourself, Stella? Would you say you were an optimist or a pessimist?"

"A realist."

Professor Dillard continued to lean forward, still smiling.

"A pessimist," Stella said.

"So, when an unexpected problem crops up, how do you handle it? What are your coping mechanisms?"

"You mean, besides vodka?"

Professor Dillard picked up her pen and made a few notes. "Yes," she said. "Besides vodka."

"I don't know that I have any coping mechanisms," Stella said warily.

"So, the problem that has cropped up between last semester and this semester. The problem that has caused your grades to slip. Can you put your finger on it?"

"No." Stella splayed her fingers, observing them carefully, waiting for Professor Dillard to fill the silence that spread out between them and, when she didn't, Stella said, "I guess I'm just overly anxious. I guess all this time I've been keeping it under wraps and now I'm beginning to feel like I'm losing it."

Outside the window, the hummingbird dipped its beak in the geraniums and then darted away. Sunlight fell in bright squares against the dhurrie rug on the floor.

"So, if you had to put it into words, do you think your problem might be a feeling that you're losing control of your life?"

"I don't know. I guess so. I guess there's some of that."

She scribbled more notes. "Well, you know there's no such thing as a bad feeling or a good feeling. Feelings are just feelings. But I wonder if you can tell me how this problem – this sense that you're losing control – makes you feel?"

"It makes me feel like shit. I can't eat. I can't sleep."

"So, anxious? Depressed? Stuck?"

"Yes. I suppose so."

"How about anger? Do you feel anger?"

"No."

More notes. Stella began to feel like she was being skillfully manipulated, and there was a part of her that looked on and admired Professor Dillard for this. If she disengaged, she could see the professor's handling of this session in purely clinical terms, like watching a training video. From time to time the little voice in her head would trumpet, *So that's how it's done,* as Professor Dillard circled back and smoothly elicited an unexpected response from her. After awhile Stella began to feel dizzy, as if she was being spun around too quickly. She found it harder and harder to muzzle herself. Professor Dillard asked her about her job, whether or not she looked forward to going to work every morning. She asked her about her fleeting moods, if she had ever read self-help books to try and lift her depression (Stella had read countless books but she downplayed this, embarrassed.) She asked Stella how she felt about change, did she set goals for herself? If she had a magic wand what positive changes would she make in her life? She asked Stella what she hoped to gain from counseling and Stella said, *To get out of having to take final exams,* and Professor Dillard laughed. Stella relaxed at this point, grinning.

And then swiftly, and without warning, she touched again on Stella's job with Alice.

"You could probably make more money waitressing or bartending," she said.

"I suppose so."

"Then why do you stay?"

"She needs me."

"So you have an emotional attachment to this woman?"

Stella hesitated. "I suppose so."

"Do you see her as a mother figure? Someone who nurtures you and cares for your emotional needs?"

"No. I take care of her."

"Why?"

"Because she's old and infirm and she's too proud to ask for help."

"Why else?"

"Because she's wounded."

"Like you?"

Stella turned her head and stared out the window.

"All right," Professor Dillard said, closing the file on her desk. "That's enough for today. But I want you back here tomorrow morning at ten."

"Tomorrow is Saturday."

"Do you work Saturday?"

"No."

"Then according to my calendar, you should be able to come every morning at ten except for Wednesdays and Thursdays."

Stella gave her a long, slightly apprehensive look. "I thought this was going to be a once a week thing," she said.

"We have a lot of work to do in a very short period of time," Professor Dillard said, rising. "I'll see you tomorrow at ten."

It wasn't until her third session that Dr. Dillard asked her about cutting herself. By then Stella had admitted that she was angry sometimes but that she rarely expressed it. She had told Dr. Dillard about living with Josh and her nomadic early life with Candy.

"In our last session we talked quite a bit about unexpressed anger," Dr. Dillard said.

As she talked to Dr. Dillard, Stella could feel a slight shift occurring inside her. It was as if parts of her had been frozen, and were coming forcefully, and painfully, back to life. She felt dizzy at times, almost sick with the emotions that pushed through her. The denial was still there but she was becoming accustomed to touching it like she might worry a bad tooth.

"Why are you angry?" Professor Dillard asked her repeatedly.

"Because life is unfair," Stella said stoutly. "You can't control what happens to you."

"True. But you can control your response to what happens. Don't you think?"

"I don't know. No. If I'm hit by a car and I'm lying in a hospital bed paralyzed from the neck down, what control do I have over anything?"

"Well, it seems to me you have two choices. You can lie there and abdicate your responsibility to yourself, or you can make a conscious decision to get on with your life in whatever way you can."

"But I'm still paralyzed."

"Bad things happen to people every day, Stella. How we respond to those bad things is entirely within our own control."

Stella shook her head stubbornly. She felt irritated with Professor Dillard, her impartial, casual way of looking at things. Her insistence that life could be explained in a rational manner. A bit like Alice in that way, in her calm belief that everything would turn out as it should in the end, as if there was some kind of benign master force at work in the universe. "But sometimes you get worn down by all the shit. Bad luck just seems to follow some people around."

"Do you really believe that? Or do you think some people's perception is merely skewed? I think I'm cursed, therefore I am."

"We're back to that glass half-full, glass half-empty argument again."

"Why are you so angry?"

No matter how many times she answered this question, Professor Dillard found a way to circle back to it, like a hound on the trail of elusive game.

"We've done that one to death, haven't we? I'm angry that I have to work so hard when so many don't. I'm angry that I keep choosing men who aren't worthy of me."

"What about your mother?"

"What about her?" Stella said warily.

"Aren't you angry with her? You told me you were sixteen years old when she drove you to Birmingham and dropped you off."

"She gave me $100," Stella said. "Which is more than most kids get."

Professor Dillard gave her a long, deliberate look. "But that's not the point, is it? How did you feel when she did that?"

"I don't know. I don't remember. Scared I guess."

"Angry?"

"I don't remember."

Dr. Dillard made several notes. "And why did she do this?"

"We weren't getting along. I wanted to go."

"But do you think that's something a parent should do? Abandon a child like that?"

"I wasn't a child."

"Emotionally, and legally, you were."

Stella's stomach bounced beneath her ribs like an acrobat. There was a bitter taste in her mouth, sharp and metallic. "She did the best she could. She had two other children at home to take care of."

"But that doesn't excuse her abandoning you, does it?"

"She didn't abandon me."

"When was the last time you talked to her?"

"I don't know. A couple of months, I guess."

"And did you call her or did she call you?"

"I don't remember."

"What about your stepfather?"

"What about him?"

"You don't ever speak of him."

"We were never close."

"How old were you when he married your mother?"

"I don't know. Nine or ten."

"And how did you feel about your mother marrying?"

"I don't remember. I was happy, I guess, that she'd found someone."

Dr. Dillard switched tactics again and asked Stella how she would rate her happiness on a scale of 0-10.

"What? No negative scale?" Stella quipped.

This brought a flurry of note-taking from Dr. Dillard. She asked Stella, *What wrongs have been done to you that haven't been forgiven?* She asked, *What relationship have you been in that you deem to be a failure?* She asked, *Would you rate your communication skills as negative, neutral, or positive?*

"Positive, I guess," Stella said.

"Positive? So you think you express your anger with people? You communicate that clearly?"

"As well as anyone else I know."

"And when did you start cutting yourself?"

This brought a pause, a moment of hesitation. Stella fiddled with the ends of her sleeves, pulling them down over her wrists. "I don't know. After I left home I guess."

"Soon after your mother abandoned you in Birmingham?"

"I told you. She didn't abandon me. It was a mutual decision."

"What happened, Stella, that made you want to leave home?"

"I don't know," she said quickly. The room shifted suddenly, tilting precariously, and she felt as if she was sliding.

She stretched out a foot and touched the leg of the desk to anchor herself. "There wasn't any room for me anymore. The house was pretty crowded. We were all on top of one another."

"That's an interesting way of putting it."

"Oh, for crying out loud," Stella said. "It's a figure of speech."

"Is there anything else you want to tell me about that time at home, just before you left?"

"There's nothing to tell. I was a rebellious teen. I was experimenting with drugs and other risky behavior and my mother thought I'd be a bad influence on my little brothers."

No matter how cleverly Dr. Dillard circled and pounced, Stella refused to give up her secret. It was all she had, really; a small, hard knot at the center of her being on which everything else rested.

"I think we'll stop here for the day," Dr. Dillard said.

By the end of June, Stella still hadn't told Dr. Dillard what she wanted to hear. Despite this, she went faithfully every day to her session. And as the sunny days of June began to slide into the hot, sweltering days of July she put on a little weight and the color returned to her face. She didn't feel remarkably different, but people around her began to notice a change. Everyone noticed, even Josh.

"Why are you so damn cheerful all of a sudden?" he asked suspiciously.

"Something's happened to you," Alice said. "You seem happier."

"Do I?"

Alice peered at her. "Did you break up with that boyfriend of yours?" She held up one arthritic hand before

Stella could answer. "No, don't tell me," she said. "It's none of my business."

They were reading out in the sunroom on a warm afternoon in mid-July. It was Sawyer's birthday. Stella had heard Alice on the monitor that morning leaving the *Happy Birthday* song on his answering machine.

"Sometimes I say things I shouldn't," Alice said.

"Don't we all."

The phone rang, startling them both. Alice picked it up and it was Sawyer. Stella could hear him clearly.

"Al? I'll be out of town until Saturday."

"Oh, you will? Did you get my birthday greeting?"

"I did."

"I always feel so silly doing that since I can't carry a tune to save my life."

"Well, it was very nice."

"I'm glad you liked it."

"So I'll be gone until Saturday. The housekeeper comes tomorrow and Jerry will come Friday to blow leaves but they're the only people that should be over here."

"Okay, then. You have a nice time."

"I'll see you Saturday."

"Bye, bye." She hung up the phone. She turned to Stella and said, "He says we should water the plants."

"I don't think he said that," Stella said.

Alice frowned and looked through the long windows at Sawyer's sprawling house. "I wonder why he would want me to water the plants. He knows I can't get over there."

"Alice, I'm pretty sure he said his housekeeper was coming tomorrow. I'm sure she'll water the plants."

"Housekeeper? No, the housekeeper comes on Friday."

"Your housekeeper comes on Friday. His comes on Thursday."

"What?"

"*Rachel* comes Friday," she said loudly. "His housekeeper comes tomorrow."

"Oh, all right then. I guess I won't worry about it."

"I don't think we should."

They both went back to reading but after a few minutes Alice mumbled, almost as an afterthought, "Why would he ask me? He knows I don't have a green thumb."

"I think I might be ready to stop therapy," Stella said to Dr. Dillard. "I'm doing a lot better."

"Not yet."

"Why?"

"You know why."

Stella flushed and looked away. She had to admire Dr. Dillard's tenacity although it was tiring at times. Tiring and irritating.

"You're better but there's still work to do."

"I can't keep seeing you for the rest of my life."

"Well, that's really up to you. We had a deal."

"Look," Stella said, pulling up her sleeves. "I'm not cutting. I'm cured. You've done your job."

Dr. Dillard regarded her attentively. "You know better than that," she said.

Absurdly, shamefully, Stella felt dampness start beneath her arms. She pulled her sleeves down and turned her face to the window.

"When you can answer *all* my questions, openly and honestly, then you're ready. When you can bring yourself to confront your mother, you're ready."

Stella swung her head around and gave Dr. Dillard a long searching look. "Confront my mother? What do you mean, call her?"

"No, I don't believe in telephone confrontations. It's too easy for one party to hang up on the other. You can't see each other's facial expressions. Face to face confrontation is the only way."

"I'm not ready for that," Stella said flatly.

"I understand. But when you are, it's an important step. Your mother did the wrong thing, driving you to Birmingham. You know it. She knows it. By confronting her, you give her the chance to express regret, and you give yourself the release of forgiveness. By communicating you open up the possibility of a future relationship with her, if that's what you want. If you don't confront her, you'll stay stuck."

Outside the window, the sky was blue and cloudless. On the deck behind Dr. Dillard's small house, a tabby cat slept in the sun.

"If you don't mind, I thought we'd end a little early today."

Stella shrugged her delicate shoulders. "I don't mind."

Dr. Dillard closed the file on her desk and rose. "There's something I want to show you," she said.

Stella followed her out into the yard and up the stairs to the apartment above. They stood for a moment on the landing while Dr. Dillard fumbled with her keys. She found the right one, turned it in the lock, and pushed the door open. The air inside the apartment was stale and the room was dark. Dr. Dillard went around opening the plastic blinds. The high-ceilinged room was sparsely furnished with a futon and a bookcase and, at the far end, a small table and two chairs framed by a large arched window. A galley kitchen lined one wall. On the other side of the kitchen, a door opened into a bathroom with a claw-foot tub.

"This is very cozy," Stella said. She could imagine Luke Morgan living here, his video equipment cluttering the room. She could feel his presence everywhere, half-expected him, at any moment, to come walking through the door.

"This is the bedroom," Dr. Dillard said, opening a door.

Long windows framed the leafy branches of a large cottonwood. It was like a tree house here, the room dappled with shade, the carpet a cool dark green color. A king size bed and a small chair in the corner were the only furniture.

"He left his guitar and a couple of boxes of books," Dr. Dillard said, opening the closet door.

"Oh?" Stella said, gazing past her shoulder into the gloom of the closet. "Is he coming back?"

"No, I don't think so," Dr. Dillard said, switching on the light. "I thought he was but he told me last week he was heading out to California."

Stella sank down on a corner of the bed with her hands in her lap, feeling an odd sense of disappointment at the news.

"So what do you think?" Dr. Dillard said, lifting her hands to indicate the room.

"I like it. It's very peaceful."

"Are you interested in staying here?"

Stella cocked her head, staring up at Dr. Dillard. "What do you mean?"

"I have an empty apartment. Are you interested in it?"

Stella looked around the tidy bedroom. "How much is the rent?"

"How much are you paying now?"

"I'm supposed to pay $250 a month plus utilities but I'm a little behind."

Dr. Dillard was quiet, considering this. "I tell you what," she said. "If you'll agree to do some light housekeeping a couple of days a week, I'll let you stay here rent free. Just until you get on your feet."

"Oh, I couldn't do that. That wouldn't be fair to you." But the whole time she was thinking, *why not?* She was already imagining her books on the bookshelves, her clothes in the closet.

"It's sitting empty right now. And I could use some help in the house. Danny isn't much of a housekeeper." She laughed and Stella grinned. Danny was her husband. He taught in the History Department.

"It's a really generous offer," Stella said. "Let me think about it." The duvet on the bed was soft and covered in small blue flowers. Stella smoothed it with a trembling hand. She said, "I've never known a guy to leave his guitar behind."

"He'll probably call and ask me to send it to him. I don't think we'll see him again." Dr. Dillard switched off the light and closed the closet door.

"Let me know about the apartment," she said.

Fifteen

§§§

In August, Professor Dillard relented and Stella met with the Dean and the head of financial aid and was reenrolled in school. Walking across campus she was filled with a sense of hope and optimism, a feeling that she was back where she was meant to be, and this time she would not fail. No matter what the obstacles, she would not fail.

She was still living with Josh, although he had taken to spending the night on the sofa in front of the TV, a move that filled her with relief. She had begun to think seriously about Professor Dillard's offer to stay in her garage apartment, although she was concerned how this might affect her counseling sessions, which were ongoing. She had begun to enjoy the sessions, the careful pacing of her confession, the sense of building pressure and release, and she was beginning to see the promise of Dr. Dillard's profession, and what this might mean to her. She could help people. She could make a difference in their lives. The thought of doing such work excited her.

She still had not told Dr. Dillard everything although she had admitted, finally, to being angry at her mother for abandoning her in Birmingham. *Depression is anger turned within,* Dr. Dillard reminded her. They met only once a week now on Tuesday mornings. Stella was no longer nervous; she understood how the sessions were supposed to work and she approached each one with a calm, passive demeanor. She kept her secret safe while the rest of it spooled out. It had become a quiet game of cat and mouse between them, a challenge, something they both seemed to look forward to.

Alice dreamed of leaving. She was on a train and Bill had gone forward to give the tickets to the porter. Sam sat beside her, nestled against her with his hand in the pocket of her traveling coat, his cheek resting on her breast. She was stroking his fine hair with her fingers. The train was empty except for a few well-dressed people she did not recognize.

Outside the window, the crowd was a blur of passing faces. The whistle blew once, a warning.

Several rows up, a young woman sat with her back to them. She was wearing a jaunty little hat with a veil. There was something oddly familiar about the back of her head and her long, slender neck, but she sat rigidly facing the front and Alice could not see her face.

There was a hiss of brakes and then the sharp blast of a whistle, and slowly, imperceptibly, the train began to move. On the front row an elderly couple sat shoulder to shoulder, swaying gently to the rocking of the train.

She could not see Bill now, and she was anxious suddenly that he had gotten off the train, and would be left behind. As if sensing her distress, Sam looked up at her and smiled.

Don't worry, mommy. It will be all right.

Gazing down into his sweet face she was overcome by a feeling of love so intense she could hardly breathe. Her heart swelled and thumped in her chest like a drum. She smiled tenderly, brushing his delicate cheek with her fingers.

The train had begun to pick up speed, shifting and swaying. She could see Bill now, standing at the front with his back to her. She relaxed and turned to the window. The crowd was gone and the train was hurtling through sunlit fields beneath a deep blue sky. Mountains rose in the distance. The warm weight of Sam against her, the drowsy scent of his hair, awakened something in her and the dream shifted suddenly, in the way that dreams do, to another scene.

She was at her grandmother's house and she could see Roddy and Sawyer playing in the yard. She was hovering somewhere above them, unseen, and she could feel herself rising, being drawn away like a feather on a breeze. Her sons were no more than two small figures now, she could see the tops of their heads as they played in the grass, and she tried to call out to them as she rose but neither one could hear her. At the last minute Sawyer raised his blonde head and looked up at her and she knew that he'd been crying.

And then suddenly she was back on the swaying train, hurtling toward some unknown destination. She felt an overwhelming sense of grief and panic at having left her two sons behind. She tried to call out to Bill, to tell him about the lost boys, but his back was to her, he was sturdily facing the front, and she knew he would not hear her. She put her head down and began to cry.

Sam looked up at her with his bright blue eyes, smiling his angelic smile.

"Mommy, don't be sad," he said in his sweet, sing-song voice.

Mommy.

Don't be sad.

Outside the window, the sky had darkened to a deep purple tinged with gold. Evening was coming on. Alice faced the front, realizing that the scene had changed again. She had the feeling that something cataclysmic was going to happen. The front of the car was flooded now with a bright light, growing ever brighter like the headlight of an oncoming train, and Alice wondered if they were going to collide. The girl at the front of the train was gone. The train lurched suddenly and the elderly gentleman took off his hat and set it on his lap, touching the old woman gently on the shoulder, and it was then that Alice, with a flutter of anxious surprise, recognized her father and mother.

It was some kind of a strange virus, the doctor told them, something they'd been seeing a lot of out on the West coast and were just beginning to see down here. It was prevalent among certain groups, he said, avoiding their eyes, certain populations. Sam had probably been sick for some time but was just beginning to show the later stages of the disease.

Alice and Bill had gone down to Atlanta to collect him and bring him home to Chattanooga. When she saw him that first time, Alice would not have recognized him. Her beautiful boy, gone. The man in the bed was pale and sweaty and his skin was covered in hideous lesions. His hair had fallen out in clumps so that the scalp showed through under the fluorescent lights, delicate and speckled as a robin's egg.

"Well, my boy, what have you done to yourself?" Bill said in a jovial voice, clasping Sam's slender hand in his own.

He looked up at his father, his eyelids fluttering. "Hello, pops," he said in a thin, hollow voice. He smiled and something of the old Sam surfaced, forcing itself into his haggard features.

Alice leaned over and kissed him. "My darling," she said. "Don't cry, Mother."

His room mate of the past five years, Charles, stood up to greet them. "Mr. and Mrs. Whittington," he said. "Thank you for coming."

Alice wanted to say, "You can run along now. His mother has come." She wanted to say, "Why are you here?"

Bill still had hold of his hand, pumping foolishly. "We'll have you out of here in no time, old sport," he said.

"Sure, pops."

His beautiful hands were lumpy and veined like the hands of an old man. "When they come to put in the IV the veins disappear," Charles told them, his eyes bright with love and awe and something else. (Relief, Alice guessed. Relief that it was not him lying in that bed.) "It's as if the vein senses the coming needle and hides itself away."

Sam was forty-two and he looked eighty. The shock of his appearance brought it home to Alice, all the words the doctor had said that she had taken in without understanding. No cure. Final stages. End of life plan.

She would bargain with God.

She searched and found a small chapel on the bottom floor. She was glad now that it was a Catholic hospital, glad for the chance to express this altered version of herself, a woman who could fall on her knees and pray sincerely and unselfconsciously for miracles. A woman who believed that miracles were possible.

The chapel was empty. She slid into one of the pews, pulled down the kneeling bench, and knelt to pray. Please God, don't take my child. I'll do anything you say. I'll become anyone you want. What could she offer? Her life for his. Her health, her wealth, her reputation. Not the other children, though. She snatched this thought away quickly. Bill? No, Bill must do his own bargaining.

The stained glass window at the front shone weakly in the dim light. It showed Saint Jude in a field of lilies carrying a golden image of Christ on his chest. Saint Jude, the patron saint of lost causes. She prayed to him. She prayed to The Virgin Mary. "You who know a mother's pain at the loss of a son, spare me."

She promised rebuilt orphanages, foster children taken in and healed, mission trips to Africa. In the end the prayer took on an angry, wheedling tone.

Not my son, not my son, so help me God, not my son.

When he died, it was Bill who fell apart and Alice who made the arrangements. She moved through the hospital, bright-eyed, competent, insistent. No one observing her heightened color, her bossy instructiveness, her ever-ready wit would guess she was a grieving mother.

They took him back to Chattanooga to bury him among his ancestors. The day was cold and wintry, the sky dark and overhanging. A perfect day for a funeral, she heard someone say, and that part of her that held itself aloof agreed. She felt as if the world was expanding around her and she was growing smaller, shrinking to the size of an atom. The minister's voice was calm, forceful in its reassurances of God's love and the promise of resurrection. She imagined herself floating away, rising up above the gathered crowd and the somber landscape, drifting high above the tree tops and the distant ridges of the mountains. Below her, the world seemed to be growing smaller, less relevant.

In the end it was Bill who brought her back. His touch on her arm anchored her, brought her crashing down to earth. She felt hollowed out by grief, a mere husk, a loose assortment of skin and tissue held together by only the most fragile web of tendons. In the car he said in an anguished voice, "Oh Al, how will we bear it?" and it was then that she let herself go. They collapsed against one another,

*shaking and weak. Despite all the things that had gone wrong in their
marriage, they had a history shared only by the two of them, and now
that history included the death of a child.*

*It was at that moment of terrible grief that she realized she had
never loved him more, had never been more grateful for her choice.*

Arriving at Alice's house on a hot August morning, Stella
found that Elaine had unlocked the front door so that it stood
open behind the glass storm door. As always now when she
entered Alice's house, walking quickly past the sunlit library,
Stella thought of *Anna Karenina* and the faded scrap of paper
nestled in its pages. She had yet to read the novel but she had
on several different occasions, taken out the translucent scrap
to stare at it, feeling that odd prickling of her scalp each time.

We forgive you.

Forgive me.

Who had written it? And why had Alice saved it all these
years? There was no doubt that the sister, Laura, had died and
that her death had caused some kind of rift in the family,
something so deep that neither Alice nor Adeline would speak
of her. But how had she died, and when? Stella had searched
the web for information on Laura Montclair but the name was
common enough for there to be many matches, and there was
no way of knowing what her married name might have been.
Without more information, an Internet search would be
fruitless.

She wondered if Charlotte might know. She wondered if
Charlotte would tell her if she asked.

Elaine was loading the breakfast dishes into the
dishwasher when she walked in.

"Hello."

Elaine glanced over her shoulder. Her hair was pulled into a thick braid that fell nearly to her waist. "Hello," she said. She pulled out the half-filled upper rack and dropped in two coffee cups. "You know you're not supposed to run this unless it's full," she said to Stella. "They don't like us wasting water and electricity."

"Oh, I never use the dishwasher," Stella said. "I wash everything by hand."

She went into the sunroom to put her purse and her backpack down on the table. When she came back into the kitchen, Elaine was writing something in the book.

"How'd she sleep?" Stella asked.

"She didn't," Elaine said, writing. "She was very restless. She kept waking up and asking me what that bright light in the hallway was."

Stella glanced over at the pile of towels that lay on the floor in front of the basement door. "Am I the only one who ever takes the laundry down?"

"No one else likes going down there."

Stella stared at her blankly. "What do you mean?"

"It's creepy down there. And it smells funny."

"So you mean they're afraid to go down?"

Elaine pursed her lips and looked up from the book, giving her a long impassive stare. "I suppose so," she said.

"You told me before there were no ghosts."

"I said I'd never seen one."

"So you're not afraid to take the laundry down then?"

Elaine smiled serenely and shook her head. "Oh, I never go down to the basement alone," she said.

Alice was sitting up in bed when Stella walked in.

"Good morning, Stella," Alice said.

"Good morning. Did you sleep well?"

"Yes. Very well, thank you." Alice had been to the beauty parlor the day before and her hair was neatly combed and styled. She cocked her head at the window, listening. "Has Elaine left?" she said.

"Yes. She just clocked out."

"Good." Alice's face brightened for a moment and then fell. She seemed preoccupied, her lips moving slightly as she stared out the window. Looking at her, Stella wondered what Alice thought about at times like this. She was a mysterious, contradictory woman. She kept her secrets well and Stella knew a thing or two about keeping secrets, and admired her for it. Yet there were moments when Stella could not help but wonder, watching an expression of deep sadness and regret flicker across Alice's face, if the effort it took to keep such secrets was truly worth the emotional damage.

"Is everything all right?"

Alice turned her head. "Yes."

"You feel okay this morning?"

"Better than I've felt in some time." Despite her preoccupied manner, her voice sounded firm and strident. She began to edge her legs toward the side of the bed, readying herself to stand. "I wonder if we might go into the library for a bit this morning."

"Sure," Stella said, hurrying to move the walker closer.

Alice rose slowly. She stood leaning on the bars of the walker, fixing Stella with a mild, deliberate expression. Her mouth trembled slightly. After a moment, she dipped her chin and dropped her shoulders as if a matter of great importance had been settled.

"I have a story I'd like to tell you," she said.

"Good," Stella said. "I love your stories."

"It's about people you won't know. They've been gone a long time."

"That's all right."

Alice looked up, her eyes searching Stella's face. "It's something I've never told anyone."

Stella straightened, returning her gaze. Her heart began to thump furiously in her chest. She felt again that odd, fleeting uneasiness she sometimes felt when hurrying up the basement stairs. As if there might be something on her heels, something unpleasant and inescapable.

Alice said, "I'm afraid it might be something of a – burden."

Stella steadied herself, forced her breathing to slow. She put one hand out and touched Alice on the arm.

"You can tell me anything, Al," she said.

Sixteen

§§§

Summary, 1935

Every time she met Brendan Burke she told herself it would be the last time.

In the beginning, she managed to keep herself detached, to look at the two of them from a distance, as if she was observing two compelling characters in a public place. He took her to out-of-the-way cafes and restaurants; she always met him at some prearranged spot, he never picked her up at the house. It was easy to make excuses to her parents, to tell them she was meeting friends for dinner or a movie. And in the beginning she still accepted dates with other young men, so it was not difficult keeping her mother off-guard.

But as the summer wore on and she began meeting him more frequently, two or three times a week, she found it more and more difficult to accept dates with others. This should have been a warning to her. An omen. He was different from the other men she had dated, more contained, less willing to reveal himself through false politeness, and she found this quality attractive. He was moody and easily offended by a word or a glance, and whereas in the beginning this hadn't bothered her, she now began to weigh her words carefully.

To celebrate the fourth of July, they made arrangements to meet at the river for a picnic. The rest of her family was attending a neighborhood barbecue and Alice was to attend, too, but at the last minute she came downstairs in her dressing gown, complaining of a cold.

"But I've told the McAfees you are coming," her mother said in a disbelieving voice. She was wearing a wide brimmed hat that shaded her face. Adeline and Laura stood behind her, properly dressed and ready to go. It was the first time in weeks that Alice had seen Laura out of bed, and she looked pale and sickly, her face swollen from the medications the new doctor was prescribing.

"A summer cold is the worst kind," her father said, coming briskly into the entry hall where his family waited. He touched Alice on the forehead and then glanced at his wife. "If she's unwell, she mustn't come," he said.

"Why must I go if Alice doesn't have to?" Laura said. She wore a shapeless flowered dress and a hat that hid most of her face beneath its brim.

"Because you haven't been out of the house in weeks and a little company will do you good," her mother said, taking her shoulders and giving them a tight squeeze as if to put an end to any argument.

Laura's pale eyes settled for a moment on Alice's face.

Alice blew her nose loudly into a handkerchief.

"Well, I don't want to go to this boring old barbecue either," Adeline said, raising her chin. She twirled the sash at her waist, staring at herself in the mirror.

"And that's enough out of you, too," Mrs. Montclair said firmly, pushing Adeline ahead of her toward the door.

"Best behavior," Mr. Montclair said, wagging one finger in Adeline's face. "Remember who you are."

It was his favorite admonition to his daughters when they left the house. *Remember who you are*, as if the family's grand reputation rested entirely on their narrow shoulders.

Mrs. Montclair pulled on her white gloves, calling to Nell over one shoulder. Nell appeared in the doorway of the dining room.

"Nell, bring Miss Alice a hot water bottle and some of that chamomile tea."

"Yes, ma'am," she said.

"Oh, mother, don't make a fuss," Alice said.

"Back to bed," her mother said, taking Alice's chin in her gloved fingers and giving it a little shake.

Adeline opened the front door and stepped out into the hot, humid day, Mr. Montclair following her to the sedan that sat idling in the circular drive.

"Come along, darling," Mrs. Montclair said to Laura, going ahead of her through the door.

Laura stood gazing at her feet; and then suddenly she looked up, tilting her head so that her face was visible under the brim of her hat. Her gaze, direct, scornful, considered, caught Alice by surprise. Even in sickness, she was beautiful, her long neck rimmed by heavy waves of golden hair. Without another word, she turned and followed her mother out into the bright sunshine.

Alice stood at the opened door staring after her. She had meant to tell Laura from the beginning that she was seeing Brendan. She had practiced a casual speech in her bedroom, but each time they were together, Laura had looked at her calmly, expectantly, and she had been unable to go on. And now it was too late; too much time had passed and such a confession would sound forced and cruel no matter how casually Alice tried to make it. The shock would be too great.

Still, it would be better if she could confess her feelings to someone. It was hard to know this much happiness and not be able to express it. Lately, she had begun to feel a lingering resentment toward Laura, a feeling that her own happiness was being sacrificed to Laura's childish whims.

But now, noting Laura's swollen ankles and her air of defiant resignation as she walked across the sunlit courtyard and climbed into the sedan behind her mother, Alice could not help but feel a fleeting sense of pity for her sister.

She took the trolley and got off a few blocks from The Chattanooga Hotel. The trolley was crowded with 4th of July merrymakers on their way up to Point Park, and as she stepped off into the glaring sun several young men in Panama hats whistled and waved streamers at her. The heat was nearly unbearable as she set off toward the red brick hotel, and she wished now she had asked Brendan to meet her at the trolley stop. The town was strangely deserted after the parade, most of the shops closed and the awnings down. Ahead she could see the small, squat Blue Bird Café and behind it the parking lot where she had agreed to meet him.

He was waiting in the car with the windows down. He had taken off his jacket and laid it across the back seat, and rolled his shirtsleeves so that his forearms were bare. His hair, stirred by the humid breeze, fell boyishly over his forehead. When he saw her he smiled and got out, going around to open her door. She thought he might kiss her, there in the sunlit parking lot where anyone could see, but he didn't.

"Let's get a breeze going before I melt," she said, sliding in and lifting her hair off the back of her neck. She removed her hat and fanned herself. He started the car and drove north through town, crossing the river and then turning left at Suck Creek Road. They followed the road for miles, the creek glinting through the trees to their right, past modest farms and houses, and later, junkyards and tarpaper shacks.

"Where exactly are we going?" she asked, drowsy with the heat. The wind roared through the car, blowing their hair around their faces.

"The Blue Hole." He glanced at her. "Ever been there?"

"No."

"Really? Never been swimming at the Blue Hole? You haven't lived until you've dipped your sweet toes into the icy waters of the Blue Hole." He glanced down at her feet when he said this, laughing, and she colored, remembering how he had lifted one foot and delicately kissed the arch, his expression one of curious and attentive devotion. It was an expression she had begun to look for during their lovemaking, an almost worshipful turning inward, a monk-like attention, an act of pure faith. It gave her a feeling of awe and power that she could be the cause of such feeling.

They turned right at the top of a rise and drove along a narrow rutted road toward the creek. Arching trees and brambles closed in around them, pressing against the sides of the car. The breeze had died and the heat was thick and close, heavy with the scent of honeysuckle and wild mint. The car bumped and jolted along the rutted track and Alice put a hand on the dash to steady herself. Sweat trickled down her back. Ahead she could see an opening in the brush and beyond that a glinting ribbon of water.

Just as the heat became unbearable, they broke through suddenly into a clearing and the breeze began again, soft and warm. They were on a rocky bluff overlooking the swiftly moving creek. A narrow path led down to the water's edge through a collection of large tumbled boulders and thick clumps of rhododendron, their flowers swarming with bees. On the opposite side, rock cliffs rose into the cloudless sky.

"Where's the Blue Hole?" she said, climbing out of the car and stretching languidly.

"Be patient. You'll see." He took the lunch pail and started down the trail, and she set her hat firmly on her head and followed him. He walked with a long swinging stride, his shoulders straining against the white cotton shirt, as sure-footed as a mountain goat along the rocky trail. Half-way down, he stopped and waited for her.

"I didn't know we'd be walking so far," she said breathlessly. "These aren't the best shoes for this."

"Do I need to carry you?"

She gave him a defiant look and leaned and slipped off her shoes.

The trail turned sharply to the left and followed the creek for half a mile before it rose again through a series of rocky ledges. The woods were dense here, thick stands of spruce and fir and steep slopes dotted with wild hydrangea. He stopped again at the top of the trail, waiting for her, and then started down on the other side. The stream narrowed, roaring loudly through rocky cliffs on both banks. Large boulders created a natural dam and a pool of slowly moving blue water, while further downstream, another line of boulders created a series of cascading falls. The bank of the creek was dark and slick and shaded by hemlocks and rhododendrons. Several wide flat rocks extended into the pool and, jumping up on one of them, Brendan crouched and set the lunch pail in the cool shallows.

He put his hand out to Alice and pulled her up on the rock beside him. Sunlight streamed between the tall trees, glinting off the blue water of the pool.

"How deep is it?" she said, leaning against him and smelling the hot starched scent of his shirt, his own familiar smell mixed with the scent of tobacco and cologne and, very faintly, whiskey.

"Deep." He pointed to the cliffs on the opposite shore. "We dive from those sometimes. To my knowledge, no one's ever touched the bottom."

"That sounds dangerous."

"Only if you don't know what you're doing."

He looked down at her and grinned. Pulling her close, he kissed her roughly, and then let her go.

She swayed, leaning lightly against him. She said, "How far is the Suck?"

"It's downstream from here, where the creek empties into the river. And it's only dangerous in the spring when the heavy rains come."

Alice had grown up on stories of The Suck, her father's tales of the notorious whirlpool on the Tennessee River where many a poor settler and his family had drowned. In the old days, settlers had come down the creek on flatbottomed barges, and Chief Dragging Canoe had stationed his warriors in the cliffs overlooking the river to pick them off as they attempted the treacherous crossing. Those that the Cherokees didn't kill, The Suck often did.

"Should we eat first or swim?" Brendan said. Looking up at his dark face, the high cheekbones, the startling green eyes, she felt a tremor low in her belly, a swelling of shame and desire.

"Swim," she said.

She had been unprepared for the intensity of the sexual act, the obliterating spasm of orgasm. She had, of course, discovered said spasm years before through a long line of ardent, imaginary lovers, but had never experienced it in the company of another. It seemed almost too private an act, too exquisitely personal to be shared, and yet each time she felt more connected to Brendan, less lonely in the world than before.

Neither one of them ever spoke of love. It wasn't necessary.

Their feelings were expressed through their actions, their ravenous mouths and hands. All was surrender and exquisite release, skin against skin, taste, smell, grateful murmurings. There was no need for words; words would disappoint, diminish, render the extraordinary ordinary.

Alice had engaged in heavy petting with boys at college, but it had never been like this. There had always been a feeling of alarm and embarrassment, followed by mild irritation. Small pleasures easily forgotten. A feeling, after it was over, that she never wanted to see the boy again.

It had never been like that with Brendan, not from their very first kiss that night at the River Rat Club. Kissing him was like falling, like stepping off a high place, a sense of letting go. And pleasure, too; the softness of his lower lip, the light but insistent pressure of his tongue. Above all, a feeling of familiarity and acceptance, as if she was where she was meant to be, as if everything that was happening to her was long-ago preordained.

And the act itself, when it finally came, was easy, too. Not something they had discussed, not something he had pushed on her (he had always been the one to stop), just a sense of sinking into pleasure, and pain too, an act as natural and necessary as breathing. Once they began there was no turning back. They made love in his car, parked along the river at night, and twice at some travel cabins just across the Georgia state line.

"I'm pretty sure the things we've just done are illegal in the Sovereign State of Georgia," he said one night, driving back to Chattanooga. He looked at her with mock gravity. "I suppose now I'll have to marry you."

She laughed.

She was careful not to be seen with him in public places where people she knew might frequent. She told her parents nothing and they didn't seem suspicious. Unlike Laura, she had never lied to them in order to throw herself at some unsuitable young man and they had no reason to doubt her.

What the future held for them, she did not stop to think. She was happy just to spend the summer in his arms, sinking ever deeper into the heart of love, blithely oblivious to the world and its workings.

The water of the Blue Hole was cold. Breathtakingly cold. The edges were lined with large rocks but the center was deep and clear, and they swam back and forth, splashing one another and diving into the frigid depths. Despite her cries of alarm, Brendan climbed to the top of the cliffs and dove, his body hanging motionless mid-air, before plunging smoothly into the blue-green depths. He dove several times, and she was relieved, each time, to see his dark head surface, sleek and shining.

Despite the heat, they were the only ones there, although Brendan warned her others might appear at any time. It was a popular swimming hole. This fact gave their lovemaking urgency, and when he pushed her beneath a rock ledge and slid down the straps of her swimming suit, she didn't protest but laughed and trembled with excitement.

Afterwards they stretched out on a warm flat rock and sunned themselves. They fell asleep and when they woke a short time later, still drowsy with the heat, he rose and went to fetch the lunch pail. She lay on her back and watched him, his wide shoulders tanned by the sun, his spare, yet muscular body. He was not overly tall, but he was quick and lithe in his movements like an athlete.

"Should I bring it to you?"

She dropped one arm lazily across her eyes. "Do you mind?" she said.

He pulled the bucket up and carried it across the rocks to where Alice lay sunning. There were four bottles of beer, and ham sandwiches and hardboiled eggs wrapped in waxed paper, and a tin of olives. She sat up, cross-legged, and they ate in silence, enjoying the whir of the insects and the faint roaring sound of the creek. Overhead through the trees, great white clouds drifted.

He drank two beers in quick succession, but she drank only one, setting the other one back in the pail.

"Have it, if you like," she said.

She lay down on her back, closing her eyes against the glare of the sun. "I wish I could stay like this forever," she said.

"We can stay like this forever," he said.

He opened the last beer and stretched out beside her, raising himself on one elbow. He touched the bottle to the bridge of her nose, the warm spot between her breasts, farther down between her thighs.

She jumped and pushed his hand away. "Behave," she said.

She hadn't told him about her plans for New York which, as the summer passed, had grown more and more distant. Clarice had gone up to Manhattan and gotten an apartment and a job as a stenographer for an advertising company, but Alice had yet to answer her last three letters.

"I can't stay much longer," she said. "I have to be home before my parents get back from the barbecue. I told them I had a cold and they'll expect to find me in bed."

He set the bottle down carefully on the rock. "You could stay if you wanted to."

She turned her head and put one hand up, shading her eyes. "I can't. You know I want to, but I can't."

He stared at her until she closed her eyes, dropped her hand. "All this sneaking around is beginning to wear on me," he said.

"You know it can't be any other way."

"Why?"

"You know why."

"Because your father thinks I'm a social-climbing rogue?"

"Because of my sister," she said gently. But it was true, although she didn't like to admit it, even to herself, that she couldn't bear the thought of telling her father about him. She couldn't bear the thought of her father's disbelief, his stern and implacable disappointment.

A troubled look crossed Brendan's face, followed quickly by an expression of sly exuberance. He sat up suddenly and, taking her hands, pulled her upright. "Marry me," he said.

She stared into his face, into his eyes which were lit now by a look of expectation and something else – fear, perhaps, or wounded vanity. She smiled foolishly at him but said nothing.

He let go of her hands and rose and walked to the edge of the rock, taking the beer with him. He stood with his back to her, gazing down at the shaded pool, tipping his head to drink. She knew she had hurt him. There had been times, in her early daydreams, when she had imagined a life with him, scenes of ironic domesticity, wedded bliss, but as their passion grew, she had let go of those daydreams. It was the price she paid for her guilt, the knowledge that the affair would end and she would go on without him. It was the only thing that made these meetings possible; her acceptance that they must eventually stop. She could not hurt her sister. She could not disappoint her parents. To marry him was unthinkable.

And yet there was a part of her that, even now, stirred with subtle anticipation and selfish possibility. Staring at his wide back, the graceful narrowing of his hips, she thought, *Why not?*

He leaned and began to collect his scattered clothes.

"We better get back," he said. His manner had changed; he was suddenly brisk and business-like.

She stood and walked over to him, letting her hand rest for a moment on his shoulder. "Don't be angry," she said.

"I'm not angry." He smiled down at her, pulled his shirt over his head. He had the air of a man who fears he has made a fool of himself and must compensate now by a show of measured indifference. They dressed in silence, their backs to each other. The sun had begun to sink above the distant ridge tops and the heat of the afternoon was dying down. Long shadows lay across the pool. The day, which had begun so bright and promising, had turned dim, oppressive. Alice shivered as she buttoned her dress. She hoped her parents had not returned from the barbecue. The last thing she wanted on this day, of all days, was a scene with her mother.

He said, "There's a place I want you to see." He tucked his shirttail into his trousers. His face and neck above his white collar were burned red by the sun. "Have you ever heard of the McGuire Farm?"

She ran her fingers through her wet hair. "Of course I have."

"Have you ever been there?"

"Once. When I was small."

"I'll take you." He stepped into his shoes and leaned to tie the laces. "When we first moved here from Kansas, my father was the caretaker. The family had moved into town but they still used the Big House on special occasions, and my father and I lived in the caretaker's cabin in the back. I still have a key."

"Won't they mind?"

He rose slowly and looked past her at the pool. "No. I'll ring Frank McGuire to make sure it's okay."

"All right." She was glad there was no more talk of marriage. Glad and a little disappointed, too, that he'd given up so easily. "When will we go?"

"Sometime next week." He continued to stare at the water, his eyes narrowed, considering. His dark hair curled wetly above his ears. "You'll like it there," he said. "It's the best spot in the valley for looking at the night sky."

And without touching her again, he leaned and picked up the pail, and started slowly up the path.

Alice managed to arrive home before her family got back from the barbecue. She hurried to her room, undressed, and climbed into bed, quickly drinking the chamomile tea that Nell had left on her bed stand. She was sitting up in bed reading when there was a faint knock on the door.

"Come in."

Laura entered, dressed in a faded housecoat and a pair of old slippers, her dark blonde hair hanging limply around her face. She was carrying a book in her hands. "How are you feeling?"

"Rested. Although a bit feverish."

"Oh? Shall I call mother?"

"Please don't."

Laura smiled, advancing slowly into the room. In the lamplight she looked pretty, but pale.

Alice said, "How was the barbecue?"

"Horrible. Mother seems determined to throw me at the Timmons boy."

"Oh God."

"Yes, exactly."

Alice grinned. "Well, it's nice to know she's taking a rest from throwing me at Bill Whittington."

"Oh, she hasn't given up on Bill. She still fancies him for a son-in-law."

They could hear their father's heavy footsteps on the stairs. The wide central staircase carried sound easily from the floor below. He walked down the long hallway and into his room, closing the door behind him. Faintly, in the distant reaches of the house, they could hear their mother's shrill voice.

Alice looked at Laura. "She isn't coming up, is she?"

"Not for awhile. She's planning the menu with Nell." Laura made a wry face. "The Timmons are coming for dinner next Friday."

"Lucky you."

"Yes. Lucky me." Laura sat down on the edge of the bed. She held the book out with both hands.

Alice took it. "*Anna Karenina,*" she said, turning it over carefully to look at the spine.

"Have you read it?"

"Yes. Well, no. I got through *War and Peace* and that was enough Tolstoy for me. What's it about?"

Laura hesitated, regarding her mildly. "Love," she said.

"Love?" Despite her sister's mild expression, Alice could feel her face warming.

"Unrequited love."

"Oh." She set the heavy book down on her lap.

The tinny roar of the radio reached their ears. Adeline was in the library below, no doubt listening to *The Adventures of Gracie,* her favorite show. Laura turned her head, listening. Alice put a hand out and tucked her sister's hair gently behind one ear. "Laura, are you all right?"

She gave Alice a brief, piercing smile. Dark crescents bloomed beneath her eyes. "Well enough," she said.

"The new medication seems to make you tired."

"Oh, yes. Very sleepy. I sleep all the time but I don't have dreams. Isn't that odd?"

"Have you mentioned it to the doctor?"

"Yes. But he says I shouldn't worry. He says I shouldn't worry about anything."

"Well, he probably knows best."

"I suppose so." She stared down at her lap. After a moment she glanced up at Alice, her eyes grave, questioning. "But what good is sleeping if you can't dream?"

There was nothing Alice could say to this. Below her, she could hear Adeline's unruly laughter in the library, followed by the voice of their mother as she joined in.

Laura seemed to be struggling with something, some interior motive that flickered for a moment across her face, and was gone. After a brief interval she said, "Are you still planning your escape to New York?"

Alice shifted the book in her lap. "Oh, I don't know," she said. "I'm beginning to think I might need to stay home for awhile. You know, to look after mother and father. They're not as young as they once were. Father's cough is no better than it was at Christmas."

"But Clarice is already there? She's written to you?"

Alice frowned, trying to remember how Laura would know this. *She knew because she'd told her.* Weeks ago, on a night with Brendan when she'd come home giddy with happiness, and had felt a need to share that happiness with Laura. A small confession, a consolation prize.

"It seems childish now." Alice ran her fingers carefully over the cover of the book, tracing the gilt lettering. "Those daydreams of running away. Something a girl might do but not a young woman."

Laura's face fell. "Oh?" she said.

"I may still go," Alice said quickly. "When the time is right."

"Yes," Laura said. "When the time is right."

"And of course, if I go, you're welcome to come with me," Alice said, placing the book carefully on the bed.

Laura smiled. "Of course."

She looked so pale and forlorn that Alice leaned and put both arms around her. Beneath her sister's unnaturally plump skin she could feel her bones, as light and hollow as a bird's.

"You can keep the book," Laura said. "I don't want it back."

Alice pulled away, holding Laura's hands and staring into her averted face. The faint, sweet scent of Laura's perfume settled over her. "Laura," she said.

"I want you to have it. It's a gift."

"Laura." Alice tugged at her hands, trying to get her sister to look at her. "Is something wrong?"

Laura slowly turned her head. She gave Alice a long, searching look. "Your face is ruddy."

Alice let go of her. "No doubt from the fever."

"No doubt," Laura said.

The approval from Frank McGuire seemed to take longer than expected, and it wasn't until a starry evening in early August that Brendan and Alice set out for the McGuire Farm. Alice had told her mother she was attending a house party. Unlike previous occasions, her mother had asked a lot of questions, wanting to know where the party was, and who was going to attend, and what time Alice would be home. She and Mr. Montclair were attending a dinner party that evening.

"Be home by one o'clock," her mother said in a mildly threatening tone. "Your father will be waiting for you."

Her mother's suspicions were to be expected given Alice's recent cavalier behavior, the fact that she spent nearly every evening out, but had not had a male escort in nearly three weeks. Or at least one that they knew about. It was only natural that Mrs. Montclair would begin to question Alice's movements. Or maybe someone had seen her and Brendan together, and had called and reported it to her mother. This seemed the more unlikely scenario. Alice felt certain that if her parents knew she was seeing Brendan Burke, they would have immediately tried to put a stop to it.

She didn't care. As each week went by her desire to see him, to be seen with him, became more and more compelling. Her parents finding out about them, the violent confrontation that would most certainly follow did not frighten her now. It would be almost a relief to confess. She was as tired of sneaking around as he was.

He had not asked her again to marry him. Not since that day at the Blue Hole. And perhaps because he hadn't asked, she had begun to contemplate it. What was so unsuitable about him? True, he hadn't gone to the right schools, he hadn't been to college, and although he dressed well, there was a crude, rough edge to him, a hint of rash insecurity. But he was a capable, intelligent, hard-working young man determined to rise in the world, and many family fortunes had been built on such men. If the country club would accept him, surely her friends and family would, too. Eventually.

And as for Laura, well, she was young. She would see that they could not help what had happened, she would forgive them both and go staunchly on with her life, no doubt falling in love with someone else before the summer was even over.

It was around nine o'clock, a warm, sultry evening when they set out. The McGuire Farm was north of the city, set back from the road across wide rolling fields. When they reached it, Brendan pulled off the asphalt and stopped the car. In the distance, the white columns of the old house glistened in the moonlight. Brendan lit a couple of cigarettes and they sat for awhile with the windows down, smoking quietly and listening to the rhythmic chanting of insects. From this angle the house seemed smaller than Alice remembered.

"I was out here once for a party," Alice said. "I went to school with Ava McGuire. I don't remember the house much but I do remember swimming in the pool."

Brendan said nothing, but tossed his cigarette out the window and started the car. They pulled slowly into the road and then took a left at a narrow sandy lane leading up to the house. An iron gate blocked the way and Brendan got out, leaving the car running. He unlocked the padlock, swinging the gate wide. They drove slowly through the gate and down the lane, flanked by rows of arching oaks. Insects, attracted by their headlights, swarmed the front of the car. A small, brown rabbit darted across the road. The trees ended suddenly and the house was visible again across a wide field, more impressive now that they were so close. They pulled into the graveled circular drive in front and stopped. The four white columns of the house were massive. Above the fan-lit front door, a small cantilevered balcony hung suspended from the second floor like an opera box. With the lights of the city behind them, the night sky was clearly visible. Pale clouds drifted like ghosts above the darkened house.

"When I was a boy, I used to stand here in the moonlight and vow that one day this house would be mine."

She smiled, trying to imagine him as a boy.

He tilted his head, giving her a cynical look. "The McGuires, unfortunately, are a large family and somehow I doubt they'll ever sell the place." She could see his features clearly in the slanting moonlight. He gazed at her, his expression fierce, proud. "I won't have this house but I'll have one like it." He said this as if they'd been arguing and he was trying to make a point. Alice, sensing that she should say nothing, stayed quiet. He tapped his fingers against the steering wheel, ran his hand once around its circumference. "The McGuires were thieves you know. There's not a single prominent family that doesn't have at least one thief or murderer in their family tree." She said nothing and he looked at her again and went on. "This house was built originally by a Cherokee chief. The Glass. They say he had a hundred slaves and over five thousand acres of rich bottomland and a house full of china and crystal that came from England. But that didn't stop old Andrew Jackson from forcing him West during the Indian Removal. It didn't keep greedy adventurers like the McGuires from moving onto Cherokee lands and stealing everything they could get their hands on, including this place."

She finished her cigarette and tossed it out the window.

"Same thing with all the families on Lookout Mountain. I'm talking about people like your beau, Bill Whittington. Sure they look and sound like Old Money now, but their forefathers were nothing more than carpetbaggers who came South after the War trying to make a quick buck."

She said quickly, "The Montclairs were in this valley long before the Civil War. Although I guess you would class them with the greedy bastards who came after Indian Removal."

"I'm trying to make a point here."

"And not very subtly either."

She slipped her shoes off and pulled her bare feet up under her, leaning against the door. The darkened windows of the old house stared down at her, dimly reflecting the moonlight.

He lit another cigarette and smoked for awhile in silence.

"I've been rude," he said.

"Yes."

"Forgive me." He put his hand out to her. After a moment's hesitation, she took it.

"Can we go into the house?" she said.

"I don't have a key to the house. Just the gate."

"Pity. It looks like the kind of place that might have a spirit or two lurking in the shadows."

He laughed. "They say it's haunted by The Glass. He put a curse on the land when he was forced to leave, and now every generation of the McGuire family suffers from a host of mysterious and tragic deaths. It's a good thing it's such a large family. There's a graveyard over there on the hill overlooking the river filled with unfortunate McGuires who died before their time."

"Well, I guess it's a good thing you didn't buy the house then."

He grinned and leaned to start the car, his cigarette dangling from his lips. "I guess so," he said.

They pulled around the house and followed a narrow drive past the swimming pool and the garden and a long weathered barn.

"Where are we going?"

"To the caretaker's cottage."

"How far is the caretaker's cottage?" she said.

"Maybe a quarter mile down this road. But there's something I want to show you first."

He patted the seat between them and she moved over. He put his arm around her and she leaned close, nestling against his side, her feet drawn up under her.

"Do you know the constellations?" he said.

"I know a few."

The fields rolled away on either side of the car. The air was heavy with the scent of camphor weed and clover, and in the distance a stand of trees rose, black against the night sky. She was aware of the sturdy weight of his arm, the slight tensing of his muscles as he plucked at her sleeve. The cigarette glowing in the corner of his mouth gave him a mocking, rakish look.

Ahead the road rose slightly and she could see a railroad crossing shining in the headlights. He pulled to the side of the road and parked in the tall grass.

"Come on," he said.

They walked hand in hand toward the crossing, her bare feet sinking in the soft dust of the road. In the moonlight the cross buck looked odd, imposing, like a brooding Celtic cross. The crossing was paved and she could see gleaming tracks stretching away in both directions. He knelt between the tracks and pulled her down beside him.

"What are we doing?" she said.

"I want to show you the constellations."

"This seems dangerous."

"The next train isn't until two o'clock." He pushed her down on her back, kissing her hungrily. After awhile he rolled over, looking up at the sky.

The stars shone in all their glory. Lit by the moon, the sky was gray and luminous, filled with drifting clouds.

"There's Scorpius," he said pointing. "And the bright star there is Antares."

"This is crazy," she said, listening for the sound of the train. Surely they would hear it over the rhythmic chant of the crickets. Or feel it in the trembling of the tracks.

"When I was a boy my father and I used to come out here and lay on the tracks and he would show me the constellations."

She put one hand on the rail, feeling for the vibration of an oncoming train, but there was nothing but heat and the smooth surface of the metal.

He said, "There are no city lights so you can see everything. And the crossing is warm and paved and gets you out of the wet grass."

"There must be less dangerous places to look at the constellations."

He put his hand up, splayed against the night sky, and dropped it back against his chest. His voice, when he spoke again, was slow, thoughtful. "You have to admit, there's something exciting about the idea of a train bearing down on you, the possibility of death coming just around the next bend."

She turned her head and laid her cheek against the warm track, gazing at him. "There was a boy I knew once who was killed walking the tracks. He must have heard the train coming but he didn't jump off in time."

He pointed at the sky. "Saggitarius," he said.

"Some thought it was a suicide but I think he was just flirting with death the way the young do, daring himself to stay on the tracks as long as he could."

"And there," he said. "There's Capricornus."

"I wonder if it hurt. I wonder if death was instantaneous."

He rolled on top of her, pinioning her beneath him. Beneath his slow kisses she began to float, filled with a peaceful contentment. After awhile he stopped, grinning down at her.

"I get the feeling you don't much care for constellations."

She put her hand up and brushed his hair out of his eyes. "I have my mind on other things," she said serenely.

The caretaker's cottage was a two-room cabin with a kitchen lean-to tacked onto the back. There was no electricity or plumbing, only a pump in the kitchen and several kerosene lamps in the front room. Out back, across a narrow strip of tall grass, stood an ivy-covered privy.

"Not what you were expecting?" he said, and she could hear a faint bitterness in his tone. Moonlight flooded the room through a pair of curtainless windows. The cabin smelled of dog and tobacco. He went over to a lantern standing on a small table and struck a match, touching it to the wick. Light flared suddenly. It was a small room, sparsely furnished with two chairs, a large table and several smaller tables. A glass-fronted cabinet holding a collection of hunting and farming books hugged one wall. The walls were chinked logs, as big around as a man's waist. *The original cabin lived in by The Glass*, Brendan had told her, *before he built the Big House*. He lit another lantern, holding it in front of him.

"Here's where we sleep," he said, indicating the room next door.

The bedroom had a mirrored dresser and an old rope bed. He set the lantern down on the dresser and then sank down on the edge of the bed, watching her carefully. She put her hand out and tentatively touched the bed post. She wondered who had last slept in the bed.

"We don't have to stay," he said coldly, noting her expression.

It was true; the cabin was nothing like she had expected. She had pictured a steep-pitched Cotswold Cottage covered in ivy. But what did it matter?

"I want to stay," she said.

He stared at her, his eyes dark in the glowing lamp light. A tremor passed through her, desire flickering between them like smoke. She pulled her dress over her head and stood there in her chemise, her hair falling around her face like a curtain.

"How many girls have you brought here?"

"Dozens," he said.

"I have no trouble believing that."

He unbuttoned his shirt and tossed it on the floor.

"Come to bed," he said gruffly.

Afterwards they lay in each other's arms in the moonlight. The lamp cast a rosy glow and outside the open window crickets chanted. Alice, drowsy from their lovemaking, lay with her back nestled against him, his arm thrown over her waist, his lips nuzzling her hair. The bedclothes were musty but smelled oddly sweet, a vaguely familiar, comforting scent.

"Have you thought about what I asked you at the Blue Hole?" he said. There was a pleading, almost threatening tone to his voice that made her uneasy. She had thought about it incessantly but to have him mention it now seemed to open a gulf between them.

"I've thought about it."

A warm breeze moved listlessly about the room. Far off in the distance, a fox yipped at the moon.

"But you won't do it."

"I didn't say that."

He pulled his arm off her and lay back, looking at the ceiling. She stared through the window at the ghostly landscape.

"You won't do it because your father disapproves of me." He was quiet for a long time. She could hear him breathing behind her. "We could elope," he said finally.

There was nothing she could say to this. She had always sought her father's approval. While Laura ran around and steadfastly refused to change her wild ways, she had always been meekly obedient to her father's wishes.

"He would never forgive me," she said.

"He would. Eventually." When she didn't respond he rose up on one elbow, staring down at her. "What does he have against me anyway?"

She let it hang in the air between them, unanswered.

He said, "I've apologized for the unfortunate business with your sister. It can't be that. It's because I'm the son of a poor man. And he wants more for you. Someone with a pedigree." He added bitterly, "Someone like Bill Whittington."

"He wants me to be happy."

"I can make you happy."

"I don't want to get married," she said, feeling a heavy sense of desperation come over her. "I want to travel."

"We can travel. We can go to Europe if you like."

"You'll have business to attend to. Men always have business."

"There'll be time for other things, too." He didn't say, *And you'll have a life of your own. I promise you that.* He didn't say it anymore than Bill Whittington would have said it. Because it was unexpected, and perhaps unbelievable, that Alice would want such a life, that she would be happy away from the domestic sphere of babies and housekeeping and bridge parties at the Country Club.

"I'll take care of you, Alice. You won't want for anything."

He had never told her he loved her. This thought had never occurred to her, although it did now. Bill Whittington had never mentioned love either. Perhaps it was too old-fashioned, too sentimental to enter into the marriage contract these days. Most engaged couples she knew seemed ideally suited on some basis other than passion; family connections, school ties, social ambition.

As she listened to him plan their future, building his argument so carefully and reasonably that a small part of her could not help but feel it had been well-rehearsed, her dreams of life in New York began to fade.

What was it that she really wanted? She couldn't say. She had built her hopes for the future on what she *didn't* want, which wasn't enough. It seemed to Alice now that she had been living a daydream, a childish fantasy brought on by – what? Her great-grandmother's death in childbirth? Her fear that a man would love her too much, smother her, kill her with his desire? But what else was there for her except marriage? A role as a girl-about-town escort for dances and dinner parties, and later as a kindly maiden aunt who could be expected to send generous birthday presents and swoop in at Christmas with her too-wide bosom and too-exuberant greetings? Women like her did not become nurses or teachers or stenographers. At least not in Chattanooga.

Brendan was still spinning his dream of their life together, and because she had already fallen in love with him and because she wanted to believe that her life might, after all, have some degree of happiness, she let him go on. They would buy a small bungalow first, but later a big house in Riverview.

Their children would be educated. They would prosper and be happy and eventually, with grandchildren, Alice's parents would forgive them. Would welcome them back into the fold with open arms.

And desire. That sweet, smoky excitement so utterly strange to her. A lifetime of lovemaking with Brendan.

There was that to consider.

They made love again and fell asleep and when they awoke the moon was high and the bed was bathed in golden light. Alice rose with a start, aware suddenly of the late time, and the fact that her father would be waiting for her. They dressed hurriedly and drove down the sandy lane past the railroad crossing and the back of the Big House. Crossing the moonlit fields, a large owl swooped above the road. Brendan stopped and locked the main gate, and they turned and headed swiftly back to town.

The whole ride back Alice felt a pinprick of apprehension in her chest, a small glowing ember. It persisted, swelling ominously into a flickering flame as they crossed the river, the streetlamps reflecting their ghostly shapes in the water. She was sustained by Brendan's strong presence, his wide shoulders, his firm and capable profile. He turned to her once, and took her hand and smiled, and she saw in his sleepy eyes that all would be all right. She was comforted by this.

Comfort, once acknowledged, began to establish itself in her heart. She felt sleepy, contented. A drowsy confidence, a sense of letting go and abandoning herself to the consequences of their decision filled her. Even her father's certain condemnation no longer concerned her. As they swept up the wide avenue toward Ash Hill, the lights of the sleeping city laid out below them, she half-expected to turn the corner and find the house quiet, dark, her father gone to bed.

But turning into the main drive, she was shocked to find the house ablaze with lights, every window starkly illuminated, a long line of cars snaking ominously around the circular drive in front, and out into the quiet street.

She had seen them pass. They did not see her parked in the shadows of the moonlit crossing. She had taken the Willys coupe after her parents left for the dinner party, waiting until Simon had driven them away and then going down to the garage to retrieve the little car.

She had overheard Alice on the telephone making the assignation with Brendan. She had followed them, not because she derived pleasure from it, but because she felt drawn to him, tethered by some invisible cord that would never break no matter how hard she tried to untangle herself. She was happy to simply drift in his presence, to be where he was. The idea of separation from him was as alien to her as the idea of separation from her own heart; there was no imagining a world without Brendan Burke, a world without his presence, his scent, his touch.

Above her Capricornus stretched like a diadem. *Look to that point there*, he had told her. *See? If you look you can see the head of a goat and the tail of a fish.*

Luna he had told her, pointing to the sky the last time they were out here, not long ago. The Moon Goddess. She had liked that. The story of a goddess who falls madly in love with Endymion, a handsome mortal who sleeps in a cave. Every night the goddess slips from the sky to lie beside him and every night Endymion dreams of holding the pale moon in his arms. A sweet tale of love and loss and reunion.

Laura stepped from the car, and walking to the crossing, she lay down between the tracks and folded her hands over her belly.

The watchman came slowly along the tracks, swinging his lantern. Dawn was coming; Warner could hear the distant chirrup of a chickadee. Further to the east, the sky was deepening into a dark purplish bruise.

Warner sighed and looked down at the body covered by a feed sack. Above him the train ticked and hissed, rising massively into the dawn sky.

"Conductor thought at first it was a calf on the tracks," the watchman said, approaching. He was a good man, an old-time railroader, a competent, trustworthy man. "Tried to slow but didn't see it in time." He lifted his lantern so the light shone weakly on the distant Willys parked in the shadows of the tall trees. "Whoever came in had a key to the padlock. And they locked the gate behind them."

"Did you contact the McGuire's?"

"They're on their way. No one was at the house last night."

They both stood looking down at the body.

"Let's get on with it," Warner said.

The watchman leaned over and flicked off the sack. They both stood quietly staring. "Funny how she could be dragged this far and her face and torso stay pretty much intact." He glanced at Warner, shrugged. "Happens sometimes," he said.

"I know this girl," Warner said.

"What?"

"I know her father."

"Oh Lord."

They both stood staring, the train hissing like some monstrous straining beast.

"What's that?" the watchman said, pointing, lifting the lantern. They were both silent, staring.

"Sweet Jesus," the watchman said.

"Pick it up and put it in the sack."

"I'm not touching it."

"All right. You go back up the tracks and collect the rest before the doctor gets here. And get this area cordoned off. Come morning there's going to be sightseers swarming the place."

The watchman had already turned, heading slowly back up the track with his lantern swinging, his head bowed as if in prayer.

Warner bent to this work. In the eastern sky Venus made her bright ascent.

Seventeen

§§§

When she had finished telling her tale, Alice sat quietly in the wingback chair beside the library window. A gentle agitation moved in her face. Sunlight slanted pleasantly through the long windows, warming the room.

Stella stood up and walked over and knelt down beside Alice and put her arms around her. "Oh, Al, I'm so sorry," she said.

The old woman trembled, but she didn't cry. She seemed sustained by something that kept her sorrowful but unbowed. Something insistent and determined.

"It was an accident," Stella said.

"Was it? My parents didn't think so. My mother thought it had something sinister to do with Brendan Burke. She was convinced he'd had a hand in it. She wanted him prosecuted. And then I had to tell them, you see. I had to tell them that I'd been with him that night, that I'd been with him all summer. I had to give him his alibi and it nearly killed them."

Stella tried to imagine Alice as a young girl, the horror and guilt of Laura's death; her own misplaced sense of duty and atonement by marrying a man she did not love. She didn't say anything but Alice saw it in her face.

"You think I married Bill Whittington out of sacrifice?" Alice said fiercely, and something moved in her eyes then, something stubborn and slightly hostile.

"No, Al, of course not."

"There's all kinds of love," Alice said sharply. "There's the kind that comes over you like a sickness, and there's the kind that comes on after years of shared struggle and companionship. And I can tell you, from my experience, it's the second kind that lasts longest. The other eventually burns away like a fever. Leaving what – guilt, regret? Would I have been happier with Brendan Burke? I don't think so. He wasn't the man I thought he was. I got the life I needed with Bill Whittington, even if it didn't seem like the one I wanted at the time."

Two young mothers pushing baby strollers passed in the street, a small ginger dog trotting at their heels.

"It took me years to realize that, of course," Alice said.

"Did you ever see him again?"

"Who? Brendan?" She was quiet for a long time, considering. "Oh, yes. But never alone. He married one of the Murchison girls, not a bad match, and they raised four daughters. She died and he inherited her money and married again. Twice, I think. Younger and prettier each time, of course."

Outside the window the drive was littered with crape-myrtle blossoms from the recent rains. On the desk, the old clock ticked steadily.

Alice stirred, calmly folded one hand on top of the other. "There's something else," she said. There was a hint of alarm in her voice, something ponderous and immutable coming slowly to the surface. She shifted slightly in her chair, her eyes flickering over the bookcase, coming to rest, finally, on Stella.

"Something I've never told anyone. Something I wouldn't admit even to myself for a long time." She raised one trembling hand and pointed to the top of the bookcase.

"Bring me that book there, the red one with the gilt lettering."

Anna Karenina.

Stella felt a vague chill of uneasiness. She went to the bookcase and pulled the novel down and gave it to Alice.

"Do you know this story?"

"Yes," Stella said, kneeling beside her.

"Laura gave it to me a short time before she died. I didn't think anything of it at the time. She was so strange those days, so preoccupied. And later, when mother searched frantically for a note to see if there might be some reason, some explanation, why she had done it." Alice stopped, closing her eyes. Her chin trembled. She took a deep breath and opened her milky eyes, setting the book carefully on her lap. It fell open to the inscription that Stella knew so well. "The coroner ruled it an accidental death and after awhile it became easier to accept that. To tell ourselves that she had simply fallen into a sleepy stupor at the edge of the tracks and laid down to rest. It made it easier for mother, although the town still talked, of course, they always do."

She fanned the pages of the book, pulled out the small scrap of translucent paper.

"And then one night I had a dream. I was pregnant with Sawyer and I woke up and I remembered the book she had given me before she died. I had forgotten it all these years. Put it away." She made a soft sound, almost a cry, and traced the faded words on the paper with a crooked finger. "And I knew when I read this, why she did it."

Stella looked down guiltily at the scrap she had read so often before, feeling again that odd sinister grip at the nape of her neck. *We forgive you. Please forgive me.*

"She was carrying his child."

Stella looked up at Alice, met her eyes. "What?"

"The note makes it clear."

"Oh, Alice, you can't know that."

"Do you see what she wrote? It says, *We* forgive you. Please forgive me. It was her final letter to me, her sister. Her sister."

"No, Al."

"She wrote it down. She was trying to tell me and I wouldn't listen."

"You can't know that."

"Because I selfishly wanted what I wanted. I didn't think of her."

"There's no way you could know that."

"I betrayed my own sister."

"Al."

She dropped her head in her hands and began to cry softly. "I've carried that my whole life," she said.

Later, Stella went into the kitchen and made them both a cup of tea. Alice was sitting quietly in the wingback chair when she returned, her hands resting in her lap, *Anna Karenina* closed now and lying on the table beside the chair. Stella set the cup down on the table and pulled a low stool closer to Alice's feet and sat down.

"Don't sit there. You'll hurt your back."

"I'm fine." Stella sipped her tea, thinking about Laura. The story was entirely plausible; girls killed themselves all the time in those days over unwanted pregnancies and faithless lovers. They still did. But how tragic for Alice to carry that burden of guilt all her life. How senseless and tragic and very, very human.

Alice sipped her tea, staring out the sunny window. Her eyes, although swollen and red, were serene. She seemed calm, resigned, as if whatever tension had held her erect and mournful had dissipated. A series of light, fleeting expressions crossed her face as she stared through the window at the neatly landscaped lawn with its formally arranged shrubs and pots of geraniums.

"I knew from the moment I first saw you that you would do me good," Alice said.

Stella, pleased, smiled and ran one finger around the rim of her cup.

"You had a look about you."

"I feel the same way about you, Al."

"We were quite a pair. We *are* quite a pair."

"Quite a pair."

Alice looked at her and grinned, her mouth tugging down at the corners, her eyes flashing with a mischievous light. She set the cup down on the table and crossed her hands in her lap. "It's funny sometimes how at the end you look back and realize how the people that come into your life influence you."

"Now you sound like a philosopher."

"God brought you into my life."

"Oh, Al."

"I know the young don't believe in God. Call it fate then. All I know is that you get to be my age and you begin to see mysterious forces at work in your life. You begin to see that certain people cross your path for a purpose." She turned her head to the window and stared fixedly at the neighbor's yellow lab, sitting in the shade of a dogwood tree. "Although my sister, perhaps, would question whether that's a good thing. Laura would say that being born my sister was one of the worst things that ever happened to her." She spoke without bitterness but with a certain hard-edged resolve as if, having begun her confession, she had no intention of stopping.

"You mustn't blame yourself for Laura. She was responsible for her own actions. She must have realized at the moment she did it, that it was wrong."

Alice turned her head slowly and let her pale eyes settle on Stella. "What do you mean?"

"She must have known it was a mistake. She must have regretted it."

"Afterwards?"

"Yes."

"So you do believe in an afterlife."

Stella frowned and looked down at her hands, feeling the heat rise in her face. "I don't know what I believe," she said truthfully. "I just know we're all responsible for our own lives. Our own happiness. At the last minute, Laura must have realized that what she was doing, the harm it would cause you and her parents, was wrong. And I'm sure she was sorry, Alice. She wouldn't have wanted you to suffer."

Alice was quiet for a long time. "No," she said. "She wouldn't have wanted that."

Stella put her hand on top of Alice's and left it there until Alice sighed, giving her a slight, apologetic smile. Stella squeezed once and let go.

Alice said, "I've told you my story. And you have a story to tell, too."

"Yes," Stella said.

"We all have a story."

"I guess so."

"And you'll trust me with yours when you're ready?"

"I will," Stella said.

Eighteen

§§§

S he couldn't stop thinking about the dead girl, Laura.
Her dreams were filled with great black dragons
belching smoke, bearing down on her with fiery eyes and
outstretched wings. And she couldn't forget Alice's face either,
as she told her story, her expression of anguish and
determination and shame. Her old-fashioned, slightly absurd
belief that fate brought people together for a purpose.

On Saturday morning Stella rose and called her mother. It
was a gray, drizzly day, the valley thick with low-lying clouds.

"I'm driving down to Birmingham this afternoon."

"Oh?" Candy said.

"I'll stop in and see you and the boys around 2:00."

"All right. And I'll make lunch! I'll make lunch before you
have to get back. You're going right back, aren't you? I'm
assuming you'll have to get back to Chattanooga." She
sounded nervous, as she always did when she talked to Stella.
Nervous and rushed.

"I have to borrow your car to drive to Birmingham," she
told Josh.

"Oh, hell no."

"All right then you drive me."

"I'm not driving you anywhere. In fact, I don't want you using my car at all. You still owe me five hundred bucks for the last two months' rent. I'm not running a goddamn charity here."

She went upstairs and called Professor Dillard. Then she packed her duffel bag and her backpack.

"Where do you think you're going?" Josh said, as she pushed past him. He stood in the doorway as she walked out into the yard, carrying her stuff to the curb.

"You can just leave the laptop," he called after her. "That'll cover what you owe me."

"I don't owe you anything, asshole."

He walked out into the yard. "I want my money."

"I paid for my keep every time I did your goddamned laundry. Every time I cooked your supper. You got off cheap."

"You're the worse girlfriend I ever had."

"Thanks. I must have done something right then."

He glared at her, shook his head stubbornly. "You're not leaving with my money."

"I'm leaving with everything I came with."

He advanced slowly towards her and she slung her backpack over one shoulder and hugged her duffel bag to her chest. He stopped, staring behind her, his attention diverted by the sight of Dr. Dillard's Audi pulling up to the curb.

Luke Morgan climbed out of the driver's door and walked over to Stella. He took the backpack and the duffel bag from her with slow, deliberate movements, staring at Josh across the dirt-packed yard.

"Let's go," he said to Stella.

And without another word, she turned and followed him to the car.

She was glad to see Luke and she didn't pretend otherwise. "I thought we'd seen the last of you," she said, grinning.

He drove slowly through the rain, past dilapidated neighborhoods and corner convenience stores. He adjusted the rearview mirror, glancing behind him. "Are you going to have trouble with dickwad back there?"

"No trouble. I don't plan on ever seeing him again."

"That's probably a good thing."

"I think so."

His arms were tanned below the sleeves of his t-shirt. His hair had blonde streaks from the sun. "Professor Dillard said you had a trip planned to Birmingham this afternoon. She suggested I take her car and drive you."

"Did she?"

"She did."

"As a bodyguard?"

"More like a driver."

Stella turned her face to the glass. Against the sodden sky, the trees seemed to be dripping, melting. "I hope she's not expecting too much. I'm just going to see my little brothers. I'm just having lunch with my mother. It'll probably be fried bologna sandwiches and Beanie Weenies. I expect you'll be bored."

He glanced at her, shrugged. "I like Beanie Weenies."

She looked at him coolly. "So why exactly are you here?"

"In Chattanooga?"

"Yes."

He kept his eyes on the road. His expression was blank, unreadable. "I came back for my guitar," he said.

She hadn't meant to, but as they drove through the rainy landscape she began to tell him about her childhood, even about her days as a street kid in Birmingham. It was easy to talk to him because he didn't ask questions; he seemed almost disinterested in what she was saying, driving quietly, seemingly lost in his own thoughts. This part of northern Alabama was pretty, rolling and green and unexpected, and shut up in the car with only the sound of the rain and the whir of the tires on the highway and the occasional murmur of her own voice, Stella began to feel a sense of relief and dawning euphoria. Or maybe it was the fact she had finally left Josh.

The only time Luke said anything was when Stella told him about her mother dropping her off in Birmingham.

"Are you saying she just left you there?"

Stella, flustered, said quickly, "She had two boys to raise."

"That's no excuse."

"She's not a bad person."

"Did she ever say she was sorry?"

"No." She could see from his expression that she'd never be able to explain this. It was a complicated relationship and one she'd never be able to make a stranger understand. Perhaps it was enough that she understood.

Not that she expected anything positive to come of this trip. She didn't. She'd agreed to it more as a concession to Dr. Dillard. And maybe there was a bit of defiance in her decision, too, a willingness to show her mother that she had survived, had prospered, in spite of her. That she was a young woman who could present a face of her own making to the world. She had a certain polish now that she had not had before. Alice had taught her that. That courage and a certain flourish were necessary, as was an ability to reorder facts, at least on the surface of life, to make them more palatable.

She was no longer a child. Her mother no longer had the power to hurt her. It would do Stella good to show her that.

They stopped for lunch at a Sonic Drive-In in a little town called Black Warrior.

"How'd you like to grow up in a place like this?" Luke said, looking around at the main street surrounded on both sides by low, brick buildings and dusty storefronts.

"I did grow up in places like this," Stella said.

"That must have been a trip."

"You have no idea."

He told her about the documentary he was working on. He'd filmed it at the Waffle House at the foot of Signal Mountain, sitting there every morning and talking to regular customers who all had their stories to tell. His favorite was Larry, a schizophrenic who proposed zany, stunningly plausible arguments in favor of quantum physics and time travel. *"Yesterday I saw J.R.R. Tolkien at the bus stop,"* he told Luke during one interview. *"And we talked about shoes."*

"Wow." Stella grinned. "He sounds awesome."

"I'm thinking I may have something in Larry. You know his father worked on the Manhattan Project. The guy's highly intelligent. He lives with his mother, of course, and I've never met her but it might be interesting to get a feel for Larry's home life. See the family dynamic."

"You mean, kind of a *Grey Gardens* thing?"

He laughed. "Well, that would be great wouldn't it?"

They had both ordered chili dogs and when they came, they ate in silence. The windows were down and a slight breeze stirred the air of the car. The rain had stopped and the sky was a pale blue, hazy with the heat.

When they had finished, Luke collected the trash and the tray and took them up to the window so the overworked waitress didn't have to come back to the car. He had left her a nice tip, too; Stella had noted several folded bills and the girl's obvious delight when she brought them their food.

"You made her day," Stella said, as they pulled away.

He smiled and looked at her curiously. "Who?"

"The waitress."

"It's hard work, waiting tables. Everyone should have to do it at least once so they know how hard it is."

"Spoken like someone who's done their fair share of food service."

They were stopped at the edge of the parking lot, waiting to pull out, and he continued to stare at her curiously, a faint smile on his lips.

"What is it?" she said.

"You have something on your neck."

She put her hand up self-consciously and said, "It's a birthmark."

He looked both ways and pulled slowly into the sparse stream of traffic, heading back to the Interstate ramp. "I have one of those," he said.

"Where?"

"In a most intimate place."

"I don't suppose I'll ever see it then."

He glanced at her and his smile widened. "Never say never," he said.

The house was nothing like she remembered it. It was small and in need of paint and the grass had grown up in the yard. Whatever pride her stepfather had once taken in the place had obviously gone. George came out onto the porch, followed by Anthony. They were both large boys wearing oversized t-shirts and baggy shorts. George came over and let Stella hug him, but Anthony hung back shyly.

"What? I don't get a hug?" Stella said, pulling Anthony close. She introduced her brothers to Luke, who shook hands with them casually. Stella was glad suddenly for Luke's presence, glad for his calm and friendly manner that seemed to put everyone at ease. The screened door swung open and Candy stepped out onto the front stoop.

Stella wouldn't have recognized her. She had put on about eighty pounds and had dyed her hair a bright red color. It hung limply around her chubby face, which was still pretty, and like her sons she wore an oversized t-shirt over a pair of black Capri leggings. "Well, look who's here!" she shouted in a false, friendly voice.

"Hi, mama," Stella said, going up on the porch to greet her.

"You made good time," Candy said, patting her back briefly before pulling away. "Well, hello," she said to Luke, pushing her hair off her flustered face. "You must be Stella's friend."

"Luke."

"Well, how do you do, Luke." Candy pumped his hand. "Come in the house, come in the house." She stood back, holding the screened door open.

There were canned Cokes set up on the coffee table around a bowl of Cheetos. Anthony and George settled down on the fake leather sofa and greedily helped themselves until Candy shooed them away. "Let Stella and Luke sit there," she said. "And don't eat all the snacks." She smiled apologetically at Luke, indicating that he should sit down on the sofa. "They're growing boys," she said. "I can't hardly keep them fed."

They talked for awhile about their lives, Stella directing most of her questions to her brothers who answered in bashful monosyllables, their lips and fingertips stained orange from the Cheetos.

"Do you like school?" Stella said.

"No," George said.

"Hell, no," Anthony said.

"But you need an education. It's important. What do you want to do when you grow up?"

"I don't know."

"Drive a truck," George said.

Candy sat on the edge of a chair sipping a Coke. She seemed nervous, asking Luke repeated questions about himself. He answered politely but there was an edge to him, Stella noted, an air of detachment. He seemed to be waiting for something, his eyes moving constantly from Stella to her mother and back again.

Stella ignored Candy, her questions to her brothers becoming increasingly more desperate and redundant. It was after three o'clock and she could smell something cooking in the kitchen. Candy had mentioned feeding them but Stella wasn't sure now she could sit at a table with her mother and eat; she wasn't sure she could handle the tension. She couldn't imagine now what she had hoped to accomplish by coming here. It had felt in the beginning almost like an act of vengeance but now it felt pathetic, almost as if she was pleading for something from her mother, something Candy was unwilling, or unable, to give. No matter how much she matured, no matter how much her life changed, she would always fall back into the same patterns of behavior around her mother. She would always be the same needy little girl. She wished now she hadn't come.

To make matters worse, Candy went and got an old scrapbook of photographs from Stella's childhood. She sat down on the sofa on the other side of Luke and opened up the book. The photographs gave her a chance to keep up a running commentary, to be jovial and falsely sentimental so that no one else could say anything or ask any questions. George and Anthony stealthily finished off the Cheetos and then settled down to playing video games.

At four-thirty Candy looked up at the clock on the wall and said, "Well, I had planned on making y'all something to eat but it's almost five and your step-daddy should be home soon." She closed the scrapbook as if that fact alone put an end to the visit. She stood up.

"That's okay," Stella said quickly. "We need to get back to Chattanooga." Luke put his elbows on his knees and leaned forward expectantly.

"Well, I'm glad you came," Candy said, smiling in relief. She held the scrapbook tightly against her chest, giving Stella a wary look. "I always knew you'd turn out good. You were such a strong girl. Just think, you'll be a college graduate and a psychologist to boot."

Stella stood up. "Well, I won't be a psychologist unless I go to grad school which seems highly unlikely at this point."

"A college graduate," Candy said, smiling and shaking her head. "Imagine that."

Stella looked down at Luke. "You ready?"

He said nothing, but rose slowly. Stella hugged her mother, briefly, and then leaned and ran her fingers playfully through her brothers' hair. Intent on their video game, they shrugged her off. She imagined her stepfather's truck pulling up out front and she had a sudden desire to flee, to escape the house and its occupants.

"We better get going," she said to Luke.

He followed her out into the yard. Candy came out onto the stoop and waved goodbye and then went back inside the house. Halfway to the car, Luke swung around and walked back up on the stoop. He stood on the porch, his face pushed closed to the screen.

"How could you leave her like that?" he said. "How could you drive off and abandon your own child?"

From inside the house, Candy's voice came back, shrill and petulant. "I knew she could look after herself."

"But didn't you worry something might happen to her?"

"I knew she'd be fine."

"How could you know that?"

"She was always a strong girl."

He bumped the door with his toe and stepped back. "Even strong girls need a mother," he said.

On the ride home, they were both quiet. The sky was streaked with red; birds flitted through the long shadows that lay over the fields. Stella huddled in the corner, her cheek resting against the window. She had never had someone defend her against her mother. It was a new sensation for her. She had not had the courage to ask her mother the questions Luke had asked, but somehow, just hearing them spoken made her feel better. She had practiced for years saying exactly what he had said.

"Do you blame me for not confronting her?" she asked him finally.

"No. I'm sure it's hard. Painful." He glanced at her. "Do you blame me for interfering?"

"I'm glad you did."

The landscape, still wet from the afternoon rains, glittered in the sunlight. Great masses of trees, heavy with Virginia creeper and wild grapevine, crowded the highway before giving way, again, to wide, rolling fields.

"Why do you think she abandoned you like that?" he said.

Stella watched the slow progress of a distant herd of cows ambling toward a feeding trough. A flock of swifts darted back and forth above the cows. *Abandoned.* A harsh, solitary word. After awhile, she stopped thinking about his question and fell into a restless sleep. She dreamed she was copulating with an unknown man, and then a series of men she knew, teachers, bank managers, fat married men, strangers who exhibited some disgusting physical deformities. Her lust was so determined and unrepentant, her attitude so cavalier and rough, her partners so completely inappropriate, (and yet she was groaning with the sweetness of release that washed over her in waves), that she could barely sustain it. She awoke exhausted and sick with shame. The sun was going down and dusk was falling. She sat upright, pushing her hair out of her face and putting her feet up on the dash.

"I lost you for awhile," he said.

"Where are we?"

"Nearly home. I stopped and bought a couple of sandwiches but I couldn't wake you." He picked up a bag on the console between them, set it down again.

She was quiet, letting go of the last remaining fragments of her dream. The dream had awakened something in her, a desire to confess, a sense that it was now or never. If she hesitated, her courage would fail her. She took a deep ragged breath.

"When I was little," she said, "I wanted so desperately to know my father. I loved my mother but I had this image of a shadowy male figure, someone who would love me for who I was. Someone who would take care of me. Someone I could love. I built my whole childhood around this fantasy of a father who would swoop down suddenly into my life and make it better. And when my mother married Moody Bates, I thought maybe he was it. But he couldn't stand me from the beginning. Maybe he sensed how desperate I was for love and was repulsed by it. People can't help but be repulsed by needy people." She glanced at Luke but he continued to drive, his eyes fixed firmly on the road. "When I was fifteen, he began coming into my room at night. At first, he would just sit on my bed and rub my back. It seemed harmless, and I was so surprised, and so desperate for his attention, that I allowed it. And later, when he began touching me other places, I allowed that, too. I don't know why. I can't explain it. There was such shame afterwards. And it didn't make him more affectionate toward me. If anything, I think he hated me even more then."

The radio was playing softly and he leaned and switched it off. "Well," she said spreading her fingers on her knees. She wouldn't look at him. "You know the rest. It's that age-old story. A cliché, really. A girl abused by her stepfather." She turned her head and gave him a fierce look, as if daring him to say anything. She could feel her face warm but she forced herself to go on. Courage was what was needed. Courage and a conviction that what she was saying was true and accountable. "But here's the thing," she said. She hesitated, breathing quietly. "I wanted him to touch me. To love me. I let him do it because I wanted him to. I don't blame my mother, really, for getting rid of me. He must have told her I was a willing participant."

"If he told her, then she should have taken your side. There should have been no question about that."

"He was her husband."

"And you were her daughter." His face was drawn, angry. His life had been so clean and fair that he could not imagine it any other way. "Look, you were what? Fifteen?"

"Yes."

"You were a girl. He was a grown man. A married man and your stepfather. He knew better."

"But so did I."

He fell silent, reflecting on this. When he spoke again his tone was low, reasonable. "You never knew your father. It's understandable that you would want a father figure to love you. It's understandable that you would be feeling confusion and guilt. Doubt, desire, self-hate. It's a classic Electra complex. I mean, you study psychology. You should know this."

She was quiet, considering. Taking it out and looking at it from all sides. "There's a morality issue here, too, Luke," she said finally.

"I'm not excusing your behavior," he said quickly. "I'm not saying it was okay that you were a willing victim. I'm just saying, given your circumstances, it's understandable that it happened and you shouldn't beat yourself up about it anymore. It's impossible at twenty-one to look back at the mistakes you made when you were fifteen and feel guilt over them. Regret, yes. A desire never to make the same mistake again. But not guilt."

The surrounding mountains rose around them, dark against the evening sky. Headlights circled the ridge like a string of pearls. Despite her nap, Stella felt exhausted. And yet filled with a curious lightness, too. A hollow sensation in her stomach, an impression of flight, like a balloon bumping along beneath her rib cage. He was right. She knew he was. She thought of Alice's face as she gave up her secret about Laura. Did her face show the same expression of regret and deliverance? Would she be able to tell Alice the story in its entirety, or only in bits and pieces, holding back out of fear and shame?

"Is there anything you would have liked to say to your mother?" In the glow of the dashboard his face was young and earnest. "Anything I didn't say?"

She smiled, shook her head. "I think you said it all."

"No really." He glanced at her and then back at the road. "Say it to me."

"Have you been talking to Professor Dillard?"

"Say it, Stella."

She crossed her arms over her knees. She put her head back against the seat and closed her eyes. "I'd say, you shouldn't bring a child into the world just to keep you company in your loneliness."

"Anything else?"

"I'd say a woman shouldn't be dependent on a man for happiness. Every woman needs her own life, her own dreams."

"Virginia Woolf couldn't have said it better," he said.

She snuggled down in the corner with her head resting against the glass. She knew now why she had told Alice she was an orphan. All her life, she had felt parentless, discarded. Alice had showed her what it was like to have a real mother. A sister. Stella had a sudden desire to confess as Alice had done, to lay her head on Alice's heart and tell her the truth. To admit to the aching loneliness she had carried all her life.

She would tell Alice when she saw her again on Wednesday. She would tell her everything.

Nineteen

§§§

Alice died in her sleep on Tuesday night. Charlotte called Stella while she was getting ready for work on Wednesday morning and told her not to come in.

Stella didn't go to the funeral. She couldn't bear the thought of it and she was sure Alice understood. The papers were filled with tributes and accolades; Alice Montclair Whittington had been even wealthier than anyone imagined and she had left multi-million dollar endowments to various arts organizations and charities. Her children, too, were handsomely provided for, as were her grandchildren, great-grandchildren and various nieces, nephews, and distant cousins. Each of her caregivers received a fifteen hundred dollar check. Stella, who had never had so much money in her life, promptly opened a savings account.

A few days later Charlotte called and said she had something to give her. Stella secretly hoped that Alice had left something private for her, a letter or a note, and she felt a stir of anticipation as she watched Charlotte climb the stairs to her apartment. They went inside and Stella made a pot of tea and Charlotte talked about the funeral and what a kind, generous woman Alice had been.

"The last time I saw her, she said she wanted me to give you this," Charlotte said, reaching for her purse. But it was only the well-worn copy of *Anna Karenina* with its familiar inscription.

"She said she wanted you to have it," Charlotte said, laying it down on the counter between them. "She said it belonged to you."

Professor Dillard got her a job in the psychology lab and as the fall semester wore on, Stella began to feel like she was back where she belonged. Her grades came up, although not enough to get her into grad school, but with any luck she'd be able to land a social services job after college and eventually (hopefully) earn enough real-life experience to make graduate school possible in the future.

Luke went back to New York to edit his movie but they talked nearly every day. He was planning on returning to Chattanooga in the spring to shoot his footage of Larry and his mother.

Not a day went by when Stella didn't think of Alice. She could still hear Alice's voice in her head, its charming inflection, heavy irony, subtle overtones of humor, and she often found herself gathering observations that she could share with Alice later. *Oh, I have to tell Alice about that*, she would think before remembering, with a clutch of grief and loss, that there would be no more shared secrets with Alice.

It occurred to her that she would always carry Alice's story in her heart, she would always hear Alice's voice in her head. She would remember Alice's anguish as she told her tale, picturing Laura sprawled on the tracks, Brendan Burke going blithely on with his life.

Perhaps that was how immortality was gained after all; by sharing our stories, by living on in each other's hearts and imaginations.

In the late spring Stella was called into Dr. Dillard's office for a meeting with Katherine Arcenaux, the head of Financial Aid. Dean Keller was there, too. Stella assumed it had something to do with a small grant she had applied for although she was surprised to see the Dean. Dr. Dillard was quiet, letting the others do most of the talking. She sat staring out the opened window, a slight smile on her face.

Dean Keller was a short, badly-dressed man with a florid complexion. He spoke to Stella in a bright, slightly pompous tone. "As you may or may not know, the late Mrs. Alice Whittington was a staunch benefactress of the University. She left a number of endowments, including one to the psychology department. She named it in honor of a deceased sister. It's a full-ride scholarship for graduate school to be given to a female student who shows a commitment to the study of clinical psychology. A three-year degree awarded at the Ph. D. level. Full tuition, health insurance while the recipient is enrolled full-time, as well as a stipend in the form of either a teaching assistantship or a laboratory assistantship." He paused and cleared his throat, looking at Stella.

"That sounds like something Alice would do," she said.

Dr. Keller continued to stare at her. "She was a very generous woman," he said. Katherine Arceneux played with a pencil, twirling it between her fingers like a baton.

Dean Keller said pointedly, "So what do you think?"

"Of the scholarship?" Stella pursed her lips. Dr. Dillard gave her a mild, encouraging smile. "I think it's wonderful. But don't you have to get a masters degree first?"

"It's an accelerated program, combining both the masters and the Ph.D."

Stella played with the hem of her jeans. "I'm sure you'll have plenty of qualified applicants," she said.

"Stella," Dr. Dillard said softly.

Katherine Arecenaux stopped flipping the pencil and began to scribble notes on a yellow legal pad.

Dean Keller blinked. "You don't seem to understand," he said.

"If you're suggesting I apply, you obviously haven't checked my GPA." She said this without bitterness, shrugging her shoulders carelessly.

"Stella, listen to what he has to say," Dr. Dillard said.

Dean Keller cleared his throat again and went on. "There are stipulations to the Montclair Scholarship."

"There always are," Stella said benignly.

"The most important being that the first Montclair Scholar will be you, Ms. Nightingale. The endowment instructions are clear on that. You can refuse it, if you wish, and we will choose someone else."

No one said anything. An errant breeze fluttered the papers on Dr. Dillard's desk. The three of them sat watching Stella who stared blankly at Dean Keller.

"What are you saying?" she said finally.

"What we're trying to say," the dean began reasonably. "What we're trying to tell you is that the scholarship is yours. If you want it."

In the quiet that followed, Dr. Dillard said softly, "Alice obviously wanted you to go to graduate school."

Stella stared at Dr. Dillard, feeling a slow swelling beneath her breastbone, a strange sensation of release and purpose. In her head, she could hear Alice laughing.

Outside the window, the leaves of the pear tree rustled in the breeze. A distant freight train passed, echoing through the valley, its horn sharp, insistent, like the cry of a great, flapping bird.

Photo © Shannon Fontaine

CATHY HOLTON is the author of
Revenge of the Kudzu Debutantes,
Secret Lives of the Kudzu Debutantes, Beach Trip,
and *Summer in the South.*

The mother of three grown children, she lives with her husband
and a rescue dog named Yoshi in Chattanooga, Tennessee.
Visit her online at www.cathyholton.com.

Photo © Shannon Fontaine

CATHY HOLTON is the author of
Revenge of the Kudzu Debutantes,
Secret Lives of the Kudzu Debutantes, Beach Trip,
and *Summer in the South.*

The mother of three grown children, she lives with her husband
and a rescue dog named Yoshi in Chattanooga, Tennessee.
Visit her online at www.cathyholton.com.

CPSIA information can be obtained at www.ICGtesting.com
Printed in the USA
LVOW131119270712

291824LV00003B/1/P